Love ~~Bites~~

"So. Are you going to see him again?" Sandy asked Tess.

"Who?"

"Cream Puff."

"I don't know. I'm not going to pursue it."

"Why not?"

"He's so young, Sandy. It's like playing."

"What's wrong with that, Tess? Just a little something sweet. Nothing serious."

"Just a little dessert?"

"Right. You deserve a treat now and then."

I popped a tiny cream puff into my mouth, savoring its sweetness. And that's how it was to be with Gregg: a little treat now and then, which never seemed quite real because I didn't understand what a treat I was for him. . .

About the Author

Sheila Dyan is a freelance journalist, the mother of two, and a good cook. *Love Bites* is her first novel. A native of suburbia, she was raised in Bala-Cynwyd, Pennsylvania, and is currently living in Cherry Hill, New Jersey, with her husband.

Love Bites

Sheila Dyan

NEW ENGLISH LIBRARY
Hodder and Stoughton

FOR MY CHILDREN
WINIFRED AND BRIAN

"In nature there are neither rewards nor punishments—there are consequences."

—Robert Green Ingersoll
Some Reasons Why, 1896

Acknowledgments

"AS WITH ANY SEEMINGLY SOLITARY ENDEAVOR, THERE ARE THOSE WITHOUT WHOM . . .":

OF COURSE: My parents, family and friends, all of whom have supported me in this consuming project.

CONSULTANTS: Fantes, cooking supply store, Philadelphia; Charles Landow, M.D.; Steve Poses of The Commissary restaurant, Philadelphia; Saverio Principato, Esq.; Vincent Sardi of Sardi's restaurant, New York; Allan Schwartz, M.D.

CONSPIRATORS AND CRITICS: Patrick Brett, Doris Chorney, Linda Fields, Harold Gross, Phyllis Gross, Roslyn Kantor, Fred Neulander, Barbara Schwartz, B. Bentley Terrace, Bill Tonelli, Stacey Wolf, and "The Brunch Bunch"—Susan Gorsen, Judy Shapiro, Susan Weiner, and Robin Weinstein.

INSTIGATOR: Helen Kushner, who, one day over corned beef on rye, said to me, "There's a book in all this . . ."

AGENT: Elizabeth Trupin of JET Literary Associates, Inc., a sparkling lady, whose warmth and support are unfailing. Above all, I appreciate her unbounded enthusiasm.

EDITOR: Jane Chelius, a sensitive and talented lady after my own wavelength, who, not surprisingly, always says to me, "It's funny that you called me . . . I was just about to call you." For her insightful and incisive skills, I am most grateful.

WITH LOVE, I THANK YOU ALL

Special thanks for a lifetime of loving, to Sam—friend, mentor, slayer of dragons.

And, to my husband, Bob, for his patience and devotion, a lifetime of love.

CUSTARD CREAM PIE

4 eggs
2/3 cup sugar
1/2 teaspoon salt
1/3 teaspoon nutmeg
1 teaspoon vanilla extract
2 2/3 cups milk
1 9-inch unbaked pie shell

Preheat oven to 425°F.

Beat eggs until completely blended. Add sugar, salt, nutmeg, vanilla, and milk. Stir until smooth. Pour mixture into unbaked pastry shell and bake 15 minutes. Reduce oven temperature to 350°F and bake about 30 minutes, or until a knife inserted about one inch from the edge comes out clean.

Let cool for 10 minutes. Refrigerate uncovered, and decorate with sweetened whipped cream before serving. Serves 8.

CHAPTER 1

Custard Cream Pie

For all its buttery crisp crust, its silky smooth sweetness, its mellow richness, custard cream pie has its downside: It sours. At the moment of the turn, when the nose and tongue can just detect its sharp edge, a custard cream pie is best tossed—at one who deserves not only the injury of the smack, but the insult of the turn.

When we first met in the lobby of the hotel, his height had taken me by surprise. I was used to a smaller man. I noted his thick, curly black hair and the graying, his large, dark-chocolate eyes and the lines radiating from their outer corners. I noted his full mouth—a sexy mouth, I thought, as a candid shot of my mouth meeting his flashed behind my eyes—and his beautifully capped teeth. Beneath his navy blazer, the slight paunch of early success strained the buttons of his blue-and-white-striped silk shirt.

Emerging from the elevator, he had found me with the help of the description I'd given him over the house phone: "I'm in purple."

"Tess? Joe Silvers."

I shook his hand firmly, with excellent eye contact and a demure smile. This man is not your average blind date, I thought, feeling not exactly average myself, catching my reflection in the mirrored wall to the left of the elevator: a vivacious sophisticate in a long, full cotton skirt and blouson top.

"Cindy's right, you are a pretty little thing," he said, smiling broadly, turning me suddenly awkward. My high heels felt too high, and my outfit too baggy—my thin, braless body lost in folds of draining purple.

This was my first date since Stephen and I had separated, and although it had been more than ten years since my last blind date, it all came back to me, including the panic: I shouldn't have had my hair cut; it was too short, accentuating my big ears, my long neck, my large teeth. I'd put on too much blush, and my long lashes, blackened with mascara, looked like spiders. And I was sure that the instant I relaxed my compulsive smile, the lines around my eyes and mouth wouldn't.

All this ran through my mind as Joe guided me by my elbow to Damien's, the cocktail lounge at the rear of the gilt and crystal-chandeliered lobby. This evening was to be a prelude to our tentative dinner date the following evening with our mutual friends Cindy and Richard "The Matchmakers" Castle. *Tentative,* as in *if This Evening goes well.*

"No, I'm not divorced yet. I've only been separated for five months," I answered his question once we were seated and served, nervously running my forefinger around the base of the wineglass before me.

Joe plucked a crimson rose from the small vase next to the tiny brass hurricane lamp lighting our corner booth in the dim, smoke-filled lounge. I nibbled at Jarlsberg and red seedless grapes from a doilied tray and tried to keep the small talk aloft, but my attention was drawn to Joe's hands as he toyed with the rose, caressed it, pulled at the dark velvety petals, and dropped them one by one onto the starched white tablecloth. Such strong, graceful hands, I thought, inventing the sensation of the touch of them on my cheek, my breast. I longed to be touched. I longed to feel the touch of a man's hand on my skin.

"Have you dated much?" he questioned gently as the red petals fell softly from his fingers.

3

"No. Not really. In fact, you're my first real date," I confided.

He's a big man in oil, a nice man, Cindy had told me. Her husband Richard's old friend from college days. From California. And his trip east was for two weeks. Plenty of time, I mused, envisioning this handsome, experienced man naked, easing me to forgotten passion.

"You must be horny as hell," he leered. . . .

Mute and unflinching, I caught his eyes with mine, searching for motive for his insensitive accusation, hating him for his raw accuracy, his jarring exposé. Pinning him with my gaze, I grabbed the shiny object nearest my right hand . . . swung upward and across . . . viscous red spewed from his throat in great pulsating globs as the silver cheese knife severed his carotid artery. His warm, unbelieving eyes were fixed on mine. His mouth opened to protest, but no words came forth, only blood. Splotches of red fell onto his hands, onto the whife cloth. I reached out to touch a warm, wet, crimson pool.

. . . Mute and unflinching, I picked up a soft red petal. Rolling it between my fingers, I sought Joe's eyes with my own, finding not a trace of remorse. But honeyed words dripped from his mouth—condescending babble about women, sublimation, Shirley MacLaine, and mind over sexual matter.

We slipped back into small talk, sipped at wine, picked at the cheese tray. He commented on my apparent sense of togetherness, my stability in the face of trying emotional times. He understood about divorce; he had been through it twice. And the noise in the lounge grew unbearable.

If he had just suggested his room, I would have said no, but what he actually said was, "Do you feel secure enough to come back to my room?" Well, after all, we had just spoken of my inner security, my psychic maturity. Could I now deny it all and say no? Yes. I said yes. We could go to his room.

* * *

4

I sat in the only unoccupied chair in his elegant room with the high ceilings and ornate crown molding, a low rocker upholstered and skirted in green and gold brocade. A handsome leather briefcase sat on the desk chair at the far end of the room. On the back of the chair, Joe carefully draped his jacket. Unbuttoning his cuffs and turning them up as he walked toward me, he asked if I would care for more wine. No, I answered, having had enough wine already to erode my judgment. He threw himself upon the massive four-poster next to my chair and, toes to heels, nudged off his polished black tasseled loafers. From The Bed, looking as though he was going to fall asleep at any moment with his hands folded behind his head on the overstuffed down pillows, Joe halfheartedly asked me about my newly founded catering business—Just Desserts—my politics, my ambitions, while I rocked, trying to look as comfortable as I pretended to be, wondering when would be the best time to leave.

Suddenly I was aware that he had stopped talking and was staring at me. Sitting up, he swung his legs over the side of The Bed to face me.

"May I kiss you?" he asked.

"No," I replied shyly.

"Why?"

"Because it would make me uncomfortable," said I without a hint of nervousness, without a shift in position, totally in control, although ambivalence was taking root somewhere in the pit of my stomach, threatening to choke off resolve.

He lay back again and switched conversational gears. He told me that my hair was pretty, though a bit short and a little out of fashion, and was I thinking of visiting California sometime?

And as I was on the verge of standing, to put an end to the evening, he slithered from The Bed, knelt in front of my chair, and he was still higher than I because he was so tall and my chair was low and he didn't ask again, he just kissed me.

Swirls of warm, swirls of soft, swirls of sensual pleasure

beginning in my mouth and spreading in concentric circles engulfed me, bound me. But I was completely in control. I wasn't doing anything that I didn't want to do . . . except that I had said no, which he interpreted as yes because I hadn't said NO! NO! NO! NO! NO!

"NO!" I said, "NO!" rejecting his seductive tongue and the tender hand that was sliding under my skirt up my thigh. He stood up obediently and lay prone across The Bed, chin in hands.

I dared not leave right after his big play because it would have looked obvious, childish, prudish, and, besides . . . I didn't want to go.

"Were you ever unfaithful to your husband?"

"No."

"You're still a goddamned virgin!" he yelled. He *yelled!* He also told me I was petite, delicate, and feminine, and so very alluring. That I was innocent and naive.

He started to get up, but once on hands and knees he hissed my name—"Tesssss"—challenged me with his eyes, reached over and took my hand. Acquiescing, as if in a dream state, I stepped out of my shoes and joined him. We knelt together on The Bed, facing one another. I started to say something.

"Shhhhh," he whispered, tracing the shadows beneath my deep-set eyes with his finger.

What am I doing here? I wondered, but didn't resist. "I'm vulnerable, and you're trying to seduce me," I said.

"You have a strong will and a strong intellect."

"Intellect has nothing to do with it."

"I am consciously going to stop trying to seduce you."

"It's time for me to go." Finally.

But he leaned to me, loosely circled his arms around me, and kissed me. Once again swirls of warm, swirls of soft, swirls of infinitely sensual pleasure engulfed me. I kissed him back warmly, thoroughly, but I was becoming aware of my hands as they hung impotently over his shoulders. I could not embrace him, I could not touch him. As if they were no longer a part of me, they would not close around him. Instead, like wet gloves they hung over his shoulders even as the rest of my body opened to him, quickened to him.

He pulled me to him and sought the soft elastic band binding panty to thigh. Reaching beyond, he touched and caressed. He pressed himself against me. I could feel his erection against my belly. . . .

NO! screamed in my head, but my knees abandoned me and we fell together into the mass of pillows on the bed. I can't! I thought, grasping at a glint on the nightstand as he rolled over me. His despicable leer once again challenged me, steeled me, allowing my trembling hands to finally embrace him. And with the embrace, the silver letter opener I clutched in my fist sank deep into his back. Shock clouded his eyes; blood welled up in his mouth mixed with saliva and spilled over his soft lower lip in a crimson thread.

. . . "NO!" I said. "I can't," I said, withdrawing my arms from his shoulders and sitting back on my heels, trying to regain my composure. He asked me something, but I don't remember what. I only remember answering as I slipped off the bed, "I'm an ambivalent person."

The elevator descended slowly toward the lobby with little jogs and bumps. Standing close, pushing me into the corner of the car, Joe asked if we would still have dinner the next evening with Cindy and Richard . . . if I'd stay with him after dinner. I smiled lamely, with my mouth. . . .

My hand found the red STOP button behind my back. The car jolted to a halt. Joe fell backward as the tip of my foot grazed the back of his ankle, hitting his head on the polished marble floor. I fell over him. Stunned, he was unable to speak, though his mouth was agape beneath me and his eyes darted about my face. NO! my eyes screamed, NO! as I crushed his mouth with mine. His wrists were caught in my grasp above his head, his long sprawled legs bowed around me. Bells were ringing as my tongue licked his into submission. I felt his erection amass beneath my thighs. Relin-

7

quishing his left wrist, I reached down to free his engorged penis and lift my skirt to a bundle between us. Hoisting up, I hung in midair just long enough to catch his wide-eyed amazement, the unchecked enthusiasm on his face. Pulling silken panty aside, I dropped abruptly, impaling myself on him. Almost immediately the quake began. Visions of barren California acres dotted with drilling rigs played behind my eyes. Up and down and up and down and the tremor that numbed fingers and toes erupted in a gush and a run of grips that closed and opened and closed and opened around him, leaving him on the brink on the edge on the verge of his own orgasm. His hands grabbed my buttocks as he continued to pump. His eyes were tightly closed, his tongue jabbed at air in and out of his dry mouth. In an instant I freed myself from him, caught his hands, and closed them around his rigid organ. Close he was, almost he was, continued he did the business by himself, yanking and stroking, pinching and pulling in a paroxysm of frenetic motion. Watching from the corner, I was in complete control. The bells stopped ringing when I pulled out the STOP and within seconds the doors to The Elevator opened to reveal a gallery that had gathered in answer to the bells, in time for them to witness the writhing hulk on the small marble floor spew forth exultations of ecstasy, spasmodic spurts of opalescent emission.

. . . "NO!" I said, "NO! I can't," just as the elevator doors opened and we stepped out into the opulent, deserted lobby.

Perplexed, he walked me to my car in the parking lot next door, kissed me lightly, and watched me drive off.

I felt I had handled everything just fine, that I had coped well, that I was in complete control—until at a red light halfway home someone in the car next to me yelled, "PUT YOUR LIGHTS ON, LADY!" Then I almost collided with a mini-van after running a stop sign. I was out of control, disoriented by passion. I could imagine the headlines in the paper the next morning: YOUNG WOMAN KILLED IN CRASH. DRIVER UNDER THE INFLUENCE OF LUST.

* * *

Since that night, I've been subject to fits of passion. I'll melt, I'll liquefy, I'll soon go up in a puff of steam, perchance to be carried by clouds to where he is, and I'll rain on him one morning. But I'd rather push a ripe custard cream pie in the bastard's lubricious face.

Smack!

The rude sound of the dollop of sweet whipped cream hitting the cooled surface of the custard jarred me from my reverie. Daydreaming again. Driven inward by the routine of whipping and spreading. So this is the single life. Weird evenings with weird men followed by ambivalent ruminations lasting for days, weeks. Lust followed by rage. I didn't think it would be this hard.

RASPBERRY TORTE

8 eggs
1 cup sugar
1/4 teaspoon salt
1/4 pound shelled filberts, grated
1/4 pound shelled walnuts, grated
3/4 cup raspberry jam
chocolate glaze (below)
powdered sugar
1 pint fresh raspberries

Preheat oven to 350°F. Butter two 9-inch cake pans. Line them with wax paper and butter the wax paper.

Separate the eggs and beat the yolks until thick and pale. Gradually beat in 1/2 cup sugar. In a separate bowl, add the salt to the egg whites and beat until soft peaks form. Gradually beat in 1/2 cup sugar and continue beating until stiff peaks form. Fold the whites into the yolks. Fold in the nuts. Pour into pans and bake for 30 minutes. Turn cakes onto a rack and remove wax paper. Let cool.

Split each layer horizontally and spread layers, except top, with raspberry jam. Put layers together. Ice sides with chocolate glaze. Dust top with powdered sugar and stud with a crown of fresh raspberries.

Chocolate Glaze

6 one-ounce squares bittersweet chocolate
4 tablespoons butter

Melt the chocolate and butter over moderate heat in the top of a double boiler, stirring continuously until smooth.

CHAPTER 2

Raspberry Torte

"Daydreamer," my second-grade teacher had told my mother. "She's always staring out the window. I can't imagine what she's thinking about."

Plotting, probably. But today . . . what was I thinking just before the banging brought me back to reality, standing at the center-island counter of my double-oven-plus-microwave Poggenpohl kitchen that my now-estranged husband had bought so I could make gingerbread children when I wasn't out selling four-bedroom, two-and-a-half-bath (with family room) homes to couples with two-and-a-half children, a dog, and a Volvo station wagon—part-time careers I had established after burning out at the end of nine years as a second-grade teacher? All those kids, and none came home with me.

I had taken well to the business of moving people around. When Stephen left, I was almost making a living with real estate sales commissions. Establishing Just Desserts had been serendipitous. The gingerbread cookies I had lovingly created for years for family and friends became a sought-after commercial product after I had donated a hundred of them to the synagogue brunch and fashion show the year before. Soon I found myself going from gingerbread to tarts, from tarts to tortes, from tortes to pies, lemon rolls, and chocolate logs. The dessert catering business filled an inner need in me as well as the holes in my finances. There's

11

something satisfying about cooking, especially desserts—the sweet end, the final taste in your mouth.

"Tess, Tess! Open up, are you there?" Sandy banging at the back door. Here to pick up the tortes for her dinner party. Was it that late?

"I'm here, Sandy, come on in," I shouted. But what had I been thinking about?

She bolted through the door, admitting a gush of crisp fall air into the pantry where two of her three raspberry tortes sat on a cast-iron pie rack. The cold air briefly filling my eyes and nose jogged my memory. I had been thinking of the smell of frost that had greeted me that morning through my open bedroom window, and how it had evoked feelings of solitude. This was to be my first winter alone. It seemed like only days, not four years, since Stephen and I had moved into this house, our dream house—my dream house.

Stephen had rushed into the kitchen unexpectedly at noon, carrying with him the crisp smell of frost. "What's for dinner tonight?" he teased, eyeing the half-unpacked boxes of kitchen equipment and canned goods on the floor, and the piles of china, pots, and pans on the countertops and table.

I scrambled down the stepladder to greet him, leaving the roll of Rubbermaid shelf lining on the topmost cabinet shelf. "Hi! What a nice surprise. You here to take me to a well-earned lunch?" I asked, embracing him, inhaling the autumn cold that seemed to emanate not from the surface of his gray London Fog, but from deep within him. His icy lips brushed mine as he patted my back with one hand, and then he headed for the desk in the open family room beyond the kitchen, dodging boxes of books and files.

"You mean you're not *making* us lunch?" he threw to me. "I thought you wanted to play house and cook three meals a day in your shiny new kitchen!"

I hated it when he was sarcastic.

"Tess, did you see the tax file for this year lying around? I distinctly remember taking it out of a box and putting it on the desk last night."

"Nope. I haven't been out of the kitchen all morning, and it isn't in here. So. How about lunch?"

After a moment he walked back to the kitchen, the file in his hand. "I thought you'd have lunch on the table for me! What have you been doing all morning?"

"Stephen, I'm serious . . . and I'm hungry, and I thought maybe we could—"

"I'm serious, too," he said, feigning a scowl. "I'm really disappointed. You've been in this big house with the big kitchen for almost twenty-four hours now, and no hot meal!"

"Would you settle for a hot wife?" I tried, seized by a need to be held.

"I would have, but since you mentioned lunch, you've got my stomach growling for food."

"Okay, so take me to lunch."

"When you have so much work to do here? Look at all the shelves you have to line!"

"Bye, Stephen," I said, turning my back to him, climbing up the stepladder, giving up.

"See ya," he said, patting my rear as he left.

"RUB! Don't PAT!" I yelled to him. But the door had shut. He was gone. And I was left to line the shelves and grumble to myself, "You pat a dog . . . you pat a friend's small child . . . you pat your buddy on the football team. You RUB your wife."

This isn't at all the way I had pictured it, I thought, no longer hungry, stepping down the ladder, clearing a space on the counter for a mug of hot coffee—installing the space-saver coffee maker under the cabinet next to the pantry door was the first thing I had done that morning. And why am I lining these shelves, anyway? I wondered, knowing full well that I lined kitchen cabinets because my mother lined kitchen cabinets, even though *she* had lined them when I was a child because the shelves then were painted wood, and she continued to line shelves—even though the cabinet shelves in her present apartment are laminated with plastic —out of habit. I lifted the receiver from the wall phone near the coffee maker, punched in my mother's number, poured the coffee with my free hand, and sat at the counter, stretching the new, white, tightly coiled wire. As the phone rang, I added sugar to my coffee from the yellow box that had been wrapped in newspaper—my mother, too, always wrapped everything in newspaper when she packed.

"Hello."

"Hello, Mom?"

"Hello, dear. How are you?"

"Okay."

"You don't sound good. What's wrong?"

"Nothing. I guess I'm just tired from the move."

"You're not doing too much, are you?"

"Well, I've been unpacking the kitchen stuff this morning, and lining shelves. . . . By the way, Mom, why do you line shelves?"

"I always line my shelves. It protects them. It keeps them clean."

"But our shelves are laminated, Mom."

"Look, I always line shelves. What can I tell you? Everything is different these days. If you don't want to line your shelves, don't line them."

"But I *am* lining them. I only asked—"

"You asked, and I'm telling you. I always line my shelves."

"So how are you feeling, Mother?"

"Fine, dear. Bernice Kaiserman—you know, the lady two doors down the hall—and I are going to lunch soon. Did you have lunch yet?"

"No. I'm not very hungry. I'm having a cup of coffee."

"You have to eat, Tess. That's why you're tired. You don't eat enough. You never ate enough. And I don't know why you decided to move into that big house. It's too much for you to keep up. You don't need all those rooms."

"It's what I want, Mom, and someday the rooms will fill up—"

"From your lips to God's ears. Tess, you're almost thirty. I don't know what you're waiting for. A man wants children, you know."

"I just turned twenty-nine, Mom. So don't worry, children are in my master plan."

14

"Your problem is you have too many plans. Real estate, a new big house. What was so wrong with your apartment? What was wrong with teaching? Tess, I—"

"Mom, I've got to go."

"All right, dear. Call me later. But don't call until after dinner tonight. I might go visit your Aunt Sarah. Remember, she's moving to Florida next week. Don't forget to call to say good-bye."

"I won't. Gotta go. Bye." I hung up and walked from the kitchen through the family room to the front hall. I walked into and out of the empty-but-for-boxes-and-drapes living room and dining room, and up the stairs. I looked into the fourth bedroom, to the right of the stairs, which was to be my office, and noted my desk, filing cabinet, and boxes of paperback books. Walking around the third bedroom, which was to be a guest bedroom, I pictured twin beds covered by rainbow-striped comforters, and a window seat holding a rainbow of throw pillows. Right now it housed Stephen's weights, rowing machine, and stationary bike. The second bedroom was completely empty, but I could picture, first, a haze of pink ruffles and white lace enveloping a twin four-poster brass bed, and alternately, a splash of primary colors surrounding a race-car bed—I had seen one in the children's furniture store in the new shopping center, where it was matched with a gas-pump chest of drawers. Yes. This would be the nursery. Well, of course—I let my mind wander—first there would be a crib, and then the fancy furniture, and then, when the second baby came, the first would be moved to the guest bedroom. And then—

And then the phone rang. I didn't want to talk with anyone. I let it ring and walked into the master bedroom feeling inconsolably alone, looked down at the unmade bed with the rosy sheets, the orange sherbet and pale blue fine wool blankets, and the creamy eyelet comforter all invitingly atangle, lay down in the middle of it, and pulled the comforter over my head. Tears ran down my nose and dropped onto the king-size down pillow. Closing my eyes, I curled up with my hands between my legs and discreetly rocked back and forth. The overwhelming intellectual anesthesia and emotional analgesia of sexual arousal quickly enveloped me, insulated me, and I rocked faster and faster. Yes. This makes it better . . . like when I was little, and alone, and afraid. Yes. The insistence of impending orgasm drew me farther and farther from my thoughts, closer and closer to that special momentary place where all wrongs are righted . . . where, for an instant, there are no wrongs. Then, driven from aloneness, I rocketed into the soft black womb of the id—

And the phone rang. Feeling consummately guilty, I answered it, out of breath . . . caught. It was the Welcome Wagon.

Yes. A time not unlike this morning—the smell of frost, the sanctuary of my bed, the palliative touch of Onan.

"Don't you ever lock your back door? Someone could break right in," Sandy scolded, startling me back to the moment.

"I don't even think about it," I said, somewhat warm and disoriented from my rememberings.

"God, Tess. You okay? You look flushed."

"I'm fine. I've just been busy. Have a seat, your tortes are almost ready. This is the last one," I said, spooning powdered sugar from the yellow and white box into the aluminum sifter I held over the torte before me.

"They look wooonderful!" she said, perching herself in a high cane-back chair at one end of the counter, propping her small pointed chin in her hands.

She shouldn't be a Sandy, the name is so incongruous with her looks, I thought, noticing not for the first time her delicate, pale skin; the high color of her cheeks, like raspberries in cream; how black her eyes and hair were, not a trace of gray. I was only three years older and . . . What was it the salesman had said to me when I took my old raccoon jacket in to be restitched? Something about how refreshing it was to see that, unlike most women *my age*, I wasn't trying to cover the gray frost streaking the front of my hair. This, as he reached out and teased a fallen lock from my eye with his finger. Pig.

"I've got news, Tess."

"News? So do I," I said.

"You first."

"Okay. What do you think about me selling my house?"

"Really, Tess? Why? You looove this house. And where would you go? And this kitchen! Could you cook anywhere else after cooking here?"

"I've been thinking about it for a while. It's too big. It makes me feel too alone now that Stephen's gone."

"But lots of divorced women live in large homes."

"Usually with children, Sandy. That makes a difference." Sandy pulled a sympathetic face.

"So I was thinking of the new townhouses that are going to go up on the old Karistan Estate. I saw a brochure. They're going to be nice. The model I like has a huge eat-in kitchen and family room combination—with a fireplace—and two large bedrooms. I can use the second bedroom as an office. And the master bedroom has a sitting room that overlooks the living room. It's very open."

"Sounds great, but do you want to rush into this? You're not even divorced yet."

"I've made up my mind. I'm putting my house on the market today. Now. What's your news?"

Sandy looked like she wanted to say more on the subject, but she didn't. "Remember Mark Weiser?" she asked.

"Who?"

"Mark Weiser, Barbara's almost-ex, the judge."

"What about him?"

"He ran his Porsche into a tree. The police are calling it an accident, but Barbara told Bob Cooperman that Mark—you *did* hear that he was caught dealing drugs, didn't you? . . . Well, he was," she continued, not giving me a chance to answer, "and Bob said it was *Barbara* who blew the whistle! She couldn't stand having the kids go with him on weekends because she knew he had stuff in his apartment. Well, anyway, Barbara told Bob that Mark had pleaded with her not to testify at his hearing, that he would kill himself before he would be humiliated in a courtroom."

"My God. Dead?"

17

"As a doornail."

"So you think he did it on purpose?"

"Absoluuutely."

"Maybe he was strung out."

"More like he was strung up. And, by the way, we're talking a million in insurance."

"For Barbara?"

"For Barbara. Probably a posthumous guilt offering."

I did not miss the narrowing of her eyes, the wisp of a smile on her lips. Yes, I too thought, maybe there is some justice in this world after all. The man was a degenerate. Black-robed, he sat on a bench steeled with arrogance, wielding the scales of justice over petty druggies and corporate thieves, while turning blind eyes to his own depravity.

"I didn't know he was selling drugs, but I knew that he used them," I said, lowering the sifter to the counter without releasing it. "You know, he tried to entice me into the bathroom for a line of coke and God knows what else at Millie's party three years ago," I confessed, adding, to point out that I hadn't taken the pass personally, "And everybody knew that he had been running around for years."

"Oh, yes," she concurred, casting her own stones. "Remember the night Charlie had an emergency at the shore hospital and I went to Barbara's dinner party alone? Remember, I was wearing a black knit sweater? You know the one, with the rhinestone bow on one shoulder and the low V-neck? Well, he followed me to the powder room and right there in the hall he put his hand into my bra!"

"You never told me about that."

"You never told me about the invitation to the bathroom."

I lifted the sifter and poised it over the torte.

"Well, he kept a lot hidden under those black robes," she continued after a short silence, shifting the guilt back to its rightful place. "And I'll tell you something else you might not know. His secretary used his American Express card to buy clothes at Best Suited. And she was always driving his car around—"

"The Porsche!"

"No. Not the Porsche, the Cutlass. He would have *died* before he let anyone touch his Porsche. Hah! He did! Maybe that's why he killed himself in it, so that they'd go together."

"So what did you do?"

"What did I do when?"

"When he put his hand in your bra."

"Well . . . I let him kiss me . . ."

I put the sifter down again and watched Sandy's eyes turn coy, then angry.

". . . just once. I was curious. Besides, I was really pissed at Charlie. I mean, do you know how many parties I've had to go to alone because he refuses to get a partner?"

You could have smacked him, I thought, lifting the sifter once again. You could have laid him out, I thought, setting my lips in a hard line. Not Sandy, I thought, she loved to be lusted after. "Mm. When's the funeral, Sandy?" I asked. "I suppose I should pay my respects—to Barbara, that is. I never had any respect for Mark."

As I gently tapped the sifter, releasing a final dusting of sugar, I felt the tiniest twinge of guilt. I supposed one shouldn't speak ill of the dead. Then again, I supposed there were exceptions. There were so many candidates for exceptions. Sandy's husband, for instance. I wondered if Sandy had heard what I had heard—that he kept a cookie in the "investment" condo they had bought at the shore. Sandy had told me it was rented, that the income would decorate their own home. Sure, it was rented, I figured—by Charlie.

"It's tomorrow at eleven. Charlie and I are going, if he gets home in time. In any case, I'll pick you up if you want to come."

Pondering the invitation, I pictured Mark in his coffin, immaculately groomed. That would be new for Mark. I wondered if it was true, what they say about dead men, that they have permanent erections. That wouldn't be new for Mark, I thought, remembering the rest of the story about the invitation to the bath, what else I hadn't told Sandy. That Mark had kissed me, too—or at least he tried to. That he had exposed himself. That I had pushed him into the bathroom. That he had pulled me in with him and kicked the door shut. . . .

"You're not really such a goody-goody, are you? You're really a lot hotter than you look, aren't you?" he slurred, grabbing me by the shoulders, pushing me to my knees. "Okay, Miss Disneyland. Do you know what time it is? It's Howdy-Doody time," he said, dropping his pants (he wasn't wearing underpants). "Hey, kids, I'm Uncle Bob, this is Howdy-Doody," he said, fondling his erection. I guessed it wasn't true, what they say about drunk men, that they can't get it up. "Let's all sing! *It's Howdy-Doody time, it's Howdy-Doody time,*" he sang, his slightly flagging erection waving before my eyes. "Come on, Tess, Howdy's wilting. Give Howdy a kiss . . . and sing! *It's Howdy-Doody time, it's—*"

"It's sopraaaano time," I warbled, grabbing the dangling scrotum before me and pulling myself to a standing position. Obediently, his voice hit C above high C as his knees cracked on the ceramic tile.

. . . I should have. I really should have. Instead, I had pulled away, totally flustered, completely mortified. "I'm sorry," I had heard myself squeal as I stood up, opened the door, and scurried back to the party.

"I'm sorry?"

"You're sorry about what, Tess? Tess? Hey, space cadet, you're sorry about what?" Sandy's whiny voice delivered me from my internal digressions.

"Sorry, Sandy, um, I'm sorry this is taking so long," I recovered as I finished the torte with a crown of fresh red raspberries. "And I've decided not to go to Mark's funeral. I'll visit Barbara at home. And maybe I'll bring a razzzberry torte, in memoriam. That's a just dessert for the judge."

CREAM PUFFS

1 cup water
8 tablespoons butter
1/4 teaspoon salt
1 cup sifted flour
4 eggs
1 cup heavy cream
2 tablespoons powdered sugar
1 teaspoon vanilla extract
chocolate glaze (use 1/2 recipe from Raspberry Torte)

Preheat oven to 450°F.

Bring water, butter and salt to a boil. Remove from heat and add flour all at once. Stir vigorously until the dough leaves the sides of the pan and a ball forms around the spoon. If necessary, beat the mixture over low heat for a few more seconds. Cool slightly. Add the eggs, one at a time, and beat until the mixture is smooth after each egg.

Drop the mixture by rounded half-teaspoons onto a greased baking sheet, leaving 1 1/2 inches between puffs. Bake for 10 minutes; then reduce temperature to 350°F and bake for about 15 minutes more, until they are golden-brown and no fat bubbles remain on the surface. The sides of the puffs should feel rigid. Cool.

Whip cream until stiff; add sugar and vanilla and continue to beat until very stiff. Cut off tops of puffs, remove excess center, and fill with sweetened whipped cream flavored with vanilla extract. Ice with chocolate glaze. Makes about 20 small puffs.

CHAPTER 3

Cream Puff

"Did I tell you he called me a virgin?"

"Um," Sandy managed through a mouthful of roast beef, coleslaw, and Russian dressing on rye.

Watching her lose the battle with the recalcitrant strand of slaw hanging out of the corner of her mouth, I decided never to order a roast beef special when on a date—if I ever had another date. "Did I tell you I decided that even though he was sexy, he was a real jerk?"

"Um-hum," she mumbled, adding, after swallowing, "I can't believe it took you two months to figure that out, or that you're still obsessing about that dumb date!"

"So, I'm neurotic," I confessed, pushing my spinach salad around on the plate.

"I have to be honest with you, Tess—from what you told me, you're lucky he didn't strangle you."

"Okay, Mom. You're right. But so was he—about my being a technical virgin."

"Don't worry. You haven't had your last orgasm."

"Sandy! Lower your voice, this booth is not soundproof." The Mykonos Diner: purveyor of fine food and superfine flash; an establishment on the cutting edge of gossip and rumor. I had my suspicions that the plush, chandeliered booths were wired.

"Sorry," she squeaked before attacking her sandwich half from a different angle.

22

The large clock over the counter showed one-fifteen. I was showing a contemporary semicustom home with an in-ground pool at one forty-five. The house was twenty minutes from the diner. If I closed the sale at the asking price of two hundred and fifty thousand dollars, it would mean a seven-thousand-dollar commission. If I sold it for two hundred thousand, it would mean a fifty-five-hundred—

"Tess. Yoo-hoo! Where are you?"

"Counting chickens."

"You should be as confident with your dates as you are with your deals!"

"I remember what it's like to make a sale," I answered sharply.

"Not to change the subject, but do you want to have dinner with me and the kids? Charlie has to be at the shore hospital early tomorrow morning, so he's staying there overnight."

"You forgot already! Tonight is my big night out."

"Aha! The music appreciation class starts tonight, right?"

"Right. It should be thrilling, since I'll probably be the only one in the class who knows a fugue from a fuck. Then again, the difference is growing dim."

"Here we go again. I'm afraid the subject of your stagnating libido is wearing thin. Now, will you get out of here before you're late for your appointment?"

"But you haven't finished yet," I protested.

"Just go. I'm fine. And I'll pay the check on the way out; it's my turn."

"So what will you do tonight?"

"I might go over to Barbara's."

"How's she doing?"

"Amazing. She looks great and seems to have pulled herself together fast."

"I think I could pull myself together pretty fast with a million dollars."

"This is a discussion for another day, Tess. You're late! Go!"

"Okay, okay. Hug the kids for me. Talk to you in the morning."

Settling into the corner of the oversize mauve cotton-velour sectional sofa in my family room the following morning, Sandy tucked her legs under her and wrapped her hands around a mug of coffee. "It's getting cold out," she said, shrugging in an attempt to shake off the morning chill.

I continued dropping tiny globs of thick batter from a teaspoon onto a greased cookie sheet in two even rows. "Puff shells for cream puffs, for Myra Freedman's father-in-law's birthday dinner," I explained from the kitchen counter. After placing the sheet in the oven, I poured a mug of coffee, added sugar from the cork-stopped glass canister on the counter, and joined Sandy in the family room.

"The sale, Tess, did you make the sale?"

I smiled coyly, settling into a nest of pastel throw pillows on the sofa, and sipped my coffee.

"You did! How much?"

"Two thirty-five."

"Fantaaastic!"

"Well, I *have* been working on that deal for four months," I said modestly. "Now I hope the buyers get their mortgage. I'd have to bake a lot of cream puffs to make six thousand dollars."

"You're such a worrywart! It'll be fine. You're sooo good at what you do, Tess. Your client must be ecstatic."

"I hope I can do as well for me."

"Six thousand isn't bad, Tess."

"No, I mean in selling my house. You know it's been on the market almost two months and only one couple has been through."

"It'll sell. I don't have to tell *you* that this is a lousy time of year to try to sell a house. Besides, they haven't even started the townhouses you're interested in."

"True, true. But preconstruction prices are always the best."

"I think you'd be better off waiting to make sure the

development is going to turn out as nice as you think it will."

"Okay, okay, enough of this. It's a moot point. I can't think of buying until I get someone interested in my house."

"You're still intent on selling?"

"I'm still intent on selling."

"So. How was the class?"

"Class?"

"Your music class last night."

"Ah, the class. Elementary, but at least I got out for an evening."

"Anybody there?" Read: Any interesting men?

"Actually, there was this adorable guy, but too young."

"So?"

"So what?"

"So, was he interested?"

"You've got to be kidding. He couldn't have been more than twenty-four."

Sandy's eyes lit up when I dropped that bit of information, and then narrowed.

Gregg Hart had the look and demeanor of a California surfboarder—six-feet-four, lean and laid-back. He had long, straight blond hair, a soft, full mustache, and huge, round blue eyes. Beneath high cheekbones were dimples big enough to sink your tongue into. In his deep, sonorous voice, he'd told me that he had graduated college as a business major, but that he was building houses—literally *building* houses. He wore tight jeans.

I was thirteen when I noticed the tight jeans of Gavin Storms. He was older, maybe sixteen, but still in junior high. He was tall, all legs, as they say; not quite all legs, I noted. He'd swagger through the halls of Hawthorne Junior High School in cowboy boots and tight jeans, the vertex of his slowly striding legs bulging. The mysteries stuffing those jeans occupied my daydreams through two semesters of Spanish I.

25

Walking home from school one spring afternoon, I spotted Gavin Storms rooted to the sidewalk a block away from me, across the street. His legs slightly apart, arms down at his sides, Gavin gazed up the street. Even at that distance, even at that age, I could distinguish his cocky sneer . . . his bulges. The object of his focus was a girl in a white blouse and short blue and green print skirt who stood wavering directly across the street from me. She stared at him, he stared at her, neither aware of me staring at them. The girl was crying. She kept wiping her eyes with her hands and moving one step ahead and then one step back until she suddenly ran forward, which prompted a somber Gavin Storms to stride toward her with his long, booted legs. When they met, the girl wrapped herself around Gavin—who was a good foot taller than she—pressing herself against his bulges. He smirked. I waited awhile for them to separate, but they stood fast, and I finally walked away.

"Tess, put your ears on, your timer went off. And you didn't answer my question. Was he interested?"

"Well, he was very attentive, and he asked for my number. He said he might need help with the assignment," I said, leaping up and sprinting to the oven to remove the browned and puffed shells that would later be filled with sweet whipped cream and topped with bittersweet chocolate. "And I'm sure that's all he wants, Sandy. He's so young, what would he want with me?" But I smiled; she smiled. I transferred the hot shells to a cooling rack, bagged cooled shells and dropped more globs onto the cookie sheet. Sandy sipped and stayed long enough to warm up before she had to pick up Rebecca from nursery school.

Two days later Gregg called to ask my advice about the theme he was writing. "It's been a while since I wrote a paper for school," he apologized.

"How old *are* you?" I asked.

"Twenty-seven. How old are you?"

"Thirty-three."

"Oh . . ." His voice dropped. "I'm really only twenty-two."

The following week he showed up at class with one of his three roommates (to check me out?). As he left, he invited me to stop in to see his apartment "sometime."

I did, the following week after class. His two-bedroom apartment resembled a college dorm—a mess of laundry and newspapers, dirty dishes and worn furniture, an unmade sofa-bed in the living room. But Gregg's bedroom was in perfect order. His bed was made, magazines were stacked neatly in a corner, clothes were out of sight, vacuum tracks streaked the carpet. Surely his neatness was a sign of maturity beyond his years, I decided. Only later did it dawn on me that he had cleaned up for me. He showed me his Bruce Springsteen album collection—a poster of the Boss filled one wall—his college yearbook, pictures of his parents and two sisters and his four-year-old nephew. I smiled in appreciation through it all, and then I left.

Gregg called several times over the next few weeks to discuss the class and the over-the-holiday theme assignment. It should have been obvious that he was interested in me, but I wouldn't believe it. He was, after all, only twenty-two and incredibly handsome. Then, on New Year's Day, he called to ask if I would help edit his theme. Yes. He came to my home late that evening.

As always, I was struck by his height, by his eyes that seemed always to find me, and by his beautiful face. His youth excited me. We edited. I had suggestions for him. I had fantasies about him—about seducing him. When he asked to see my paper, "It's in my study," said I. "Would you like to see my study? It's upstairs."

"Shur," said he in his laid-back drawl.

As we climbed the stairs, I experienced the oddest sensation—that this wasn't really happening, that I was making it up, watching a movie. I couldn't believe I was going to seduce this young, young man. I didn't believe I *could* seduce him.

Sitting down beside him on the love seat next to my desk, I handed him a rough draft of my paper—paralleling great works of art and music by dates of composition. I watched him read and pictured myself falling into his arms, swooning from his baby-fresh aroma, feeling his firm young flesh beneath my fingertips, my lips, the tip of my tongue. Suddenly, my fantasy became reality as he looked up and placed his long, strong fingers on my thigh. I remained quite cool, quite the sophisticated woman, and placed a hand on his wrist. He leaned over and kissed me hungrily, his mustache brushing the tip of my nose.

"I've wanted to kiss you for a long time," he said when our lips finally parted.

"Yes," said the sophisticated woman, not missing a heartbeat. "You're very attractive."

But he noticed the smoldering lust beneath her cool exterior. "You're warm," he said, running a hand around the back of her neck.

"Yes," she said.

I wondered, as he kissed me again, should I or shouldn't I? I was in complete control, I wouldn't do anything I didn't want to do. In fact, he was probably as scared as I—maybe more so. After all, he was dealing with an experienced older woman. He probably couldn't wait to get back to his apartment to tell his roommates all about it.

"Do you want to stay for a while?" the experienced older woman enticed.

"Shur," drawled the smooth young man. "Do you want to get into bed?"

I hesitated long enough to make him feel like he was skating on thin ice.

"That's okay, you don't have to . . . but *I* want to," he reassured me.

Sweet. The question still was, did *I* want to? It had been eight months since Stephen left, since I'd made love to a man. Maybe I was thinking that I had to prove to myself that I could do it, that my body was still in working order, that I wasn't scared of men or sex or being hurt, that I could do anything I wanted to do and that I wanted to do what everyone else wanted to do, that I was still desirable . . . *that I was real*. Maybe I was thinking about how few people get to live out their fantasies. Maybe I was thinking that he was indeed the most delicious-looking man I had ever seen. If anyone was skating on thin ice, it was I.

Yes, I wanted to.

I led him to my bedroom, left him by the bed—"I'm going to slip into something more comfortable," said I— and retreated to the bathroom, grimacing as that old, old line rattled around in my head like a tire wrench. But I forgot about my trite exit when struck by déjà vu while changing. Pulling a loose-fitting black silk camisole over my head, I remembered.

I was in a hospital, six years ago. I had showered and washed my hair, as per the nurse's orders, and was pulling a green cotton hospital gown over my head—the shroud I would wear the next morning to the operating room where I would undergo plastic surgery on my fallopian tubes, to make them more attractive to my husband's sperm. Anesthesia terrified me: I felt I might die. As I dressed, I thought, How cruel to require one to prepare one's own body for death. But the terror was tempered by an odd excitement, an excitement based in an old memory.

I was in a hospital. I was five years old, standing in a crib, in a long, cold, gray hall, holding on to the cold metal rail, screaming in terror, waiting to be taken into the operating room to have my tonsils removed. I remember being carried to the bright operating room and laid on a table. I screamed, *"NO!"* as my arms and legs were held down, *"NO!"* as someone put what looked like a strainer over my face—like the kind my mother used in the kitchen—and a white towel over the strainer, *"NO!"* as a fog of ether smothered me. There was no air, only the acrid fumes that penetrated my eyes, nose, and mouth, that made my skin tingle, go numb, my ears go deaf even to my own shrieks, that blotted out my reality as the world blackened around me. Although my arms were held fast, I reached out with both hands and grasped at the black, tried to pull holes in it, tried to pull myself from the mounding black that engulfed me, lifted me into the silent abyss.

I can remember this because I came back: It wasn't physically painful—this small death—in fact, it could have been an exciting, pleasurable trip—this going and coming —but for the terror, but for the force, the binding of choice.

As I checked the fit of my new camisole in my bathroom mirror, I felt bewildered by the craziness of my remembrances—at a time like this.

Returning to the bedroom, I found Gregg naked, lying on his side across the bed, his head propped up with his hand, his very long penis draped across his very long leg. His smooth, youthful, almost hairless body was subtly muscular and tanned from the waist up. *Cheesecake* crossed my mind, but it didn't quite fit. I sat on the bed and leaned down to put my lips to his. After that it was all rushing hearts, flushing skin, flailing arms and legs.

"I'm sorry it was so quick," he apologized when he had finished, falling asleep as the words left his mouth.

"Short but sweet," I lied, still feeling the pain of his final thrust.

But that was not the end of it. Sweetly is how we ended it . . . after he woke . . . when we made love again . . . without the confusion of fear and the unfamiliarity of foreign bodies.

"See, I tooold you!" Sandy said with an approving smile, pouring herself a mug of coffee the following morning. "So?"

"So, what?"

"So, how was it?"

"Fun . . . and kind of scary. He's so beautiful— inexperienced, but beautiful," I said, remembering how inexperienced I must have seemed, being as frenetic as he. "He's as yummy as these cream puffs," I added, dribbling melted semisweet chocolate over the tops of Toby

Handleman's four dozen cream-filled miniature puffs on the counter.

We tittered.

"I'm so glad your first time was a nice one, Tess. I've heard sooo many stories!"

"I know," I said, and related my neighbor Millie's story about her friend in Pittsburgh who ran from a date's apartment—leaving her fur coat in his closet—when he started to push her around, telling her that she was a bad girl and had to be punished. *And he'd seemed so normal,* Millie's friend had said.

Aghast, Sandy asked, "Did she get her coat back?!"

"Nope. He hung up when she called him, and she was afraid to confront him alone and embarrassed to call the police. So she reported it lost to her insurance company. They pointed out that the coat was five years old and paid her enough to buy the left sleeve of a new coat. She bought a puppy for her kids."

Sandy shook her head, looking genuinely disturbed, although I wasn't sure what aspect of the story had bothered her the most. Giving her the benefit of the doubt, I said, "There are a lot of scary people out there. Luckily, I've never run into any real wackos. Of course, my experience is rather limited. When I was in college I dated guys in my class, and I didn't lose my virginity until I was a junior."

Sandy got a settled-in-for-the-season look about her as she listened to my rather ordinary tale of my infatuation with and defloration by Stuart Singer, an ordinary-looking, ordinary student in my abnormal psych class who I decided was extraordinarily interesting by virtue of the fact that he was the only guy who showed an interest in me, and how, after a monthlong separation for winter semester break which had turned us both into rabid autoerotics primed to pounce upon one another, it all ended the split second I saw him: He had changed his hairstyle; I changed my mind.

"So what about after college? Didn't you sleep with any guys before you met Stephen?" she asked when I had finished, which was not the question I would have asked.

"Nope. Stuart Singer was the only one. And it wasn't until

31

years later, when I decided what a nerd he was, that I finally stopped feeling guilty about dropping him because of a change of part."

"Oh, Tess. What a terrible pun!"

"Sorry. I couldn't resist."

"So whatever happened to Stuart Singer? Maybe he turned out to be a really great catch, Tess."

"Are you trying to say I was ahead of his time?"

"That's two!"

"Sorry. Well, as I was saying, I decided he was a nerd when I bumped into him shortly after Stephen and I moved into this house."

"Oh. You were already married. That's funny."

"That's defense. I was trying to make myself feel better about being with Stephen and not Stuart. You're right, you see. He actually was a great catch. He married a pediatrician and had four kids and runs a very successful advertising agency."

"And you weren't happy with Stephen?"

"I guess it was when I moved here that I began to wonder if marrying Stephen might have been a mistake."

"Really? From what you've told me, it sounded like you were *never* sure about Stephen."

"What I mean is, I guess it was the first time I began to think I could live without him, regardless of whether living *with* him was a mistake or not . . . and that maybe I was wondering if he really wasn't who I thought he was . . . and that maybe I didn't like who he was, as opposed to not liking some of the things he did. Kind of Haim Ginott turned inside out. Understand?"

"I'm not sure." Sandy looked at me and screwed up her face. "Tess, why *did* you marry Stephen?"

Now there was THE question . . . the one to which I had no answer, not even for myself, I thought, remembering when I had first met Stephen.

Contrary to the opinion of many of my single friends, I believed that there was always something positive about a blind date, even if it was only the excitement of anticipation. So when Aunt Sarah told me that Uncle Martin, who was an attorney, was involved in a business deal with a young, single attorney, and that she had told Uncle Martin to give him my number, if it was okay with me, I said sure, even though I couldn't believe that anyone associated with Uncle Martin—who, according to my mother, conducted most of his business on the underside of a rock—could possibly provide anything more than a single evening's diversion with a lower life form. Stephen Fineman—the blind date—was, however, impressive. He dressed impressively, he dined impressively, he talked impressively about his clients and his business, using figures that read like long-distance telephone numbers. He was slim, attractively graying, and aloof enough to hold my interest. He was also almost thirty, which, to me at twenty-two, made him an older man . . . and therefore even more interesting. On our first date he told me a lot about himself, including the fact that he hadn't married yet because he was too selfish, a comment that I chose to ignore, ignoring, too, my belief that a woman should pay heed to what a man tells her on a first date, because he will invariably tell her who he really is.

The *first* first time I made love with a man—that was Stuart Singer—had been on a date that was after too many to count, and until I met Stephen, I hadn't dated anyone since Stuart long enough to decide it was long enough to make love to him. The first time I made love with Stephen was on our third date, which seemed long enough because when I was near him my heart thumped and my mouth was dry, and when he touched my hand I felt the world stop, and when he kissed me the world disappeared. So I guess it's not so surprising that once he made love to me, he became my world. I was very young.

"I was very young, Sandy," I finally replied to her question.

"That's an answer?"

"It's the best I can do."

We slowly nodded at each other.

"So. Are you going to see him again?" she finally asked.

"Who?"

"Cream Puff."

"Oh, I'll see him in class."

"I mean, are you going to *see* him again?"

"I don't know. I'm not going to pursue it."

"Why not?"

"He's so young, Sandy. It's like playing."

"What's wrong with that, Tess? Just a little something sweet. Nothing serious."

"Just a little dessert?"

"Right. You deserve a little treat now and then."

"Right."

"Right," she echoed.

I popped a tiny cream puff into my mouth, savoring its sweetness. And that's how it was to be with Gregg: a little treat now and then, which never seemed quite real because I didn't understand what a treat I was for him.

LEMON MIRROR CAKE

FROM: Commissary Restaurant, Philadelphia

Angel Cake

4 egg whites
6 tablespoons sugar
1/2 teaspoon vanilla extract
1/3 cup flour

Preheat oven to 350°F.

Beat egg whites until frothy. Gradually add 3 tablespoons of the sugar and beat until soft peaks form. Add vanilla; beat until peaks just barely stand (not stiff). Quickly sift 3 more tablespoons of sugar with the flour over the whites. On mixer's lowest setting, beat batter until just combined, scraping sides of bowl (mix thoroughly, but avoid overworking). Pour batter into ungreased 9-inch false-bottomed cake pan. Spread it quickly from the center, making batter flush with the pan's sides. Bake 20 to 25 minutes. Cool cake completely in the pan.

Lemon Mousse

1 cup lemon juice
1 envelope unflavored gelatin
1 tablespoon grated lemon rind
1 cup sugar
2/3 cup heavy cream
5 egg whites

In a saucepan, sprinkle gelatin over the lemon juice; let sit for 5 minutes. Stir gently over medium heat until dissolved (do not boil). Stir in rind and 1/2 cup sugar; stir to dissolve. Pour the mixture into a large bowl. Refrigerate until it is the texture of an unbeaten egg white, stirring every 10 minutes. Meanwhile, whip heavy cream until stiff and refrigerate. Once lemon mixture is ready, work quickly. Beat egg whites and 1/2 cup sugar to soft peaks; then fold into gelatin mixture. Fold in whipped cream. Pour mousse over the cake in the pan, making the top smooth. Cover pan with plastic wrap and freeze the cake until the top is hard, about 1 to 5 hours.

Raspberry Glaze

2 tablespoons water
1 1/4 teaspoons unflavored gelatin
1/2 cup raspberry puree (5 ounces frozen, sweetened, whole raspberries, pureed)
fresh raspberries

Sprinkle gelatin over cold water in a small saucepan; heat just to dissolve. Whisk in the puree; pour immediately over frozen cake, tilting back and forth for even coating. Refrigerate cake for 1/2 hour to set glaze. Transfer to serving dish. Decorate with fresh raspberries. Serves 10.

CHAPTER 4

Lemon Mirror Cake

Sunday morning brunch conversation at Mykonos with Sandy and Janet was predictable: sex and money—usually the lack thereof. Listening to each other's tales of deprivation, we were hyper-empathic; that is, no matter how bitterly one of us might complain, the others understood only *too* well, each secretly feeling at least *as* deprived, if not *more* deprived.

This morning was no exception. Janet was relating an episode of her continuing financial battles with her ex-husband (Leonard Meyer, M.D., an obstetrician/gynecologist who, if you were to believe his depositions to the family court, was so impoverished he was forced to live in a HUD-subsidized apartment house—complete with roaches, he told their son, Sean, who told Janet, who, in an unfortunate fit of frustration and rage, told Sean that his father was an asshole). Sandy greeted this debasement of the medical profession with defensive incredulity, citing Charlie's long hours with his patients, resulting in disappointing (although she seemed not to be wanting for any necessity in life apart from a sable coat and a Jaguar) recompense. Truth be told, Leonard, too, was not wanting for any necessity in life, including a forty-some-foot sailboat that he'd "sold" to his brother Albert—a man who got seasick eating in a waterfront restaurant—for one dollar shortly before he left Janet and "borrowed" from his brother almost every weekend when the weather was nice, and a fifty-some-thousand-dollar Mercedes Benz, which Leonard told the court was not his personal property but was leased by the corporation for which he worked, failing to mention that "the" corporation was "his" corporation.

Thirty-two years old, five-foot-five and not thin, Sandy's cousin Janet had moved to the area from upstate New York five years ago with Sean—now age nine—looking forward to the closeness of family, and a part-time job as a dental hygienist in Sandy's dentist's office—that's Terrance Applebaum, D.D.S.—following her divorce, an event, Janet had related, precipitated by "Leonard's sleazy affair with the little twit from his office who would give him all the love and attention he deserved and none of the aggravation." Read: Leonard left Janet to marry his very young—twenty, to be exact—very impressionable, nonigravida receptionist. "Would you believe an obstetrician who hates women and kids!" she had said, further explaining that he'd made The Twit sign an agreement that they wouldn't have children. "I don't need any more children. I need a wife who'll take care of *me*," he had cried to Janet, who had cried to Sandy, who later told me, who couldn't understand why anyone would want to leave this warm, funny woman with wildly wavy auburn hair streaked with silver, hazel green eyes made greener by tinted contact lenses, and a perfect set of never-braced, big white teeth. Perhaps it was because Dr. Leonard Meyer couldn't handle the fact that his son was handicapped, a victim of cerebral palsy. I had first met Janet and Sean the morning of Sean's fifth birthday.

Sandy and I went over to Janet's to help with Sean's party for sixteen five- and six-year-olds. I had been in my new house about two months and was already fast friends with Sandy, whom I had met at the supermarket when I oohed and ahed over Rebecca in her infant carrier while waiting in the express line. So one day, when Sandy told me she was going to help at her cousin's son's birthday party and asked if I knew how to make a birthday cake, I said I'd make the cake for her if I could help at the party, too. I never could resist a roomful of kids.

Sean was a charmer, and a typical five-year-old—on wheels—which, I came to understand after knowing them awhile, was surely as much a tribute to Janet's strength as it was to his. The party was a success, i.e., the kids went home happy and the three of us were done in. So. After the party, after dinner, after bath and bed for Sean, and after Sandy nursed Rebecca and put her down on Janet's bed between two king-size pillows, the three of us shared a bottle of wine and three dozen of my chocolate chip cookies in Janet's living room while Janet told the story of Sean's catastrophic birth. It was a story Sandy had heard before, and one that Janet would tell over and over throughout her life—a kind of litany of acceptance. "Lenny was devastated when it happened," she started. She always started obliquely—with her husband's pain. She told us that it was months before Lenny could admit that Sean wasn't going to get better. "Actually, he never said that," she clarified, "he just stopped talking about it. You know, it's so incredibly ironic—I was married to an obstetrician, and I had this major, MAJOR problem at Sean's birth." Abruptio placentae, one of obstetrics' most dangerous complications, she explained, had robbed Sean of his potential to walk and many other motor skills, and Janet of her uterus. "Sometimes I think doctors have a harder time with this kind of thing than other fathers, just because they *are* doctors and they can't do anything to make it all right," she said with greater compassion for Leonard than she would ever express for herself. "We were really lucky," we would hear Janet say many times over the years. To Janet, *lucky* meant that she hadn't bled to death, that Sean hadn't died of oxygen deprivation, that Sean wasn't mentally retarded as well as physically handicapped, that Leonard could afford to provide the special care that Sean needed—even if she had to take him to court to compel him to provide it. Watching Sean and Janet in their individual struggles—he with his

39

uncooperative muscles, she with her uncooperative ex-husband—I never had the feeling that she and Sean were at all lucky, just very, very brave.

Today the struggle was about a special-needs summer camp Janet had found for Sean, where a wheelchair was neither out of place nor an impediment to an enriching camping experience. It sounded good, Leonard had agreed, but it was expensive.

"Sooo," Sandy piped up.

"Sooo," Janet mimicked, "Fuckface told Sean that he can't afford to send him to overnight camp this summer."

"Jaaanet."

"Saaandy. Grow up. I'm being kind. Do you know what he had the gall to tell his son? 'Don't worry, your *mother* can send you to camp.' Now, why can't Fu—why can't F.F. afford it? you may ask. Well, because he and The Twit—unencumbered as they are—are going to Italy for three weeks in May," Janet started.

"They're probably going to a medical meeting, so it's all deductible. Doctors don't make as much as you think," Sandy lectured. "You know how decrepit my car is? Well, we can't afford a new one until Charlie's Mercedes is paid off. I, too, used to think that doctors' wives were able to have whatever they wanted," she sighed, changing the subject.

"You were only half right: doctors' *second* wives get everything they want!" Janet said with possible malice aforethought, sending Sandy into a pout.

Sandy is such a baby, I judged . . . and Janet sounds so bitter. But the fact is that Janet is what is called "painfully honest" by those who know, and "bitter" by those who have no idea. I knew she wasn't the only ex-wife of a professional to fall from homemaking and motherhood, triyearly vacations, charge accounts at Saks and Bloomie's, a new car every two years, and fine restaurants and theater on Saturday nights . . . to an entry-level job, a week's vacation at home with the kids in December, bills from Marshall's and Filene's Basement, a new muffler or brakes for the old car

40

every year, and pizza and a videotaped movie on Saturday nights with the kids—thank God for the children! And despite it all, from what I could see, Janet had remained the warm, caring mother, the interested, generous friend that Sandy had said she was before her divorce—if sometimes a little too honest.

It was Janet who interrupted my star-skipping with, "So how was your blind date last night?"

"Not bad, but nothing special. He's just a salesman," I answered—understanding that, for Janet, the subject of Leonard Meyer, M.D., in any form, was over for now—and I shared with them the hours I had shared with Marv Kravitz (a man who had gotten my number from Phyllis Becker, a woman who carpooled with Sandy for Rebecca's ballet class and whom I hardly knew, but who'd known Marv since high school) at Le Petit Champignon, including a description of our dinner: I had sweetbreads in Madeira; he had escargot in burgundy; we shared a rack of lamb in mustard, with baby veggies; a small mixed salad vinaigrette followed the entrée; with pots of tea—Earl Grey for him and chamomile for me—we relished a small plate of white chocolate mousse in raspberry sauce garnished with fresh raspberries and slices of kiwi, and a lemon mirror cake for two. This elegant layering of angel cake and lemon mousse is frozen, and then topped with a hot raspberry glaze that's cooled in the refrigerator to a shiny clear mirror finish. "Oooh, look at that pretty lady in the mirror! She looks almost good enough to eat," Marv had crooned with a sly smile as we peered at our reflections in the top of the cake.

"Nothing special, she says! Actually, we *all* eat like that *all* the time!" Janet teased.

"I mean *he* wasn't special."

"So, are you going to see him again?"

"Next Saturday."

"Special enough."

"Better than being alone."

"Alone? So where's Cream Puff?"

"I see the name's sticking," I answered, not answering,

silently savoring the memory of Gregg's second visit two weeks ago.

"So, have you seen him?"

"Not in two weeks."

"Why not?"

"Janet, this is not an ordinary relationship. It's an ephemeral kind of thing," I said, sounding as pretentious as I felt.

"You mean he calls you when he's horny?"

Leave it to Janet to cut to the bone, I thought. "Well, I get horny too," I said.

"So why don't you call him?"

"Because I don't want to make more of this than it really is." How it *really* was, I realized as I said it, I *really* didn't know.

"You know, Tess, I don't think you *really* know how it *really* is," Janet said, understanding how I really am.

"God, Janet, don't play shrink."

"Maybe you *need* a shrink."

Sandy, who had been sitting sucking at her coffee, chimed in, "I think you *both* could use a good shrink. At least you get a little excitement in your lives. All Charlie does is work."

"So, how's Harvey?" I asked Janet, ignoring Sandy, but wondering if the vague rumor about Charlie's mistress in their shore apartment was, in fact, true.

"Harvey's Harvey," she answered, ignoring Sandy.

"Who's Harvey," Sandy asked.

"I've told you about him . . . haven't I?" Janet said, drawing Sandy back into the fold.

"If you did, I don't remember."

"Well. Harvey Cohen is a financial planner who does work for Terry, and ever since I cleaned his teeth about five months ago, he's been coming on to me."

"Oh, Janet, you think eeevery guy who smiles at you is coming on to you!" snipped Sandy.

She should talk! I thought.

"Then, about three months ago," Janet continued, "Harvey was in to see Terry about some business, and on the way out he pulled me aside and asked me to have lunch with him the next day, which I did. And then he asked me to spend the following Saturday with him."

"Oh? So how was it?" Sandy asked.

"All I can say is that he pushes all the right buttons for me."

"See that! And you keep saying that all the good men are married."

"They are. He is."

"Jaaanet! No wonder you didn't tell me about him before."

"Well, if I didn't, Sandy, it was probably because I didn't want to hear 'Jaaanet!' "

"It's just that I don't understand—"

"The only thing to understand is that I didn't go after him, he came after me. And if I hadn't accepted, someone else would have—he was looking. And, besides, there's no one else around, so why should I be celibate?"

"You mean you only see him because you're horny?" I sniped, missing the mark a bit.

"I'm glad I'm married. I couldn't deal with the single life," said Sandy.

Neither could I, I thought, mentally trying to sort out the difference between sleeping with a married man who plays around and sleeping with a single man who plays around. There was, of course, the issue of marital infidelity. There was also AIDS. Married men could get it and give it to their unsuspecting wives. Married men were definitely losing points. As to what all this said about the "other" women who consorted with them . . . well, that needed further sorting out.

It was David I called as soon as I got home from brunch.

David Ross, Stephen's officemate, occasional business partner, and closest—make that *only*—friend, was one of the nicest people I had ever known, and with his honey blond hair and brown eyes lighted by specks of gold, one of the most attractive, almost pretty beneath his carefully trimmed beard. David was also warm and caring, a svelte six-foot-one of sensitivity carefully honed by years of soul-searching through encounter groups and several modes of psychotherapy. He did not, however, stitch himself into any of the disciplines that he tried on, but gleaned the softest, most giving traits from each. So, despite his years of training, he was not commercialized, not molded into a smooth, slick, glowing social machine; he was sort of fuzzy around the edges. And when you listened to him, you felt that he was listening to you. Stephen once commented that in David's practice of law, he was smart enough, but in a dumb sort of way: He had some great ideas, but he didn't know how to carry them out. David was smart in a dumb way when it came to women, too. Women loved him, but he didn't seem to know what to do with them. He dated a lot, but at thirty-one he had no wife, no steady girl. In fact, in the five years Stephen and I had known David, he had never had a significant relationship with any woman. But for the strong sexual vibrations I felt when I was near him, I might have thought him gay.

"I need the name of a good shrink," I cried over the phone.

"A shrink? What for, Tess? You're a rock, one of the few women in the world I can count on for rational behavior," he praised.

"I don't think I'm coping well with single life," I confessed.

"Are any of us?"

"You seem to do okay."

Silence.

"So, who's the shrink?" I asked again, not knowing what else to say and beginning to feel uneasy.

He gave me the phone number of Dr. Michael Lerner, and then said, "Tess, I want you to know that I'm here for you. This has nothing to do with Stephen. I care about you, and I want to help you in any way I can."

"Thanks, David. I know you're there."

"Okay," he teased, forcing the softness from his voice, "call Lerner, but don't let him mess with your terrific

44

neuroses. You know I love you just the way you are! Understand?"

Understand? What? That he loved me? Could he love me? Maybe he's been waiting for *me*, I thought, remembering our years of friendship, the times he'd joined Stephen and me at dinner or a movie, with or without a date, the many times he'd stopped over for a drink, a cup of coffee, unannounced . . . always warm, always caring, never out of line.

"Tess! You home? Knock, knock!"

"I thought I heard a rapping at my door," I had greeted David in the pantry that afternoon with a smile, panting slightly from the dash from my office. I kissed him lightly on the side of his mouth and he gave my arm a rub. David never pats, I noted.

"How ya doin', kiddo? Bake anything irresistible today?" he asked, heading straight for my cookie jar—a mammoth ceramic creation shaped like a house, complete with two children holding cookies, standing under a tree.

"Only chocolate chips," I warned before he lifted the lid, referring to the Toll House cookies I make all the time, for myself, from the original recipe on the back of the chocolate chip package—the ones my mother made for me when I was a child.

"*Only* chocolate chips, she says," he said, diving in and coming up with a handful, and then heading for the refrigerator, a cookie already in his mouth. "Milk?"

"I'll get you a glass . . . and a plate."

Once settled at the kitchen table with his milk and cookies, David told me what a lucky guy Stephen was to have found someone who was not only beautiful and smart, but who could cook. He was always telling me that. He was always telling Stephen that. Neither of us believed him.

"Honestly, David, I can't understand why some lovely lady hasn't swept you off your feet long ago."

"You did. But you were already married to Stephen."

"Right. With that attitude, you'll never get married. Don't you ever get serious?"

"I am serious. You just won't believe me." And he laughed, devoured a cookie in one bite, and washed it down with a gulp of milk.

"So, how is my husband?" I asked, wondering if he'd be home on time tonight . . . for a change.

"Oh, right. I told him I was stopping here on the way home, and he asked me to tell you that he'll probably be a few minutes late. The man is so disorganized."

"Tell me about it!"

"Don't worry. I keep my eye on him for you. I told him that I was going to join you two for dinner and that *I* didn't want to be kept waiting." He hesitated for a moment, then added, "That okay with you, Tess? Mind a tagalong?"

"What? No date tonight?"

"It's a slow season."

"You know you're always welcome, David."

Watching him in my kitchen, munching on cookies like a little kid, being as pleasant and supportive as I could imagine a man could be, I tried to imagine what it would be like to be married to David instead of Stephen. He was so attractive . . . and when he got up to leave—"I have to stop at home for a minute. I'll see you at Antonio's at six-thirty," he said—and gave me a hug, I kept the feeling of his arms around me after he had gone. *You swept me off my feet. You shouldn't be married to Stephen,"* I imagined him saying to me while he buried his soft beard in my neck. And I grew warm imagining his hands on my back, on my backside, his mouth on my neck, on my mouth, his long white fingers slipping between my . . . An image of David and Katrina plastered itself over my fantasy. Katrina, the long-legged, long-haired dancer from the Pennsylvania Ballet Company who spoke in whispers—when she spoke at all—was the last lady I had seen David with. We were celebrating David's birthday at the Fountain Room in the Four Seasons Hotel. She couldn't keep her hands off him, in her own quiet way, and they didn't come back to our house after dinner— Katrina had said she had a present for David at her apartment. I pictured David making love to Katrina . . . her long slim legs entwined with his . . . her long, straight, golden hair swirled around the two of them. . . . And I cringed at the thought of my short legs, my short boyish hair, and . . . Katrina. She probably made that name up for the theater, I decided. And why was Stephen always late? I wondered, now totally annoyed. And as much as I enjoyed having David around, why did Stephen not mind that David was always around? It was as if he used David as a buffer, so he didn't have to get too close to me. Yes. Stephen had trouble being close, I thought, believing that Stephen loved me very deeply . . . so deeply that it scared him. Yes. It felt nice to be loved so deeply. And I continued my fantasy, but replaced David with Stephen . . . Stephen telling me that he loved me so much that it scared him.

Yes. *I'm* never out of line. But David. Do I understand David—who he is? how he feels? what he's saying? I always believed it was Stephen that David wanted to be close to, a strong male bond to stave off the loneliness of singleness. Then again, David and I had remained friends even after Stephen and I separated. But David was like that, able to divide his loyalties successfully. Of course, I fought with myself, it *could* be me. No. I'm not his type. Not at all like those young, leggy, blond creatures who ran through his life leaving no fingerprints on his soul, barely lifting the dust from his id. Surely he was just being his usual caring, sharing, nurturing, warm, sensitive—

"Tess? Are you still there?" I heard David question over the phone, over the buzz of my inner monologue. "Tess, I want to be sure you understand what I'm saying."

"Of course I understand," I finally answered, not understanding at all.

I wanted to make something special for Jacqui Berkman's Friday evening dinner party, something that would reflect the pretensions of one who spelled Jackie *Jacqui*. So I called Le Petit Champignon and got the recipe for their lemon mirror cake. I was picturing Jacqui admiring the finished cake, admiring herself in its shiny glaze, when I was struck

47

by an odd thought seemingly from nowhere: What would Jacqui see? Tall, extraordinarily thin (she always had five pounds to lose, but no one could figure out where), with blunt-cut, short, straight brown hair to her earlobes, parted in the middle, accentuating her sunken cheeks and sharp nose, her thin lips: One of Tom Wolfe's social X-rays, the way I see her; chic, exotic, the way she sees herself. "Don't you think I look exotic with my hair this way?" she had asked me at a cocktail party, stealing a glance at herself in a large oval mirror on the wall behind me. I remember thinking at the time how her high-fashion taupe dress hung on her bones, drained the color from her gaunt cheeks, how there was no possible way her thighs could touch. Exotic? No. "Yes," I said, "it gives you a really different look." Different from what you see in the mirror, I thought.

Setting out the ingredients for the cake, I considered that even in mirrors we probably don't see ourselves as we really are. This idea crystallized the nebulous mental meanderings that had plagued me since my first meeting with Dr. Lerner—Michael—almost a month ago, on a Tuesday, at eleven.

Remembering my first visit with Michael made me want to hide in a closet. I had tried to impress him with my intelligence, generosity of spirit, charm, sense of style, my youth (surely I was younger than he)—my image of myself as a totally desirable woman in complete control of her being. Right. That's why I was sitting in a shrink's office. Surely he saw right through me, understood that I was a total fraud.

By our third appointment, this past Tuesday, I was a little more comfortable—a little less comfortable than I am in a dentist's chair—comfortable enough to notice that Michael was actually younger than I by three or four years. Then again, perhaps he looked younger than he was. Average in height and build, Michael was above average in looks. The waves in his black hair hid early strands of silver. His dark eyes were alive behind clear-framed glasses. I liked the way he sat in a black leather Eames chair, in *front* of the desk rather than *behind* it, so that he sat facing me, close to me, as

48

I crossed and uncrossed my legs on the sofa across from his desk. Behind the desk, against the back wall, a trough of tropical trees and plants—some nearly six feet tall—were warmed by a row of track lights in the ceiling. Light from a row of tall casement windows on the right covered with old-style wooden venetian blinds formed glowing stripes across the floor behind Michael's chair.

"So, how do you see yourself?" he asked after I had shared a few vignettes from my growing-up years.

Yes, I look pretty. Yes, I'm having a good time, I remember thinking as I checked the hall mirror of my girlfriend's home. I was nine, maybe ten, and I was dressed up as a Dutch girl for a Halloween party. And my mother had put bright red lipstick on my mouth and circles of red rouge on my cheeks and shiny black mascara on my long eyelashes. But I had to keep looking in the mirror to know that I was.

Attractive, I remember thinking as I walked by the wall of mirrors at one end of the girls' gym, stealing a look at myself wearing a fluffy blue and silver strapless prom gown. But the boys, whose attention I begged as I walked daintily to and from the girls' room, appeared oblivious to me.

Yes, an eye-catcher, I remember thinking, glancing at my image in a tall, ornate pier mirror in a hotel lobby, perceiving a lovely young lady in black taffeta at a college dance. But it seemed that the young men whose attention I was trying to will were totally unaware of my presence.

"Oh, yes, we've met before," said the middle-aged lawyer's middle-aged wife when we were introduced at some professional function I was attending with Stephen several years ago. "You're noticeable." Was that a compliment? Does "noticeable" mean "attractive"? The men in the room didn't seem to notice me at all.

"I don't know, Michael. Isn't that why I'm here? Do you want to hear something weird? I'm not even sure if I know what I really look like."

"That's right," he said, leaving me wondering what he meant by that.

"Several people have told me that I don't photograph the way I actually look . . . and someone—the first husband of an old friend—once told me I was many women in one, always changing. I don't see myself as that complicated. He also told me he loved me," I babbled on. "And another friend, Alan Garfield, my friend Millie's husband, once said, 'You have a thousand faces in you.' . . . Does that mean he loves me? And he told me I was memorable. Is that anything like noticeable? And how does one remember someone who's always changing?"

"Perhaps that's why one remembers," Michael offered gently.

I looked at him blankly and did not respond, but something somewhere inside me clicked and I felt the back of my throat tighten, my eyes become myopic behind a film of moisture, my ears fill with soft static as I pulled myself in.

The buzz of the oven timer roused me from memory to the warm, sweet aroma of baked cake and the drone of the mixer. I turned the mixer off, retrieved the golden sponge cakes from the oven and set them on a rack to cool, and put the bowl of whipped cream in the refrigerator. Sandy walked in—on her way home from dropping Rebecca off at nursery school—as I was sitting down at the counter for a coffee break.

"Hiii! I see coffee's on," she said.

"Morning. My! Don't we look glowing! What's up?"

"Oh, nothing much. It's just that the nicest thing happened," she said, pouring herself a mug of coffee and opening the refrigerator to look for milk. "Anyway," she continued after sitting at the counter, pushing the mixer to the side, "I was coming out of Rebecca's school and I bumped into Danny Foster—remember him? Ruth's husband? You know . . . Ruth, the potter? I've got one of her pots in my living room by the fireplace. Well, Danny was dropping Matthew off at school—Matthew's the youngest of, would you believe, five! Can you imagine! Five! I can't find time enough for two. . . ."

No, I couldn't imagine all those warm little bodies, those sticky sweet hands, those loving little arms.

Catching the shadow that crossed my face, Sandy caught herself. ". . . I mean, you know I'm thankful for two healthy kids, it's only that I find it hard to imagine *five*—"

"I know," I said, offering a helping hand. "It's always hard to place yourself in someone else's shoes."

"Right. Anyway, we almost literally bumped, and he made a big fuss about how nice it was to see me, how wooonderful I looked. . . . Tess, I think he was coming on to me. I mean, the way he grabbed my arms when we bumped, like he didn't want to let go, and he made such a fuss—"

You probably had your lashes going double time, I thought to myself. "You do look bright today, Sandy," I said honestly, noting her canary yellow cashmere sweater-blouse—opened to the third button.

"Yes, I think so. His wife doesn't do a whole lot with herself. She wears those long skirts and heavy sweaters . . . she neeever wears any makeup, and her hands are so rough from throwing pots. I'll bet her nails never saw a coat of polish—what nails she has!"

"Sandy," I groaned, watching her slender hands flutter around like birds with scarlet-tipped white feathers.

"Oh, Tess, I'm not trying to be mean, but Danny actually said something about how put-together I always look."

"My, my!"

"Oh, it wasn't really anything . . . but I'll bet he would like it to be something."

"You may be right," I said, softening my attitude, feeling a sting of jealousy. "You know, men don't make passes at me. I always hear women talking about all the married men who make passes at them. Not me."

"Tess, I can't believe that."

"No, it's true. Maybe I give off the wrong vibrations."

"You mean you want married men to come on to you? You'd have an affair with one?"

"No. I'm only saying that it would be nice to believe that I'm desirable."

"Oh, come on, Tess. You're so attractive. You just don't know what a pass is!"

"Do you think so?"

"Absoluuutely. Guys look at you all the time when I'm with you."

"Never. They're always busy looking at you."

"Are you kidding? You turn heads, Tess. I've been green with envy lots of times. And I marvel at how you stay so cool and unaffected."

"That's because I'm unaware." I got up to turn the cakes out. Running a knife around the edges of the pans, I recalled one incident: "Well, there was one guy, when Stephen and I were still together—"

"Who? When? Where?"

"Didn't I ever tell you about the French doctor? At the Legal Aid Society dinner dance . . . oh, it had to be two, three years ago."

I related the story to Sandy while making the lemon mousse, which was as silky as the soft yellow satin dress I had worn that night.

Clingy, backless—a no-underwear dress. Stephen hated it. I loved it. It made me feel alluring, although I was sure no one ever took notice of me.

Stephen and I walked slowly among the crowd, stopping before familiar faces, reacting automatically to automatic conversation. Soon bored, I toyed abstractly with my inner switches. The right stance, a measure of inner tension . . . I turned on, flashing a smile toward Stephen.

"What's the matter?" he responded predictably, disappointingly. I faded, turning my attention to the crowd herding toward the tables for dinner.

Although I had planned to maintain my usual low profile, I changed my mind when seated. Above the haze of legal jargon, a treatise on the color and clarity of fine wine was being delivered by the man to my immediate right, René Breton, a plastic surgeon from France and the brother-in-law of a local judge, whom I had met briefly about a year before. Although he had been in this country for more than

52

ten years, he had retained a heart-melting accent. Switching on, I felt my eyes light up, my heart pump a blush to my cheeks.

The slight, middle-aged doctor turned his inquiring blue eyes to me. "Some wine?" he offered.

"Thank you, yes," I said, smiling.

After filling my glass, he stood up and proposed a devastating toast in the spirit of his profession: "Here's to flapping thighs, sagging breasts, and falling faces."

Immediately I became aware of my tiny breasts, gelatinous thighs, and the faint smile lines on my thirtyish face, but managed to maintain a measure of inner tension as the Frenchman sat down and touched his glass to mine. When he asked me to dance, I was startled and confused for a moment, not knowing if I should ask Stephen for permission, or just say yes . . . or no. With the finesse only a totally nonplussed woman can summon, I cast a dazzling smile upon René, turned to Stephen, and, placing a hand on his, asked, "Do you mind?" Without waiting for an answer, I offered my hand to René.

He took me in his arms, grasping me closer than I thought possible while still dressed, and I suddenly realized that I hadn't danced with a man other than Stephen in years. When I first heard the compliment, it whizzed by my ear like a snatch of someone else's conversation. I thought I heard it, then wasn't sure, then was sure but didn't want to be, then was not sure and wanted to hear it again.

"I'm sorry, what was that?" I queried obtusely.

He said it again—slowly, deliberately: "You are a very beautiful woman."

I pulled away slightly to search his eyes. Surely he sensed my surprise, I thought. Surely he loved my surprise, I later thought. Managing a quiet "thank you," I allowed him to gather me in his arms once again and whirl me about. The compliment was beating in my ears. He'd called me beautiful, a beautiful woman. Then it was fluttering inside me, tickling a giddy smile to my lips. The compliment, a small bird with large wings, beat under my heart as I became aware of the Frenchman speaking.

"You are beautiful, stunning."

Oh, the deliciousness of it! Don't stop, don't ever stop, I thought to myself as the bird thrashed around wildly inside me.

"Of course," he added decorously, "I mean it sincerely, and without any improper intent."

"Of course," I echoed, embarrassed and flustered, not quite sure if he meant it or not, not quite sure if I wanted him to mean it.

Dancing with René through a second musical set, I slowly became aware of Stephen standing just a few feet away, his eyes following me and my admirer as we laced through and around the other couples on the dance floor. In a moment he was beside us, a hand on René's shoulder.

"Pardon me, this is our dance," Stephen said coolly, reclaiming me from the arms of my surprised partner.

I fell into comfortably familiar steps, and preened mentally.

"I know tomorrow is Sunday, but the accountants have arranged a tax meeting, so I'll be gone most of the day," Stephen announced.

"Oh, that's all right, I have plans for tomorrow," I parried with sangfroid as I pictured myself and the French doctor doing incredibly lewd and lascivious things in one of those motels with the water beds, video cameras, and hourly rates.

"What a greaaat story, Tess. So, did he call?"

"You are incredible." I laughed at Sandy, putting the now completed cakes in the freezer. "I never considered that I would ever bump into him again, and I certainly didn't think he'd actually call me. But, guess what."

"He called."

"He called. One afternoon after Stephen and I had separated, ostensibly to find Stephen. At first I thought he really wanted to find Stephen. Then I thought, A business call? In the afternoon? At home?"

"So did you see him?"

"You've got to be kidding. I gave him Stephen's office number."

"It could have been fun."

"I doubt it. But the point is, I fell for his line. I didn't even know it was a pass! I really thought he had meant what he said." I began cleaning up, putting the pans and bowls, beaters and spoons into the dishwasher. "Then he called and I realized . . . I felt so dumb!"

"Tess. How do I explain this to you? Why do you think he complimented you?"

"Because he heard I was newly separated and figured I'd be easy."

"But you weren't separated at the dance. And he didn't call until after you were separated."

"But *he* was still married!"

"So, what did you want him to do—divorce his wife so he could say something nice to a pretty lady who caught his eye at a dance?"

I noted exasperation in her voice. Was I exasperating?

"God! Tess, you're exasperating."

"But am I attractive?!"

"Look in the mirror!"

"Mirrors don't work."

"They work for some things," Sandy said, then broke up in a howl of laughter. I threw my arms around her and we laughed until tears ran down our faces, remembering what I had related to her the previous Sunday.

"So how did your date go last night?" Sandy had questioned at Sunday brunch (Sandy and I were alone; Sean was being treated by a school friend's family to a day in Philadelphia, including a show at the Fels Planetarium in the Franklin Institute, so Janet had treated herself to a day in New York City with Harvey, who had told his wife he had to attend an investment seminar). Sandy was referring to my third date with Marv Kravitz.

In my head I quickly reviewed the developing gestalt.

Marv was a nice man, terribly hurt by a wicked wife who ran off with the director of her little theater group at her synagogue. Well, she didn't exactly run off with him. My dentist's hygienist's husband ran off with her brother's wife. They ran off to Australia. Marv's wife moved into The Director's center-city apartment—about twenty minutes from Marv. Marv's fourteen-year-old son, Zachery, visited his mom every other weekend and Wednesday nights for dinner.

A manufacturers' rep for boudoir mirrors, Marv was every inch the salesman—the inches that he had. When he had pulled up to the house for our first date a month ago in a very long navy blue Lincoln Town Car, I watched from my kitchen window as he descended from the plush velour front seat to the driveway. About five-foot-four and slight of build, Marv looked like a little boy. We reached the front door at the same time, but I waited for half a minute after he rang the bell before I opened it, taking time to check myself out in the art deco mirror above the chocolate-marble-topped credenza in the foyer. Hair okay. Makeup okay, although the dark shadows under my eyes attested to a lack of sleep the night before. And I did look awfully thin. So I smiled vigorously to appear more alive as I opened the door. "Tess?" "Hi, Marv," I greeted him, extending my hand as he walked through the door. His small hand gripped mine overly hard. We both smiled a lot, made our way through the formalities of how lovely my home was, how lovely I was, what a lovely evening it was. He held my coat for me with an exaggerated flourish—"Your coat, madam!" The car door was opened for me with the same flourish. Watching him walk briskly around the car to the driver's side, with his head held a little too high, his arms swinging a little too wide, I was reminded of Spanky of the Little Rascals, and I wondered if tucked away in a closet in Marv's home was a beanie. He was sweet, though, and it was nice talking to a man who wasn't overtly weird, so at evening's end, when he walked me to the door, kissed my hand—with a flourish— and asked me for another date, I accepted.

And after a second date—we saw the latest Woody Allen movie and ate dinner at a local Italian restaurant, and he gave me a peck on the cheek at my door and rubbed my hand as he told me that he had found it hard to concentrate on his work since our first date—I accepted a third date.

"It was bizarre," I finally answered Sandy, and shared with her the hours I had shared with Marv on our third date.

After an intimate dinner and a bottle of wine at Charades, a nouvelle cuisine restaurant in the area ("We should eat light," he had said cryptically), Marv asked me back to his home—to show me his line.

"Is that anything like etchings?" I teased him.

"Do you mean, is my line just *a line?*" he retorted.

I laughed nervously and wondered if I should go, because, after all, wouldn't that mean that I was willing to . . . and was I willing to . . . ? No, I wasn't ready to . . . but no, I didn't want to appear the prude, and no, it wasn't very late, and no, I wasn't ready to go back to my big, empty house, so, yes, I would go, have a cup of tea, see his line of mirrors, and then it would be late enough to call it a night.

So there we were in the early American country kitchen of his three-bedroom, two-bath ranch home, with the plate rail above the dark wooden cabinets and the Pennsylvania Dutch hex signs on the wallpaper. Marv was fixing me a cup of Earl Grey tea, which I love but don't drink at night because it's loaded with caffeine, but which I said was fine because it was all he had and I wanted to be agreeable. And I was leaning against the built-in phone center—a kind of raised desk in an alcove with a wall telephone—when he set the tea on the table, came over to me, put his arms around me, kissed me lightly, and pressed his body to mine. He was just about my size, which felt nice, and he smelled good, and when he kissed me again, seriously, his mouth was warm and soft. I felt my blood stir.

"Oooph! What you're doing to me!" he said, slowly grinding his pelvis against mine, pushing me against the desk behind me. "Oooh! Feel that? Feel what you're doing to me?" he said, pushing harder, his eyes closed, his face puckered up in ecstasy. But the only hard thing I felt was the

57

knob of the desk drawer poking me in the ass. He kissed me again, passionately, running his little hands up and down my back. "Oooh, yes, yes," he whispered in my ear. "Feel it, feel it," he rasped, pushing into me. But the harder he pressed, the harder the knob bit into me, until, in pain, I pushed away from the desk—into him. "Oh, yes, that's good!" he responded, misinterpreting my movement as passion. "Come with me, *mon cherie,* I want to show you my line," he said, suddenly pulling away, holding my hand, leading me toward the bedroom wing off the front hall. What was intended to be the third bedroom, between his son's room and the master bedroom, was Marv's showroom. The walls were hung with mirrors in brass frames, wooden frames, carved frames, mirrored frames. There were full-length mirrors for walls and doors, and wide mirrors to go over bureaus and dressing tables. Marv showed me around the room, guiding me by my shoulders from behind, stopping before particular mirrors to point out favorite designs —"Look at the detail on the French baroque piece"—and to nuzzle my neck. Did he, in fact, roll his eyes upward to look into the mirror as he kissed my neck? I wasn't sure the first time, but he did it again. Yes, he definitely looked at us posed in front of the mirror, his face in my neck, his hands running down my arms—and he closed his eyes quickly when he saw me looking at him looking.

"Very nice," I finally said, pulling away from him. "It's a lovely line, Marv."

"But you haven't seen the best ones yet—my private collection," he said, taking me by the hand again, leading me to the master bedroom.

A king-size mahogany four-poster bed with a mahogany canopy stood against the back wall. On the wall, between the low headboard and the canopy, a large mirror in an unusual bronze and brass frame—"Isn't it fabulous?" said Marv. "I got it at an estate auction in New York"—appeared to be improperly hung so that the top tilted slightly away from the wall. In front of the windows on the right was a love seat covered in a floral fabric matching the drapes on the windows. Next to the love seat stood a small round antique table, and on it was a tiny crystal lamp and a six-inch oval mirror in a hand-cut glass frame—"I found that in an antique shop in Connecticut," Marv said. In the corner across from the foot of the bed, to the right of the love seat, was a handmade brass brazier from India, the top of which had been electrified and hung from the ceiling on a long brass chain. Its shapely dome, hanging low over the footed bowl planted with ivy, was punched out in an intricate design, throwing an eerie light over the room and snowflake patterns on the soft-rose walls. This was the only light on in the room. Next to a mahogany triple dresser on the left wall was a matching highboy. Above the triple dresser hung a huge mirror in a gilt wooden frame—"From my grand-mother's home. It was her mother's," he explained. Along the wall in front of the bed, next to the brazier, were three antique cheval mirrors—"My prizes," he said proudly as he paraded me before them, touching each one, causing them to tilt slightly in their freestanding frames. Two were rectan-gular: One, in a heavy brass and iron frame, had been imported from Italy; the other, elegant in a simple cherry frame, was English.

"This is my favorite," he said, stopping in front of the last glass. The large beveled oval mirror was framed in heavily carved ebony and mounted on solid brass swivels in an ebony stand that was taller than the glass itself, its sides terminating in thick, eight-inch finials. Here and there on the glass were small patches of gray where the silvering was eroding. "This is a very old piece, from the eighteenth century. The wood feels wonderful. It's so smooth and hard," Marv said, reaching up to stroke one of the finials slowly with his left hand. Grinning lasciviously in the mirror, still stroking the finial, he took my hand with his right hand and pressed it into his groin. My heart skipped a beat and then began to race. I saw everything at once in the mirror—his eyes, my eyes, my hand in his hand in his mushy crotch—and before I could move, his arms were around me and he was kissing me tenderly, smelling won-derfully of something musky, and then he was behind me unbuttoning my cream silk blouse, kissing my neck. And I just stood there letting him, watching him undress me in the mirror in the dim, eerie light. It was all quite strange. We were disembodied from He and She in the mirror, but the feelings of those bodies remained with us.

I watched Her standing naked and flushed. He took Her hands and ran them along the sides of Her body. I felt Her hardened nipples as He steered Her hands across Her breasts, which appeared larger than I had remembered them to be, but the touch of Her hands sent a familiar charge through me. "You are beautiful . . ." He said, ". . . look how beautiful . . . so smooth . . . so tight . . ." drawing Her right hand toward the dark triangle, pressing closer behind Her. I felt the soft, the wet, as He guided Her fingers . . . I felt the waves of pleasure, the tension as He slipped Her fingers to and fro, as He rocked behind Her. My knees gave way and I found myself on the floor, on the soft gray carpet, looking up at Marv, who was suddenly out of His clothes, moving the cheval glasses on their casters out from the wall, forming an alcove of mirrors, tipping them slightly downward on their swivels so that I could see Her looking down at me. And He spread Her legs gently so I could see Her soft hidden parts. . . . I watched as He knelt, His small penis hanging limply, and touched Her swollen pink flesh . . . and I quivered and moaned softly . . . and He lay down between Her legs and put His mouth to Her flesh and I felt the unbearable velvet of His tongue, the tiny spasms in the muscles of Her tense legs and arms—and I did not miss the small bald spot on the back of His head reflecting the tiny flakes of light from the brazier—and just when I was lost in pleasure, when I thought I would explode with pleasure, he suddenly stood up.

"Don't stop!" I heard myself cry out.

"Wait, it's not over," he said, pulling me up, kissing me, coaxing me to my knees, pushing the mirrors upright. We watched as He moved close to Her. "Touch me," He said . . . and She reached out to touch Him, to stroke Him until I felt His member slowly swell, filling Her hand, growing hard and smooth, growing and growing much beyond what one would have expected of a thing so small

. . . or so it appeared in the looking glass. I watched as He moved back and forth, forcing the great burning cock up and back in Her small fist. "I love a woman with small hands," He said. "Look how big it looks in that small hand. . . . Look how big and hard it is. . . . Feel how hot it is. . . . Oooh, what you do to me," He said, rocking up and back. But suddenly He stopped, pulled me to my feet, took me to the bed. And when I lay crosswise on the bed and looked up, I saw the secret mirrors of the canopy reflect Her smooth, shapely, outstretched body. He took Her hand and placed it between Her legs. . . . "Oooh, doesn't that feel good, isn't that hot," He said. And I was watching Her caress herself . . . yes, She knew how, She knew where, how fast, how hard, when to stop so it wouldn't end . . . when a soft sound drew part of me to another dimension coming toward me—the reflection in the great ebony cheval mirror that Marv wheeled to the edge of the bed. And shortly I was surrounded by reflections so that when he lay next to me, we two had become twelve. He watched, I watched, They watched, as He stroked himself to mythic proportions . . . as bodies touched and turned and played and burned . . . as the headless woman in the mirror lowered herself onto Him. I felt the filling the stroking the exquisite pleasure and I closed my eyes and flattened my body full of him against him and he watched as She moved creating wondrous friction inside and outside and he began to move and he came in a long loud cry and I watched as She stroked His body with Hers until my fingers and toes went numb and my inner eyes went black and I was swallowed into the abyss.

"Wow," I whispered in his ear.

"Oooh, what you do to me," he said to . . . to me? . . . to Her in the mirror?

And it did not end there. The night went on for eons as the mirrors multiplied the seconds the minutes the hours as they multiplied our bodies over and over and over . . .

When I said good night to Marv at my front door, he asked us out for the following Saturday night, and we accepted.

* * *

61

And last Sunday Sandy had listened intently to my adventure and said only, "Wooow," when I had finished.

And now Sandy and I were practically choking with laughter. "Have a good time tomorrow night!" she managed through her cackles as she was leaving to pick up Rebecca. "And to think you said he's nothing special, just a salesman."

"That's right," I said, "he's just a salesman. A damn good one. He does it all with mirrors."

FLOATING ISLAND

The Islands

2 cups milk
1 teaspoon vanilla extract
5 egg whites
2/3 cup sugar

Over low heat, warm milk and vanilla in a deep skillet to a simmer. While milk is heating, beat egg whites until foamy. Slowly add sugar, continuing to beat until whites form stiff peaks. Off the heat, drop egg whites by large, rounded spoonfuls into the milk. Return skillet to very low heat and poach islands for 2 more minutes, until firm to the touch. With a slotted spoon, remove the islands and drain on a towel. Refrigerate on a platter.

The Custard

2 cups milk (from the islands plus fresh)
1 teaspoon vanilla extract
5 egg yolks
1/2 cup sugar
1 tablespoon apricot brandy

Strain milk into 2-cup measure and add fresh milk to fill. Heat milk and vanilla in top of a double boiler to a simmer. Blend egg yolks and sugar. Stirring constantly, slowly add hot milk. Return mixture to top of double boiler, add brandy, and cook, stirring constantly, until mixture thickens. Plunge the top of the boiler into ice water, and stir occasionally until the mixture is cool. Strain custard and refrigerate.

The Caramel

1 cup sugar
1/2 cup water

Cook sugar in a heavy saucepan over low heat until it melts and turns golden brown. Off the heat, stir in water. Return pan to heat and simmer for about 10 minutes, until the caramel is smooth and slightly thickened. Cool at room temperature.

The Assembly

Float islands in custard in a crystal bowl. Drizzle caramel sauce over each island when serving. Serves 8–10.

CHAPTER 5

Floating Island

On a blustery Friday in March, I pretended I was engrossed in whipping egg whites into meringue and poaching them into tiny islands that would float on sunny vanilla custard in a crystal bowl at Paula Reuben's dinner party that evening. The snowy archipelago on the cooling rack reminded me of the chains of islands illustrated on maps. It's not true that no man is an island, I mused. We're all islands, and the water around us is deep, and cold, and treacherous. I was really waiting for Stephen.

I had said *NO!* the night before when he called, waking me at eleven-thirty. *NO! I won't take you back!* But I knew he wouldn't accept no. Sure enough, at a little after four, just as I had set the finished sea of custard in the refrigerator to chill, the doorbell rang. Reaching for the doorknob, I saw Stephen through the glass panes, and the wisp of a smile that had crossed my lips dissipated. My heart began to race, my skin to tingle and go numb as I pulled within myself, away from him, remembering, in an instant, all at once, all the times before when he had come and gone . . . the promises . . . the betrayals.

"Stephen, where are you?" I had questioned him one night in bed as he lay on his side beside—not around—me. "You're not with me."

"Oh, I don't know," he answered, gazing at a spot between my chin and my shoulder.

"Something's come between us," I said. The small clues were there—the little things that appear unimportant when listed, but are, in fact, the very things that define the ebbs and flows of a relationship. Sentimental songs on the radio, such as "You Don't Send Me Flowers Anymore," prickled me. Like pop psychology or pop art, pop songs often hold essential truths in their clichés. Stephen had stopped holding my hand in the car. We were making love quickly— fucking; there were no lingering Sunday mornings in bed with brunch at four, no predawn, dreamlike conjoinings. It was more than the bloom off the rose, the honeymoon being over; it was deeper than that. We had been married only three years. Surely, I hoped, he wasn't bored with me yet. Surely, I felt, he was bored with me. "Are you bored with me?" I asked.

When we first met, I had believed him when he told me how much he wanted a home—his own home, with his own lawn, not a rented *unit* or a condo with a *collectively owned* lawn. And I had believed him when he told me he loved children. We talked a lot about children—I guess *I* talked a lot about children. But I also believed him when he told me that he was an island, floating from one woman to the next, that he never let anyone into himself, that he got bored easily. So why did he keep calling? So why did I continue to see him? Our bodies loved, melded when we made love, when we slept, when we held fast to the warmth of each other, that's why. We felt safe with each other when it was only skin between us, because his skin my skin became our skin. So I believed him when he went away on business trips and called me every evening to say he missed me, intimating that he was dining, and sleeping, alone. I believed him when he went on mini-vacations to this island and that mountain, not to be away from me, he said, but to be by himself—a fine line that I chose to believe in.

And I believed him when he promised me he spoke to

Dorothy Oberman—his former bookkeeper and former lover—"occasionally . . . on the phone, not in person, and only because she needs to talk to me. . . . I told her I'd always be there for her, as a friend." Even when he came to me reeking of perfume one evening—the personification of a cliché—I believed him when he swore he had seen Dorothy "just this once, to give her some money to help her out of a jam" . . . that he hadn't made love to her. I remembered a character in a Doris Lessing novel telling how she'd smelled another woman on her man when he came home to her one night. She *knew* he had been unfaithful. Forget the temporal scent of *another woman* on the hair ends, the pore rims of a man; confronted with Opium pressed into a white-on-white cotton shirt, all *I* knew was that I wasn't going to believe anything I didn't want to believe. So I allowed Stephen to "prove" his fidelity to me: He made love to *me* that night—passionately. A cliché that should have proved something, but it wasn't fidelity.

I suppose I knew it; I know I felt it. I simply chose not to believe what I felt: that there was a lot he didn't tell me, that he was breaking promises to me. Until even when we were skin to skin I felt apart from him—then I chose to be away from him. And it was painful. Like a burn victim, living without skin, all nerve ends exposed, nowhere could I find comfort. This must be love, I thought, never having experienced anything like it before. So I believed him and forgave him for his unconfessed sins when he cried to me that he, too, was in great pain and begged for another chance.

And so we married, to provide skin for each other's charred souls. But the soul is merely the spindle around which the rest of us winds: the day-to-day, the experiences of a lifetime—that thread from which we each weave our private beliefs, our public tales. And skin provides no armor against our deceptions.

"Of course I'm not bored with you," he had answered after a while, but added, "Maybe I'm just not the kind of man who can be married."

I was silent.

"I love you," he said, trying to hold back the crashing void. "I want to be with you, but maybe I can't be married."

"What are you trying to tell me, Stephen?" I asked, ignoring the fact that he'd already told me.

"Nothing. Nothing. Only that I'm trying to adjust, and it's not easy. But it'll be okay. I'll adjust."

"You'll adjust to what? Is it that we're alone? That we don't have children? We've tried so hard, Stephen. I feel a void, too," I said, assuming that he felt a void. "But at least I have you. I'm grateful for that. At least we have each other. I thought you felt that way, too."

"I do, Tess. I do. In fact, maybe it's better that we don't have children. I want to be with you, but I don't want to be in a place where I have to be every day because I *should* be or I *have to* be."

"You want me but you don't want responsibilities? You mean you don't want to be responsible to *me,*" I answered in anger, aware that I was dragging him into deep waters and we were going to drown. "Please try to be honest with me," I pleaded over his silence. "You have to let me know where I stand with you. That's only fair," I ended, ignoring the fact that he had already been honest.

But soon after there was that Wednesday morning phone call from Carley "Wonder Woman" Statten's husband, who was even more honest with me. I suppose I wasn't surprised to learn that Carley, who had been Stephen's secretary for almost two years, was having an affair with him, not really surprised, that is. Stephen readily confessed to his yearlong "dalliance" with Carley, but begged for forgiveness on the grounds of "stupidity," "male ego-gratification," and "vulnerability"—to her big tits, I reckoned. He'd fire her, he'd never see her again, he said. He couldn't bear the thought of losing me. "You've already lost me," I lied to us both, and told him he'd have to move out. He did, into one of the sleazy investment apartments that he and David owned on the fringe of respectable society. But I missed him desperately, and I consoled myself by believing that he needed to leave in order to stay. And when he called every morning to plead for time and understanding, and every night to tell me that he loved me, I finally consented to go to a marriage counselor with him.

Marty Steinheiser, M.S.W., was a small man, about fifty, with pale blue rheumy eyes, livery lips that collected bits of white foam at the corners when he talked, and a balding head. I spent considerable moments contemplating the stripes of long hair that spanned the top of his head, ear to ear, wondering if they reached his shoulders in the shower, whether they stayed put when he made love to his wife, *if* he made love to his wife. He came highly recommended.

In our initial, joint session in Marty's dim office, sitting in heavy mahogany and leather armchairs across from his heavy mahogany desk that held the single light in the room—a brass apothecary lamp with a green glass shade—I yelled about Stephen's dishonesties, his infidelities. Stephen listened, staring at his fingers meshing and unmeshing around his crossed knees. I interpreted his silent listening as agreement, contrition. Sitting behind his desk, Marty listened, bobbing his head now and then, lowering his seemingly lashless lids, thumping his receding chin with a stubby forefinger. I interpreted *his* silent listening as agreement, sympathy. When alone with Marty, I cried about Stephen's infidelity and my infertility, and Marty soothed, "I understand how you feel. . . . This must be very hard for you. . . ." and excused, "Consider the fragile male ego. . . ." and judged, "Perhaps the greater sin is to be unforgiving." When alone with Marty, Stephen listened as Marty told him about his own marital difficulties with an unforgiving wife. When Marty separated from his wife, Stephen and I separated from Marty.

We dated. We went on weekend trips to New York City to see the ballet and to Vermont to ski. Still angry, I drew a line behind which I was determined to stand, and wait, and watch. Until I felt sure of him, I wouldn't let him come home. But I needed his skin. So we lived apart and we slept together. I had the illusion of control. It was probably what he'd wanted all along.

Then one Thursday night when, after eight staunch

months, I was inexplicably feeling flutters of trust and the need to relax, to fall against the man who continually expressed a desire to be there for me, Stephen called from Chicago, where he'd been on business since Monday. "Come to me from the airport tomorrow," I appealed, "I miss you."

We hugged when he arrived Friday evening, but we didn't really kiss. He didn't seem hungry to see me. He made himself a drink, told me quickly of the business of his trip, and asked about my week. I was quiet, content in having him beside me, having the comfort of his presence, trying to ignore the ghost of a wall that I sensed around him. "I just needed you near me," I explained.

"I had an interesting flight home," he said abruptly as we sat on the sofa, his hand resting on my knee. A red flag waved in my head. "Sitting next to me was this woman . . ." *NO!* wailed in my head. ". . . thirty years old, divorced, blond . . ." Red flares shot off. *NO!* I don't want to hear this. ". . . a paralegal for Leiber, Armstrong, Block, and Cohn— you know, Bart Armstrong's firm—the guy who wanted to involve me in that crazy bond deal last year. Small world."

I felt all the blood in my body race to my hands and the cavities behind my eyes. "Oh?" I said, trying to control the quiver, the quake, the red rushing up my neck, the pounding in my ears. "And I suppose you took her card?"

"Yep." *BASTARD!*

"And you gave her yours?"

"Sure. . . ." *SADIST!* ". . . She said maybe she could be of some help to me with—" But I didn't let him finish. Falling on him, I pummeled his shoulders and arms with my fists. His arms flew up protectively, and I retreated, more shocked than he by the incredible anger that had been summoned from somewhere inside me. He looked at me, half smiling. "It was only business!" he defended himself.

"Bullshit!" I yelled. But feelings of guilt for my lack of reason, my hostile and uncharacteristic assault, dampened my rage. And the paralysis of ambivalence set in: *He* wasn't responsible for his seat assignment; or was he? People *do* talk on planes; but most people don't exchange business cards. Or do they? Isn't that what business cards are *for*, for *business*? Isn't that how *business* is carried out, deals are created, fortunes made? But Stephen had more connections with that law firm than *she* could possibly have. And I noted that she had given him *two* cards—a corporate business card designating her a paralegal for the firm, and a personal business card, emblazoned with her home telephone number, designating her a "consultant," a clearly ambiguous term advocated for use on such cards by magazine advice columns on "the single life." Better than writing your name on the wall of a telephone booth, I reasoned.

We went to bed early. We didn't make love. I felt betrayed, but I wasn't sure how.

Stephen said he was trying to be honest with me when he told me, a week later, about the lunch he'd had the day before with Elayne Darby, the blonde from the plane, who, he said, had called *him* because she wanted to share some information with him about the bond deal, information that only *she* was privy to because she was on *intimate terms* with one of the law partners. Read: She was sleeping with him. Then, in an effort to coax her into sharing more of this information with him, which, it turned out, was nothing he didn't already know—which was nothing *I* didn't already know—he took her to dinner one evening, and then to lunch again. And then—small world—a few weeks later they met again on a plane, this time on a trip *to* Chicago. So he had dinner with her one night in Chicago at this excellent little Thai restaurant she knew of, and maybe lunch one afternoon—he couldn't remember for sure. Of course, it was all business.

All of this he told me one night when I was in enough psychic pain to question him about the distance once again growing between us. And, as he is wont to do when I ask the right questions, he told me part of the truth. But *she* told me the *whole* truth when she called to tell me that she was having an affair with Stephen and that I shouldn't try to hold on to him because she intended to fight for him. What is this? I wondered, falling down my own private rabbit hole. Am I living in a grade-B movie, an afternoon soap opera? I, who groaned at such clichés in television sitcoms I refused to watch and best-selling novels I refused to read, was living in one. Maybe *this* is real life. Maybe *I'm* not fighting hard enough for my man, I concluded desperately.

So I yelled at Stephen and told him that I wasn't going to let go that easily—easily?—that I was determined to put our marriage back together because I believed we needed each other. After two weeks of passionate browbeating—by me—and penitent chest-beating—by him—I listened on the other phone when he called Elayne from my apartment to tell her that he loved me and that he wasn't going to see her anymore, that it was (I shuddered at the triteness) just one of those things. I listened as she called him a fucking pig and told him that he'd never have any further dealings with Leiber, Armstrong, Block, and Cohn, that she wouldn't miss him at all, and that, by the way, he was devious, withholding, and untrustworthy. I would have bowed out more gracefully, I thought, victorious. And, although I felt he *was* devious, withholding, and untrustworthy, we started dating again. And, after a while, when I was beginning to believe that we could never be together because he could never be honest with me, I decided that we should be together because as long as we were apart he had no reason to be honest with me. So he moved home. So we moved to a new house. And I believed him when he said that *this* time it would be different, *this* time he would be honest with me, *this* time he knew what he wanted.

Until the next time, which was three and a half years later, when, after a particularly edgy week, Stephen came home late with a curious story concerning a traffic jam, a traffic ticket for speeding, an old friend from college days, his friend's girlfriend, and a few drinks in a hotel lounge, although not necessarily in that order. These facts were clear: Stephen was upset; he had been drinking; he reeked of perfume. Again! Remembering Doris Lessing, I accused him of being with another woman. "I danced with my friend's

72

girlfriend," he insisted. I told him to leave. He spilled: He had seen Dorothy. . . . She had called him; she needed money again. . . . She was hysterical. . . . He agreed to see her, once, in a public place. So they met in a bar and had a few drinks, and he gave her some money . . . and of course he hugged her when he left, because she was so upset . . . and he got a ticket on the way home for speeding because *he* was upset that he had broken his promise to me not to see her again. "She looked so old," he said. I don't know what Lessing's character would have done, but I put my arms around my man and held him. I felt so sorry that he had to face that disgusting remnant of his degenerate past. I felt so good that he had been honest with me.

But he had been more honest with Dorothy—when he told her that he would always be there for her, but he would never marry her, even if he left me . . . which he was thinking of doing. This *she* told me when she called me the next day—Why do they all call me? Why can't I figure these things out myself?—to tell me that David had found out that Stephen was sleeping with her in the same sleazy apartment Stephen had occupied three years earlier, where, unbeknownst to me, she had taken up residence when he moved back home. And in a seizure of guilt under David's condemning eye, Stephen had met with Dorothy to tell her that she'd have to move. "So," she said to me, "I thought you should know *all* about it." *All* included a quick synopsis of her former husband's infidelity and the bitch who took him from her and the bitches who kept taking Stephen from her.

I quietly placed the receiver in its cradle—I couldn't believe I had listened for as long as I had—even as she continued to cry to me—to *me!*—about Stephen's unfaithfulness. Her point was an interesting one: Stephen had not been unfaithful to *me*, he had been unfaithful to *her*. And that made all the difference. So *this* time when he begged for forgiveness, *this* time when he told me he loved me, that he couldn't live without me, I didn't believe him. *This* time, even though I still loved him, even though I could have forgiven him again, I told him no, because *this* time I could not forgive myself.

"Stephen." I closed the door behind him and turned to face him in the foyer, frozen with resentment.

"I want to come home. I'll do anything you say. I need to be here. It's all I ever wanted," he stumbled.

His pathetic demeanor stoked my anger to the point of release. "It's not what you *ever* wanted!" I raged. He cringed, cowered as I overwhelmed him with abhorrence, with hateful accusations, venomous imputations: "You're treacherous! You disgust me! You can stand there and tell me that while you were fucking *her*, all you wanted was to be with *me*? Liar! Cheat! Perfidious prick!" Yes. I liked that one. But the eruption left a void inside me into which my outside began to sink, and I felt his arms go round me—structure for my collapsing being. His sobs were in my ear, his tears on my cheek, tears that primed my own, and my tears arrested his. But he held me still, tighter than ever before, tighter than I have ever been held, and I clung to him, though it seemed that I could never be held long enough, or hard enough.

Not hard enough to dispel the encroaching ogre, the unnameable terror that had visited me in the night in my fever in my mother's arms . . . never long enough, always a hunger for more, just a moment more, to make it real.

But he held me that hard, that long, long enough for me to feel finished and that I could let go first.

I noticed that it had darkened outside as we sank to the stairs where he sat one step below me, his arms wrapped around my legs, his head in my lap. And I bent over him, cradled his head in my arms, laid my cheek on his hair, the soft touch of which always surprised me—prematurely gray, it looked like steel wool, a metallic quality that matched his wiry body, his steel gray eyes, his cold, hard edge. I wept again, easily, quietly, for a long time, long enough to wash away the fantasy, to say good-bye to the man I had wanted him to be, pretended he was. "You have to go now," I said gently, but with a conviction that moved him to his feet and out the door without so much as a whisper. He was gone. We both knew he'd be back. I knew it would be different.

"Let me understand this," said Michael Tuesday morning, "he put his head in your lap and you cried on him?"

I nodded.

"That's wonderful."

Why? I wondered, but didn't ask because I was overwhelmed with sadness. Why? I didn't ask. "I think I was saying good-bye," I said.

Michael saw my face contort, my shoulders hunch over as if I had taken a blow to the gut. He left his seat, sat down beside me, and put his arm around me. Was this to be it: the opening up; the letting go? Was I going to allow myself to allow him to comfort me? No. I was too aware of him next to me, of the awkwardness of our juxtaposition—what to do with my crossed legs, what to do with my shoulders, what to do with my arms, my hands, my limp hands that couldn't just hold on to this small island of peace. Although frustrated now, as well as in pain, I fought the tears that choked me. Michael stood up to remove his jacket—this was to be a production, my breaking down—then returned to sit beside me, and this time I turned to him and put my head against his shoulder. He removed his glasses and gently held me. Then it struck me: Michael had removed his jacket, he had removed his glasses—he was undressing! No, of course he wasn't. What a strange association. I was in pain, Michael was trying to comfort me, but I was distracted by motions. My emotions were stifled by motions. I was discomfited, but I was no longer moved to the threat of tears, no longer moved. Frozen with inhibition, I felt graceless, ungrateful, ugly. I . . . I . . . I! What about him? What about Michael? Now I felt guilty as well as frustrated and in pain. I hadn't given a thought to how Michael was feeling. I had assumed: He didn't feel; he was just trying to do his job—building bridges from island to island.

ROCKY ROAD ICE CREAM CAKE ROLL

5 eggs
1 teaspoon vanilla extract
1/2 teaspoon salt
1/3 cup sugar
1/3 cup cornstarch
1/3 cup flour
chocolate marshmallow ice cream
4 one-ounce squares semisweet chocolate
1 1/2 tablespoons solid vegetable shortening
1/2 cup chopped almonds

Preheat oven to 375°F. Line a 10 1/2 x 15 1/2-inch jelly-roll pan with wax paper.

Separate the eggs and beat the yolks with the vanilla. In another bowl, beat the whites until foamy. Add the salt to whites and beat until soft peaks form. Slowly add the sugar and beat until stiff peaks form.

Spoon the whites over the yolks and sift the cornstarch and flour on top. Fold the mixture to blend, and spread it over the wax paper in the pan. Bake for 12 minutes, or until a toothpick comes out clean.

Turn the cake out onto a towel and remove the wax paper. Trim crumbs away and roll the cake up lengthwise with the towel. Let it sit for a minute, then unroll. Roll it again with the towel in it and let cool. Unroll it and spread a half-inch of softened chocolate marshmallow ice cream on the cake to the edges. Cut it in half and roll up the two halves. Wrap in wax paper and freeze.

Melt semisweet chocolate squares in the top of a double boiler with the shortening. Mix in chopped almonds. Lay the frozen rolls in the middle of a sheet of wax paper. Glaze each roll with melted chocolate mixture. Return the rolls to the freezer until ready to serve. Serves 12.

CHAPTER 6

Rocky Road Ice Cream Cake Roll

"Big News . . ." Sandy had promised me when she called at ten o'clock Friday morning to ask me to meet her at the diner for lunch. News meant a juicy piece of gossip about someone we knew well, or something perfectly horrible about someone we barely knew at all. Occasionally a single item encompassed both criteria. This constituted Big News.

". . . But first we've got to find Janet," she had said. I had no idea where Janet was—she was off on Friday when she worked Thursday evening, which was the case this week. Sandy said she'd explain all at lunch.

I finished baking two sheets of sponge cake for the Rocky Road ice cream cake rolls Charlene Platt had ordered for her seven-thirty dinner party, showered and dressed, met a real estate client—Vincent Salvatore, business broker, bodybuilder, gourmet cook . . . and single—at his two-bedroom, two-bath, condominium townhouse that he wanted to sell for two hundred and twenty-five thousand dollars, and made it to the diner by one o'clock. Sandy was waiting.

"You won't belieeeve what's happening," she started even as the hostess was leading us to our booth. We ordered quickly—two small Greek salads, coffee—without looking at the menu, and then Sandy continued. "Do you remember a woman I mentioned to you months ago? I met her at Rebecca's nursery school? Eileen?"

I shook my head, totally unfamiliar with the name, somewhat distracted, considering the desserts I had to put together after lunch, and the new listing I'd just got, and the very attractive man who'd given it to me.

Sandy ignored my lack of enthusiasm and began to relate the most bizarre tale: It seemed that she had become friendly with Eileen, who was the mother of one of Rebecca's nursery school friends, Karen. After a time, Eileen began confiding in Sandy about her husband's inattentions, inconsiderations, inabilities—the latter of which he blamed on her being six months pregnant and "gross." Now, Sandy (she tells me this for the first time) had had experience along these lines in that Charlie had handled her pregnancies with the sensitivity of a yak—"He said he got the creeps when the baby moved . . . and that my breasts were too big."

"Charlie said that? But he's a doctor," I said, sounding really dumb.

"He's shy, though, I guess," she stammered quietly, coming to the defense of . . . her husband? her choice of husband? I contemplated the difference as Sandy continued her story. Eileen hadn't bought Sandy's attempts at assurances that "he'll be okay after the baby is born. . . ." Neither had Sandy. "I was trying to make her feel better, Tess, but I was sure her husband was playing around."

"Why?" I asked.

"Well, he made a pass at me!" Sandy answered.

Hah! I knew it! This is going to be another banal tale of suggestive conversation and eyeball fucking, I thought, shoveling anchovies and feta cheese into my mouth to keep from saying something I'd regret.

"It was a couple of weeks ago—it was the only time I met him—at the spring celebration at school," she said. The Pass was a bit of flirting by the snack table when Sandy had dropped that "Charlie is sooo busy we're like two ships passing in the night"—I couldn't believe she actually said that—and he had replied that she better be careful that she didn't "dry up."

"Sandy! I can't believe he said something so disgusting!"

"He didn't mean it that way. He was just trying to be friendly."

I closed my eyes momentarily and shuddered. "Okay. So go on with the story."

"Well. Eileen was sure her husband was seeing another woman, so she lifted his paging beeper from his briefcase before he left the house yesterday, and picked up his calls as if she were the answering service, then forwarded the messages to the real answering service. And this morning Eileen was very upset because, of the nine calls she picked up yesterday, three were from a woman who wouldn't leave her name, but on the third call left a message: 'Reservations at the Wayfarer are all set. Dinner is at seven tomorrow night.' That's tonight, Tess," Sandy explained. "But Eileen's husband had told her at the beginning of the week that he was flying to Pittsburgh tonight for a weekend investment seminar, and the Wayfarer is a small restaurant and bed-and-breakfast place in Cape May. So guess where Eileen will be at seven o'clock tonight."

"The Wayfarer."

"Right."

"Gutsy lady," I cheered.

"Not so fast, Tess. You haven't heard the other side of the story," Sandy warned, pausing to catch up on her salad. And then, "I called Janet to chat last night—I forgot she was working—and Sean told me he was going to visit his grandparents for the weekend because Janet was going to be away, but he didn't know where . . ."

"Oh shit," I said, catching on.

". . . and then this morning, when Eileen tells me about her husband—did I tell you his name is Harvey?—going away for the weekend—"

"Say no more. Harvey is Janet's Harvey Cohen and Eileen is Mrs. Cohen. Right?"

"Right."

"So much for Janet's rationalization that *this* married man is okay to date because he hasn't slept with his wife for

79

over a year . . . that his wife is cold, unaffectionate, and hates sex . . . that she's a weak, incapable woman and that as soon as he finds a way to break the news to her without driving her to suicide, he's going to leave her. Did I leave anything out?" I asked in a rising voice.

"Well, Janet said that when you date a married man, at least you know he isn't fooling around with anyone else. And you know the way things are nowadays, Tess."

"Oh, yes. Well, I guess Janet doesn't count the wife as 'someone else,'" I spewed with considerable bile, understanding more than ever that I didn't understand the way things were nowadays. "So, where's Janet?! I suppose we do have to find her to warn her," I allowed.

"That's the big question," Sandy said. "I've been calling all morning, but there's no answer."

"Why doesn't that woman get an answering machine?!" I asked the chandelier. Why is everyone so hurtful? I asked myself, picturing poor Eileen (whom I've never seen in my life) crying into her hands above her belly big with child. I felt angry not only with Harvey (whom I've never met), but also with Janet for embracing the contemporary credo that *(a)* it is justifiable to do something hurtful if it will be done by someone else anyway if you don't do it, and *(b)* the justification of a hurtful act is increased proportionately by the number of people practicing said act. I felt angry, too, with Sandy for buying into Janet's rationalization . . . and with myself for feeling so damn self-righteous.

I left Sandy to finish her salad and tried to call Janet from the pay phone near the rest rooms. The telephone rang and rang and . . .

"Hello."

"Janet! Am I glad I caught you! Are you planning to drive to Cape May this evening?"

"How did you know, Tess?"

"Don't go!"

"What?"

80

"Don't go. Harvey's wife found out and she's going to be there!"

"Oh, Tess, thank you! I'll never do married again . . . I promise."

. . . and rang. Defeated, I went back to the booth and joined Sandy for one more cup of coffee before I had to return to my kitchen.

"You seeing Mirrors tomorrow night?" she asked.

"No. Marv has to be in Chicago to see a client. But I have a date."

"Ohhh. Who?"

"David. We're going to the movies."

"Oh, he's not a date."

"I know. But he called last night to tell me that his Saturday night date canceled and he was dying to see this movie—"

"So good old Tess will baby-sit," Sandy sneered.

"Actually, the way I look at it, he's baby-sitting me," I retorted, feeling hurt. "Why so resentful?"

"I'm not! But don't be so coy, Tess; you know you have a crush on him."

"Sandy! He's only a friend. Besides, I'm definitely not his type."

"Don't you wonder what his type is, Tess? Have you considered it might be *male?* I mean, aaall those arm-hangers he dates—"

"Really, Sandy," I said. Bitch! I thought. *You'd* like to have a go at David yourself—and you probably would if you knew about the bimbo Charlie's got shacked up in his shore condo . . . a story known to everyone, *except* to you . . . because you're so involved with your *imagined* intrigues that you can't see the real thing.

"Tess, what are you thinking? You have the oddest look on your face." But she didn't wait for an answer. "I'm going to the bathroom, and then I've got to get to my haircut," she said. "George gets furious when I'm late."

"Right. I'll pay the bill; it's my turn. And then I'm going

home, so I'll try calling Janet," I said, already feeling guilty for my unstated anger, my unfair mental indictment of Janet, Sandy, and Charlie, who, for all I *really* knew, was a good, hardworking, faithful husband—even if he was a nerd.

Back home I tried Janet's line again, to no avail, and then set about rolling chocolate marshmallow ice cream in sheets of sponge cake, coating them with bittersweet chocolate glaze and chopped almonds, wrapping them in wax paper before freezing, and trying to reach Janet between steps. When I tried Janet's line at about five o'clock, I got a busy signal. Thank goodness, I thought, redialing immediately. Still busy. I tried every four or five minutes for about a half hour until, finally, it rang . . . and rang . . . and rang. . . . I couldn't believe I had missed her.

Driving over to Charlene Platt's to deliver her cake rolls, I thought I saw Janet's car headed toward the expressway. I followed it for a block until I could see for sure . . .

And then I stepped on it, following her onto the expressway. I drove close behind her and sounded my horn. I saw her look into her rearview mirror, but she speeded up. I pulled up next to her in the left lane and sounded my horn again. Alarmed, she looked over, and I motioned for her to pull off at the next exit. Half a mile up the road she exited and I followed her to a gas station just off the ramp. We both jumped out of our cars.

"What's going on?" she asked.

"Janet! Am I glad I caught you! Are you on your way to Cape May?"

"How did you know, Tess?"

"Don't go!"

"What?"

"Don't go. Harvey's wife found out and she's going to be there!"

"Oh, Tess, thank you! I'll never do married again . . . I promise."

* * *

. . . but it wasn't her. Defeated, I turned right at Charlene's corner, dropped the desserts off, and returned home.

I was dozing in front of the television in the family room that night when the phone rang. At first I thought the ringing was coming from the television—an old Barbara Stanwyck movie, *Sorry, Wrong Number*—but it persisted beyond Barbara's answering the telephone in black and white, so I fumbled for my telephone, noting that it was eleven-forty.

It was Sandy. She was quite beside herself. "You won't belieeeve what I've been through tonight. Tess, I had to call you. I hope it's not too late."

It was. "No, of course not. What happened?" I asked, coming to as I remembered this afternoon's conversation . . . and Janet. "Did you find Janet?"

"No. Just listen, Tess." She related a bedtime story even more bizarre than the lunchtime tale: Eileen had called Sandy hysterically about nine-thirty to ask if Karen could spend the weekend at Sandy's house. A terrible thing had happened: Harvey had been killed in an accident . . . she didn't know whom else to call . . . her parents were flying up from Florida late that night, Harvey's parents were flying in from Ohio in the morning . . . she had no family in the area. So Sandy went to Eileen's to comfort her and bring Karen home with her as soon as Sandy's mother arrived to stay with Sandy's children. "Where was Charlie?" I asked. Charlie had an emergency at the shore hospital and was staying overnight.

As Sandy was driving to Eileen's she remembered Cape May, the Wayfarer, and Janet, and realized that she had no idea how any of it fit together, so by the time she reached Eileen's, Sandy was in quite a state herself. And when she walked into the house, Eileen collapsed into Sandy's arms, sobbing out her incredible story: Eileen had gone to the Wayfarer at seven o'clock after walking on the rocky beach and wandering around the Victorian town for a good three hours in an attempt to compose herself. She inquired about the Cohen reservation and was taken to a table where, already seated, was a woman who, because of her diminutive size, short, curly chestnut hair, triangular face, and almond-shaped hazel eyes, could have been taken for Eileen's younger sister—if she had had one, which she didn't. The woman took no notice of Eileen walking toward the table, but when Eileen sat down, recognition and then alarm registered on her face—

"It wasn't Janet!" I interjected.

"It wasn't Janet."

"So where's Janet?"

"I don't know, but is she going to be pissed when she hears this story!"

"So go on," I said, fully awake now, picturing the scene as if it were an old movie on television: a quaint little restaurant, pink roses and baby's breath in a crystal vase and a tall white candle on the table for two . . . the pregnant wife, the other woman.

"I'm Eileen Cohen. I believe we're waiting for my husband," Eileen said.

The other woman froze, white-faced.

"I hope you don't mind my intruding, but I thought we should meet," Eileen said.

The other woman opened her mouth but said nothing.

"You're the only one I can learn the truth from . . . and I'm the only one who can be truthful with you," Eileen said.

The other woman's pallor gave way to flush. Her eyes filled with tears as if the infusion of color were a physically painful process. "I didn't know you were . . . Harvey didn't tell me . . . I didn't want anyone to be hurt—"

"I understand," Eileen said, completely controlled, resting her arms across her obvious belly. "How long have you been seeing my husband?" she asked, a question that evoked a lengthy life history from the other woman, the salient points of which were as follows: Penny Jamison, divorced mother of five-year-old twin boys, an accountant for an insurance firm in Philadelphia, had been seeing Harvey for about two years. She had met him two years after her own husband, an attorney, had left her for his office manager.

"I would never date a married man before I met Harvey. I never wanted to hurt another woman the way I'd been hurt. But Harvey was so persistent, and I felt so sorry for him . . ." Penny stopped momentarily and stared at Eileen. "I don't understand. . . . You're so pretty . . . and you're expecting a baby! Harvey told me that you and he hadn't slept together for years, that you weren't well—mentally, that is. I can't tell you how sorry . . . but I honestly believed that he was going to leave you," she said, desperation crowding her voice. "I thought my prince had come. You don't know what's out there, Mrs. Cohen."

"I'm beginning to find out . . ." was all Eileen said before the police arrived.

"The police?" I questioned.

"Oh, Tess. Be still and let me finish the story. I haven't told you the worst of it!"

"Mrs. Cohen?" the short, dark state policeman asked, to which Eileen nodded. "Ma'am, I'm afraid there's been an accident . . ." Now both women blanched. When the officer told Eileen that Harvey's Saab had gone out of control in the southbound lanes of the Garden State Parkway and had plowed into the back of a flatbed trailer hauling a mobile home, that he had been thrown through the windshield and had died instantly, that the authorities had tried to phone her at home and finally reached the baby-sitter—who had taken Karen to the playground after dinner—who told them where she could be found, that he had felt it best to come personally to tell her, that he would drive her to the hospital, if she wished, or home, she stared at him in disbelief. The officer put a hand on her arm to steady her as she stood up, facing him, but she pulled her arm away, swinging around toward Penny, who sat unsure of her role—after all, what does one say to the widow of one's dead lover, especially when one is in at least as much pain as the widow herself?

"SLUT! It's your fault that my husband is dead. He was coming to see you!" Eileen roared, shocking the officer and the diners in the intimate little restaurant, and helping Penny to find her voice.

"Don't call me a slut, you—you BITCH!" she said, rising from her chair. "If you knew how to hold a man, he wouldn't be dead. He wasn't running *to me* . . . he was running *from you.*"

"Stop! Hold it, Sandy. I don't think I can take any more of this. The whole world is a goddamned cliché!" I yelled into the phone. "Just tell me the bottom line here: Was there a fight to the death? Or did the officer arrest them both for disturbing the peace . . . or for unjustifiable stupidity?"

"Bottom line: The officer took Eileen home after a terrible shouting match—"

"No blood?"

"No blood. Just guts."

"How's Karen?" I asked, suddenly remembering the littlest victim.

"She's sleeping. She has no idea what's happening."

Nobody has, I thought. A man lies to his wife, lies to his mistress, and in the light of truth, does their loving image of him wither like a vampire in the light of day? No. The women blame each other for their pain. He alone is absolved, bleached white like a stained sheet in the light of the sun. "Sandy, I'll talk to you later. *I've* got to go to sleep," I said, hanging up, falling quickly into a fitful slumber. . . .

In the diner at Sunday morning brunch, Janet listened to Sandy relate Friday's events while I fought with a blinding sunbeam intruding into our window booth. As the story unfolded, Janet grew more and more distressed until, in a rage, she yelled as loud as she could, "That two-timing BASTARD . . ."

"Three-timing," I muttered to myself, squinting against the offending sliver of light.

". . . It's a good thing he died, because if he hadn't I would have killed him myself—AFTER I castrated him!" Janet finished in tears.

Incredibly, everyone in the diner stood up and cheered

and then began tapping their water glasses with their spoons. I wanted to join the crystal ensemble, but the sun was in my eyes and I couldn't find my spoon . . . and the ringing glasses continued to get louder and louder . . . and the sunbeam kept finding my eyes no matter where I turned.

. . . And the ringing telephone finally awakened me to the glaring rays of the morning sun from the skylight above my bed, burning through my closed lids. Groping for the phone, I remembered the weird dream I had just had and noted that it was no weirder than the events of the day before. "Hello?" I said, thick-tongued.

"Tess, it's me. I hope it isn't too early. Did I wake you?"

Yes! Of course! "No, it's okay," I mumbled to Sandy. "What time is it, anyway?"

"I did wake you. I'm sorry, but I had to call. Janet just called me. She heard about Harvey on the radio last night on her way to New York—"

"To where?"

"She was on her way to White Plains, New York. Harvey had told her he was going there for a weekend seminar, and she decided to surprise him. Today is—was—his birthday."

"It looks like the surprise was on Janet."

"You're sick, Tess. Look. Janet's really strung out. She couldn't sleep once she got home, but waited until a decent hour to call me."

"What time is it?"

"Six-fifteen."

That's a decent hour? I thought. "So go on," I said.

"I told her I'd come right over, but she said she wanted to take a shower and be alone for a while. She's coming here at nine."

Janet and Sandy were already drinking coffee at the kitchen table, and Sandy's mother, who had slept over, had taken the three children to the playground by the time I got to Sandy's house at nine-thirty. My mother had called to tell me that after seeing a news special about AIDS on television last night, she couldn't sleep a wink . . . and that I should go back with Stephen. "A wife has to learn to close her eyes to certain things," she'd lectured. A long, rambling defense of my position served only to increase my mother's conviction that I was a failure as a woman, to decrease my sense of self-esteem, and to increase the profits of the telephone company, that powerful entity that makes it possible for someone in Florida to reach out and smack someone around in Pennsylvania. So I was not only late but distracted when I sat down next to Sandy. "Sorry I'm late," I muttered.

Janet, who had obviously been crying before I arrived, started anew, holding her napkin to her face. Sandy started to catch me up: Janet was twenty minutes from White Plains when she had heard the news broadcast about the accident. She almost ran amok on the Tappan Zee Bridge when the words "Harvey Cohen, dead from injuries" bored into her ears, when the words "southbound lanes at five-thirty this afternoon" threw her into a state of confusion. But she made it to the hotel where Harvey was supposed to be staying—of course he wasn't—and she sat dazed in the lounge long enough to down a brandy and two cups of black coffee before driving home. Now she blamed herself for the accident and—

"Whoaaa! Back up. You lost me," I said.

By this time, Janet had stopped sobbing, and she told me the rest of it herself: At about five o'clock yesterday afternoon, Harvey was wheeling south on the Garden State Parkway toward Cape May, New Jersey—although Janet thought he was wheeling north toward White Plains, New York, and his wife was supposed to think he was flying northwest to Pittsburgh, Pennsylvania—when he called Janet on his new car phone. "Hi! Baby! No more long lonely road trips!" he said, explaining that this newest toy—a birthday present to himself—had been installed the day before, and she was his first call. Janet had walked in from a long day of vanities only seconds before her phone rang. She'd gotten a haircut and manicure, then bought a sexy black lace teddy with a snap crotch at the Perfumed Garden.

She had stopped at Castlemeyer's to pick up the small chocolate chip birthday cake she'd ordered earlier, with traditional sugary white icing, blue and yellow flowers, and blue HAPPY BIRTHDAY HARVEY. She bought blue birthday candles at Gifts and Greetings and spent three-quarters of an hour poring over their birthday cards filed under "Love" until she found the perfect one, more than an hour picking out a pigskin ticket and passport folder at Travels, and another half hour agonizing over the style of the monogram that the saleswoman then embossed in gold on the folder's lower right corner. All this for a man who, if you listened to Janet tell it, was only a good fuck. "It's nothing. I'm in charge of this relationship," she had assured Sandy and me on more than one occasion.

So. The phone had rung and it was Harvey calling from his car phone, and Janet, who was all excited about her plans to surprise him later that night at his hotel in White Plains, decided to tease him a bit, to get him primed, aroused for her arrival.

"Haaarvey," she whispered over the phone, setting down her packages, settling into a comfy chair, "do you know what I'm doing right now?"

"Tell me, honey."

"I'm thinking of you, sweetheart. Do you know why?"

"Tell me, doll," he answered, being sucked into the mood by the sex in her voice as he sped south in the fast lane of the Garden State Parkway at just under seventy miles an hour.

"Because I just got out of a hot, hot bath . . . and I'm lying on my bed all warm and tingly . . ."

Harvey fumbled to turn down the radio and turn on the cruise control so that he could pay close attention to the sweet sounds coming over his phone.

". . . and I thought how nice it would be if you were here beside me . . . how good your skin would feel on mine . . . how good it would be to have you touch me like only you can . . ."

Harvey grunted small sounds into the phone as he listened intently, lost in the fantasy.

". . . I'm on top of my satin comforter . . . and I've got all my pillows piled up around me . . . and the shades are drawn . . . oh, Harvey, it's like being in a warm, soft nest. And my skin, Harvey, it's so soft from the hot bath oil. I'm rubbing some of the oil on my tummy right now. It feels sooo good, Harvey, so slippery smooth, and warm and wet—"

"Your tits, doll, rub it on your beautiful tits. Tell me what it feels like."

"Oh, Harvey. It feels wonderful . . . my nipples are getting so hard . . . they're standing right up . . . I'm running my fingers around and around my nipples, Harvey—"

"I'd love to be there to rub them for you, gorgeous."

"You are, Harvey. You're right here with me, touching me . . . and, Harvey, you're getting so hard . . . Oooh, I want to suck it, Harvey . . ."

By now Harvey had his fly open and his wang was sticking out acutely, just below his seat belt. He told Janet to hold on a sec while he cradled the phone between his left ear and shoulder so he could grasp the steering wheel in his left hand and his considerable erection in his right. Yesiree! He had the world by the balls: a hot rod in each hand and a hot bitch in his ear.

"Christ, sweetheart! I feel like I'm eighteen again. Did I ever tell you about the White Shadow," he asked Janet, gripping his dick, flirting with memories of his first car—a pre-owned, white Austin-Healey with a soft, red leather interior that his parents had bought for him when he graduated from high school.

"Sure, honey. She was your best girl, wasn't she?" Janet said, feeding his fantasy.

"You know, I can still remember the silky feel of that six-hour compound and wax job I gave the old girl. God, I was a cocky bastard stretched out in her low-slung seat, one hand on the steering wheel, the other on the gearshift, peeling out at lights, downshifting around corners. . . . What a turn-on!" And as he pictured the White Shadow speeding through the old neighborhood in the wee hours of the morning, his right hand shifted his dick up and back . . . until he found a rhythm . . . and he was drawn back to the voice in his ear . . .

". . . Yes, lover, you're getting me so excited. I can't keep from touching myself. . . . I know I shouldn't touch myself, but, oooh, it feels sooo good . . . and the oil is running down my belly, Harvey, and, ooooh, Harvey, it's running into my honey pot. Oh, Harvey, I can't help it . . . I have to touch myself . . . Yes . . . It's so hot, Harvey, it's so soft and wet . . . and my fingers are in it . . . and I'm imagining it's you, Harvey, rubbing up and back . . . Can you feel it, Harvey?"

Now Harvey was really going at it . . . up and back and up and down . . . he was having one helluva time. But he kept his eye on the road, his left hand on the wheel as he approached his supreme moment.

". . . Harvey . . . lover . . . I can see how big and hard you are. . . . I'm slipping my fingers into me and it's you, honey . . . I can feel you in me, Harvey . . . in and out . . . faster, honey . . . oooh, Harvey . . . oooh, lover . . . oooooh . . ."

And with this momentous moan of pulse-pounding passion, Harvey stretched his legs out as far as he could and started to jerk in his seat, trying to get enough body English into the act to finish himself off, but his seat belt wouldn't give him the necessary leeway. . . . "I'm comin', doll . . . I'm comin'," he rasped through the phone, while fumbling with the seat-belt latch, trying to free himself. "I'm comin', doll!" as the latch finally gave way and his pelvis thrust forward and his dick hit the steering wheel so his left hand jerked in a kind of reflex action, which pushed the wheel sharply to the right, steering the Saab into the right lane, which at the time was, unfortunately, occupied a short distance up by a mobile home on a flatbed trailer, and what with Harvey's cruise control set at seventy . . . well, the last thing Harvey saw was the back door—and the bumper sticker JESUS LOVES YOU.

"JESUS!" was the last thing Janet heard over the phone.

"Oooh, Harvey, was it as good for you as it was for me? . . . Harvey? Harvey? Are you there, honey?" The line had gone dead. "Those fucking car phones!" was all she said before slamming her phone down, scooping up her packages, and running to the bedroom to shower and dress for the evening.

"I guess I left the house about eight-thirty so I'd get to Harvey's hotel by ten-thirty," Janet continued. "He had said he'd be back in his room by ten and he was going to call me to say good night. I had it all planned . . . how he'd be so excited from the phone call . . . and how he'd be so pissed that I wasn't home when he called at ten . . . and how I'd knock on his door . . . and . . . but I killed him, Tess!" she sobbed, grabbing my hands across the table.

Yep! You blew the bastard right off the road, I thought. "You didn't kill him, Janet," I said, squeezing her hands tightly. "It wasn't your fault. Do you know where he was going? Didn't Sandy tell you where he was going?"

"White Plains," Janet cried.

Obviously Sandy had not told her.

"No, Janet. He wasn't going to White Plains, and he wasn't going to Pittsburgh like he told his wife, either. He was on his way to Cape May," I said, throwing a piercing glare at Sandy, who leaned back in her seat, rolled her eyes upward, and pressed her lips together.

"What are you talking about, Tess? That's not possible."

"He was on his way to Cape May to meet someone else, another woman, for his birthday celebration."

"How do you know?"

"His wife told Sandy."

Sandy found her courage about there and she finished the story, which finished Janet.

"That BITCH!" Janet choked out.

"Which bitch?" I asked, not without a touch of sarcasm.

"Both of them!"

"Oh! A brace of bitches!" I informed Sandy, who squinted

contemptuously at me. "And I suppose Harvey was their innocent victim?"

"You don't understand, Tess."

"From what I could see, it wasn't I who didn't understand," I whined to Michael on Tuesday, pouting in a corner of his leather couch, my shoeless feet tucked under me, my arms folded. "Maybe it is me. Am I nuts? Or is the whole world nuts?"

"You're not nuts," was all he offered.

"So everyone else is nuts, right?"

"I love it when you're black and white," he said, laughing.

"What's that supposed to mean?"

"It means that for some reason you must have it one way or the other. There's no in-between, no gray."

"Why?"

"I don't know why."

"Yes, you do. You're supposed to help me when I get stuck."

"Why do you think Janet, and others, get involved in no-win relationships?"

"Because she, they, don't think very much of themselves."

"And why do they make excuses for their lovers who treat them poorly?"

"Because they have to . . . so they don't see what ugly people they've allowed themselves to get involved with . . . so they don't see how ugly they've become."

"You think Janet's ugly?"

"No," I said. *Yes*, I thought, and then suddenly felt ugly myself. "Not ugly; sad. She's so smart and she's acting so dumb, like she doesn't understand how demeaning that relationship was to her. I don't understand it, I don't understand any of it . . . what goes on out there!"

"Out where?"

"There! In the world."

"Out *there*? Where are you?"

"I feel like I'm on another planet."

"And the men on your planet are so wonderful? Like your husband, for instance?"

That cut deep. Tears welled up, but I put my head back so they wouldn't spill over, so they'd drain back behind my eyes and run down my throat in a hot stream of contempt. I wanted to answer him, but I was afraid that I'd choke on my pain, so I just glared at him until the feeling was pushed back down.

"That hurt, didn't it?"

"Not really," I lied. "I know you're right." What I meant was it hurt like hell *because* I knew he was right.

"So, men are a pretty scummy lot."

"That's a trick question," I said, understanding that it was, in fact, a question, not a statement, and that if I said yes, which I was inclined to do, Michael could infer that I thought he was scummy, too. I didn't think Michael was scummy. Of course, I didn't know Michael that well. For all I knew he might be wonderful to his clients, but scummy to his wife. After all, he didn't get personal with his clients. Of course, if I said that to Michael, it would hurt his feelings because that would be denying the extremely personal relationship that's supposed to develop between therapist and client. Then again, it probably develops on the side of the client but not on the side of the therapist. I mean, after all, a client only has one therapist, but a therapist has many clients, and one could not expect one's therapist to be personally involved with every client. Talk about burnout! And surely it would be conceit for me to think that I would be one of a chosen few whom he felt personally involved with. On the other hand, I wasn't feeling extraordinarily personally involved with Michael . . . so why was I going through these mental machinations when the man asked me a simple question . . . that wasn't really a question?

"Oh? How's that a trick question?" he asked.

"Well, you want me to say either yes or no. That men—all men—are scummy, or are not scummy. It's not as simple as that."

"I see. You mean it's not all black and white."

"Right. Now. In my experience, I've come across a lot of scummy men."

"That sounds like a fair statement. Have you met any men who aren't scummy?"

"One or two."

"One or two?"

"Well, one besides you."

"I'm not scummy?"

"I don't think so."

"Thank you. And who's the other?"

"David. David Ross. Stephen's friend. You know David —he gave me your number."

"Yes. I know David."

I waited to see if he had any further comment. After all, he had been David's therapist for two or three years. He was, in fact, David's last therapist. But Michael wasn't talking— professional confidence, of course. He waited for me to continue. "Well, I don't think David is scummy," I said. "In fact, he's got to be one of the sweetest people I know. I consider him a close friend. I feel I can trust him. Sort of."

"What do you mean, sort of?"

"I mean, as far as I can see I can trust him. I haven't had any really personal dealings with him, so I'm not sure I can really trust him."

"Personal dealings. You mean you haven't slept with him?" Michael was leaning forward in his seat now. He was into this conversation. He had an opinion. I could tell. He wanted me to know something. Oh, God. Maybe he knows David is gay! I thought. If anyone would know, Michael would know.

"No. That's not what I mean."

"Oh. You *have* slept with him?"

"No! What's going on here? Why are you pushing this?"

"I'm not pushing anything. You said you haven't had any personal dealings with David. But you also said he's a close friend, that you can *sort of* trust him. So I was trying to understand what you mean by 'personal dealings.'"

I sat there and glared while caterpillars and ants crawled

around in my stomach making me teary-eyed, uncomfortable. Cotton filled my ears. I wanted to scream, "YOU DON'T UNDERSTAND." But I knew he understood far better than I, so I decided to trust him because it was too painful not to. "Okay. Personal dealings, as in sex," I said quietly.

"So, men get scummy when you have sex with them."

"It does seem to bring out the worst in them," I said, growing more uncomfortable, wondering where this was going to lead. Afraid of where this was going to lead? Afraid of what?

"And David? Where does he fit into this?"

"I'm not sure. He's kind of an enigma. We're friends. I find him attractive. Sometimes I think he finds me attractive. But I'm not at all his type."

"What's his type?"

"You should know that better than I."

"I know what he's told me."

"Has he told you he's gay?" I dared to ask.

"No. Why do you ask that?"

"Well, it's just that his social behavior with women is so superficial."

"You mean your friendship with him?"

"No. I mean his dating habits. He dates these . . ." I didn't want to say "bimbos," because that's such a demeaning term to women, and I'm a woman, and I didn't think I should join the scummy men who use it. ". . . these superficial women. He has superficial relationships with them and then goes on to others. It's almost as if he doesn't want to be involved with them at all. Like he's only doing it for appearances. Like maybe he's really a closet gay?"

"It's possible."

Aha! "And he's so sweet and nurturing. Men just aren't like that!"

"I see. Women are sweet and nurturing. So if a man is sweet and nurturing, he must be gay. Well. That's black and white!" He laughed again.

"You're laughing at me again! That's twice today. You're going to give me an inferiority complex!"

"I'm going to give you a complex!" He doubled over in laughter. "Hah! That's rich! I'm going to give this model of self-esteem an inferiority complex!"

An attempt to suppress the smile pulling at my face was in vain, and the effort made me blush hot and crimson.

So there I sat burning red with this stupid grin distorting my heretofore indignant demeanor, and he sat on the edge of his chair, and taking my hand in both of his he looked directly in my eyes, smiled, and said, in the most gentle, nurturing, loving way, "You're a neat lady, Tess." A soft, warm glow enfolded me, and for a moment, for just an instant, I felt like a little girl . . . and very, very special. "I don't think David is gay, Tess," Michael continued seamlessly, letting go of my hand, sitting back in his seat, getting back to my question. "I found David to be an extremely sensitive man who, in fact, likes women very much."

"But all those women he sees? If he likes women so much, why doesn't he stick with one?" I asked, feeling like Michael and I were comrades in an intrigue, in a secret hideaway, talking secret things, things we'd never tell anyone but each other.

"Maybe the women he dates aren't his type."

At home that night, I unplugged the telephone in my bedroom, curled up in bed with a large dish of chocolate marshmallow ice cream that I topped with a scoop of chopped almonds left over from the Rocky Road ice cream cake rolls, and started to watch a videotape of a vintage Sherlock Holmes movie, *The Woman in Green.* As the familiarity of the old movie wrapped around me like the comforting arms of a gentle, trusted grandfather, I slowly lapped at the smooth, sweet ice cream. And I tried to remember the comforting aura at Michael's office, to recapture the sweet taste of being special, but I bit into a chunk of almond, filling my head with an unbearable crunch, breaking the mood. I felt cranky. I didn't want the almonds in my ice cream disrupting my peace. I felt annoyed at myself for dumping them into my dish. And as I tried to pick them out, to push them aside, I understood: Life starts out okay—smooth and sweet—but we manage to mess things up . . . we put hard things in our way. And growing more perturbed at the offending almonds pervading my ice cream, I realized something else: Once you crap up your life, it's not easy to smooth it out. Descending to the kitchen, I dumped the whole bowl of homemade Rocky Road into the sink and started over with a fresh dip. Elementary, my dear Watson.

Life should be so easy.

CHECKERBOARD CAKE

3 ounces semisweet chocolate
4 cups sifted cake flour
2 cups sugar
2 tablespoons baking powder
1 1/2 teaspoons salt
1 cup unsalted butter (softened)
1 1/3 cups milk (room temperature)
1 tablespoon vanilla extract
4 eggs

Preheat oven to 350°F.

Melt chocolate in top of double boiler and set aside.

In large mixing bowl, combine flour, sugar, baking powder, and salt. Mix on low speed for one minute, until well blended. Add butter and 1 cup of milk and beat at medium-high for 1 1/2 minutes, scraping sides of bowl.

In another bowl, combine vanilla, eggs, and 1/3 cup milk and beat lightly. Add to batter in three parts, beating at medium-high for 20 seconds after each addition. Scrape sides of bowl after each part.

Divide batter in half. Stir melted chocolate into one half of the batter.

Grease and flour the bottoms and sides of the special cake pans from the "Bake King Checkerboard Cake Set" (#1200) (manufactured by C. M. Products, Inc., Subsidiary of Chicago Metallic Products, Inc.), Place the divider into one prepared pan and pour in the two batters (dark and light) as described in the instruction booklet "How to Use Your Checkerboard Cake Set" that is included in the set. Repeat procedure for each pan.

Bake pans in the center of the oven for 25 minutes, revolving the pans once after 12 minutes.

Allow cakes to cool in pans, sitting on racks, for 10 minutes before removing. Assemble the cake according to directions in the instruction booklet. Serves 10.

CHAPTER 7

Checkerboard Cake

I was having a terrible day. It had been a terrible weekend, and before that a terrible week . . . when I stopped to think of it, I couldn't think of when it hadn't been terrible. Of course, that wasn't how it was, but that's how it felt the Monday afternoon in May I struggled with the checkerboard cake I was trying to perfect for my new clients, the Chessmen, a group of men and women who met at the library the first Thursday of each month to play chess. I hadn't been aware of their existence until one of the members, Gus Kolodner, got my name from Linda Bliss, the special events director at the library, who had mentioned to Gus that Coffee, Cake, and Criticism had its refreshments catered by Just Desserts on the third Thursday of each month.

The idea of featuring a checkerboard cake on the dessert table for the Chessmen made me feel extremely clever, but after a morning of preparation and concoction, I stood in front of a counter covered with dirty dishes and a lot of crumbs. Something had gone wrong.

I had borrowed the special round pans with the circular metal insert and the recipe for the cake batter from Sandy's mother, who had inherited them from an aunt. She said she had never made the cake herself, but she remembered that her aunt's cakes were in three layers, each consisting of three concentric circles of alternating chocolate and vanilla, looking very much like a bull's-eye. Supposedly, once the layers were baked and stacked together, cemented by chocolate icing, slices of the finished cake would have a checkerboard design. Personally, I couldn't picture the whole thing, but, on faith, I made the cake batter. Then, finding only one insert—consisting of two concentric circles on an odd frame—for the three pans, I assumed the other two inserts had been lost, and figured I'd make one layer at a time. After removing the first layer from the pan, I was faced with the bizarre metal contraption embedded in the cake. An attempt to extricate it neatly failed. Stubbornly, I tried a second layer . . . and a third. Finally, I was left with three large chocolate cupcakes—the centers of the bull's-eyes—and a pile of crumbs. I no longer felt clever. And the failure added to my already agitated mood, which had been precipitated by the events surrounding the death of Harvey Cohen almost three weeks ago, and further exacerbated by several lovesick phone calls from Stephen—I refused to see him—and a disastrous Sunday night date.

"Disastrous, Tess? How bad could it have been?" Sandy had questioned over coffee and a bagel earlier in the day when I had just started to make the batter for the checkerboard cakes.

"Trust me."

"From what Cindy told me, this guy sounded like a winner."

"Alan Persky, another blind date from the folks who brought you Joe Silvers, the California Kid."

"Oh, Oil Wells!"

"Yep. Alan is another of Richard's old college friends, also nice-looking, also lots of money—"

"But?"

"Boooooring!" I trilled. "He took me to Atlantic City to have dinner at one of the gourmet restaurants in Caesars Palace, but once we got there he spent hours at the craps table, totally ignoring me."

"Did you finally eat?"

"Oh, sure—at ten o'clock! And all he talked about was himself—all the way to Atlantic City, all through dinner, and all the way home. You know, he never asked me one question about myself. 'Richard tells me you bake cookies and sell houses,' he said early in the evening, and then made some sexist remark about how that probably gives me lots of time to play tennis with the girls."

"Yuck!"

"And you can't imagine how hard those stools at the blackjack tables can be, when you can find one to sit on, which I finally did after standing for an hour and a half watching Alan crap out."

"You played blackjack?"

"No. I found a stool at an empty table and watched the crowd."

"Anyone interesting?"

"Actually, yes. I saw George Cantelli."

"THE George Cantelli?"

"Uh-huh."

It really was him, I remembered. turning the mixer on medium and watching the spinning beaters blend the raw ingredients into a smooth batter. George Cantelli, a comedian of international and transgenerational renown . . . and I was no more than fifty feet from him! That I could see him at all was surprising because there were so many people hovering around his table on the cocktail platform, and there was so much smoke in the casino that my eyes were tearing. But it was George Cantelli all right. I had heard he was performing in Atlantic City, and there he was, a lot smaller than he looked on television, but a lot better-looking. And it certainly appeared that he was staring back at me. Then again, he was probably looking at someone behind me, I thought. But it did seem that whenever I looked over to him, he caught my eyes with his. No. Unless he walked over and knelt before me, I wouldn't believe he was actually looking at *me.* Not that I looked bad. It was a mild night and I was chicly romantic in a bone linen midiskirt and a matching, long, silk sailor blouse. When I looked over again, he wasn't talking to anyone . . . and his eyes did seem to stop on mine. This is crazy, I thought, a mixture of hypoglycemic hallucination and boredom. What was really crazy was that I didn't grab a cab and go home instead of sitting on that high chair like a dunce, waiting for an inconsiderate blind date to lose his money. I only hoped there'd be enough left for dinner. Well, Georgie, I thought, it's just you and me. So, where's your wife? I was sure I'd read that he was married. Of course, what would that mean to a Hollywood type? Then again, what would *I* mean to a Hollywood type? Moot question, but there was nothing better to think about. So. There. It happened again. Eye to eye. I wonder if he thinks I'm someone he knows. I have been told that I look like a million different people. What would I do if he actually came over to me? Another moot question. But I played with it as I straightened my back, suddenly aware of my tendency to slump when I sit. Head up, shoulders back . . .

"George Cantelli, I presume."

"I'm afraid you have the advantage."

"Tess. Tess Fineman."

"I've been noticing you, Tess Fineman. You're a noticeable person. Perhaps you were aware that I've been watching you from across the room."

"Oh? No, actually not. I thought I was watching you."

"I'm flattered. You're alone. Are you waiting for someone? You shouldn't have to wait for *anyone.*"

"Just my blind date. But I've grown quite weary of him."

"Perhaps we could have a drink?"

"I'd like that enormously."

"Won't you step this way," he said, taking my hand, leading me toward a small private booth in the bar area, straining to keep his hands, but not his eyes, off my incredibly delicate unpadded shoulder.

"Thank you. I . . ."

. . . Oh, oh. He's getting up. There goes my entertainment, I thought, as George Cantelli walked away from his

103

table and down from the bar platform. Losing sight of him in the crowd, I turned my attention to the nearby blackjack table. I had watched the dealer draw twenty-one three times in a row, to the disgruntlement of the four men at the table, when I became aware of someone standing just behind me, a little to my left. I turned my head to find George Cantelli standing there smiling and waving toward the table to my right, but before I could turn away he looked at me and smiled anew. I smiled back and then turned my eyes, if not my attention, back to the blackjack table. This was it, my chance to be really cool, really sophisticated. I could hear myself telling Sandy about my big adventure in the casino with—are you ready?—GEORGE CANTELLI. As I sat coolly watching the men at the table win then lose then win then lose, I could feel George's eyes burning the back of my long, alabaster neck, velvety with blond fuzz. "Love fuzz," Marv called the fine, fuzzy little hairs at the nape of my neck that George Cantelli watched glisten golden in the bright light of the casino. I could feel the hairs stand up to meet his lustful gaze as a blush crept by them, tinting that svelte, graceful curve. *Perhaps we could have a drink,* he'll say, touching me lightly on the back of my neck, barely ruffling the fuzz. *I'd like that enormously . . . very much. . . . I'd like that. . . . Certainly. Thank you, that would be delightful. . . . Of course. That would be very nice. . . . How kind of you. . . . How . . .* Should I just leave my date at the table, I wondered, or should I tell him I was going? Nonsense. George wasn't going to talk to me. Then again . . . Perhaps if I turned and smiled again. There. He responded with a smile of his own and stepped forward, placing himself—I couldn't believe it!—beside me. *Nice day, isn't it? . . . Nice casino, isn't it? . . . Are you staying here?*—no, that's his line. *Are you enjoying your stay? . . . You are a marvelously inventive entertainer, a creative genius. . . . A drink? I thought you'd never ask! . . . Of course. I'd like that enormously. . . . It would be my pleasure*—no, that's his line . . . As I turned once again toward the blackjack table, I could see George out of the corner of my eye staring at my profile, my left profile with its sharp, sophisticated edge. Now's my chance, I thought—head up, shoulders back—as I shifted my eyes to the left, catching his, then turned my head slowly, sensually, till we were face to face.

"Mr. Cantelli"—I extended my hand—"Tess Fineman. I . . . I'd very much like to have your autograph." My God! I'd asked for his autograph! Clod! Jerk! I couldn't believe I'd said that!

"Certainly, if you have a pen, I don't seem to have one on me," he said, letting go of my hand, patting his pockets in search of the mundane object.

"I don't either, but I'll find one. I enjoy your performances very much."

"Thank you," he said politely, the fire in his eyes extinguished by my insipid request for his autograph instead of his body.

Utterly embarrassed by my gauche, star-struck behavior, I hopped off my stool and hurried away to find a pen. When I returned, he was still standing there, held by the inertia of disappointment, no doubt. He took the pen from me and mechanically signed his name, *George Cantelli, with best wishes to Tess*—he did remember my name—on a cocktail napkin. Still smiling, he walked off, leaving me to hop upon my stool once again, clutching my booby prize.

"Tess. Tess! You're lost somewhere."

"Sorry," I said, turning off the mixer.

"So? Did you get his autograph?" Sandy asked.

"Whose?"

"George Cantelli! Didn't you just say you saw George Cantelli at the casino?"

"Oh. Yes. Of course," I said, digging the crumpled cocktail napkin out of the pocketbook I had left on the kitchen table the night before.

"That's exciting!" she said, smoothing the napkin on the table, impressed. "Did you get to talk to him?"

"Just briefly. I told him I liked his act. He shook my hand."

"Well! That had to make your evening."

"It helped," I said. To make it a disaster, I thought.

I dumped the crumby mess in the trash, setting aside the giant cupcakes for Sandy's kids, washed the pans, and then sat in the family room with a cup of coffee and a tranquilizer: the crossword puzzle in the Sunday *New York Times Magazine*. I find peace in the knowledge that the puzzle has a black and white solution. There's no gray in a crossword puzzle. It helps to focus me, draws me together when my thoughts pull me in myriad directions. Control. As I work toward a solution, I feel in control. I must remember to tell Michael about my puzzles, I thought, penciling "AMAH" in 27-Down, for "Japanese nurse." Sitting quietly filling in squares, I relaxed. The checkerboard cake conundrum would wait till tomorrow. Yes, tomorrow is another day.

"She's left home and is having an affair now," said one therapist to another on his way out of the conference room in Michael's office suite. I heard this over the *swishhh* of the white-noise machine in the waiting room Tuesday morning.

"Was she having an affair while she was still at home?" questioned the other therapist.

"No," he answered. "I wouldn't let her."

I wouldn't let her. That's control. It's not the kind of control that I have guarded so furiously, the kind of control that makes motion transcend emotion in a kind of bastardization of Marshall McLuhan. They're talking control where it counts, over others' emotions.

I thought about the conversation I had overheard as I settled into my favorite spot on Michael's sofa, drew my legs up, and tucked my feet under me. But all I said was, "It's starting to rain pretty hard out there." And then I proceeded to bitch about my life, my inability to seize the moment, my failed cake. He listened silently. Then, finding nothing else to say, I decided to try to take the wheel, exhibit a little control in our relationship. I asked him about his life.

"I'm at a good time in my life right now," Michael

answered openly. "I'm happy. I'm doing work that I love, I have love in my life."

I have love in my life. He was referring to his wife, a woman who equaled him in impressive credentials—an award-winning artist who held a chair at the university—and good looks. And I'd bet her cakes didn't fall apart.

I have love in my life. He could do anything. Control.

Envy. I felt envious of Michael. He had love in his life. He had it all. I wanted it.

"I can teach and do research. I'm at a point where I only have to see the clients I want to see," he continued his musing.

"I feel privileged," I said obediently, letting him know that I caught the mirrored compliment, and that I would hold it to me because I, too, thought he was outrageously bright and talented.

"You *are* privileged," he said, reinforcing his point. No mere musing, this was control. He was in control. "Yes," he was saying as he lolled back in his easy chair, cradling the back of his head in his hands. "I'm doing what I want. I'm where I want to be."

God, he looked open, inviting. Smug. It struck me that he wasn't wearing a tie, which he usually did, just a yellow shirt open at the neck and a camel sport jacket. He was casual. Actually, he was a little mussed up. It was becoming. The gray in his wavy black hair showed in its slightly tousled state. He looked comfortable. He was comfortable with his life. Maybe too comfortable. Yes. There it was. The chink in the perfectly crafted being. Complacency. A toehold into the control center of the inner man. Bravo! for arrogance. Here! Here! for egocentrism. But beware complacency. The bogeyman will get you if you don't watch out!

Driving home, I had an epiphany: Take the rings out of the pan *before* baking the cake. Thank you, God.

Back in my kitchen, I readied my ingredients and equipment for Checkerboard Cake II, and set about my task with newfound fervor. Totally in control, I scooped and measured, mixed and poured—one layer at a time—and then slowly, carefully, I removed the metal rings from the pan and watched the three circles of thick chocolate and vanilla batter wed, but, lo and behold, they did not blend! Perfect bull's-eyes met my proud gaze as I set the three pans in the oven.

As the kitchen filled with the sweet smell of baking cake, I wiped the countertops and put the bowls, spoons, and other utensils into the dishwasher, turned it on, and sat down with my as-yet-uncompleted crossword puzzle. There was 16-Down: a seven-letter word for "dominate" that ended in "OL." The answer had been eluding me. Then, 16-Across: a three-letter word for "food fish." Of course! "COD." And the c in "COD" gave me "CONTROL." And the drone of the dishwasher in the background reminded me of the drone of the noise machine in Michael's waiting room . . . and the conversation between the two therapists about control . . . and my conversation with Michael, also about control. Funny coincidence. Cod. Funny word. Cod . . . as in cod-piece, a kind of sixteenth-century fly for men's tight breeches, I thought, picturing Shakespearean players in their tight breeches and exaggerated codpieces. And the thought of codpieces, tight pants, men's bulges, made me flush. And I thought of Michael and wondered about his complacency, his possible lack of control.

"I love my work, too, Michael," I had said. "My business is growing, slowly but surely. It's the rest of my life that I can't handle," I had complained, referring to the lack of love in my life.

"Of course, I'd rather be a success than have some meaningless affair," I had said, meaning, of course, give me a good fuck and I'll be a success if you want me to . . . I'll be anything you want me to be.

He knew what I really meant. He always knows what I really mean even if I don't say it.

"I understand," is what he had said. . . .

* * *

"I always understand you," he said, moving from his chair to the sofa, taking my hand in his, pressing it to his lips. I knew his lips would be soft. "I've understood you since the first day we talked," he said, brushing my tousled hair from my eyes with his fingers. I knew his touch would be tender. "You do have love in your life," he said, moving closer, close enough for me to see the tears behind his glasses. I knew he would be vulnerable. "You see, Tess, I love you. I want to make love to you," he said, taking me in his arms, kissing me fervently. I knew he would be passionate. And the waves crashed on the rocks.

. . . The splash of water on my bare feet pulled me from my daydream. Water, sudsy water everywhere. The dishwasher. Something with the dishwasher. The dishwasher was out of control. I was out of control.

By the time I cleaned up the floor, called the repair service, unloaded the dishwasher, and rinsed its contents in the sink, my cake layers were baked and cooled. They plopped out of their pans neatly. All's well, I thought, stirring the smooth, bittersweet chocolate icing. I assembled the layers, scored the top of the iced cake with a crisscross design, placed the finished cake on a pedestal plate lined with a paper doily, and set it aside. Then I iced the three cupcakes from the day before, planning to take them all to Sandy's house after dinner for a taste test. As I cleaned up the bowl and utensils from the icing, my mind kept drifting back to the tender tears of vulnerability I had imagined in Michael's eyes. Horny. I was definitely horny. Out of control . . . hostage of hormones . . . victim of viscera.

Vincent Salvatore called about five-thirty. He had gotten a telephone call from Lorraine Farber, a divorced attorney I had brought to see his townhouse Monday evening. She told him she wanted to work out a deal to buy the townhouse directly from him for less money. He was appalled, he said. "I think she was trying to screw you out of your commission," he said. "But I wouldn't have any part of it. Maybe you should come over and we can review the figures and see if we can't put together a deal the lady can't refuse."

Interesting, I thought, as I remembered the two of them flirting with each other at his house.

"Sexy bedroom. Yes? Decorated for the romantically inclined," he had teased, smiling broadly, revealing straight white teeth amidst his heavy black beard. He was referring to the Pablo Picasso erotica hanging on the midnight blue walls, the midnight blue satin sheets on the low platform bed, the small stereo speakers secured in all four corners of the ceiling. Lorraine wet her lips and smiled. "This is the master bedroom," was all he had said to me when I first saw the house. "And you'll love the bath," he said to Lorraine, taking her by the elbow, leading her into the master bath, which featured a large, clear-glass-enclosed steam-shower with four shower heads and a long marble bench built into the back wall. "Big enough for two . . . or three," he said, holding her arm, his black eyes watching me watch him and her in the mirror. Not a chance, I thought, inferring an invitation to a *ménage à trois*. Then again, he was only flirting with Lorraine, I thought, trying to show her what a macho guy he was. I was just a prop. I did not miss that she moved almost imperceptibly closer to him, tilting her head slightly toward him. Did she blush? I wasn't sure. But she took her glasses off and fluttered her eyelashes. "Veeery nice," was all she said.

"How about seven-thirty, Vincent? That should give you time to have dinner."

"You don't eat dinner?"

"Well, it will give me time to grab something, too," I answered.

"Tell you what. Why don't you come over at six-thirty and we can eat dinner together. I hate to eat alone. And you'll find I'm a very good cook."

"That's very nice, Vincent," I said, taken aback, not sure

whether I should say yes . . . or no . . . or . . . "I'll bring dessert!" I said, eyeing the checkerboard cake on the counter, knowing that Sandy would understand. Anything for a sale, I thought. But what I was feeling was unsettled . . . and the soft warmth of Vincent Salvatore's hand in mine when we had shaken on the listing of his home.

". . . and so I hope you don't mind if I don't bring the cake tonight," I told Sandy over the telephone while putting a fresh coat of polish on my nails.

"Of course not. Is he cute?"

"Sandy! This is business."

"Right. Is he cute?"

"In a rough sort of way. He's dark and solid-looking. He lifts weights. Oh, and he's got a beard."

"Sounds interesting. Call me when you get home tonight."

"Sandy, this is business."

"Right. Call me. Bye!"

As soon as I put the phone down, it rang.

"Hello? Just Desserts? I want to order a pineapple cheesecake." It was Marv.

"Sorry. We're out of cheesecake."

"Okay, then I'll have a cherry cheesecake."

"Sorry, we're out of cheesecake."

"Okay, then I'll have a blueberry cheesecake."

"Sorry, we're out of cheesecake."

"So then I'll just have a plain cheesecake!" he finished our ritualistic telephone conversation, a holdover from our brushes with *Sesame Street*—he with his son, and me with Rebecca and Jonathan on Saturday mornings at Sandy's house.

"How about a fuck?" I said, surprising both of us.

"Oooh, what you do to me, sweetheart! You know what's best about our relationship? Regular sex. . . ."

Surely he jests! Sex with Marv is not exactly what one would call regular, I thought with relish for a split second, until I realized that what he meant was regular as in *steady*, not regular as in *standard*. And I suddenly felt used.

111

". . . It sure makes life less complicated. Cuts out all the games," he continued.

"Right," I said. Wrong, I thought, becoming aware that I didn't like his game anymore. I wanted to be wanted for my flesh and blood, not my illusive image, which is a reflection of not only the beheld, but also the beholder. Go fuck yourself, Marv! I yelled in my head. That's what you've been doing all along, anyway.

"So, when will I see you this weekend, Tess? I thought we could spend Saturday together and go to the zoo. Spring is here! The animals are starting to mate. It's a great show!"

"Oh, Marv. I'm so sorry, but I'm going to be out of town this weekend. I'm going to . . . a seminar. Yes, a real estate seminar in . . . White Plains. I won't be back until late Sunday night."

"Oooh, am I disappointed. Well, that's the way the mirror cracks! I'll call you next week. Okay?"

"I'm going to be pretty busy next week, Marv. How about if I call you when I see a break."

"All right," he said softly after a long pause. "I understand. Hope to hear from you soon."

"Sure, Marv. Thanks for calling. Bye."

So much for that, I thought, putting the telephone down gingerly.

Cake in hand, I arrived at Vincent's townhouse at exactly six-thirty. Up to that point, my interactions with Vincent had been all business, and even as I stood at his front door, I insisted to myself that this was a business call. But when he opened the door, I was seduced by the sight of his Reeboks, blue jeans, and sweatshirt depicting Mozart, the strains of a Bach Brandenburg concerto, the bouquet of sautéed garlic. I left my pretense on the patio and allowed myself to drift into this business of sensuality.

Vincent greeted me with a glass of wine, relieved me of my cake, and led me to a barstool at the counter in the small kitchen with the butcher-block countertops and white ceramic tile backsplashes. "The chef is at work," he declared, picking up his own glass from the counter and draining it as he turned to the stove. He pushed up his sleeves, revealing sizable forearms, and with a long-handled, flat wooden spoon proceeded to orchestrate our dinner amazingly in time to the very, very quick concerto in G major that surrounded us. He manipulated the implement in his right hand while deftly maneuvering the pots and pans with his left. White clam sauce simmered, angel-hair pasta churned in boiling water, plump capers rolled about in white wine and lemon juice thickened by a lump of sweet butter, and the music played on. I watched with admiration as Vincent drained the pasta, sauced the veal, and tossed the salad, thinking, A man in control of his kitchen is a man in control of his life.

"Dinner is served," he announced, carrying the dishes to the small, square, glass and stainless steel dining table. Once I was seated, Vincent lit the candles on the table, dimmed the hi-tech steel and enamel light overhead, and placed a basket of hot garlic and cheese bread before me . . . leaning close to me . . . telling me that the recipe for the bread came from his grandmother who lives in Sicily. And I could have fainted from the exquisite aroma of the bread . . . of the after-shave? cologne? soap? that emanated from Vincent.

I tasted everything. "It's wonderful, Vincent. I'm impressed."

"Then I've succeeded," he said, smiling a very quiet smile, giving the electricity between us room to build. "I wanted to impress you."

"Oh?"

"You attracted me the first time we met. I tried to flirt with you when you brought the lady lawyer over, but you were tough. Ve-ry pro-fes-sion-al. So I figured I had to get you out of your business suit . . . so to speak."

That did it. As good as dinner was, it was over for me. I remembered all at once all of those scenes in movies where the man rubs the woman's foot with his under the table, rubs his leg against hers under the table, puts his hand on her knee under the table, touches her hand as he passes the pasta, touches her face as he dusts a crumb from her chin, and I felt Vincent all at once all over me. And he hadn't even touched me.

"You're not eating!"

I flushed. "I'm not as hungry as I thought I was."

"Yes. Appetites tend to supplant one another. I feel it, too."

That's saying it like it is, I thought, flushing deeper.

Bach filled my ears. Vincent filled my wineglass. "To a sensual evening," he said, touching his glass to mine.

I drank the wine quickly in an effort to hydrate the desert that had taken over my mouth.

"You have a fine body, Tess."

That's direct, I thought—a pass even I can't miss. "Oh, it's fine, all right," I said, laughing nervously, "for a teenage boy."

"And I'll bet you're going to complain that your thighs are too chubby, too. Most Jewish girls say that."

Very direct. No games played here. "Well. My legs aren't my best feature." I couldn't believe I was discussing my body as if it were a piece of equipment with this . . . this stranger!

"I personally don't like a woman with chicken legs. Soft thighs make soft cushions."

I couldn't respond. Tumbleweeds were blowing around my tongue.

"I'm looking forward to this evening, Tess."

Dinner wasn't This Evening? Of course not. *Dessert* was This Evening. I guessed *I* was Dessert. No. I changed my mind. *He's* Dessert.

"It's going to be fun," I heard myself say.

"Fun?" He sounded hurt. Maybe *fun* was too frivolous an adjective for this Macho Guy, this Latin Lover.

"Yes. Fun," I repeated, feeling my spinning wheels click into gear. "It's always best when it's fun."

"You're okay, Tess." He laughed, putting his napkin on the table. Dinner was over. Vincent stood up, took my hands, and pulled me to my feet. He put his extremely muscled arms around my waist and kissed me. It was nice, relaxed.

Okay. So far I was okay. I was also dizzy—from the wine, the Bach, the garlic, Vincent. "Oooh, Vincent, what you're doing to me," I said, totally in control of my loss of control.

"This looks serious," he said, his arms around me, walking me backward, toward the stairs.

Serious? Could he possibly mean *serious* as in *I could really get serious about you?* No, no. He means *serious* as in *We're going to do It.* Kicking off my flats, I put my stockinged feet on his Reeboks, letting him carry me to . . . whatever, accepting with abandon that walking backward on his feet was about as serious as this was going to get.

Upstairs, he gently placed me on the bed and pulled my bulky cotton sweater over my head. Lying beside me, his mouth latched onto my right breast, he somehow dealt with my slacks and panties, and the next thing I knew Vincent was between my legs doing something so incredible with his tongue that I came in a flash with a yelp, and then again . . . and again . . . and again. . . . The man was impressive—and he didn't even have his pants off. It didn't occur to me to wonder if I was impressing him. Then we were both naked, and I found out just *how* impressive he was. And then it was morning and I awoke with Vincent plastered to my back, his black beard nestled between my neck and my shoulder. I smiled. He stirred. He was on top of me, kissing me, and all I could think of was my morning mouth . . . *garlic* morning mouth. He felt my reticence, wiped *his* mouth on the midnight blue satin sheet, and kissed me again. And then he was behind me, his hands all over the front of me. It felt like Sunday morning.

Sunday mornings with Stephen were warm and wet. I'd wake slowly, encased in Stephen, and we'd made love before I even opened my eyes. Behind me, his arms around me, his morning erection rooting between my thighs for acceptance, he'd kiss my neck, rub my breasts in a spiral of circles starting wider than they deserved. The first fuck of the morning was slow and hot. Then we would doze . . . tease and play . . . doze . . . tease and sometimes play again . . . and sometimes we wouldn't get up until two or three in the afternoon.

"You do okay for a teenage boy," Vincent teased, after.

When he left the bed to open the aluminum mini-blinds, there, in the wash of sunlight, I finally saw the full splendor of his beautiful body. From my reclined position, he looked like a marble statue, larger than life, every muscle, every feature chiseled to silky definition. Imagine! Michelangelo's David . . . in bed with me, Tess Fineman.

"Brunch?" he asked.

"Of course."

"Mykonos okay?"

"Sure." And I thought of Sunday brunch at the diner with Sandy and Janet, watching the singles come in with their Saturday night dates. Well, at least this was the middle of the week. No one would know.

At brunch, I couldn't eat very much, again. And again, he noticed. "It's exciting, isn't it? Being with someone new."

"Actually, I find it uncomfortable," I said honestly.

The rest of the meal was quiet, until the waitress asked, "How about dessert?" Vincent immediately replied, "We're having it at home."

I looked at him and he winked at me, and that wink undid me, again.

"Your cake, Tess. We didn't eat your cake last night."

"Yes."

But as soon as we walked in the door of his house, his arms were around me again, and there I was on his feet again as he walked me backward to the stairs again and he carried me up to the bedroom again and this time I didn't wait for him to undress me, I pulled off my sweater and pants and panties, and before I could see that he, too, was undressed his head was between my legs and his impressive organ straining its latex jacket was in front of my eyes and all I could do while he did whatever it was that he did so well

116

was to hold on to his staff for dear life as I came over . . . and over . . . and over . . . and over . . . until, exhausted, I cried, "UNCLE!"

"Wha?"

"Uncle!" I said, then gave him his due until he spilled in a gush. And then—yes, and then—and then he turned and we thrashed and heaved until, hooting and laughing, we were both spent . . . again.

"You were right," he said, lying back in exhaustion.

"About what?"

"It was fun."

We did finally get to my cake . . . after we rested, after we showered and dressed . . . after we made a pot of coffee.

"You do the honors," he said, handing me a knife and a plate.

Faced with my experimental creation, I was pulled back to the real world where I felt a little unstable, a little unsure. I approached the checkerboard cake with trepidation, wondering if, this time, I had gotten it right. The knife cut a wedge in the three layers. Slowly I inched the wedge out of the cake. . . . "STRIPES!" I cried.

Preparations for Checkerboard Cake III included pencil and paper. But as I sketched cake layers and three-dimensional bull's-eyes at my kitchen table later that afternoon, I found I couldn't concentrate. I went to the phone and dialed. "Sandy?"

"Tess! Where have you been? I've been trying you all day. Didn't you get my messages on your machine?"

"Sorry. I forgot to look at the machine when I came in."

"I waited for your call last night, and then tried you this morning, early . . ."

"You want company for dinner? I'll bring dessert."

"Sure. Charlie's working late. So where were you?"

"Playing chess."

"Chess?"

"See you in an hour. Bye."

I played the tape on my answering machine. There were eight messages:

BEEP. "Tess! Where are you? You were supposed to call me back last night."

BEEP. "Good morning, sunshine! It's Marv! What an early start! Just wanted to tell you that I'm going to miss you this weekend. So, if you'd like to have dinner tonight, tomorrow, or Friday, I'm at your service. If not, have a productive weekend in White Plains. Ciao!"

BEEP. "It's me again. Thought maybe you were in the shower earlier. Where are you? Do you want to have lunch? Call me when you get in."

BEEP. "Tess? It's David. It's one-forty. Just checking in. I'm okay. You okay? Peace."

BEEP. "Just Desserts? This is Gus Kolodner from the Chessmen. I wanted to tell you that we're looking forward to your goodies Thursday night, and on behalf of our membership I'd like to extend an invitation for you to join us for the evening. You don't have to call me back. See you Thursday, either way."

BEEP. "Tess, it's three-thirty. Now I'm worried. Call me!"

BEEP. "It's Stephen. I want to see you. Please, Tess. Unless you call me, I'll be over at seven. It'll be okay. Really. I love you."

BEEP. "It's Mother, dear. Why aren't you home? There never seems to be a right time to call you. Call me when you come in. I'll be at home."

What she meant was, *I'll be home, where I belong, unlike you, who are off to God knows where! doing God knows what!* You're right, Mother, there never is a right time for you to call me, I thought.

I dialed Stephen's office number, but hung up when his secretary answered. I just won't be here, I thought, remembering that I'd be at Sandy's. That's better. That way I won't even have to talk to him. What to do about Marv? Nothing. And I'll call David when I get home tonight, before I go to bed. Gus. The cake. Tomorrow. I can't think about that

118

now. Maybe I'll just make the fudge bars and honeyed granola . . . and I have two sour-cream coffee cakes in the freezer. That should do it. Right.

At five thirty-five I embedded a cherry candy heart in the iced top of each of the three oversize chocolate cupcakes, boxed them, and left for Sandy's.

After dinner, after story time—when I read Rebecca and Jonathan *my* favorite book, *Put Me in the Zoo*—after bath time washed chocolate icing off grateful faces and chocolate crumbs down the drain, after bedtime quieted the house, Sandy and I sat down to mugs of tea and the third chocolate bull's-eye.

"Well?" Sandy said, picking the cherry heart off the cake and popping it into her mouth.

"Well what?" I teased.

"Well, so where were you, what happened?"

"Well . . ." I started slowly, "I was at Vincent's townhouse for dinner . . . and I stayed for brunch."

Sandy couldn't contain herself. "So, so, so?" she begged, on the edge of her seat.

"So. He had invited me to dinner to talk about the sale of the house—you remember I told you about the lady lawyer I took to see the house? Well . . ." and I related the whole story, leaving out not one juicy morsel. And Sandy giggled and tittered, laughed and clapped her hands like a little girl hearing a favorite fairy tale where the beautiful princess has her cake and eats it, too.

"Tess, you're incredible! So when are you going to see him again?"

"I'm not."

"What! You've got to be kidding. You knooow he's going to call you again."

"It doesn't matter. I don't want to see him again."

"Why not? He sounds faaabulous!"

"So was Gregg . . . and Marv."

"Was? What's this *was?* Did they appear in the obit column this morning?"

"I pretty much told Marv yesterday that I didn't want to see him anymore. And Gregg . . . well, he called last week and I told him I was *involved.* I felt weird with the idea of sleeping with Gregg while I was still seeing Marv. So I said I'd call him when I was free."

"That was monogamous of you."

"Well, that's what made me comfortable."

"So now you're not seeing Mirrors or Cream Puff, why can't you see the Italian Stallion?"

"The Italian Stallion? You do come up with them!"

"It's my most major talent. But, actually, it's you who comes up with them, I only name them. So how come?"

"How come what?"

"How come you won't see him again?"

"Because it was just sex. That's all. We have absolutely nothing in common, nothing to talk about."

"How do you know? You didn't talk!"

"I know. Trust me."

"Okay. So what's the matter with pure sex?" she demanded.

"I don't know. It was fine for what it was, but there was so much missing. It was like Chinese food. Three hours later you're hungry again—deep down."

"So?"

"I guess what I'm trying to say is that it happened because of the right chemistry, the right circumstances, the right tensions. . . . It was totally spontaneous. I went over because I thought it was business, and I certainly couldn't do that again. . . . I mean, if he called and I went out with him again, it would be tantamount to saying, 'Okay, I want to fuck, too. Do we eat dinner first, or do we just get naked and do It?' Look, it was great fun, but it wasn't a performance that would hold up in a rerun. . . . What I'm trying to say is that I don't think I'm a casual person, Sandy. I don't want *just* sex . . . I want *the rest.*"

"I'm not saying you should *marry* him! You know, Tess, I think you're scared."

"Of Vincent? Not a chance!"

"Not Vincent. Someone much more formidable: YOUR-

SELF! Of admitting that you get horny like everybody else and that good sex now and then is good for you."

"Not so. How about Gregg? Remember? Just a little dessert?"

"That's different. Cream Puff stood for something else. You thought he wanted you for your intellect, your maturity, your life experiences. You felt like the Romantic Older Woman. The sex wasn't even that good. You were his mentor, so you had a rationalization other than libido to sleep with him."

"God, Sandy. You're beginning to sound like Janet. You make me sound so neurotic."

"Hey. We all have something."

By then the mugs were drained. I felt drained. I picked up the last crumb of cake on the end of my finger and licked it off. "I think I'm depressed. I'm going to go home and sleep for a year."

"You know what your trouble is? Too much sex. You've been overorgasmed, orgasmed out. You're too mellow! Go home and sleep and have some nightmares . . . tense up again and you'll feel great in the morning."

Very early Thursday morning I pulled the coffee cakes out of the freezer for the chess club meeting that night—just in case. But after I made the fudge bars and the granola, I decided to take one more shot at the checkerboard cake. It was such a good idea; I couldn't let it go.

The phone was ringing when I walked into my kitchen after gathering ingredients from the market for Checkerboard Cake III.

"Hello," I answered, putting the grocery bag on the counter.

"There you are! I thought maybe you moved and didn't tell me." It was David.

"Uh-oh! I forgot to call you back last night. I did get your message. Sorry. Anything special?"

"Only that I was thinking about you. The last time we talked, you were pretty upset about Janet and her boyfriend.

121

You going to be home for a while? I met a client at the diner, and thought I'd stop over for a last cup of coffee before I go back to the office."

"You look okay," David said, giving me a brotherly kiss and an awkward hug about ten minutes after we hung up.

"I'm fine." I poured us each a mug of coffee and sat at the kitchen table with David. The yellow legal pad full of bull's-eye drawings was still there from the day before.

"What are these?" he asked.

"A puzzle. I'm trying to make a checkerboard cake," I said as David picked up the pad, turning it this way and that, trying to understand.

"Explain."

"Okay. Men are supposed to have a good sense of spatial relationships. See if you can figure this out. . . ." And I explained the pans to him, and the three layers, and the chocolate and vanilla batters, and the bull's-eyes. ". . . but I ended up with STRIPES!"

It didn't take him thirty seconds after I had finished my spiel. "You have to alternate the colors, Tess," he said.

"But I did. That's how I got the bull's-eyes."

"No. I mean you have to alternate the order of the colors in the layers. The top and bottom should be the same, but the middle has to be different. Black, white, black . . . white, black, white . . . black, white, black," he explained, drawing more bull's-eyes on the yellow pad.

"I can't believe it's that simple."

"It is. Here, I'll show you," he said, drawing a three-dimensional diagram of a cake with a slice cut out of it.

"Checkerboards! Amazing! Why couldn't I think of that?"

"Perspective, my dear girl. You got stuck on those chocolate-centered bull's-eyes. You needed a new perspective."

"You're a genius!" I raved, giving his hand a squeeze.

"I'm just a fresh pair of eyes. You've been staring at the problem too long."

I smiled at the drawing for a while, and then at David, and then at the drawing again, and then my smile faded.

"Speaking of staring at problems too long. . . . Do you think I'm terribly neurotic?" I asked, turning serious.

"Time out. What's going on here? I thought you said you're okay."

"I lied."

"So what's the matter?"

"Everything."

"Everything is very big."

"Well, almost everything."

"I'm here. I'm all ears," he said, leaning toward me, elbows on the table, holding his mug in one hand, his beard in the other.

"I don't know. It's just that . . . why do things have to be so complicated? Why can't I go out and have a good time, come home, and forget it? Why can men be that way and not women? Why is there always more to it for a woman?"

"I'm not sure what you're talking about."

"Sex. I'm talking about sex!" I blurted out, suddenly sorry that I'd started the conversation, suddenly blushing and uncomfortable.

"Can you give me a few more clues as to what, specifically, this is about?"

Unable to turn back, eat my words, start over, I stumbled out a quick explanation about a date with a guy who meant nothing to me, but I slept with him anyway because . . . "I don't know why," I lied.

"And now you feel guilty about satisfying a few animal urges."

"That's what Sandy said."

"Perspective. It's all perspective. I guess men don't feel guilty because we've been brought up to believe that we're *supposed* to have animal urges detached from human feelings. But all people have the same needs, Tess. And, shocking though it may be, the truth is that women have a need for fucking, and men have a need for loving. Life isn't as black and white as a checkerboard," he said, picking up the pad and dropping it on the table with a smack. "And people aren't as black and white as chessmen." He said this with an edge of . . . anger? pain?

123

"You're right," was all I could think of to say. Although what I wanted to do was stand up and come around behind him, and hug him, and tell him that I didn't mean to hurt him, that I knew he was different— No, no. That's not what he wanted to hear. He's *not* different, is what he said. Men are not what we think they are. They're not what a lot of men think men are. And I guess the same goes for women.

"Got to go," he said, standing abruptly. "Got a lot of work to finish. Chin up, everything will work out okay. Just don't be so hard on yourself. Talk to you next week. Got a hot date this weekend," he said as he walked out the door. "She's going to take care of all my male animal needs. Owwooooo!" he howled to the sun and then laughed and then was gone.

Checkerboard Cake III was a success. I cut it into thin wedges that I arranged on a thick cardboard plate stapled with white doilies. Checkerboard slices! They were beautiful. And Gus was delighted. Just Desserts had another regular customer. I wouldn't stay at the meeting, however.

"Oh, I can't blame you, it gets pretty tense here," Gus said. "Chess is a game of power, you know. The people who play it are into control."

I wanted to say, "Is that anything like being into leather?" but, instead, I smiled sweetly and went home.

HONEYED GRANOLA

3 cups rolled oats
1 cup wheat flakes
1/2 cup wheat germ
1/2 cup bran
1/2 cup sesame seeds
1/2 cup cashews
1/2 cup sunflower seeds
1/2 cup shredded coconut
1/4 cup peanut oil
1/4 cup honey
1 teaspoon salt
1/2 cup raisins
1/2 cup chopped dried apricots

Preheat oven to 225°F.

Mix all of the ingredients except the raisins and apricots in a bowl and spread thinly on a cookie sheet. Bake for about one hour, until golden brown, turning once. When cool, add the raisins and apricots. Serves 20–25.

CHAPTER 8

Honeyed Granola

Michael always had his own agenda. I could tell by the way he would cut me short when I started on something he didn't consider relevant that day, how he steered toward something he had a mind to and fought me when I tried to override him. I let him win, aware that I usually covered my agenda as well as we sidestepped and bowed, advanced and retreated, turned this way and that in a dance that drew us ever forward, ever closer to The Truth . . . and to each other. That glorious Tuesday in May, it was my attraction to him—the inevitable attraction a client develops toward a successful therapist: that is, a therapist who is succeeding with the client. It is what must happen to a client—being attracted to one's therapist—to prove the therapist's skill and the client's cooperation, the failure of which to occur proving . . . what? failure of the client? or failure of the therapist? Moot question. I was attracted.

I had said something that held him, and he stared at me, smiling.

"Why are you looking at me like that?"

"Like what? I don't understand," he said, leaning back casually in his chair, his hands on his thighs.

"Of course you understand. What's going on?" We were both smiling, but I was squirming because he kept gazing at me, waiting for me to catch on? or to crawl into a corner and hide? or to demand that he stop? What?

"No, I don't understand. What do you think is going on?"

I tried to cooperate: "You're staring at me."

"Staring?"

"You're staring and smiling at me."

"So?"

"So why are you staring and smiling at me?"

"Oh, I don't know. What do you think?"

Truth. Tell the truth. Cooperate. "You're flirting with me."

"I'm flirting with you?" His smile broadened to a grin.

Tortured, I burned in a blush. "You're appreciating me."

"Yes. I'm appreciating you, and you think I'm flirting with you. That's interesting."

Stay honest. "You *are* flirting with me, aren't you? Trying to get me to like you." Wipe that silly grin off your face or I'll hate you forever, I thought. "You know I like you," I tried to appease him.

His grin melted into a grimace of feigned puzzlement. "Are you flirting with *me?*" he asked. "Do you think something's happening between us?"

That's it! He asked for it. Honesty, right in the face: "Are you asking me if I want to have sex with you?" I asked bluntly, leaning forward in my seat. "If I want us to get naked and do It, right here on the sofa, on the floor, with the door unlocked, with your colleagues just steps away? If that's what you're asking, the answer is no. No, not here, not now. But in some other world in some other time? Of course." I hesitated and searched his being for a response. Whatever it was, it didn't show. He is good. I continued: "I'm supposed to be attracted to you, aren't I? It's part of the therapy, right? So don't flatter yourself, I'm not trying to seduce you. I don't do married. Remember?"

Of course he remembered. Still no response. Control. Maybe too much control. Maybe that was the response.

"Besides, it's a lot easier to find a good lover than a good therapist," I finished.

Just then I thought I detected a glint of excitement in him. Maybe it was the way the light hit his eyes as they flitted away from my face to fall momentarily upon my naked shoulder, bared accidentally by the shifting wide boat-neck of my cream cotton sweater when I folded my arms in front of me. An almost involuntary shrug of my shoulder boosted the sweater back to its proper place, and his eyes back to mine. He might have love in his life, but perhaps he also had a need for flight from the ennui of complacency.

"So you think I'd be a good lover?" he asked.

What about the good therapist part? I wondered.

"Well, maybe it is easy to find good lovers," he mused to the ceiling, leaning farther back in his chair, linking his hands on top of his head. "After all, you found Stephen, and he was a good lover. Right?"

Hoist with my own petard! I didn't want to do this conversation. Not now. Not when I had an edge. Of course, that's why he'd started it. "Stephen wasn't an especially good lover," I said. "We've been over that before."

"Have we? It must have slipped my mind. So tell me, Stephen wasn't a good lover?"

"Nothing slips your mind."

"Why would you choose a lousy lover if good lovers are easy to find?"

"I never said Stephen was a *lousy* lover."

"Oh. I must have gotten it wrong. What was it you did say? He was inattentive, permitting but not participating, squeamish—"

"I was really responsive to him, and he never failed me," I parried sheepishly.

"Right." He nodded, suddenly shifting forward, elbows on knees. "Like an inflatable plastic doll. Yes, I understand. That's really what a good lover is all about, being available for service. The rest isn't important, right?"

"What rest?" I asked, not really needing to ask.

"*What* rest? The *rest!* Caring, appreciating you, appreciating your body . . ."

He thinks he would like my body. He's imagining the rest of my body.

". . . wanting to please you, showing *his* need for *you* . . ."

He needs me, he wants to please me. He thinks Stephen

128

must be a schmuck. He wants me to know that he wouldn't be such a schmuck. He wants to show me that he's a good lover.

"Forgive me. I got carried away for a minute. You don't need to be cared for, appreciated. You're independent."

Sarcastic bastard. I glowered.

He glowered back. His glower was darker than mine. He rolled his chair farther toward me so his knees touched mine. His glower enveloped me. "You were fucking, not making love. You don't make love alone. You were alone! Got that?!"

That's assuming that he is a good lover, I continued my thoughts, fighting off the truths he shot at me, the possibility of his passion for me momentarily supplanting the fact of Stephen's lack of it. Yes, he must be a good lover. He's so sensitive, intuitive. Then again, maybe not. Maybe he's not like that when he's really close, personally, not professionally. After all, he's only human, only a man.

"Alone, Tess," he continued quietly, gently tapping my knee with a forefinger, letting me know that I wasn't alone in there, when I was with him.

I felt tears well up and spill over, carrying satin-black mascara down my cheeks. I supposed swimmer's mascara was de rigueur for women in therapy, and my refusal to use it was my arrogance. Since my first visit to Michael's office, when he'd dropped a box of tissues next to me on the sofa, I'd refused to cry. I would wince and grimace, choke and sigh, but I wouldn't cry. I'd think, *Ya can't make me cry! So there!* So there I was crying, for my aloneness, for my fear of a really good lover . . . a really good love-er.

Driving home with all my windows open, the sun sparking on every shiny surface filling my eyes with blinding gold, the birds chirping unmercifully in my ears, the smells of wet earth, cut grass, and growing things bloating my head, I was in pain . . . painfully aware of my unattachment in the world, my unattachment to the world. The angst of spring, a yearly occurrence, was worse than usual this year. My neighbor, Millie Garfield, had told me her allergies were especially bad this year, too. I wondered if the two were related. Maybe I was allergic to life.

Spring proved to be as short as it was furious, exploding into the heat of summer by the third week in May. June and July all but melted by, leaving disjointed, surrealistic recollections, like mirages in the heat waves of the desert.

I sold three homes, including Vincent's townhouse, although I was careful to be ve-ry pro-fes-sion-al whenever I saw him or spoke with him. He was clearly confounded by my attitude. He asked me out on an actual date once (after he had asked me to dinner at his house again and I had refused). I said I was busy. But he telephoned on business more than was necessary, and he stopped by my house one evening to drop off some papers that could have been mailed. I began to understand the flattery-cum-annoyance a man must feel after having enjoyed a one-nighter with a woman, receiving cutesy studio cards and flirty phone calls. And Vincent must have felt like the woman who wasn't respected in the morning.

I didn't sell my home, although a terrific family—Stan Leibowitz, his wife Michelle, and their three small children —came to see it in June. I was awestruck by their beauty— as individuals and as a family. Stan was the quintessential tall-dark-and-handsome stranger, and Michelle the quintessential natural beauty, with rich, curly brown hair to her shoulders, big brown eyes framed by naturally dark brows and lashes, a glowing complexion, and a terrific figure— despite the fact that she had given birth only six weeks before. She held baby Max, who had a head full of black hair; her husband carried two-year-old Tiffany, a child as delicately lovely as her name; and five-year-old Pamela, reminiscent of a Degas dancer, held fast to Michelle's free hand as I guided them through a tour of my home: "This is the kitchen and breakfast area, and the fireplace in the family room over here works great . . ." et cetera. When we got to the second floor, Michelle took over: "The master bedroom is so roomy! Look, Stan," she directed, walking through the french doors to the sitting area, "we can put a bassinet in here for Max, and there's room for my rocking chair. . . . Pamela, honey, wouldn't you love this room? Look at the window seat," she said when she came to the second bedroom, which, except for the closets, had remained empty since Stephen and I had moved in. The third bedroom, my guest bedroom, she decided would be for Tiffany, and the fourth bedroom, my office, would be for Max, when he outgrew the bassinet. I guess she won't need an office, I thought, watching her with envy as remnants of my dreams of white lace canopies and red and blue race cars swept around me. "She's really something, isn't she," Stan whispered, leaning close to me. Such pride. How nice, I thought. But I did not miss that while *she* was giving my *house* the once-over, *he* was giving *me* the once-over. And after they left I thought about them all, especially Stan, with his dark good looks, his family pride—the way he winked at me in the master bedroom. My God, I thought, now I'm sounding like Sandy! This man with the model family is a MODEL HUSBAND, for goodness sake—a model with a tic in his eye. Are there no faithful men in this world? I cried inwardly, disillusioned.

But when he called three weeks later asking to see the house again, I must say I looked forward to seeing him—the beautiful man with the beautiful family and the tic in his eye. When I caught a glimpse of him through the living room window as he approached my front door, my heart jumped, I blushed; and when I opened the door I was sorry that he hadn't brought the children, and sorrier that he *had* brought his wife. Then, walking quickly through the rooms, I soon realized that *she* no longer seemed interested in the house . . . and *he* no longer seemed interested in me. He was cool, businesslike, asking questions about the neighborhood, schools, shopping. She was impatient, tense, cutting off my answers with her own: "There'll be plenty of time to find that out once we decide on the right house." *No Sale* rang up in my head as I shut the front door after them, disappointed by the capriciousness of home buyers, but relieved by the restoration of Stan Leibowitz as Model Husband, concluding that The Flirtation had been only in my head after all . . . possibly the result of some misdirected longing to belong . . . probably overwhelming jealousy of Michelle Leibowitz.

Marv had been easy. He had taken my hint—I never returned the two calls he left on my answering machine—and stopped calling.

I finally answered Stephen's calls and agreed to see him when he told me he wasn't well. His diabetes—kept under control with insulin injections—was giving him trouble. He had protein in his urine and his doctor said it might mean kidney involvement. He was going for tests. He looked scared. Maybe it was his illness, but I could have sworn there was something else. I was surprised by my own lack of compassion for him, my overall lack of feeling when I was with him, although the hours before and after his visit were loaded with confusing tensions. Maybe the torrents of conflicting emotions canceled each other out, I reasoned, leaving me feeling nothing at all. When I saw him a second time, he told me that the kidney tests showed nothing significant, but the doctor said he should be watched. I slept with him the third time I saw him. It wasn't like I had remembered it. Where's the passion? I wondered as his body heated up next to mine. Where's the involuntary gush of bodily fluids, the rush of blood? Why does he smell different, unfamiliar? He seemed unaware of the change . . . in himself? No. It wasn't he who was different, it was I. "I want us to be together, Tess," he said, after. "We belong together." And my heart pounded and my stomach felt like kneaded sourdough. Nauseated. I felt repulsed. I wanted to be away from this man to whom I was married, for whom I'd thought I had a love that was endless, by whom I had been so hurt that sometimes I feared my anger would consume me. I didn't let him stay the night. And three days later he left for two weeks in the Greek islands . . . alone, he said

. . . with Dorothy, I found out from Janet, who had heard from another hygienist in Terry's office whose husband owned the travel agency that arranged Stephen's trip. Was there no end to this man's treachery? I wondered. "I can't believe you slept with him again!" Sandy screeched when I told her . . . *after* I had found out about Dorothy.

Janet healed from her unfortunate liaison with the late Harvey Cohen. To help speed her recovery, she sent Sean to the special camp she had found, and planned to start suit against her ex-husband to pay for it—an expense he had agreed to cover the summer before (although not in writing), extracting a promise from Janet to pay for all the camp clothes and equipment, and then backed out of, pleading a "cash-flow problem," which, she had explained to us back in February, meant that Sean's summer camp had become a trip to Italy, and (Janet found out in April from a fur salon salesman whose heavily plaqued teeth she cleaned every three months) a down payment for a new lynx coat for The Twit.

"Do you really want to go through another legal battle?" we asked her, remembering chilling tales of her past experiences, from her naive acquiescence to Leonard's demands in their divorce settlement, at the urging of her attorney, "to avoid the trauma of court" . . . to a couple of protracted and expensive bouts of showy posturing between his and her attorneys, including letter sending, affidavit writing, and deposition taking, in an attempt to get Leonard to do for Sean what any normal father would be embarrassed *not* to do, but ending up in settlements where Janet caved in, at her attorney's insistence, "to avoid the trauma of court" . . . to Janet picking up the shortfall for Sean's expenses ever since, again "to avoid the trauma of court." But this time was different, she said. Sean, she explained the facts of life to us, was too young to understand that Mommy couldn't afford to send him to the camp, and too young to be told that Daddy didn't care enough about him not to disappoint him, but old enough to be crushed with disappointment and to blame it on she who was nearest to him—Janet. "So I'm going to have to take my chances in court, although I can't really afford to hire an attorney any more than I can afford to pay for camp!" she told us.

I told David about the trauma of divorce attorneys one night after we had kept each other company at a movie . . . and he was incredulous. "The kid's in a WHEELCHAIR, for God's sake! The man's a DOCTOR! That's DESPICA-BLE!" he yelled. "She shouldn't have to fight this guy. He's Sean's FATHER! The man's got problems, Tess—SEVERE problems! What a SLEAZE! This OFFENDS me PER-SONALLY. . . . What's Janet's number?" he demanded, picking up the phone, calling her right then—eleven-thirty at night—and there—in my kitchen. Quite out of char-acter, he told her to "drag the bastard into court," that there wasn't a judge in the country who wouldn't make sure Sean was taken care of in the style to which a doc-tor's son should have become accustomed. In high dud-geon, he promised, "And it won't cost you a thing, sweet-heart, because I'm going to be your lawyer and I'm not going to charge you a penny. My compensation will be seeing that piece of shit lose his balls in court!"

Well! Janet and I were both taken aback by David's vitriolic tirade, his chivalrous proposal, his voluntary involvement . . . and we were very impressed.

David occasionally fed me Thai food, gentle jazz, Chopin nocturnes, and only the best movies at the Ritz Five—the subtitled, the offbeat, with Vivaldi and Bach between features—and then left August 1 (after filing papers for Janet's lawsuit against Leonard) for a month of backpacking in Europe. He sent me one postcard while he was gone, from the music festival in Salzburg: "Having a wonderful time. Wishing you a month of Mozart second movements." He couldn't have wished me anything nicer—sublime beauty, pure joy, peace—or anything less attainable, it seemed.

Michael, my oasis of rationality in a desert of madness, abandoned me in August when he left for a three-and-a-half-week seminar/vacation with his wife and children in California, via the Grand Canyon and other seeable sights.

Sandy struggled to recover her balance—which was a bit off after Janet's ordeal with the late Harvey Cohen, and my blowing away Cream Puff, Mirrors, and the Italian Stallion, while allowing Stephen back in my bed, even for the one night—by chasing her children around the pool at the swim club in a bikini, drawing a great deal of attention from the lifeguard and the tennis instructor. "I'll say it again," she said again and again, "I'm glad I'm married. I wouldn't know where to begin in the singles world. It's all veeery confusing." She got *that* right.

September brought the first gust of cool air, the first hint of fall, a wake-up call. And suddenly sanity prevailed . . . or so it seemed. I was preparing for Millie Garfield's monthly writers' club, which was meeting that night. Cinnamon-raisin coffee cakes were made early in the morning; oatmeal chocolate chip cookies had been made the day before. All that was left to do was the honeyed granola for munching.

A writer of esoterica, Millie Garfield enjoyed local renown. Her column on astrology appeared in the *Daily News* every Saturday, and her offbeat full-length features were published in *The Philadelphia Inquirer*'s Sunday magazine every now and then, her latest being "The New Brand of Professionals," a story about the growing popularity of tattoos among doctors, lawyers, and other professional men and women. Millie's writers' club meetings were one of my growing number of monthly catering contracts, and I particularly looked forward to those Wednesday evenings, usually attending and staying until the end. The dessert table was simple to prepare—Millie's standard order was, "Anything you think would be nice, Tess, as long as you include plenty of your marvelous granola!"—and the people were friendly . . . weird, but friendly. Millie always managed to put together an interesting program, like the one in June when Jerry Swerdlow spoke about dreams and how writers could tap into their unconscious through dreams to create believable fantasy.

Jerry was a writer of sci-fi stories and nonfiction magazine articles, a creative writing teacher at Temple University, and very, very smart. He was also very, very cute. Tall and lanky, with long dark hair and thick straight bangs, eyes like pieces of polished coal, and a smooth, translucent complexion, he was about twenty-eight, looking eighteen.

After his talk—which was carried out in a darkened room to promote the listeners' relaxation and dreamlike state, a technique that worked so well that one of the gathered (a soft-spoken, confusion-bound woman in her early fifties with unruly gray hair carelessly tied in a knot on top of her head, a woman who wrote of cosmetic fads, medical oddities, and such for supermarket tabloids) nodded off, jolting to wakefulness with a high-pitched shriek and a wild look in her pale gray eyes when the lights were turned on—after his talk, I gave Jerry my telephone number when he told me he was looking for someone to cater a monthly meeting of some other writers' organization. He was, he also told me, single-but-living-with-someone.

Now, single-but-living-with-someone was akin to married in my book, but after he called me a couple of times, first to tell me that the group didn't want desserts catered after all, and later to tell me that he was sorry about the disappointment he might have caused me, and, by the way, could he stop over for a cup of coffee some evening on his way home from his office, just to talk, because I was, after all, such an interesting woman, so easy to talk to, I finally consented to a tête-à-tête because, of course, it was going to be absolutely innocent and, after all, he seemed like such an interesting man, and so young, and so eager . . . and I was flattered.

So he came. And we talked. And he loved that I had fruit and cookies and cocoa, and leftover chicken and spaghetti in the refrigerator. He was hungry. And he told me about his parents dying in a plane crash when he was eleven, how his uncle and his uncle's second wife, who was very young and very attractive, took him in, and how at fifteen his adolescent lusting for his uncle's young attractive second wife was satisfied when she came into his room on a day he was home from school with a fever, rubbed his back, and gave him his first blow job. And that he now related fever with sex and that whenever he got sick he got horny.

The fourth time he visited he told me about his live-in girlfriend, a psychologist, who'd been his best friend since he was eight, and how even though she was his best friend he couldn't talk to her the way he could talk to me—as if he'd known me all of his life—and how capable I must be running two careers and a big house all by myself, and how deep I was, and how attractive I was. How hungry he was. How scared. When he kissed me, I thought his heart was going to burst right through his starched white shirt. Curious, I thought, that I could have this effect on him. I'm always surprised when I have an effect on someone. I want to look over my shoulder to see who's standing behind me.

The tall casement windows on both sides of the family room were open to the breezy summer night and the cross currents pulled a warm draft across the plush putty-colored carpet where we squirmed and fumbled in a half-clothed attempt at lovemaking. What a wonderful body he had: long-limbed and almost childlike in its pale, unbuilt-up leanness; how unchildlike its manliness! What a shame he didn't know quite what to do with what he had. But how good to feel hot skin. How good to feel arms around me; how good to feel him filling me.

"I'm going," he said suddenly, opening his eyes, lifting his upper body to arm's length from me.

"You're gonna come?"

"No, I . . ."

"You came?"

"I gotta go."

"You have to pee?"

"No, I'm going."

"You're going?"

"I'm leaving."

"I want to come!"

"You came!"

"I didn't come."

"I'm going."

"I don't understand."

"I gotta go." And he sprang to his feet, pulling his shorts and pants up in one motion. He was still erect.

When I stood up, my hitched skirt fell, and I just left my panties lying on the floor as I ran to the front door after him. He was halfway down the walk, his shirttails hanging out, and he was struggling to get the keys out of his pants pocket. "Jerry!" I called, and he turned but kept on running—backward.

"I gotta go!"

"This is weird!"

"You knocked my goddamned socks off!" he shouted, one hand deep in his pocket, one leg in his white Volkswagen Rabbit.

As I watched him drive off, I became aware of wet running down my leg. He had come . . . and gone.

Then there was Dr. Daniel Daroff, another very smart man. He was a physics professor and an amateur astronomer who spoke to Millie's group about the summer sky and then ran off before I had a chance to meet him. But he was attractive, and Millie told me he was single, so I enrolled in his summer evening lecture series in astronomy held at the high school in August. Not just to meet him, of course; I thought it might be a nice place to meet other single men and learn about black holes and entropy all at once.

It turned out that I was one of seven women in a group of eight. The only man there was with his wife. They were into stargazing and had a telescope on the roof of their beachfront home in Longport. So I flirted with Daniel Daroff, who was handsome in a poetic way. That is, he was, behind his soft bushy mustache, finely featured, pale, and delicate. I carefully watched his dark eyes, beneath a mop of wavy, light brown hair, darting back and forth from student to student as he lectured, how he walked back and forth across the front of the room in long strides, his arms gesticulating this way and that like a stork attempting to take flight. And when he passed by me, my eyes caught his. He sort of lurched, hesitating on the syllable in his mouth, elongating it, holding it, and though he continued to move forward, away from me, my eyes held his, causing his head to swivel around as he walked. When I smiled, ever so faintly, he abruptly turned his head forward and continued the word, and the lecture.

At the door after class, the Longport couple pelted him with questions about supernovas, but his eyes never left mine as I stood back waiting to meet him. ". . . and I hope you'll explain black holes before the end of the semester," I remember finally saying. Two hours later, sitting on the edge of his desk, I could have taught Carl Sagan something about black holes.

Two weeks later, after three dinners, one movie, and two lunches with Daniel, when I found myself in his apartment kissing him on his Danish modern sofa flanked by two leggy dracaena plants in black rubber tubs, the term "entropy" began to take on new meaning.

He had a wonderful mouth, and he smelled nice. He didn't use after-shave or anything, he just smelled nice. But I thought he was going to just kiss me all afternoon. "Well, I guess we're gonna do It," I heard myself blurt out.

His eyes went wide and wild for a moment—surprise? fear? confusion?—but he took his cue and led me to the bedroom. There he gently unbuttoned my blouse and then, while I finished undressing, started undressing himself. Nice, tight, narrow body, I noted, arranging myself on his bed. Long, pretty legs. Not obviously aroused, he lowered himself onto me anyway. For a minute or two he just kissed me—with his eyes open. Then things got kind of frantic . . . his heart was beating a hundred thousand billion times a minute . . . he kept trying to enter me but he couldn't . . . I was really excited and tried to push up against him in a vain attempt to make something happen . . . he made some funny noises and dropped to one side. "Did you come?" I gasped.

"Sort of."

"Sort of?"

"I think we have to talk."

"Talk?"

We dressed self-consciously and met in the living room. Taking my hand, he sat on the sofa and pulled me onto his lap.

"So talk," I said gently.

"Well, here goes," he started, staring across the room, and all of a sudden his heart started beating a hundred thousand billion times a minute again. "I really don't do too well with women. With sex, I mean. I mean, I really get scared. . . ."

No shit, I thought. His eyes grew large and dark as fancy black olives. He was sweating. He looked ten years old.

". . . And, well, what I've done before is just give massages, you know, like back rubs, and . . ." His voice trailed off along with his attention. He seemed to be lost somewhere momentarily. Then, quite abruptly, he smiled broadly at me. "So, do you want a back rub?"

"Okay," I said, trying to be understanding, trying to understand, wondering just how weird he might get.

"Great!" he said, relieved, energized. Easing me off his lap, he led me, once again, to the bedroom. "So, do you want to take your clothes off?" he asked on his way to the bathroom.

I wasn't sure if I wanted to or not, but I did. Maybe I was curious. Maybe I was crazy.

Minutes later he returned, naked, carrying a paper cup. "My secret formula," he explained, sitting on the edge of the bed where I lay prone. "Now, close your eyes."

I can't believe how trusting I was of this possible lunatic. I closed my eyes. The next thing I experienced was his long fingers sliding across my shoulders on a film of something warm and wet, and the heavy aroma of cloves filling my head. Is this kinky? I wondered as the sweet vapors put me a little off-center.

"It's Baby Magic lotion and baby oil and oil of cloves warmed in hot water. Isn't it great?" he chirped.

It was. I luxuriated in the feel, in the smell, wondering what kinky was.

"Want a front rub, too?"

140

I turned and watched him. He looked intense as he worked, slowly, gently, carefully avoiding nipples and groin.

"Okay. Now you do me," he said after a while.

This, then, was not to be foreplay, to lead up to; this was to be instead of. I couldn't believe I was there. I can't believe I went out with him again.

Yes, indeed, it had been a surreal summer, I thought, spooning granola into white cardboard boxes lined with wax paper, tying the boxes with thin gold ribbon, and sealing the flaps with self-sticking white labels bearing the gold imprint JUST DESSERTS. It was four-forty. I had to drop off Millie's goodies for her meeting that night—the usually Wednesday meeting was a Friday this month, a meeting I couldn't attend because I had tickets for a concert—and the concert was at seven-thirty, so I would have to leave my house about six-thirty to have time to stop at Millie's and get to the concert in time to get a good seat, so I'd have plenty of time to get dressed and grab something to eat if I finished Millie's order by five. No problem, I thought, signing the boxes with a gold pen, "Just for You, by Tess." *Success is all in the packaging,* I remembered from a college marketing class. No problem, I thought, *if* the phone doesn't ring, which it did, and I considered letting my answering machine pick it up . . . but what if it's Millie, about the meeting tonight? or Janet? Maybe she decided to go to the concert with me after all. I really didn't want to go alone. "Hello."

"Tess?" It was Millie. She had bumped into a man she had known for years through the Friends of the Philadelphia Museum of Art . . . a nice man, an energy consultant, thirty-one . . . two small children . . . his wife had died in a car accident ten months ago; he was dating . . . did she know anyone, he had asked her.

A nice, stable widower with two motherless babes—a possibly sane man! "Sure! Give him my number. In fact, maybe he wants to go to a Chamber Players concert to-night," I half teased.

Five minutes later, I was still packaging granola, the phone rang. "Hello."

"Hello. Is this Tess?" It was Elliot Spector, the Sane Man. I laughed.

"Keep laughing," he said, "because I'm really calling to tell you that I'm *not* your date for tonight, I already have plans, but when Millie called to give me your number, I decided to call and introduce myself and see if we could get together another time."

We chatted and bantered—I was getting better at that— he said he was intrigued, and could we meet for brunch in the morning? No, I was meeting some friends for brunch at the diner. Dinner? No, I already had plans—with Janet. It wouldn't be fair to Janet to cancel . . . and besides, I didn't want to appear too available.

"Well, how about tonight after your concert?" he tried.

"I thought you had a date."

"I do, but it's for an early dinner. She's traveling and has to leave early. What time do you think you'll be home?"

She's *traveling?* "I don't know, probably about ten."

"I'll call you when I'm free."

"This is crazy. I'm not going out that late."

"It's not so late," the Sane Man insisted.

Who was I to argue with sanity? And besides, none of my friends would go with me to the concert so I felt angry and disappointed, and knowing I would be coming home to someone—anyone—would make going to the concert alone not so lonely. "Okay. But don't call after eleven."

Three minutes later, I was still packaging granola, the phone rang. "Hello."

"It's me again. . . ." It was Elliot again. ". . . I'm really excited, I feel like I'm back in high school. Two dates in one night! Don't disappoint me! I'll call you when I get in."

"I won't disappoint you if you call before eleven," I warned, mindful of the shred of control I attempted to retain in this scenario.

Finished the packaging, dressed, ate, stopped at Millie's, got a good seat at the concert, home by ten-fifteen. The message the Sane Man had left on my answering machine informed me that he was "running late," that I should "not

142

wait up," that he would "call in the morning." Read: *I got lucky.*

"So, can we have breakfast?" It was Elliot at nine-fifteen—AM

"I told you I was meeting friends."

"Call me when you get home. Maybe we can squeeze a cup of coffee in before your dinner date tonight."

"I'll call you," I promised, flattered that he was being so persistent, but knowing full well that I wouldn't have time to meet him.

"So I promised to call him when I get home," I told Sandy and Janet at brunch. We giggled like teenagers. My, wasn't dating fun? Sandy still thought it must be as she lived vicariously through me and Janet, but Janet and I knew the truth: The population of single men is like a bowl of granola—what ain't fruits and nuts is flakes.

We were deep into whitefish salad, toasted bagels, and the disappointments of the summer when, out of nowhere it seemed, a strange man grabbed Janet's arm. "Tess?"

Shaking her head, Janet smirked at the man and pointed to me.

Releasing her arm, he took my hand. "Tess!"

"Elliot, I presume," I said darkly.

"I hope you don't mind my interrupting."

It's intrusive and rude, I thought. "Not at all," I said, smiling, holding his hand briefly. "Janet, Sandy, this is Elliot. Elliot, Sandy and Janet."

"Well, I was also meeting someone for breakfast, and when I saw you girls I knew that one had to be you, Tess, so I thought I'd say hello. Nice to meet you all. Call me when you get home, okay?"

He wasn't bad-looking, I thought. He'd rather take out Janet.

"Elliot?" I had called him as soon as I walked into the house.

143

"I'm on the other phone, let me call you back, okay?" he answered, and hung up.

Five minutes later the phone rang. "Hello."

"So how's it going?" It was Elliot.

"Well, considering that last night you called me to tell me that we didn't have a date, and then you called me to break the date that we didn't have, and then you made a pass at my friend at brunch, to which you were not invited in the first place, and then you practically hung up on me when I called, I'd say everything is going about par," I answered with honesty, honestly irritated.

"Uh, well . . . *cough cough* . . . oh, excuse me, but I seem to have picked up something. In fact, when you called I was . . . uh . . . talking to my doctor. I really feel lousy . . . *cough* . . . so I guess I won't be able to make it today after all. I don't know what it is, but I've felt it coming on."

"Mmm. I've felt it coming on, too."

"You mean on me?"

"Look, Elliot, cut the bullshit."

"Hey! Chill out, sweets! You know, you mature women should learn to loosen up."

"FUCK OFF, ELLIOT!"

Slamming down the phone, I burst into tears. "THEY'RE ALL CRAZY!" I screeched aloud. "THEY'RE ALL A BUNCH OF WEIRDOS! THEY SHOULD ALL BE LOCKED UP!" I was screaming as I dialed Sandy's number.

"Hello," she answered unsuspectingly.

"HOW COULD YOU LET ME GO OUT WITH ALL THOSE CREEPS!" I yelled at her.

"Tess? What's going on? Are you okay?"

But all I could do for the longest time was sob, until, finally, "No, I'm not okay—no, that's not right, *I* am okay . . ." and I explained the Elliot phone call. "It's *them*, Sandy. *They're* not okay. I finally figured it out. It's not me. I'm not crazy. It's not that I'm easily confused, it's that they're confusing because they're crazy."

"You're confusing me, Tess."

* * *

144

"And that's the way it's been going. They're all so crazy. I mean, women aren't that crazy, are they?" I asked David.

Sitting next to me at my kitchen table Wednesday afternoon, he lifted his drink and studied it through a tight-lipped smile. "Well," he said, turning to me after a moment, "it's all in the way you look at it. I've met some crazy ones, but crazy can be interesting . . . for a while."

"Not for long. Trust me. I used to think it was me. These guys would confuse me and I assumed that I was missing something, that they were tuned in to the real world and I wasn't . . . so I'd go along for a while . . . but things wouldn't clear up. But after this absurd little dance with Elliot—Sandy calls him Datus Interruptus—it finally hit me: They're nuts. They don't make sense . . . not my kind of sense."

"I have to tell you, Tess, I was wondering how long it would take you to come to your senses . . . so to speak," David said, smiling.

"So. Where are all the sane men?" I rambled on, embarrassed by his perception. "They're married, of course," I answered my own question. "I've never done married. Maybe I should try married," I said, remembering my attraction to Stan Leibowitz.

"It depends on what you want from the relationship. Now, if it's just sex . . . well, married men are basically safe. They usually don't want to leave their wives, they just want a little something more," said David, playing devil's advocate.

Closing my eyes, sighing, I contemplated his words and wondered bitterly if it were all as insipid as it sounded. Were there no faithful *and* sane men in the world? Were there no real meaningful relationships—the kind that are attached so deep down that they aren't pulled loose by every lusty vibration that prickles the skin? Not according to my mother, I thought, the image of her tearstained face fleeting before me.

"Men!" she railed. "None of them are any good." It seems that good old Mr. Hammerman, our next-door neighbor, had stopped in while I was at school and his wife was at work to help my mother unjam the garbage disposal. And he made a pass at her. "The nerve of him!" she cried to me when I walked in that afternoon and found her busy busy busy cleaning closets. "'I'm hungry,' he said to me. So I offered him some pound cake. But he said, 'You don't understand. I'm hungry for you, Miriam.' *I* understand! I understand that men are animals. They're all the same. And your father was no different," she threw at me.

My God. I was only twelve! Was that any kind of thing to say to a child? But I now understood her anger. I plucked a Wheat Thin from the small tray of cheese and crackers I had laid out for lunch and fiercely pulverized it between my molars, remembering my own recent brush with adultery, with Stan Leibowitz when he had come to see the house, for the third time, one day near the end of August—alone.

"Sure. Come on over," I said when Stan Leibowitz called at one-thirty on a steamy August afternoon to say that he hadn't bought a house yet, that he was still interested in my house, if it was still for sale. And I said that it was. And he asked if it would be all right if he came right over, since he had just left a lunch meeting in town and didn't have to return to his office. And I said, "Sure. Come on over." And then I ran around the house making sure toilets were flushed and closed, my dirty clothes were in the laundry basket, and the counters were neat. I went into my bedroom to make the bed, but I found the colorful slept-in disorder of the bed alluring, so I left it . . . and in a blatant fit of sexism, I threw a black silk nightgown on the foot of the bed and sprayed perfume around the room. What a clever sales ploy, I thought, although I wasn't at all sure what I was intending to sell.

"It's nice to see you again, Tess," he said, taking my hand at the front door. "I brought you these." He pulled a small bouquet of flowers from behind his back.

"For me?" I squealed, hating the sound I made.

146

"They were on the lunch table at my meeting."

"That's very sweet. Would you like a cup of coffee? Or would you like to see the house first?" I asked, quite aware of the invitation to visit I had offered. Quite aware of how *really* nice it was to see him again. Quite aware of my self-disgust.

"Coffee would be great. The coffee at lunch was terrible."

We sat at the kitchen table, had coffee and chocolate chip cookies, and chatted for at least half an hour, during which time he told me that Michelle was having difficulty making up her mind about a house, but that he was going to take the bull by the horns and choose one he felt was best for them. And I commented that when we first met it had sounded as though she knew exactly what she wanted. And this gave him an opportunity to tell me of the troubles they'd been having, about her unpredictable moods, her unkind words . . . her coldness. "I'm trying to get her to talk to someone, a psychologist or something like that," he said, and then went on to tell of his pain, his loneliness, his frustration—highly sexual man that he is, he explained. My response to all of this was not what I might have expected: not a dash to my phone book to give him Michael's number . . . not empathetic mumblings about postpartum blues, the inevitable difficulties in even the best of marriages, the worthiness of making the effort to hold it together. No. My response was a tilt of my head and a soulful gaze, a fluttering of my eyelashes and a quiet sigh. "It must be so difficult for you," I murmured.

"Yes," he replied with lowered eyes.

But then, with the ball back in my court, I became aware of my inner conflict, my confusion of illusions. Was Stan Leibowitz making a pass at me after all? Was *I* making a pass at *him? Me?* Tess I-Don't-Do-Married Fineman? And I thought of all the unkind thoughts I had for others who indulged in extramarital affairs . . . and I thought about my ideal of the Model Husband—the Faithful Husband. Looking at Stan, I saw the illusion fade, leaving a man, just a man, sitting across from me . . . a very attractive man . . .

an attractive, uncrazy man. And, as I already feared that maybe I attracted crazy men because *I* was crazy, sitting quietly in my kitchen with attractive, uncrazy Stan, I realized my need to know if I could attract a sane man . . . a basically decent family man who, when the going around home got rough, felt a need for a shoulder, a reassuring arm, a tender hand, I rationalized. Sure! I argued with myself, give them a shoulder and they take a hand! No, I retorted, everyone needs a hand now and then. And why shouldn't we help each other? I was convincing, but I still wasn't convinced. "How about if we take a look through the house now," I wimped out, letting my head go numb.

So he followed me up the stairs and I was very aware of him behind me, studying the back of me. And I took him through the three *other* bedrooms first, saving the master bedroom with its unmade bed and perfumed air for last. And he seemed a lot more interested in the movement of my hands as I pointed out windows and closet space than in the windows or closet space. I did all the talking. And when we walked into the master bedroom, even I was taken in by the seductive smell, but it was he who said, "There's something awfully inviting about this room." I noted with pride how his eyes went straight to the tangle of colors on my unmade bed and rested for a time on the nightgown. Without a further word, Stan took me by the elbow and walked me through the french doors to the sitting area where the mirrored closet doors reflected the two of us taking entirely too long to reflect on the love seat, barrel chair, two end tables, and television console. "Great little room," he said, sitting on the love seat. "I'll probably spend most of my evenings here."

"You'll have to wait until the baby moves to his own room."

"Well, he's sleeping through the night now, so by the time we move in, he'll already be in his own room."

"It sounds like you've made up your mind about my house," I said, sinking into the barrel chair, swiveling it suggestively from side to side.

"I've made up my mind," he said, standing, taking two steps toward me, kneeling in front of me, taking my hands in his. "Tess, I've thought about you every day since I met you."

I'm not really going to fall for this, am I? I asked myself, already falling, my head spinning, my blood coursing through me, warming me, dampening every part of me except my mouth. "Stan, this isn't . . ." I tried through that arid orifice.

"Be nice to me, Tess. I promise, you won't be sorry."

I was already sorry, but it was too late. I was overcome by the musky smell of him, by the touch of his lips on my cheek, my chin, my lips.

So even when he uttered the despicable words "I know you, Tess. I could tell the minute I met you that you weren't afraid of married men. You've got that look in your eyes," momentum drove my arms around his neck, my mouth to his. But somewhere in the remnants of my sanity, the word *married* registered, invoking images of *his wife* and *their three babes*. . . .

And as his warm, fluid tongue washed the cobwebs from my mouth, setting off tiny spasms in my lips, my arms, and my fingers, my foot, flanked by his bended knees, swung upward in a solitary jerk. His lips left mine and he fell backward, writhing and breathless, grasping his injured parts with both hands. An image of ripe figs bursting, spewing ten thousand golden seeds, exploded in my head.

. . . That's what I wanted to do . . . for his wife, his children . . . for me . . . for dashing my illusions. But instead I put my hands to his shoulders and gently pushed him away. "Stan, this isn't right. You were wrong. I can't do this. I'm sorry," I said, jumping up and running from the sitting room, from the bedroom, down the stairs, to the kitchen, where I waited for him at the pantry door . . . waited until he caught up to me looking very annoyed, and told him that I'd decided not to sell the house, after all. "So please don't call me again," I said, feeling very crazy, and very angry—at us both.

"Have you ever done married?" I asked David.

"Only once. It was a mistake and I felt terrible about it. It didn't last very long."

"None of your ladies last very long. Don't you ever get involved?"

"Not really. Well, for a short while, when it's new, when it's exciting. But it doesn't stay that way, so after a while it just finishes on its own."

"Don't you ever want anything more?"

"I didn't know you cared, Tess."

"But I do," I answered, feeling my anger fall away like a molt, leaving a soft, vulnerable part of me exposed. This is probably the only decent man left in the whole world, I thought—perhaps overstating his goodness somewhat—and I do care about him. Yes, I do care, I thought. "I do care," I said.

"I don't think you want a married man. You'd get hurt. And you'd feel very guilty," he said, veering from my confession . . . for a moment.

"You're right." I indulged his obvious discomfort. "So I'm stuck with the crazies. No guilt, just bewildered and horny."

He was quiet and still for a long moment, and then: "Horny can be taken care of."

"Easy for you to say."

"No, Tess. This isn't at all easy for me to say. Do you know what I'm saying?"

I thought I knew, but I didn't want to . . . or I was afraid to. Sex. He wants to have sex with me. No. He wants to make love to me. He loves me! *Does* he love me? Or does he want to be a Friend Plus Sex? Could I have sex with David? My God! What about Stephen? Doesn't he care what Stephen would think? Do I care what Stephen would think? Warm. I'm getting warm. I'm blushing, I can feel it creeping up my chest, my neck, he'll see it. Caught.

He caught my hand in his. "We'd be good together, Tess."

I can't believe he's saying this. This is real, it's happening, he's trying to seduce me. What to do? What to do? "I—"

"Really good." He put my hand to his lips and teased a finger with his tongue.

Hot. I felt hot and squirmy. Sex. Love. Yes. I need sex and love. In that order? This isn't happening. "I—"

His arms were around me. When did he stand up? When did I stand up? Was I standing? There was no floor beneath my feet. He's holding me up. He's so tall. Don't I have a say in this? "I—"

He smells so good, his mouth is so soft on mine. How can thin lips be so soft? What a dumb thing to think at a time like this. Do I want a say in this? Oh, this would be a good one on Stephen! The phone! Let it ring, I'm busy. Go away, world, I'm not in, I'm out, I'm gone. "I—"

"I want you, Tess. I've wanted you for so long. I want to take care of you."

Yes, take care of me. Take me. Take me. "I—"

His mouth again, on mine. NO! I can't do this.

"NO! I can't do this!" I said, pulling away.

"But, Tess . . . I thought—"

"You thought wrong," I said. But seeing his crushed expression, all I wanted to do was wrap myself around him and kiss him again. "No, not wrong, but—"

"I don't understand, Tess, but I'm sorry. You have to believe that I'm sorry if I . . . I wasn't trying to take advantage of you. I'm not very good at this."

"I think you're *very* good. I almost—"

"I mean I'm not very good at telling how I really feel. Do you understand what I'm saying, Tess? Do you understand any of this?"

"No, I don't understand," I said, finally telling it like it really was.

"Neither do I," he said, cautiously rubbing my shoulder. "But I do know that I don't want to lose you. Promise me you'll just forget this happened. We'll pretend I wasn't here today. Someone else was . . . my evil twin brother, Lenny the Lech."

"I promise, I promise," I lied, laughing nervously with

151

David, trying to wade through the bog of awkward desire, back to the familiar shores of friendship.

I hadn't seen Michael since his return the first week in September. A twenty-four-hour stomach virus had kept me close to my bathroom the first Tuesday he was back and I chose to skip the week altogether and come the following Tuesday, a day he was going to be away for some teaching obligation. So I made the appointment for Thursday. After the weekend fiasco with—without—Elliot, I felt an intense need to whine to Michael and was angry that our Tuesday appointment wasn't going to be until Thursday. But then, after Wednesday with David, I was glad the appointment had been put off until Thursday. What was I going to do when I no longer had Michael to dump on? I wondered while driving to his office.

"What am I going to do when I don't have you to dump on anymore?" I asked Michael after I'd politely inquired about his vacation, and then waited for him to ask how I'd gotten along without him, which he didn't, which made me feel he didn't care, which made me feel angry and dependent, which made me ask him what I was going to do when he was no longer around, understanding how abandoned I felt when he wasn't around, not yet understanding that I wasn't always going to feel that way.

"You're planning to quit therapy?" he asked.

"No. Not now," I answered impatiently. "But I won't have you forever."

"How about if we worry about that when the time comes," he said, and then, after a pause, "So what's been happening?"

"Not a lot," I lied as my inner eye scanned the mirages of summer.

"How's the business going? Making anything new?" he fished.

"It's going well. I've been involved with granola lately," I said, not knowing why I said it.

"That's a fruit and nut mixture, isn't it?"

"With grains and honey. I use it a lot for fill-ins. You know. Bowls of honeyed granola instead of pretzels or potato chips."

"Sounds healthy."

Healthy! Hah! I laughed.

"What's so funny? What did I say?"

"Just that granola is healthy. It's an inside joke."

"Can you let me in on it?"

"Well, the summer's been rather strange, and the other day I found myself comparing men to granola. You know. What ain't fruits and nuts is flakes."

Michael laughed. I laughed. I turned red. Michael sat there chuckling at me, shaking his head. "So not a lot happened this summer?" he asked.

I sat squirming, not knowing how to respond to his snare.

"I guess granola is a step up from scum," he challenged.

Oh, God! He remembered our conversation from months ago! He probably writes it all down, I thought. "It can get scummy if it stays around too long," I said cryptically, wanting to leave.

Instinctively he changed the subject. "How's my friend David? What's he been up to?"

I told Michael about David's trip to Europe, about the postcard . . . about the day before, which was what I wanted to tell him all along.

"So not a lot happened this summer," he said again after a time, settling back in his chair. "So what is this? Budding romance?"

"More like blooming insanity!"

"Why's that?"

"He's Stephen's friend, remember!"

"I see."

No, he doesn't see, I thought. "And besides, if this goes any further, I'll probably end up losing a good friend," I illuminated quietly.

"Oh. Now I see. David will get scummy."

"If he hangs around long enough, which he probably won't."

"So he'll just disappear after a fling?"

"Well, maybe not exactly. We *are* friends. But maybe we won't be friends anymore."

"Sex and friendship don't mix?"

"Not from what I've seen."

He sat watching me be contradictory.

"So you don't have to worry," I continued. "I'm not going to seduce you because I need you as a friend." Now, why did I say that? How did we get back to last month's conversation? I'll bet he thinks *I* write it all down.

"Well, I'm glad to see you consider me a friend," he said.

I guess my hour is up, I thought, catching him glancing at his watch. Michael: my friend . . . for an hour a week. I knew I wasn't being fair, but I held on to my thought as I wrote out a check, as I walked out the door, as I drove home, feeling like a flake in a sea of granola.

CHARLOTTE RUSSE

1 envelope unflavored gelatin
1/4 cup water
1/3 cup sugar
1/2 cup milk
1 1/2 teaspoons vanilla extract
1 cup heavy cream
sponge cake (see Rocky Road Ice Cream Cake Roll)
1 pint strawberries
3 tablespoons kirsch (cherry brandy)
1 tablespoon sugar

Sprinkle the gelatin over 1/4 cup cold water and let it stand for 5 minutes. Mix the sugar and milk in a saucepan, add the gelatin, and cook over medium heat until the sugar and gelatin dissolve, stirring constantly. Remove pan from heat and stir in the vanilla. Chill in the refrigerator. When thick and syrupy, beat the mixture until it is fluffy.

Whip the cream to soft peaks and fold into the chilled gelatin mixture.

Line the bottom and sides of a 1 1/2-quart mold with slices of sponge cake. Spoon in the filling and chill for several hours. While it's chilling, slice strawberries and set in kirsch and sugar to marinate. Unmold; garnish with sliced strawberries. Serves 6–8.

CHAPTER 9

Charlotte Russe

It was inevitable. It had been only a matter of time until Charlie blew his cover. The time came, as always in these matters, too soon . . . or too late . . . and the revelation was more like the peeling of an onion—layer by layer—than the lifting of a lid.

Sandy had walked in so quietly I wasn't aware that she was standing in the doorway until I turned off the mixer and looked up from the softly peaking mound of whipped cream in search of vanilla extract. Her skin was paler than usual, her puffy eyes underlined with black smudge. She had been crying. Before I could get a word out, before I could reach her, she folded into the nearest chair and sobbed out the worst of it.

"Charlie's been screwing his operating room nurse in our shore apartment!"

Sitting down beside her, I put a hand on her arm. I knew the pain. "Is that it, then? I thought someone was sick or dying. This can be fixed," I lied.

"No, you don't understand. The apartment is theirs. Charlie's been paying for it, furnishing it. . . ."

I shook my head slowly in disapproval.

". . . And that's not the worst of it."

"So what's worse?"

This naive query triggered a new spate of tears and sobs.

I put my arm around her shoulders and tried a different question. "How did you find out?"

Amidst hiccups and sniffles, Sandy sputtered out a classic small-world tale: Charlie had hired a decorator—who billed Charlie at his office—to put the shore apartment together . . . a black marble table had arrived from Italy and the decorator wanted it delivered before he left for two weeks in the Caribbean . . . his secretary tried to call Charlie at his office, but he was in the operating room . . . Charlie's secretary gave the decorator's secretary Charlie's home phone number, saying, "I'm sure Mrs. Solomon can take care of this for you" . . . and the decorator's secretary called Sandy to tell her that her black marble table had arrived from Italy and was sitting in the warehouse awaiting delivery . . . and Sandy said, "My black marble table is sitting in my living room" . . . and the secretary checked her records and read the delivery address to Sandy . . . and Sandy said, "To where?!" . . . and the secretary repeated the address and Sandy hung up and called the hospital, demanding to speak with Charlie, who was still in the operating room . . . and when he finally got on the phone she demanded that he come home immediately or their marriage was over . . . so he did . . . and, being the weak, repressed, guilt-ridden creature that he is, he spilled . . . but being the dishonest, spoiled, cowardly toad that he is, he spilled slowly—over three days—with all the requisite histrionics, while Sandy listened tearless in disbelief, until this morning when she woke up and understood that it wasn't going to go away.

"Sandy, I'm so sorry," I sympathized.

"But that's not the worst of it."

"What could be worse?"

"Tess, he wants a divorce. He was setting the apartment up for himself and his . . . his—"

"How about 'slut'?" I offered.

"And that's not the worst of it."

"So tell me already, what's the worst of it? Don't tell me she's pregnant!"

157

"I only wish. You see . . . the fact is that . . . well . . . oh, Tess, *she* is a *he,*" Sandy said finally, burying her face in her arms on the kitchen table.

Right. Operating room nurse . . . as in male nurse. How we all do assume. So Charlie was gay. So Charlie was leaving Sandy. I knew some of the pain.

I remembered when I got the call from Jim Statten, Stephen's secretary's husband, early one Wednesday morning: "Did you know that your husband and my wife," et cetera . . . how the words had echoed in my head even after I hung up the phone . . . and how I'd looked in the mirror to see if I was real, if this was really happening . . . how I saw myself crumple, like wet crepe paper . . . diminishing, bleeding, disintegrating. And *I* had only lost out to a pair of great tits.

Days later, Sandy and I sat interminably in a diner booth over turkey clubs and endless cups of coffee, rehashing. I tried to be alternately cheerful, furious, indignant, and nonjudgmental.

Sandy was alternately silent, tearful, baffled, and belligerent, but consistently pale and depressed as she struggled with the triangles of sandwich that grew dry before her. "I had no idea, Tess. . . . I mean, he gave me absolutely no idea. Everything had gone on as it always had. . . ."

How *had* everything gone on before? I wondered. In all the years I had known Sandy, I had never really gotten to know Charlie. He was nice to me, but aloof. Without contradiction from Sandy, I figured that behind closed doors, she and Charlie had something good going, despite the rumors to the contrary, which I chose to believe or disbelieve on any given day. How we all do assume.

". . . How could he do this to me? It's so humiliating. What am I supposed to do? What do I say to people? What do I say to the kids? How am I supposed to feel?"

"How *do* you feel?"

"I don't know. One minute I'm embarrassed, then angry,

then hurt. And I'm scared, Tess . . . you know . . . about AIDS."

"Maybe you should have a blood test, Sandy."

But she continued, not hearing me, "Sometimes I miss him, and sometimes I'm just glad he's gone and I don't have to wonder where he is and what he's doing."

"You used to wonder?"

"Well, yes," she admitted. "I guess I knew something wasn't right for a long time."

"Did you suspect someone else?"

"No. Well . . . I guess I did suspect there was someone because he . . . well, I just figured if he wasn't making love to me, there had to be someone. Of course, that was only after a long time. For a while, I thought he was just overworked or something."

"How long are we talking about here, Sandy? You never indicated anything was wrong."

"A looong time."

"A few weeks, a few months?"

"How about two years." She shrank in her seat.

"TWO YEARS?" I heard myself blurt back at her in amazement as candid shots of Sandy at parties, dinners, and such started clicking off in my head: shots of Sandy batting eyes at others' husbands; of Sandy in low-cut blouses and clingy sweaters brushing up against would-be adulterers; of Sandy in tiny bikinis splashing water on assuming young men. My usually critical attitude was tempered by the picture of Sandy now before me: neglected, humiliated, wronged.

"Ever since Jonathan was born. He never came near me again."

"What did he say?"

"First he said he was depressed, that the responsibility of being a father of two was hard on him, that I should give him time. So I gave him time. Then he said that while I was nursing the baby I didn't turn him on. So I stopped nursing Jonathan after two months. Then he said the night feedings were keeping him up, and he started sleeping downstairs on the sofa-bed in his den. Then Jonathan started sleeping through the night, but Charlie stayed downstairs because he said he was afraid I'd get pregnant again. So I had my tubes tied. Remember how sick I was after that surgery, Tess? Then Charlie stopped making excuses."

"You mean he still sleeps downstairs?"

No answer.

"Did you talk to anyone about this? Your mother? A doctor? Someone?"

"I wanted to see a psychologist, but Charlie wouldn't go with me. He said it was my problem. He was happy."

Charlie was happy. Charlie was gay. Charlie was a prick.

"I don't know how you get over something like that. What a rejection. Another man. Sandy said she feels she can't be much of a woman if *he* married her," I related to David over lunch in my kitchen the following day.

"Maybe she should look at it as a compliment," he tried.

"Maybe she should kill him! And why are you defending him?" I shot back.

"Why are you so angry?"

"I can't stand seeing Sandy so humiliated."

"That's all?"

"It's just that there seems to be no end to it."

"To what?"

"To . . . to . . . SCUM!"

"Scum?"

"SCUM. As in Shallow Callous Unfaithful Men."

"As in Charlie?"

"As in Charlie, Leonard Meyer, Harvey Cohen, Mark Weiser—and let's not forget Stephen!"

"Quite an ignoble fraternity."

"Scum. All of them."

"Stephen, too?"

I didn't answer.

A slight shrug of his shoulders failed to dispel the concern that had clouded his face. "Tess, are you finished with Stephen?" he asked.

"Of course," I lied. "Why?"

He didn't answer.

Taking advantage of his silence, I changed the subject back to Sandy. "Do you think Sandy's sexy?" I asked.

"I think you're sexy."

"David, I'm serious."

"So am I."

"Well, do you?"

"Sandy's very attractive."

"But do you think she's sexy? I mean, do you think she has a sexy body?"

"I think your body's sexy, Tess. Can't you tell? Just looking at you . . . just thinking about you arouses me."

His words aroused me. I felt my heart stop and then practically jump from my chest. I flushed.

"You're flushed, Tess."

I started to tremble as he reached across the table and took my hands in his. "David, I—"

"No. Don't say anything yet. Let me—"

"I—"

"Please." He was quiet for a moment. And then, "Tess, I can't stop thinking about that day last month when my evil twin brother embarrassed you. I can't tell you how sorry I am that it happened. No, not that it happened, but that it happened that way. Tess, I want to make love to you. I want more than anything in the world to hold you and take care of you. I've never felt this way about anyone and I don't know how to do it right, but I have to tell you how I feel. And I'm not insensitive. I'm sure you have some feeling for me, too. Tell me I'm not wrong."

I was dumbstruck. Such honesty . . . such caring. "You're not wrong, David," I said, not quite dumbstruck.

"I haven't been with anyone in a long time, Tess. I can't even remember the last time I had a date."

I smiled, remembering the last time I had made love to a man. Daniel Daroff. Well, *almost* made love to a man. And I blushed, remembering the last time I kissed a man. David. Yes, I thought, we have some unfinished business, David and I. But what about our wonderful friendship? What will happen to our special feelings for each other, feelings not clouded by sex . . . by sex and jealousy . . . by sex and jealousy and dishonesty?

Confused by my silent smile, David cried, "Oh, God, Tess. There isn't someone else, is there? You never said . . ."

"No. No one else. I haven't even had a date since August. I was just thinking of kissing Lenny the Lech in my kitchen . . . how good it felt . . . how I want to kiss you again, but I'm afraid."

"Of what? Of me?"

"Of whatever it is that makes scum."

"I think I'm being insulted."

"No, no. It's just that I don't want to lose our friendship. You're the best friend I've ever had. We care about each other and we go out together and enjoy each other and we're attracted to each other and we're honest with one another and we're not jealous of each other's relationships. I'd say that's just about perfect."

"Not quite, Tess. I *am* jealous when you tell me about a date, about your problems with men."

"Ah . . . so. What do you think we should do about this?"

"I think you should let me carry you upstairs and make mad, passionate love to you."

"But will you respect me at five o'clock?"

"I'll even take you to dinner at six o'clock."

"But . . . will we still be friends?"

"The best of friends."

"Promise?"

"Cross my heart and hope to die in the scum pond."

And he carried me upstairs and we made mad, passionate love . . . Well, we made love, but mostly we giggled and blushed when, being so nervous, neither of us could get it quite right . . . except that when there's so much good feeling, nothing could be really wrong.

"God! You have a beautiful body," he said after this and that, running his hand along my flank, across my buttocks.

"David, you don't have to—"

"You have a great body! Look at yourself," he demanded,

pulling me to my knees, turning me toward the mirror over the dresser across from my bed.

"Okay. So I'm not fat."

"Lots of people are *not fat*. But *you* are sexy," he said, squeezing my thigh. "Look at these gorgeous legs!"

"You *like* my chubby thighs?"

"A great ass, too."

"And my tiny boobs are a real turn-on. Right?"

"Do you think I should get my boobs siliconized?" I had asked Stephen one December evening after the office personnel Christmas dinner party had put me face to face with Carley Statten for the first time since he'd hired her six months before. Actually, face to face is not an accurate description of our meeting, as her height and spike heels set her shoulders about level with my eyebrows, and her very large breasts swelling over the decolletage of her very short red satin sheath directly in my line of vision—or so it seemed at the time. "Nice meeting you," she had said, looking everywhere but at me. "I have this terrible cold," she added quickly, putting a tissue to her face, hiding her eyes from mine. And sitting across from me later at the long, narrow banquet table, she was fidgety. "I really shouldn't be out tonight. I don't feel very well," she informed me, putting her hand to her face, across her bosom, as if suddenly feeling her exposure. "I'm glad we've finally met. I've heard so much about you," I offered with an edge. I had heard Stephen brag to colleagues, "Have you seen my new secretary?" I had heard Stephen repeat his clients' remarks about the new secretary—appellations such as "Amazon," "Woman of Steel," "Playboy bunny." It seemed that the legendary Great Legs of Alex Gordon's secretary were being supplanted as the building's resident-fantasy-object by the Great Tits of Stephen Fineman's secretary. "Wonder Woman" was my choice, I decided, watching her choke down a shrimp cocktail. Her dry-endy hair was nonetheless long and black, her oily uneven skin only a slight detraction from her dark, almond-shaped eyes, well-arched eyebrows, and sharply defined nose and chin. Yes, I could picture Carley in

163

a Wonder Woman costume looking every inch the cartoon character—and just as one-dimensional.

"Silicone? Now I'm really worried about you," Stephen had answered my late-night question. "I think you're becoming psychotic. Maybe you should talk to a shrink."

"You've got great nipples," David soothed, running a finger around the left one, which stood up instantly. I closed my eyes, succumbing to the soft warmth of his tongue and lips, the exquisite nip of his teeth that sent a current of pleasure right through to the end of me. Touching here, there, we delighted again, anew, in the delicious juxtapositions of the hards and softs of our bodies.

"It was absolutely the last thing I would have expected to happen," I swore to Janet and Sandy Sunday morning in the diner, feeling the need to defend my liaison with David, which felt as tentative as it was passionate, leaving skid marks on our psyches.

"Sure," Sandy said, looking very jealous indeed.

"What's with the face?" Janet chided her.

Sandy rolled her eyes.

"I'm sorry, Sandy. I guess it's not too tactful of me to talk about this right now."

"Stop patronizing me, Tess. It has nothing to do with me. I just can't stand to hear you be so . . . so *surprised* about David. After all, you've been flirting with him foreeever. You should hear yourself! 'Can you imagine, girls! David and meee!' Surely the lady doth protest tooo much!"

Look who's quoting Shakespeare! I thought venomously. "Maybe I did want it, but I never thought it would actually happen," I defended myself. "It was a fantasy for me. It still feels like fantasy."

"Well," she concluded, "I guess it settles one point: He's not gay. Then again—"

"Then again, I'm glad somebody's getting something," Janet jumped in. "And, Tess, stop being so defensive! You're allowed to have a feast while all around you are starving. So enjoy it for all of us! And, I have to tell you, he's real pretty. And I *don't* have to tell you what I think of him! He's been a prince dealing with the camp thing."

"So when will it be finished?" I asked, pulling in my spines.

"Well, you know how Leonard's managed to get the hearing put off a few times? The judge finally demanded that the motion be heard right after New Year's. That was *after* David sent a letter to the court explaining that I have to sign Sean up for camp again soon, and they still haven't been paid for last summer. The camp director's been a doll about waiting for his money. Would you believe that David wrote that he'd be personally responsible for the fee if things didn't work out in court? Tess, if things don't work out with you and David, I have dibs on him."

"By the way, Tess," Sandy started again, "how's Stephen taking your affair with David?"

"Stephen's not," I said. "As far as he and the world are concerned, David and I are just the good friends we always were. Actually, I think that's where it's at . . . sort of."

"A Friend Plus Sex. Have I got it right?" Sandy sneered.

"Right," I avowed, not believing it for a minute.

"So, Sandy, what's with your divorce? Is the good doctor being decent?" Janet changed the subject again.

"So far. He said he's going to keep depositing household money in my account each month, and he'll take care of the taxes and everything. But I also know that he's hired an attorney. A big gun. I guess I should get one, too."

"I'd say that's a good idea," Janet agreed. "Save yourself some energy; let the lawyers battle it out. You have nothing to lose, because the only thing you have is the kids . . ."

". . . And you know he won't want the kids!" Janet and I said in unison. We all laughed, including Sandy.

"It's going to work out, Sandy. You'll see. You won't have to live vicariously through Tess and me anymore," Janet teased. "You'll be able to experience firsthand the glamour, the excitement . . . the horniness of single life!" We all laughed again. "We'll show you around. We'll buy you an answering machine—by the way, ladies, the answering machine you got me for my birthday is great. We'll fix you up with all our old blind dates!"

"Aaaagh! I thought you were my friends!" More laughter.

"If you find something good, I'll watch the kids!" I added.

Sandy turned and hugged me. "You *are* good friends."

"Nah! Tess just loves your kids," Janet said.

"Thanks, guys." Sandy sniffed back a tear. "I don't know what I'd do without you. And, Tess, I'm really glad for you . . . about David, I mean. I'm sorry about what I said. I haven't been myself lately."

"Don't worry about it, Sandy," I said, wondering who she'd be next.

"How's it going with David?" Sandy asked over a chef's salad at Mykonos, where they were about to condo our booth. She was looking better now that the word was out, now that the rumor rush had boiled up and subsided, now that her day in court—which had become a necessity when Charlie's lawyer succeeded in convincing Charlie that Sandy was going to clean him out and advised him to cut his voluntary support of his family in half, and Sandy's lawyer succeeded in convincing Sandy that Charlie intended to force her out of her big home and into a full-time job—had provided her and the children with a monthly support check that would do nicely (although Charlie and Sandy each thought they were being taken) until a settlement could be reached.

"Nice. But I keep waiting for him to disappear," I answered.

"Why do you say that?"

"As we've all noted, he never stays with anyone very long."

"But this is different. He's your friend—at least, that's what you keep telling me. 'He's just a friend,' remember?"

"Well, obviously he's not *just* a friend anymore, and I'm sure it's getting in the way. I mean, I can still talk to him and everything, but . . . well . . . it feels different."

"I should hope so."

"What I mean is that, before, when we were just friends, I felt we'd *always* be friends, no matter what. But now that we're lovers, I have the feeling that at any given time he could decide that he's bored . . . or something."

"That you're not so great after all? Now that he's finally conquered you?"

"Something like that."

"You're weird, Tess."

"You noticed."

"You're weird . . . but you're cute . . . and you're not horny. So lighten up. Don't be so hard on yourself."

"You're right. I'm not horny," I said, cracking a smile. "The sex is really good."

"The sex is always good for you," she said, laughing.

"So, how are the kids?"

"Tess, you don't have to change the subject. I know you think I've been deprived all this time, but you don't have to feel sorry for me. Because I haven't been. Deprived, that is."

"Oh?"

"I have a lover."

"Oh?!"

"George."

"George? Not George who cuts your hair! I thought he was—" I stopped myself.

"That's the one, and he's not."

Then again, she hadn't known her husband was gay either, I thought. George. I had difficulty focusing on this new situation. With each new twist, my kaleidoscopic view of Sandy's life changed. "How long's this been going on?"

"Six years."

"SIX?"

"Well, I've known him six years. I've only been sleeping with him for two years." She came into color as she answered my puzzled expression in a spirited duet with her hands: "There was this instant attraction when we first met. I mean, he looked like he couldn't wait to get his hands on me, and he always took a looong time with my hair. He'd been recently divorced, and I felt a little sorry for him, so Charlie and I had him over for dinner one night . . . and

167

then I had lunch with him occasionally . . . and he would stop in during the day for a cup of coffee now and then . . ."

She sucked him right in, I thought.

". . . and after Jonathan was born and Charlie was so cold . . ."

I listened intently, trying to put it—my reaction, not her story—together. I was thinking that maybe I shouldn't be feeling so sorry for her. After all, she and Charlie were each playing their own little games, and who knew which had come first? Sandy was such a flirt, and she always seemed so needy. Now I was wondering who else she . . . My mind flipped through the candid shots again and came to a screeching halt at one of Sandy and Stephen in my kitchen —embracing. Just a friendly hug, he had said when I walked in from the dining room. I wondered then, and I was wondering now. Guilt-stricken, I tried to stop thinking. "I'm glad you haven't been deprived, but I'm surprised you never said anything about it. Does Janet know?"

"She didn't, until last night. I had dinner with her and Sean. It was kind of fun having a little secret."

Little secret? Try *double life*, I thought, wondering what other little secrets she had, feeling hurt that my good friend had been holding out on me. I was always so honest with her.

I bumped into Sandy on a miserable day three weeks later in the parking lot of the shopping center. I was between a settlement and an appointment to show a house—which, this being two days after Christmas, represented an unusual flurry of real estate business for that time of year—and I had stopped to pick up flour, sugar, and eggs at the supermarket for some baking I had to do that night—which was the usual flurry of dessert business for that time of year. She looked tired, disoriented.

"I have to talk to you, Tess."

"Step into my office, Mrs. Solomon," I said, leading her out of the freezing drizzle into my four-year-old maroon Toyota four-door, where, for the next twenty-five minutes, she explained to me how Charlie had come over the night before to beg for her forgiveness, to tell her that he must

168

have been crazy to leave . . . that he really loved her . . . that he wanted to work it out . . . that he wanted to come home . . . while the motor of the Toyota hummed to keep us warm.

"But what about The Guy?" I asked.

It was insanity, he had told her . . . a midlife crisis . . . a remnant of some adolescent homosexual craving . . . that being away from Sandy had made him realize that he really desired her.

"Do you believe him?"

"I want to."

"Maybe you should get some professional help on this."

"It's going to be fine, Tess. Just the way it used to be."

I wondered how it used to be. I wondered if she really knew how it used to be.

"What time are they coming?" David asked, licking the beaters from the mixing bowl of whipped cream.

If dessert is the most satisfying part of a meal, surely the last of the batter on the beaters is the most satisfying part of the dessert, I thought, remembering my mother's kitchen, and how, when I was a good little girl, my reward was licking sweet goodies from the beaters. And I remembered the day my mother discovered the rubber spatula, and how cheated I felt as I watched her manipulate the cruelly efficient implement, leaving nothing at all to lick from the beaters or bowl. Yet I had been so very, very good. Whoever invented the rubber spatula must hate kids, I had thought, promising myself that when I grew up I'd never use one, a promise I hadn't kept, with one exception: When it came to beaters, the good guys always got the last licks.

"Tess?"

"Hmm?"

"What time—"

"Oh, seven-thirty," I answered. This post–New Year's dinner was a command performance. Sandy had asked me to invite Charlie and her for dinner as a show of support for their renewed relationship. "Besides, Charlie and I have

169

some news," she had said, refusing to divulge The News until we were all together.

"What's the big secret?" David asked.

"I can't imagine. You know Sandy. Everything with her has to be dramatic."

"More important, what's for dessert?"

"A yummy custard molded in sponge cake and topped with whipped cream and strawberries marinated in kirsch and sugar. It's a special dessert for Charlie. He loves sweet things," I explained.

"Is that supposed to be a pun?"

"Unintentional, I assure you. But the dessert is quite intentional," I said.

"What's that supposed to mean?"

Smiling my most Mona Lisa smile, I continued stirring the custard over a low flame.

That evening, Charlie was, as usual, aloof but obligingly pleasant. A smile stamped his soft, scrubbed-looking face that was reminiscent of the faces on Campbell's Soup cans. Sandy, as usual, hung on him like a mantle. David and I kept up a steady flow of inane conversation.

As I poured the coffee at the end of dinner, Charlie cleared his throat for attention and pronounced The News. "Tess, thanks for having us here tonight. You've been a real friend to Sandy, so I know you're going to be happy to hear that I'm going to be your neighbor again." Sandy cuddled closer to him, taking hold of his hand. the one playing with the coffee spoon.

I don't know why I felt surprise. What had I expected? Then again, the surprise was not the reconciliation, which was obviously expected, but that Charlie was moving back into the house. Perhaps I thought they would date while each living out their own private fantasies in their own private worlds in a kind of collusion of mutual delusion. "Well! Welcome home, Charlie. We'll celebrate with a dessert I made especially for you," I said, placing the dessert in front of him. "It's a charlotte russe," I added. smiling a wicked little smile.

Charlie's small khaki eyes met mine for an instant that had to be counted as a first. In them, disbelief dismissed comprehension. An almost imperceptible knit in Sandy's eyebrows signaled her vague sense of something gone awry.

David choked on his coffee. "It's nice to hear things have worked out for you two," he finally managed, silencing the unspoken consideration of intent.

"Thanks, David. I think we're going to be okay. Right, Sandy?" Smiling, Charlie gave Sandy a little push with his body—sort of an inverted hug.

Fitting, I thought. "Dessert, Charlie?" I asked, mounding a sizable portion on a plate.

"Yes, ma'am."

"Sandy?"

"Of course! When did you ever know me to pass up something so sinfully good?"

Never. Absolutely never, I thought as the candids started to flash in my head again.

"Tess, I have more news for you. There's going to be a new addition to the family," she said. Did she blush?

"You're not pregnant!"

"No, no. George Davidson. Do you remember George? The guy who does my hair. . . ."

I can't be hearing right, I thought.

". . . Well, I was getting my hair cut last week and he was saying how his lease was coming due and they raised his rent, and I was just saying how I was looking for someone reliable to baby-sit for the kids sometimes so Charlie and I can have more private time together, and he was teasing about how he'd baby-sit if it meant cheap rent, and I was saying how there was an apartment over the garage—"

"You didn't—"

"I most certainly did. George is moving in next week. Isn't that great?"

Was that a sneer on her lips as she leaned back against Charlie's shoulder? "Great," I agreed obediently.

"I thought it was a great idea, too," Charlie chimed in. "We're going to use the rent money to buy Sandy a new car. Hers is a good five years old and takes forever to warm up."

"Sometimes I have to start the engine and then come back to the house for a second cup of coffee before I leave," Sandy added, confirming the need for a new car . . . and therefore the extra income . . . and therefore the new tenant.

"So. George. He's single?" I poked.

"Yes," said Sandy, appearing a bit alarmed at my pursuance.

"And he doesn't live with anyone?"

"No. Actually, he did have a roommate, but it didn't work out. Charlie thinks he's gay, but I don't think so. You've met him, Tess. Do you think he's gay?"

"Not from what I've heard." Bitch.

"How's it all working out?" I asked Sandy when I met her for breakfast at the diner two weeks later. I knew that the moves had gone smoothly. Sandy had kept me abreast of Charlie's moving back . . . and George's moving in. I had to admit, the scenario appealed to my sense of irony, justice, and intensely black humor.

"Weeell . . . everything's going just great! Charlie is positively ecstatic about being home. He just loooves being with me again. He can't keep his hands off me!"

"And George?"

"He can't keep his hands off me, either! I can't believe I pulled this off."

I couldn't either. And I was beginning to wonder who was pulling what off whom.

"It's so exciting. George and I have this signal, you see. If he's home and wants company, he leaves his window shade up. I can see it from my kitchen window."

Company? Read: A Fuck.

"He's a very private person, Tess. He's an artist, you know. And not only with hair. He's a sculptor. And he promised to do a bronze of me."

In the nude, I presumed.

"I know it's risky, but—"

"Sandy, wouldn't it be easier to use the telephone?"

"Not really. He never knows if Charlie is here or not. You

172

know Charlie walks to the train when he goes to University Hospital."

"I see," I said, trying to make sense out of nonsense. "So why don't you call him?"

"Well, I do, if his shade is up. But I'd neeever bother him if his shade is down. Even if his car's there, he might be sculpting. As I said, he's a veeery private person."

"I guess I don't know a lot about these things, Sandy. But it sounds strange to me. Are you sure you know what you're doing? As your friend, I have to tell you, you really sound off-the-wall."

"Don't worry, Tess. It's like a game. And I have to tell *you*, it's wonderful fun."

"Right." Almost as much fun as Russian roulette.

"What more can I do?" I asked Michael the following Tuesday. "And, remember? She called *me* weird!"

"No. I don't remember. She called you weird? You? Hah!" He leaned far back in his seat, chuckling.

"Oh, wonderful! Just what I need! My therapist thinks I'm weird!"

He didn't respond, but he stopped laughing.

"You didn't say that, did you?" I asked meekly.

"What *did* I say?"

"You laughed at the idea that Sandy called me weird."

"Right."

"But it wasn't because you thought *I* was weird; it was because you thought *she* was so weird. You were agreeing with what I had said to you."

He didn't respond.

"Right?" I begged the question.

"But you thought I was laughing *at* you, not *with* you. Who thinks who is weird here?"

"I think Sandy is weird. I think I'm weird."

"Right."

"Am I weird?"

He made a fist. "Do you want a shot in the arm or in both arms?"

I felt shy, dumb, but most of all, I felt young. And, looking at Michael through the fine mist in my eyes, I felt his loving aura wrap fleetingly around me.

One bitter cold morning that felt more like February than March, I sat at my desk working out income tax figures on my calculator while listening to Sandy rationalize her situation over the phone uncomfortably cradled between my shoulder and ear. Nothing added up, not the figures, not Sandy.

". . . After all, considering what Charlie did to me, there's almost nothing that I could do that would be unjust. Right?"

She had a point.

". . . And all I'm really doing is protecting myself. I mean, suppose Charlie decided to leave again? At least this way I have someone to fall back on. . . ."

Oh, you mean just like before, I thought.

". . . And, besides, what am I supposed to do with this wonderful friendship between George and me? Throw it away? Would that be fair to George? Or me? I mean, forget the sex part . . ."

First she'd have to; hearing about the sex was my favorite part.

". . . we have this reeeally close relationship. He's been my best friend . . ."

I thought I was. Now, why doesn't this column add up?

". . . and I've inspired him to a creative zenith. . . ."

Creative zenith?

". . . He's doing things he's never done before. . . ."

I'll bet. How I hate numbers.

And as she prattled on about how nobody was going to get hurt because George was so clever, and she was so careful, and how she really did love them both, I kept coming up with wrong answers on my adding machine.

After about forty-five minutes, Sandy suddenly exclaimed, "Uh-oh! I got so involved in our conversation I forgot about the car! Tess, let me call you back, I was going

174

to go shopping this morning and I left the car warming up in the garage." Click.

I don't think I had said one word during the entire call. Sandy was wrapped up, but not in conversation,

George died the next morning in the intensive care unit of University Hospital. Charlie had died twenty hours earlier in George's arms, above the garage . . . above Sandy's running car . . . above suspicion. The sweet sleep that overcame them both was not the swoon of posterotic passion, but the coma of carbon monoxide poisoning.

LADYFINGERS

3 eggs
1/2 cup + 1 tablespoon sugar
1 teaspoon vanilla extract
pinch of salt
2/3 cup sifted cake flour
powdered sugar
6 squares bittersweet chocolate

Preheat oven to 300°F.

Separate eggs and slowly beat 1/2 cup sugar and vanilla into egg yolks until they form a ribbon and are thick and pale.

In another bowl, beat egg whites with salt until they form soft peaks. Add 1 tablespoon sugar and beat until they form stiff peaks.

Spoon about a quarter of the whites onto the yolks, sift on about a quarter of the flour, and fold gently. Repeat until whites and flour are all partly blended into yolk mixture.

Use a pastry bag to squeeze lines of the batter onto two buttered and floured baking sheets (about 4 x 1 1/2 inches). Sprinkle with powdered sugar and bake in middle and upper levels of oven for about 20 minutes, until lightly crusty and light brown under the sugar. Remove with spatula and cool on rack. Melt chocolate squares in a fondue pot or the top of a double boiler. Dip the tips of cooled ladyfingers in melted chocolate and set to dry on wax paper. Makes about one dozen.

CHAPTER 10

Ladyfingers

Standing pallid by Charlie's coffin at the graveside funeral service, Sandy was a portrait of pain. Her white face was a scream held in a frame of black hair, her eyes black eddies of pain. I wanted her to be angry, to take satisfaction in her just, if inadvertent, revenge on her two faithless lovers. But guilt enveloped her; loss, like her long black coat, overwhelmed her.

She had called me about eight-thirty two evenings before. She was crying. "Tess! I need you! Come now!" she managed, and then hung up. Spurred by the urgency in her voice, I sped to her home, running a red light and two stop signs. Two police cars, their lights flashing, were in front of her house; an ambulance was pulling out of the driveway. All I could think of was the children. The front door was open. I ran in and found Sandy sitting at the kitchen table, ashen, clutching Rebecca. A police officer was talking on the telephone.

Sandy looked up. "Oh, Tess! He's dead!"

My heart stopped and a knot grew in my throat, choking me, forcing tears from my eyes as I thought of Jonathan. "JONATHAN!" was all I got out.

"He's asleep, Tess; he doesn't know," she answered, allaying my worst fears.

177

"Sandy, what's going on?" I asked, able now to run to her and put my arms around her.

"It's Charlie! He's dead! I killed him!" She began crying anew.

My eyes found those of the officer who was hanging up the phone. "What's happened?" I implored.

"It appears to have been an accident, in the garage apartment, ma'am," he started. "It seems that Dr. Solomon and Mr. Davidson"—*George?!*—"were asleep in the apartment when they were overcome by carbon monoxide coming from a car running in the garage below them. . . ."

Recalling the morning's telephone conversation with Sandy, a wave of nausea washed over me . . . remembering my inattention . . . my silent criticism . . . her quick exit. Her words—*"I left the car warming up in the garage"*—echoed in my head.

". . . They took Mr. Davidson to the hospital," the officer continued, "and the paramedics said he might make it. We didn't reach Dr. Solomon in time."

"OH MY GOD, SANDY!" I exclaimed, hunching over her, burying my face in her hair. We wept. My tears were as much tears of relief for the children's safety as they were tears of sympathy for Sandy's pain.

When the officer left, Sandy asked me to call her parents. "I have to lie down," she whimpered, relinquishing Rebecca to me. I sat with Rebecca cuddled against me on the sofa in the family room until she fell asleep. After carrying her to bed, I called Sandy's parents.

I called Janet when I got home, drained, about eleven-fifteen . . . after Sandy's parents arrived . . . after Sandy was coerced into sleep by a whopping dose of Jonathan's Benadryl, the only thing in the house with a sedative effect. Janet was, of course, shocked, but not too shocked to see the scales of justice swing into balance: "BLASTED IDIOT! He deserved it, Tess. I mean . . . so, he was gay. FINE. But he had no right to treat Sandy that way. So, he chose the life he wanted. FINE. But why couldn't he be honest with Sandy and let her choose hers? Because he wanted it all, THE

BASTARD! They ALL want it ALL! Poor Sandy must be devastated. . . ." And Janet ranted on for quite a while. And we both grew very, very angry. "I hope the CREEP had a lot of insurance!" Janet ended.

Then I called David. He wasn't shocked. I don't think anything shocks David. He was concerned, for Sandy . . . for the children . . . for me. Most of all for me. "Are you sure you're okay? Do you want me to come over?"

"I'm okay," I lied. "I just want to go to sleep."

The next morning I called Sandy. She didn't want company, she didn't want to talk, but she talked . . . and talked. What she told me was that George had died a few hours before . . . that her mother was making funeral arrangements for Charlie, it would be a graveside service the next morning . . . that she had no idea who was taking care of George's arrangements, and she didn't care . . . that she was confused, and scared. . . . "Suppose the police think I did it on purpose!"

"Not a chance," I told her, all the time wondering, What if they do?

"Two people, Tess. I killed two people!"

Déjà vu crept over me. When had I had this conversation before? Janet. Yes, after Harvey died. Why is it that when a man is literally consumed by adulterous passion, the wronged woman is consumed with guilt?

Dinner at Janet's house that night was tense as we waited for Sean to go to sleep so we could Talk. Finally, at nine-thirty, "I can't believe this has happened, Tess," Janet started.

"Neither can I."

"Do you think Charlie and George were seeing each other before George moved in?"

"Who knows? But I'd say, no. Remember, Charlie was involved with the guy from the hospital."

"True. But it's possible he wasn't any more faithful to his boyfriend than he was to Sandy. Remember Harvey?"

We shook our heads. There was little else to say . . .

except, "How do you think they were found?" Janet queried.

"Well, University Hospital called Sandy looking for Charlie, and—"

"No! I mean, how do you think the police found Charlie and George? Do you think they were naked?"

"Janet! Only you would think of something like that!"

"Oh, no, Tess. Only I would *say* it!"

Yes. I had to admit, there is a bit of the voyeur in us all. Even so, I decided to let Janet accept the responsibility for *our* thoughts. "Well, anyway, the officer said they had been sleeping," I said.

"Right. That's what they *said*. What did you expect them to say—'Dr. Solomon and Mr. Davidson were found in a lovers' embrace'? What do *you* think they were doing?"

"I guess what everyone else does—one way or another."

Janet slouched into the sofa and nodded in agreement. Suddenly she giggled and then mugged a serious, brow-knitted face. "Now," she said, "I can understand Charlie being hot for George. He was quite a hunk. But what I can't understand is what George would want with bland, chubby Charlie!"

We both giggled. The wine we were nipping from Waterford crystal goblets—Janet had pulled out the good stuff in a warped gesture of support for Sandy—was doing its job, easing the pain . . . until we thought of Sandy, which was what we had been avoiding all night. And then Janet started to rage against MEN—their insensitivity, infidelity, undeveloped sense of fair play. And then Janet started to cry for Sandy, for herself, for all the pain. And I joined her, until we were both tuckered out, and I went home. David and I would pick her up at ten o'clock for the funeral. It was going to be dreadful, we had agreed.

It was dreadful. The morning was cold and blustery. Almost two hundred people showed up, and most stood because only about forty chairs were set up around the mahogany coffin perched on a sling over the open grave. A worn, green canopy covered the grave site. Janet, David, and I stood at the back of the last row of chairs facing Sandy and the children. David held my left hand; Janet held my right. The whispers in the crowd were deafening, only bits and pieces of which could I hear clearly. *". . . Do you think she'll sell the house? . . . She's so pretty, she'll do all right. . . . Lots of money there. . . . Doctors are no better than the rest. . . . Of course she knew. A wife knows. . . ."* God! People are cruel. I looked around at the faces. Most looked curious, not sad. Necks craned to see the bereaved widow. Only when the rabbi spoke was there quiet, and when he had finished his short service, the whispers roared louder than before. *". . . queer . . . only an orderly, or was it a nurse . . . did Sandy's hair . . . justifiable homicide . . . next year we'll dance at her wedding. . . ."* I hated them all.

At the close of the service, Sandy, holding Jonathan, stood up, as did Rebecca, Charlie's parents, his two brothers and sisters-in-law, his grandmother—on his mother's side—and Sandy's parents, who stood next to Sandy. Filing past the coffin, each picked up a stone or fistful of dirt and placed it on the lid. Sandy remained standing by the coffin, a portrait of pain. Jonathan, a blue-snowsuited fireplug, straddled Sandy's left hip; Rebecca clung to her mother's black-booted leg. A strong unit, they would survive, I thought as I watched them be brave. And then the coffin was lowered. Horrified, Rebecca cried out, "NO! THAT'S MY DADDY!" —an exclamation that tore through the cold, clear day. Sandy's mother pulled the startled Jonathan from Sandy's arms, allowing Sandy to drop to her knees and envelop her screaming daughter. For all my penchant and facility for bizarre and hyperbolic fantasy, nothing I could imagine could come close to the grief and terror I saw in that child.

The scene reminded me of the absence of my own father, who had died in a car accident with my two-year-old brother, Jamie, when I was five, and I started to cry, for Rebecca, for me, a spontaneous outpouring that was quickly squelched by a question: Had I really been better off without my father, as my mother had told me, as I thought Rebecca might be without Charlie? I hoped Sandy would never say anything like that to Rebecca. She would never forgive her mother for that.

Rebecca's macabre cry brought to mind another time, another funeral.

The very first funeral I remember attending was only a few years before, for someone I didn't know—the grandmother of Jack Moskovitz, a longtime business associate of Stephen's. Stephen couldn't be there, he had to be in Atlanta on business . . . would I please go in his stead . . . it would mean a lot to Jack—although I had met Jack and his wife only twice before they'd moved to Arizona several years ago. And of course I said I would go. After signing the book in the foyer of the funeral home, I entered the small, dimly lit chapel. It had a faintly musty smell. The front wall was paneled with redwood; the Eternal Light, hanging above and to the right of the dais in its contemporary brass holder, glowed an eerie red-orange. Most of the seats were already filled when I walked down the center aisle toward the front, toward the first row of seats on the left where Jack sat with his wife, two teenage children, his mother, and three others I couldn't identify. In front, on the right, propped up at an angle in the corner, was the beige coffin. The top half of the lid was open, displaying an elderly woman in a starched blue lace dress with a small spray of blue silk rosebuds pinned at the center of the frilly high neck. Her gray hair was in curls, her lips and cheeks pinked, her eyes closed. Pink spotlights cast a kind of plastic life on the face of the corpse. I imagined it being a scene from a horror movie about a doll shop for the elderly, where life-size, aged dolls were bought by old people for companionship in their second childhood. I stopped halfway down the aisle, waiting for . . . what? . . . the old doll's eyelids to pop open and reveal bright blue glass eyes? her arms to suddenly pop up, reaching out for me? Finally moving forward, I kissed Jack and his wife, reintroducing myself as Stephen's wife, and, with a sympathetic smile, briefly pressed the hands of the other mourners in the front row. And all the while I could hear nothing of what was said to me because my ears were filled with the buzz of flowing blood. I found a seat, close to the front of the chapel on the right. My eyes never left the doll in its lacquered box. I only vaguely remember the service—the rabbi's eulogy, the congregation's whispers and recitation of the Twenty-third Psalm, the mourners' silent weeping. But when attendants closed the lid of the coffin, lifted it from its corner, and placed it on a dolly, and the pallbearers walked it slowly up the center aisle, a single voice pierced the thickness of the moment: "GOOD-BYE, MAMA!" This came not from a child—that is, not from a child young in years—but from Jack's mother, the elderly child of the dead woman, who lunged from her aisle seat to wave a frantic farewell to her mother. My heart stopped. My eyes filled. My body hair stood on end. I felt nauseated. Funerals are barbaric, I thought.

I didn't go to the cemetery. Instead, for no conscious reason, I drove to my mother's apartment—she hadn't yet followed her sister Sarah to Florida. I told her—for the first time, although I had known for a while—that she would have no grandchildren . . . that the surgery I had had was an attempt to correct misshapen fallopian tubes, not a D and C for excessive menstrual bleeding, which is what I had told her at the time of the surgery so she wouldn't know I couldn't do even such a natural thing as conception right . . . but that apparently the surgery was a failure, because here it was two years later and I was still a barren woman. Somewhat distracted, my mother told me that I never did eat right, that I didn't get enough sleep, that a man wants children, which seemed to be an odd thing for her to say since she had so often told me, "Your father—may he rest in peace—never had time for his children." What I wanted was her touch. I seemed to remember it from somewhere in my past . . . when I was feverish . . . when she'd press her long, soft fingers to my forehead, to my cheeks, to check my temperature. Sitting with my mother after Jack's grandmother's funeral, I cried in my head, "Mommy, I'm hurting." But all I felt was her distance. That's when I first noticed the deepening wrinkles around her eyes and mouth, the fine lines developing on her over-rouged cheeks, the kink in her short, gray hair. When did she get old? I thought. I still felt like a little girl—her little girl. I felt that she might die before I grew up . . . that I might never grow up.

All this I recalled about a month after Charlie's funeral as my electric mixer traced deep furrows in the thick batter that would soon be delicate, chocolate-tipped ladyfingers for Gail Shusterman's younger sister's baby shower. Roses of homemade strawberry and lemon ice were already made and boxed, and I'd baked an orange-glazed pound cake the night before. The ladyfingers were the last of the order, and they would be done in plenty of time for the eight-o'clock shower. My mother had called about eleven to remind me that I hadn't called her for over a week. Stephen had called soon after to "check in." Although he was calling every other day or so, he made no effort to see me. I was beginning to feel that maybe we could be friends after all. And then Sandy had called to see if I'd be home about two, and would I like company for a cup of coffee? She was fine. The kids were fine. "Sure," I said. And then I started to think about how surprisingly well Sandy was handling the horror that had taken over her life, which brought to mind Charlie's funeral . . . and so on.

"Friends? You and Stephen? Are you craaazy?" Sandy asked later that afternoon, sitting at my kitchen table over our coffee and the few misshapen ladyfingers that hadn't made the cut.

"Maybe it's spring fever," I answered. "You know. Trees bud, flowers bloom . . . I sprout wings of fancy. I lose my mind."

"I'm serious, Tess. You don't want to be friends with Stephen, you want it to be the way you thought it was . . ."

I wondered how she thought it was, how she thought *I* thought it was.

". . . and if you think *he* just wants to be friends . . . Well. Maybe you have lost your mind." Sandy had toughened up over the last few months.

"I haven't seen him. Not for a while. But he hasn't been feeling great, and I think it helps him to know that he can talk to me."

"It matters to you how he feels?"

"We were . . . *are* married, Sandy. Obviously I still have some feelings for him. But I know it's over. Don't worry. I'm just trying to be civil."

Sandy rolled her eyes. "Not to change the subject," she changed the subject, "how's David these days?"

"Amazingly still around."

"Does Stephen know?"

"If he does, he's not letting on."

"Tess, are you and David in love or something?" she asked after a long pause.

What's with the edge on that question? I wondered. "What's love?" I asked, wondering why I was being evasive.

"I don't know. I thought you'd know. You have more experience than I do."

"Maybe in finding out what *isn't* love," I said.

"Oh. I've had my own experience along those lines," she said, growing pale and teary.

I wondered if it was pain she felt, or just emptiness. She'd seemed happy when Charlie had moved back home. And she'd had something—I didn't know what—with George. Ego, maybe, or revenge. But love? The truth was, only Sandy knew how Sandy felt . . . no matter how *truthful* she was with anyone about her feelings . . . including me, her best friend. Well, usually her best friend.

"Do you want to know how I really feel about everything that's happened, Tess?"

"If you want to tell me," I said, surprised by her sudden need to share her feelings, something she hadn't done at all since the funeral. And the coincidence of our thoughts startled me, as it always did, whenever it did, which was often. Sandy would say I was witchy. I would say that we weren't good friends for no reason.

"Relieved. I feel relieved. Does that sound strange?"

"No."

"I know I was caught up in craziness, and now I'm

relieved that it's over. I mean, I guess I loved Charlie when I married him, but we didn't share very much. You know I told you about how we didn't have sex after Jonathan was born? Well, the truth is it wasn't a whole lot better before Jonathan, or even before Rebecca. You know, like maybe once every few weeks? Even when we were first married. I didn't think it was normal, but he kept telling me everybody's libido is different. How could I argue with that? So I figured I was oversexed. Actually, *he* said that. He even told me to see a psychiatrist because I was a borderline nymphomaniac. And of course I took it to heart, because, after all, he was a doctor. I thought he should know about these things. And all the time it was him! Why couldn't I see how strange our relationship was?"

Why couldn't you? I thought, and then quickly answered my own question when I thought of my own assortment of aberrant relationships. "You're asking *moi?*" I asked.

"Actually, I never could figure out why you put up with Stephen."

"Right. Well, that's sort of different."

"Why?"

"I'm not sure. But it is. Hey! We're not talking about me. We're talking about you."

"It's all part of the same conversation, Tess. I mean, I have to find out what's normal. It's obvious that I didn't know abnormal when I was in it. So . . . what's normal!"

"What do you mean?"

"I mean . . . well . . . sexually. You tell me that sex is good with David, and it was good with Stephen . . . and there were the others. They may have been strange, but the sex was good, wasn't it?"

"Some of it was fun. But it wasn't always so great. Sandy, what are you getting at?"

"I'm confused, Tess. I don't know what I'm supposed to feel."

"What, specifically, is so confusing?"

"Tess . . . I've never had an orgasm with a man."

I was taken aback by this confession, as candids of sexy

Sandy clicked through my head, but I tried to be understanding. "Well, it sounds like you didn't have a whole lot of opportunity," I said. And what about George? I wondered to myself.

"I thought it was going to happen with George. But it didn't turn out that way."

"Yes. What about George?" I asked, now that she had brought it up.

"Mostly George and I talked a lot. I was flattered because he was always telling me how wooonderful I looked, how exciting I was—"

"So?"

"So it was all talk. I mean, we kissed a lot and I kept waiting for him to get into some really great sex—whatever that is—but we only did it a couple of times and it wasn't anything great."

"But the way you talked about him—"

"I know. I guess I was trying to convince myself. So . . . how do you?"

"What?"

"Get off with a guy?"

"You mean have orgasms?"

"Um-hmm."

"It depends."

"On what?"

"The guy, my mood, a lot of things."

"But you can do it."

"Not every time. But I always did with Stephen. . . ." I said wistfully, my mind drifting momentarily away from Sandy's concerns to my own.

"I can do it myself," she filled my pause in a small voice.

"Well, that's a start."

"But it's not normal."

"Why not? What's normal?"

"I don't know. I'm asking you."

"First you have to have a normal guy."

"Like your gallery of freaks was nooormal!"

"Let me restate that," I said, cracking the tension with a

laugh. "First, let's drop the word *normal*. Now. Good sex requires two people who like each other—"

"Like you like Stephen?"

"Okay. Let's say two people who like each other's bodies—"

"Two people as in any two people?"

"What do you mean?"

"I mean as in a man and a woman, or two men, or two women."

That threw me, made me feel dumb. This wasn't going to be as easy as I thought. "Well, yes, but for me it's a man and a woman."

"But it could be two men or two women."

Something's not right with this conversation, I thought. "Sandy, what are you trying to say?"

She flushed. She got up from the table, poured herself another cup of coffee, and hung around the center island, picking up ladyfinger crumbs and eating them one at a time.

"Can I help?" I asked.

"It's just that . . ." She was close to tears. "Tess, I'm not who you think I am." She turned her back to me as she swept the remaining crumbs into a neat pile. "I think I'm gay . . . and I don't know what to do . . . and . . ." And the tears came.

"Sandy . . ." I soothed, jumping to her side, putting an arm around her quaking shoulders. She turned to me and hugged me hard.

Sandy gay? I wondered. Well, her men are gay. That doesn't mean anything. Then again . . . And I felt her full breasts against my own flat chest. It startled me. It felt nice. I wondered if men missed that when they hugged me. And then I wondered if it felt *too* nice. They were a lot different from what I had . . . not so different . . . a lot different. Could Sandy be gay? What if she kissed me . . . what if she just took my face in her hands and kissed me. . . . What would I do? . . . Why would I think that? But if she did, would I like her full lips on mine? . . . I like a man with full lips . . . would I like a woman's? . . .

* * *

188

She took my face in her hands. "I knew you'd understand, Tess, because we understand each other, we're the same, you and I," and she kissed me, her full lips pressing mine.

. . . No. I don't think I'd like that. But her breasts . . . would I like to touch them, press them like I press my own when I feel horny, when there's no man around, when I do it myself? I like the feel of my breasts as I imagine a man would like the feel of them . . . but wouldn't hers feel nicer? They're so much bigger . . . so different from mine. Is that why I'd like to feel them, because they're different? What am I feeling? What is she feeling? Does she want to touch me? What would I do if she tried? Could we ever be friends again? Would I punch her out? Worse yet, would I like it? . . .

And she ran her hand down my side and rubbed my thigh and she took my hand and put it on her breast; it felt soft and alive . . . and she put her hand on my tummy . . . and lower. I felt myself blush . . . flush? "Do you want a back rub?" she asked . . . and I was on a sofa and she rubbed my back. . . . "Do you want a front rub?" she asked . . . and I turned and she touched me the way I would touch myself. . . . "I want to finish you off," she said—I read that in a book once—and she put her mouth to me and as I felt her tongue on my flesh I pictured her flesh and it was my flesh and when I touched her I felt my touch . . . like in a mirror . . . like for myself.

. . . It would be like doing it for myself, I thought, so how bad could it be? A woman knows a woman's body. . . . But what about the rest? Yes, for me there would have to be *the rest*, I thought as Sandy clung to me in my kitchen by the pile of crumbs on the counter. How familiar she felt . . . like my modest mother, whose ample bosom—which I'd never seen unclothed—cushioned me as I hugged her in the airport when she left for Florida . . . like when I was a child. And Sandy's sobs ebbed to sniffles and hiccups, and I held her like a child . . . like my child.

"What should I do, Tess?" she asked, pulling away, wiping her eyes and nose on a kitchen towel.

"About what?"

"About . . . who I am."

"Who do you think you are?"

"I guess I don't know."

"Well, I know you're a sweet, caring, beautiful woman, a wonderful mother, and a dear friend who's been through a lot lately and who needs some time to sort it all out. Sandy, do you think you're gay just because you don't have orgasms with men?"

"That's part of it. But . . . well . . . it's just that I'm so much more comfortable with women."

"But you seem to like men. You're always telling me about this one and that one making passes at you, and how flattered you are."

"I know. But I never said I was comfortable with it, did I? Well, I'm not. I feel like I'm on display, and I have to smile and act flirty because that's what they like."

"So you do it because *they* like it?"

"No. Well, yes. I mean, I like to have their attention, but at the same time it makes me really uncomfortable. What I really like is coming back to Janet or you and telling about it. That has to be considered strange." She looked at me askance, embarrassed. "Tess, do you think I'm gay?"

"I think you're confused. And I'll throw one of your speeches back in your face: I think you're scared of yourself."

"I'm sorry about that, Tess. I guess I must have sounded terribly pompous."

"No. I think you were right. And you probably understood how I felt because you felt the same way. Birds of a feather, they say." I pulled a stool up to the counter. "Sit here," I ordered, uncovering a plate of perfect ladyfingers. "You're going to help me give these a manicure." I removed the white wrappings from several semisweet chocolate squares and placed the chocolate in an electric fondue pot set at low, and we watched the squares melt around the edges, eventually engulfing themselves. Then, one by one, we dipped the tips of the ladyfingers in the hot chocolate—like brown nail polish—and placed them on sheets of wax paper to cool and harden.

"You know, Tess, I really love you," she said, smoothing a sheet of wax paper on the counter.

"You do, do you?" I said noncommittally.

"You're a good friend, Tess, and I want you to know what you mean to me."

What do I mean to her? I wondered. What does she want to mean to me? What if she is gay. What does that mean? Birds of a feather . . . does that mean I'm—no. And I wrestled with my feelings of caring for my friend and worrying about how I cared for my friend, and wondering why I had to wrestle with any of it at all. Maybe I'm an unconscious gay. Unconscious, maybe. Latent. That's the word. Maybe I'm a latent gay. Maybe that's why I choose poor relationships with men. But then there's David. . . . But he's just a friend, a friend plus sex . . . and I'm still not so sure about his gender identification. Maybe he's bi. A friend plus sex? So couldn't two women have that? Is that what Sandy wants? Would I want that? Maybe I'm bi. Could I do that? Maybe . . . on a desert island . . . with no men . . . after a long, long time. But I'd rather be with David.

"What are you smiling at, Tess?"

"Me. I find myself amusing, Sandy," I said, relieved that I found myself to be, after all, straight—well, as straight as anyone really is.

"Sandy, what you have to do is find a man who loves you and you'll be able to work out the rest." Of course, I understood that I was talking from my own newly confirmed heterosexual bias, and that if Sandy was, in fact, gay, I was not being of very much help to her. But I didn't think Sandy was gay. She couldn't be. Birds of a feather and all.

"I have to tell you, Michael, it was unsettling. There I was trying to comfort my closest friend—female friend, that is . . ." I added for Michael's benefit, because I didn't want him to think that I thought Sandy was a better friend than he, even though he was a clinical friend. . . . Perhaps that's a bit austere, I corrected myself to myself: even though he was a *professional* friend, as in *paid* friend . . . No, no, Michael is a friend—just a friend, I lied to myself, deciding to debate the inequality of our friendship some other time; there were more pressing issues right now. ". . . and all these lusty thoughts, supposings, fantasies, whipped through my mind. It scared me a little."

He didn't say anything, but he looked very serious.

"And now you're scaring me. Why do you look so serious? Do you think I have any reason to believe those thoughts were to be taken seriously . . . as in maybe I have some latent homosexual feelings?" I asked, my latent insecurities twisting my stomach into a four-in-hand.

"Why are you so concerned about what I believe?" Michael asked.

"You're the expert. You know. You know who I am better than I do."

"Nobody knows you better than you do."

"So if I think something about myself, even for a moment, it could be true?"

"Do you believe that?"

"I don't know what to believe! You're supposed to help me decide what to believe, what's real and what's made up. If I knew what to believe, I wouldn't be here!"

He rolled his chair forward until he was inches from me. Leaning forward, his elbows on his knees, his head tilted up to me, he said nothing for a long moment. "Is that why you're here," he asked finally, "for me to tell you who you are and how to live?"

Yes, I thought, that's what I want. . . . Yes, make it easy for me. . . . Yes, because I don't believe what I tell myself. "No," I answered. He waited for me to finish, even though I thought I had nothing more to say . . . but I finished. "You only know what I tell you . . . one way or another. You're my Captain Marvelous Magic Mirror and Secret Decoder Ring, the one I sent for from the back of a cereal box when I was seven . . . and it never came . . . until now."

His mouth stretched slowly into a smile, and he started to rise, to move toward me.

Oh, God. He's going to hug me. He liked what I said. I learned something important and he's going to hug me for it. My reward. Reward? So why do I hate it so? Why, when I see him stop and think, when his closed-lip smile spreads slowly and he puts his hands on the arms of his chair, pushing himself up and forward, why do I squirm inside and outside and want to put my arms out, my hands up . . . why? *No, don't, don't hug me, don't,* I entreated silently.

"Why won't you let anyone hold you?" he'd once asked, sensing my discomfort. Good question. "That's not true," I had lied. I hug people, I let them hug me, in greeting . . . in farewell . . . in sex . . . in pleasure. But not in pain. A hug is a momentary melding, a sharing of body and soul. I can share my pleasure, I can share others' pain, but I can't share my pain. In pain, I wrap my arms around myself, shield myself from others' arms.

So . . . here he comes. He seeks to compliment, not console. He seeks to share with me this pleasure, not knowing that to me it's pain. So . . . he's going to hug me . . .

"No! Don't do that. Don't touch me!" I implore. Hands up, a shield against his advance, I cower in the corner of the sofa. I push away his challenging hands. I stand and push away the intruding body rising to meet me, push away the demand for reason for calm for obedience. "Go away! Leave me alone!" But he's persistent, he's determined, he'll have his hug, he'll not let me be neurotic about this, he'll make me like it, show me it's okay, it's nice, it's what I really want. Squared off, eye to eye, adrenaline finely focuses attention and I feel the dissociation, the numbing as all energy turns inward, then spews forth in one brilliant line of force, strengthening arm, contracting fingers to fist. I am steeled, I am stone; my arm alone can move and it moves on its own. Such power, such release, relief as stone fist meets flesh.

* * *

. . . So . . . I let him. I let him hug me as I put my head down—in deference? to avoid an imagined kiss? to what?—as I obediently lean forward in my seat and carefully place my limp hands on his shoulders or around him or . . . what to do with them? where to put them? while he hugs me. Why don't I just hug him back? I want to, I really want to. So why would I rather smash him in the mouth?

"Impotent rage," he said, mind-reading again.

Is that anything like entropy? I wondered, fiercely trying to organize the chaos swirling in my head. But the more I thought, the more chaotic my thoughts became. Control. I was losing control, I thought. Michael seemed to be disappearing down a long hole as he sat back down in his chair . . . his voice echoed as he quietly spoke words I didn't hear . . . and I wondered if it was I who was falling into the abyss, not Michael. I felt frustrated, angry, as adrenaline-induced blackness started to close in on me. I leaned forward and reached out to tear at the black, to grasp reality. I grabbed Michael's jacket sleeves, and from somewhere inside me a most awful demon erupted: "YOU'RE TRYING TO DRIVE ME CRAZY! I CAME TO YOU FOR HELP! YOU'RE NOT SUPPOSED TO DRIVE ME CRAZY!" I yelled. "Do you know what I want? What I REALLY want? I want to be FREE! Free to say what I feel and not give a SHIT what anybody thinks! I want to feel what I feel and not feel WRONG about it! You're so DAMN SMUG sitting in your chair, DIRECTING our conversation, CONTROLLING our relationship, PLAYING with my head. WHY am I so concerned about what YOU BELIEVE? Because you DO know more than you say. Because, although you'd like me to believe we're friends, we are, at best, UNEQUAL friends! And why do you insist on hugging me when you know—you MUST know—that it makes me uncomfortable? Are you some kind of SADIST?! If you're so GODDAMNED SMART, why can't you MAKE ME COMFORTABLE . . . so that I can hug you back and not worry about what I'm feeling, what you're feeling? Because that's what I really want to do, Michael. I want to hug you and tell you that you're the only person in the world who has ever loved me . . . who has ever REALLY loved me. AND I HATE YOU FOR IT. I HATE you because it's a kind of in vitro love, not for outside this room. And nobody—DO YOU HEAR ME?!—NOBODY outside this room knows how to do it! You're a TEASE, Michael! A FUCKING TEASE! You're SPOILING me for the REAL world!"

As I bellowed my last words, I realized the black was gone and I was standing in front of Michael in his chair. And I thought that I had blown it all, I had finally shown him what a jerk I was . . . what a spoiled, ungrateful woman—little girl—I really was. I stood before him wide-eyed, waiting for retribution . . . for him to be stern with me and tell me that I was obviously an immature, narcissistic bit of flotsam asea in a vast universe of more important matters.

"Are you finished?" he asked.

"Yes."

"That was great." And he stood up and applauded, clapping his hands slowly, nodding his head. And when he stopped clapping he stood there gazing at me, appreciating me. And I finally understood. Unequal friend? Of course not. Michael wasn't an *unequal friend,* because he wasn't a *friend*—at least, not as in *friend* who could become *friend plus sex.* I had had it all wrong. But that was only natural. After all, doesn't every little girl fall in love with her daddy? And if he loves her well enough, then she can love, and trust—which is, after all, the better part of love—another. She can become a woman . . . and an equal. I stepped forward and put my arms around him, my surrogate father, rested my head on his shoulder and held tightly for a moment, feeling not yet an equal, but very much loved.

"Am I hard to hold?" I asked David Wednesday afternoon. He had arrived around one o'clock at my request—I'd left a message on his answering machine the night before. It didn't seem to me a particularly complicated question.

"That depends," he answered.

"On what?"

"Whether you mean it literally or figuratively."

"Oh?"

"There's a school of psychology that takes after some Eastern thought . . . that to have is not necessarily to hold, but is to enjoy. For example, you see a beautiful flower, but if you pick it to hold as your own, it will die. But if you don't try to own it, you will have it to enjoy."

I must have missed something, I thought. I asked a simple question and I'm knee-deep in something I'm not sure I want to explore. "So I guess I meant literally," I said.

"Well, that's an entirely different matter," David said, smiling, moving closer to me on the sofa, putting his arms around me, holding me close. "See how easy you are?"

Yes, this did seem easy, letting David hold me. He could hold me forever . . . but it won't be forever, I thought, wondering just how long it *would* be, and I held tighter . . . and the more I thought about him letting go, the tighter I clung . . . and I was sorry I had started the conversation.

We made love right there on the sofa. It wasn't in either of our plans for the day—he was going to be late for a deposition, I was going to be late for a meeting with the owner of an expanded Cape Cod who was moving to New Mexico and wanted to sell quickly. I felt more passionate than usual, and after David left I felt more alone.

What was it that David had said about holding, figuratively speaking? Did Sandy really want to hold me, figuratively or literally? Why wouldn't my mother hold me? There were some things about this loving business that weren't going to be easy . . . even for a loving, lovable person, I thought.

"SHIT!! SHIT!! SHIT!! I'M LIVING IN A FUCKING SOAP OPERA!" I screamed aloud in the shower, while the driving hot water numbed me, the billowing steam filled my eyes and nose, puffed my skin. Then I remembered how I felt when I yelled at Michael . . . how I felt he loved it, loved me for it, because it was honest . . . because loving isn't only about sweetness and light. And I remembered feeling that no matter what I chose to say or do, Michael would love me . . . because I deserved to be loved. And anyone who tried to be unlovable to me had better WATCH OUT!

196

Stepping from the stall I caught my reflection in the mirror above the sink.

Eyes flashing, skin flushed, steam emanating from my enlarged form, I raged from my cubicle: SUPER BITCH! Ready to fight for Truth, Justice, and the Loving Way!

Stephen had called while I was meeting with the Goodmans —owners of the Cape Cod—and had left a message on my machine asking me to call him back, which I did, after I made a few early inquiries regarding a buyer for the Goodman house—Maggie Pritchert had told me weeks ago that a client of hers was looking for a Cape Cod in the area, and I had a client who was looking for a ranch home, and, after all, what is a Cape Cod but a ranch home with guest quarters?—and after I threw a salad together for dinner. It was seven-fifteen. Stephen said he wanted to talk, not on the phone; could he come over . . . for just a few minutes? "Sure," I said, totally in control.

"I just wanted you to know something, Tess," he said, sitting at the kitchen table, after some small talk, after I fixed him a tumbler of bourbon on the rocks and sat across from him with my diet Sprite. "I realize how much I've hurt you in the past," he said. He took a sip of his drink and held the cold glass to his cheek. Something gold sparked between the slightly open ends of his starched white collar, beneath the loosened knot of his navy and green silk tie. "I want you to know that the business with my trip to the Greek islands last summer taught me something. . . ."

The mention of that trip with—with The Pig tensed me, sent flares rocketing through my head. And then, as he shifted his shoulders, I could make out the shapes of tiny naked golden women, hands to feet, encircling his neck. A souvenir from Greece, no doubt, I thought. A trophy chain, I speculated, picturing myself hanging with the rest of them, promising myself I wouldn't ask him about it.

". . . I've been ashamed ever since. And you have to have noticed that I've left you alone, Tess. I've tried not to

197

intrude into your life, because I understand how awful that must have seemed to you . . . *I* must have seemed to you. And you were right. It *was* awful. *I* was awful. . . ."

The rockets fizzled.

". . . I guess I'm just here to say I'm sorry. I know I've said it before, but I wanted to say it again, to your face, with no ulterior motive . . ."

Red flags waved. Stephen did nothing without an ulterior motive, I thought.

". . . other than to let you know that I still care about you. That I want us to have something together. Whatever it is you choose, Tess. I want you to know that I haven't seen Dorothy in months. I ended it. For good this time."

"How'd she take it?" I asked, immediately wishing I could take back my words.

"Not great. But that's not important."

It shouldn't be, but it is, I thought, thinking that he had treated her as badly as he had treated me. Not that I felt sorry for her, except that I did, somewhere deep inside where, when push came to shove, I sided with my species. "Good," I said. "She doesn't deserve anything great."

He didn't respond.

"New necklace?" I asked.

"Just something I picked up in Greece," he said, further loosening his tie and opening his collar so I could have a better look.

"It's you," I sneered.

He didn't answer.

"So how are you feeling?" I changed the subject.

"Much better. The doctor thinks that I probably had a virus or something. My kidneys are in great shape. It had me worried for a while."

"What happened to your thumb?" I then asked, although I had seen the bulky bandage on his left hand when he first walked into the house.

"Nothing much. I jammed it in my desk drawer—the drawer got stuck and I was trying to shut it. I thought it was just bruised, but then it got really sore. The doctor said it's cellulitis—some kind of infection in the skin. You know,

198

because of my diabetes these little injuries can blow up," he said, smiling a crooked, scared little smile. . . .

And as he spoke, holding his hand on the table for me to observe, I saw his thumb begin to swell, straining the white bandage. Dots of red appeared as the tiny square holes of the gauze filled with blood. The dots spread out until they connected and the entire bandage was weeping red . . . and the thumb continued to swell, constricted in the middle by a thin band of adhesive . . . and the gauze grew fat and logy and suddenly Stephen cried out in pain as the thumb BLEW UP, sending blood and bits of flesh and gauze about the table, the floor, the ceiling as he screamed in pain, in agony. . . . "You DESERVED that," I barked sadistically. . . . "That's what you did to my heart!" I shrieked. . . . "Now you know what it feels like," I squealed.

. . . "It's okay, Tess. Really. I'm taking an antibiotic. It'll be fine," he said, trying to assuage the seemingly uncalled-for shock that showed on my face. He put his hand on his lap, out of sight.

I must be mad, I thought, standing and fetching a plate from the counter. But he would deserve no less, I rationalized my madness. "Some ladyfingers?" I offered, removing the plastic wrap from the plate of chocolate-dipped ladyfingers left over from Monday.

"Will they massage my insides like only you can massage my outsides?"

"Don't get cute, Stephen," I said. Very tough, Super Bitch, I complimented myself.

"Okay, okay. I was only joking . . ."

And now he's going to tell me that I can't take a joke, I thought, arming myself for rebuttal.

". . . but, sorry, Tess. I shouldn't have said that."

Disarmed.

"Listen, I really have to go. I said what I wanted to say. I hope you can find a place for me somewhere in your heart, if not your life." And he stood, scooping three ladyfingers from the plate.

"Thanks, Stephen. Take care," I said, watching him leave, feeling the emptiness of my home close in around me as he drove down the driveway, away from the house . . . away from me.

"Whatcha doing, Sandy?" I said into the phone in the family room, setting the plate of ladyfingers on the cocktail table, settling into the sofa, piling the throw pillows around me.

"I just put the kids to bed. What's wrong, Tess, you sound funny."

"I don't know. I feel . . . lonely. I feel all alone and I wanted to hear a friendly voice."

"I'd come over but I can't leave the kids."

"I know."

"Do you want to come here?"

"No."

"Why don't you call David?"

"I don't know. I have some thinking to do before I see him again."

"Sounds heavy. Do you want to talk?"

"I don't know what I want. Listen, I'll talk to you later. Okay?"

"Sure, Tess."

"Okay. Later. Bye." I hung up before she responded, and sat in the family room without turning on the television. Feeling needy, but not sure of what I needed, I picked up the phone and pushed some buttons. "Hello, Mom?"

"Tess? What's wrong, dear?"

"Nothing, Mom. Why should something have to be wrong?"

"Because you rarely call me just to say hello."

She had a point. "Well, nothing's wrong. I just called to say hi. How are you?"

"I can't complain. How are you and Stephen doing?"

Here we go again. "We're not doing. I really don't want to talk about this again!"

"All right. But you don't have to bite my head off. Are you very busy with your baking?"

"Yes. Actually, I'm getting new jobs almost every week now, and a few monthly jobs. I can't believe how this has blossomed."

"That's wonderful, dear. It's just a shame that—"

"What, Mother?"

"Well, that you're alone."

Like a knife in the heart, her words struck me down. That's why I called, Mother, because I'm alone! Because I'm lonely! You're my mother. You're supposed to make me feel better! I thought. "It's not my fault about Stephen! I tried! It didn't work! I did everything I could and it wasn't enough! So stop trying to make me feel guilty!" Super Bitch yelled through the phone, my body hot and trembling.

"But, Tess—"

"And another thing, Mom, how come you never tell me that you love me? All you ever do is criticize me, tell me what I do wrong. You even criticized me when I told you I couldn't have a baby. You never even said you were sorry . . . that you hurt for me. Didn't you know how much I was hurting? You're never there for me, Mom. Where are you? With Jamie and Daddy? They're gone! But I'm still here. I'm still here, and I need you to love me!" My God! Where did all that come from? I thought, waiting with stopped heart for a response.

Silence. There was silence on the other end of the phone. . . .

And after a moment a voice, a strange voice: "Tess? This is Mrs. Levy, your mother's neighbor. I was here watching television when you called, and all of a sudden she fell over! I'm going to call the hospital! She looks terrible, all blue and distorted, I think she had a stroke . . . or a heart attack! What did you say to her? What did you do to your poor mother? I think she's dead!"

. . . "Tess?" my mother finally said. "I'm coming up. I'm coming up on the first plane I can get tomorrow. I'm sorry, dear. I'm sorry if I didn't do things right. It's not always easy—"

"Okay, Mom. Okay. Everything's going to be fine. We'll talk. It'll be fine."

"Are you going to be all right tonight?"

"I'm okay, Mom. I just had to let you know."

"I can't talk now, dear," she said, her voice trembling with bridled emotion. "We'll talk tomorrow, when I see you."

"Okay, Mom."

"Tess . . . I love you."

"Thanks, Mom. I needed to hear that. Bye, Mom."

After I hung up I turned on the television and reached for the plate of ladyfingers. Like puffy fingers, old-lady fingers, they lay on the plate. I picked one up and ate it, savoring the softness, the sweetness mingled with the salt of my tears.

PINEAPPLE UPSIDE-DOWN CAKE

1 very ripe pineapple
1 1/2 sticks butter
1 cup dark brown sugar
1/4 cup juice from the pineapple, or canned pineapple juice
red maraschino cherries
1/2 cup milk
1 egg
1 1/2 cups flour
2 teaspoons baking powder
1/2 teaspoon salt
1/2 cup sugar

Preheat oven to 400°F.

Pare, core, and slice the pineapple into 1/2-inch slices. Over low heat, dissolve the brown sugar in 1/2 stick of butter in a 9-inch cake pan. Off the heat, add the pineapple juice. Arrange about five slices of the pineapple in a single layer on the bottom of the pan. Place a cherry in the center of each ring.

Melt one stick of butter in a saucepan. Off the heat, beat in the milk and egg. Add the milk and egg mixture to the flour, baking powder, salt, and granulated sugar in a mixing bowl and beat until smooth. Pour the batter over the pineapple slices and bake for about 35 minutes, until a toothpick comes out clean. Cool in the pan for 10 minutes. Turn the cake out, pineapple slices up, on a serving plate. Serves 8–10.

CHAPTER 11

Pineapple Upside-Down Cake

Mondays I experimented. This Monday it was pineapple upside-down cake. I had sold a colonial condominium townhouse to a middle-aged widow the month before—a sweet Italian lady who loved to bake for her three sons and their wives, and her two grandchildren, children of the middle son, the ophthalmologist. From that deal I walked away with a nice commission and three wonderful-sounding recipes. The secret of her grandmother's pineapple upside-down cake, she had told me, was fresh pineapple. "My grandmother would *never* use *canned* anything . . . unless she had canned it herself!" Mrs. Tassoni had boasted to me.

The phone rang just as I had cut into the hard, prickly skin of the pineapple, piercing my finger on one of its sharp barbs. It was Stephen.

"I have to see you, Tess. Will you be home about four?" he asked.

I sucked at my injured finger, drawing a salty drop of blood into my mouth before I answered. "I don't know, Stephen, I have a lot of errands to run," I lied, trying to decide whether or not I should see him . . . whether or not I wanted to see him.

"Please, Tess. This is very important. I promise I won't stay long. I really have to see you."

"What time did you say?"

"About four. But I could come later if it's better for you."

"No, not later," I said, thinking that if he came later it might turn into dinner, or if he came later yet it could turn into . . . I didn't want to think about it. . . . No. I don't want you here, I thought, feeling uncomfortable and conflicted, wanting to drop the phone and run out of the room, out of the house, to run away. But instead I said, "Four is okay, Stephen," and then I hung up, cutting off whatever he said in response. I returned to the deliciously sweet pineapple covered with perilous barbs.

I was glad my mother had left the morning before. After all, how would I have explained Stephen's visit after I had so painstakingly explained why we weren't seeing each other, why it was over, why it was, in fact, best that way? She had said nothing; but at least this time she didn't disagree, she didn't criticize. As I pared and cored the pineapple, I recalled my mother's weekend visit and felt pleased with myself. She had come. She had cried and told me she loved me, that I was the most important thing in her life. She also told me how hard it had been being a widow . . . how hard it is to lose a child . . . how sorry she was for me that I had no children, that she had no grandchildren. I saw how different she and I were, and that neither of us would ever be what the other wished. But we reached an understanding—that we were very different, but that the love between a mother and daughter transcends differences. And that was enough for now. It had been a good visit.

"Something smells good," Stephen said when he stepped through the front door. "What is it?"

"Pineapple. I tried a pineapple upside-down cake this afternoon. An experiment. I think it's a winner," I answered, leading him through the living room into the kitchen.

"I'm leaving my practice, Tess," Stephen blurted out, before he sat down, before he even took off his jacket. He looked awful. He'd found out about David and me! I thought. A blush of guilt burned my face.

"You're what?" I asked, already formulating excuses and apologies in my head. But I was wrong. It had nothing to do with me. It had nothing to do with David.

"I'm in a lot of trouble, Tess. I'm probably going to be disbarred."

"I don't understand." *David never said a word to me! I thought, feeling betrayed.*

"Of course you don't. You don't know about any of this. Nobody does."

"Doesn't David know?" I asked selfishly.

"No."

"Stephen, what's it all about? Sit down. I'll get you some coffee . . . or would you rather have a drink? Tell me what's happening."

Stephen took off his light gray suit jacket, hung it on the back of a kitchen chair, loosened his yellow-and-gray-striped tie, and sat at the head of the table. "Coffee would be good," he said, slumping in the chair, staring at his hands tightly clasped on the table in front of him. "I don't know how all this happened, Tess."

"How all what happened?" I asked as I measured coffee into the filter, filled the reservoir of the coffee maker with water, and pulled two mugs from the cupboard . . . trying to stay busy, to avoid having to sit near him, to look into his eyes.

He began to talk, and his story sounded like page one of the *Philadelphia Inquirer:* ATTORNEY INVADES TRUSTS— *Investigation Reveals Multimillion-Dollar Embezzlement— Forty-year-old Charter Acres attorney Stephen Fineman has been indicted for invading clients' trust fund accounts in amounts totaling more than two and a half million dollars, according to Montgomery County district attorney Harold Bradford. If found guilty, Fineman could face disbarment, fines, and up to fifteen years in prison. . . .*

As I listened, I found it difficult to reconcile the illusion of Stephen with the reality of Stephen for two reasons: his need for the illusion . . . and mine. Always immaculately attired in a custom-made suit, silk tie, and shined shoes, in the eyes of his friends and business associates Stephen appeared the

206

epitome of success. Listening to him talk about his maneuvering and manipulating of funds, one could take Stephen Fineman for the Machiavelli of venture capitalism. Successfully building tremendous gross returns, fabulous investment potential, Stephen seemed to enjoy unassailable business acumen. But beneath the panoply of sartorial splendor and slick self-assurance, Stephen Fineman was no more than a gambler, and beneath the solid facade of fancy figures, his investment fortress was no more than a house of cards.

It had started innocently enough, Stephen recounted. He had borrowed a little from one trust to cover the losses of another—and his personal accounts—when things hadn't moved as quickly as he had calculated. And then some deals went sour, and Stephen's *borrowing*, which was really *stealing*, increased to cover new quick-profit deals made under the unrelenting pressure of debt . . . and those deals had also soured. "I had everything planned. It was going so well. And then it all fell apart." With this, his fingers unmeshed and his hands fell to the table palms up, like small dead creatures.

I felt sorry for him. "I guess it's hard to see a bad investment coming," I offered.

But his ego got in the way. "They weren't bad investments! I know a bad investment when I see one," he defended himself.

"Well, they must have been risky."

"Not really. You see, there's liabilities, and there's contingent liabilities," he started. This was to be a lecture of business buzzwords intended to excuse, to obfuscate.

I sat down next to him and listened attentively for a couple of minutes as he explained contingent liabilities, debt service, cash flow. "Okay, Stephen, okay. Now talk to me about the bottom line," I said, growing impatient. "The bottom line is one business term I understand completely. And if I understand anything you're telling me, the bottom line is that you stole a lot of money from your clients and you can't return it. So you might go to jail."

"I could lose everything I have, Tess. Everything."

There was a time when I felt Stephen could figure a way out of any kind of mess, but before me now was a defeated man. I got up and poured coffee into the mugs on the counter. I put two teaspoons of sugar in mine and one teaspoon of sugar in his, the way I had done hundreds of mornings, and then sat at the table again, placing the steaming mugs before us. "Do you want a piece of cake?" I asked, as if I were speaking to a hurt child. And the child in him nodded an assent. I got up again, cut into the still warm cake sitting on the center island counter, and slid a slice onto a plate along with a fork. As I set it before Stephen, I began to wonder what he wanted from me. As always, I made it easy for him. "Stephen, can I help?"

"I don't know, Tess."

Of course you do, I thought.

"I want to get this all settled. I want to start over again. I want another chance," he said forlornly.

With business? With me? "I don't have the kind of money you need, Stephen."

"No, Tess. Honest—I didn't come for money. I know you don't have it. But there may be something you can do . . . for both of us."

For both of us? The only thing I could do for both of us is shoot him, I thought, feeling immediately guilty for the rearing up of such unsympathetic feelings. "For *both* of us, Stephen? I didn't know I was involved in this," I said.

"You're not. Well, not really . . ." Something in his face changed. I could almost hear the *click, click, click* of a calculator, the *whirrr* of a computer emanate from his being. A hard glaze slipped over his eyes as he reached across the kitchen table for my hand. "I want to put my property into your hands for safekeeping. For us."

He got my attention. "What do you mean?"

"When the shit hits the fan, they're going to come after everything I have. Tess, I've managed to put away some cash and bonds over the years, and I need you to keep it safe for me."

"Safe?"

"I want you to hold it for me . . . you know . . . until this whole legal mess is over."

Of course I knew. "Do you mean *hide* it for you? Can we really do that?" I questioned with a carefully executed note of naiveté, while my heart picked up tempo and blood coursed through my veins, through my brain, waking the sleeping shrew within.

"Of course. It's no big deal. I had it in my bank box; now I want you to keep it in yours."

"How big a deal is it, Stephen?"

"About a hundred thousand in cash and . . . uh . . . two million in bonds."

I softened to his words, but I didn't miss that although he could be facing disbarment, even jail, what was foremost in his mind was his money. "That's a *very* big deal, Stephen," I said, allowing my eyes to grow wide.

He put his other hand on my hand and tried to let his face go liquid, resulting in an insipid grimace. "I need you to help me, Tess. See me through this and I'll be yours forever. I'll be everything you've ever wanted me to be."

Ah. A hook was baited. The question was, whose hook, whose bait, who would bite?

Carefully I pulled. "I don't know, Stephen."

"Tess, please. Anything. Ask me anything and I'll do it. Whatever you want me to do . . . any way you want me to do it . . . I trust you with my life. Please, just promise you'll think about it."

"I'll think about it."

I didn't miss the barest hint of a smug expression that animated his pasty face. He thought he had won, and he pulled the plate holding the slice of cake toward him, picked up the fork, and cut into the sticky sweet. It looked good. It looked right. Stephen swallowed it in seconds. "Good, Tess. Very good."

Very good indeed.

"I saw Stephen last night."

"Last night? You saw him last night?" Michael prompted.

"He called yesterday morning to ask if he could come over and I said yes. I didn't want to see him, but I couldn't say no."

"You didn't want to see him?"

"Well, I guess I did want to see him or I wouldn't have said yes, but I didn't *want* to want to see him."

"That's perfectly understandable."

"Okay. I did want to see him, but I didn't want him to know that I wanted to see him."

"So you said yes so he'd think you didn't want to see him."

"Stop twisting everything I say!"

"I'm sorry. I'm just trying to get this straight."

"I saw him last night and listened to him complain about his financial problems and his plea for help. I said I'd think about it. And then I slept with him."

"Oh! So you fucked him."

"We made love."

"It was okay?"

"It was okay. I hate Stephen but I love his body. And I told him that."

"You told him what?"

"Well, I kicked him out in the middle of the night. 'So you used my body and now you're tossing me out,' he said. But I told him, without a bit of pretense, that he was right. That I never had a problem with his body. I loved his body; I hated him."

"That's great," Michael stroked, "that's great. So what kind of help did he ask for?"

"Well, it started with business—he wants me to help him save his fortune." And I related the details to Michael.

"Are you going to help him?"

"I don't know. I don't want to help him. I don't want to get involved. But I thought that if I could help myself, then maybe—"

"Great! Turn it around on him! Get his money and send him to jail! Con the con man! How could you do it?"

"Michael! That's horrible!"

"Oh. You didn't think about it that way. I see."

"I didn't say I didn't think about it. In fact, as we sat talking, I had it all figured out in my head . . . just as you said. But I'm not sure I could do anything like that. It's not in me. Besides, he's too smart to let anyone get the best of him. I'm sure he has this all mapped out. And anyway, I don't want his money. I don't want anything from him."

"Nothing at all. That's why you keep seeing him."

I sighed. "Well, that's a little harder to sort out."

"How's that?"

And I told Michael about the rest of the evening—well, I gave him the gist of it while rerunning *all* of it in my head. "After he finished the cake, he came on with the old seduction act," I started.

"I miss you, Tess," he said, his face collapsing into the soft folds of self-pity. "I think about you all the time. I think about how you look, how you feel, how you taste."

How I taste? Stephen's shrink must be writing his material, I thought—*if* he's seeing a shrink. Then again, he probably got it from some pop-psychology book. In any case, I didn't like his newfound sensitivity. It seemed insensitive.

"Don't you miss me at all?" he asked, rising from his chair and stepping behind mine.

Yes, I wanted to say. Yes, I miss fucking you, I miss your body curled around mine at night, I miss your mouth, your tongue, I miss your skin. "No," I railed, "I don't miss your lies, your disrespect, your lack of consideration, of compassion. . . ." My denial grew in intensity, usurping my sense of control, my embarrassment at his ill-fitting words, ending in a scream of pain. ". . . No, I don't miss you! I hate you!"

". . . with the usual pleas for forgiveness . . ."

"Don't say you hate me, Tess. Don't. I want to love you. I want to make it all right again."

"It was never all right."

. . and I folded . . ."

Bending over me, he wrapped his arms around my shoulders and kissed my neck. I felt the rush, the stirring, the quickening of my blood. My head fell back and he kissed me, upside-down. He ran his tongue along my lips until they parted, allowed him in. Tears spilled from my eyes down the sides of my face, little whimpering sounds escaped from my throat as he licked the tears from my cheek.

. . and we made love . . ."

We hadn't made love in almost a year. And unlike that singular episode last summer—that singularly unsatisfying episode—making love to Stephen this time was wonderfully familiar, exquisitely heated by his absence. I wanted to stuff him inside me and keep him there, where he could be a part of me, where he could only pleasure, not hurt, me. After, we fell into the perfect sleep of sated sexual desire. Waking around three to the heat of Stephen's body, the pressures of his chin in my neck, his leg on my leg, I felt like a cradled babe, unaware of the cold hard world to be met . . . eventually. Holding back reality, I concentrated on pacing my breathing with Stephen's to avoid the warmed sour puffs of night breath emitted by his rhythmic gaspy exhalations. I didn't want to reposition myself; I wanted to stay wrapped in Stephen's body. The heat of it, the weight of it, the presence of it comforted me. How to keep his body there and yet not have to face him in the morning? How to avoid reality? These were the burning issues of the night.

". . . and I woke up about three in the morning. That's when I told him that I didn't want him there anymore."

"So he left?"

"Yes."

"And then?"

"And then I fell asleep. . . ."

212

I fell asleep quickly after he was gone, but not before I recalled our lovemaking . . . and then our evening's conversation. We had made love, but he wasn't fucked . . . not yet.

"Why are you looking at me so funny?" I asked Michael, whose eyes seemed to be boring through mine as he tapped the index fingers of his folded hands against his bottom lip.

He loosened up and smiled. "Why do I always have the feeling there's a whole lot going on in your head that you choose not to share with me? That's just a feeling I get . . . it may not be true at all. I'm not always very accurate about these things," he said.

Bullshit, I thought. "Bullshit," I said.

"I just thought I'd ask."

I held out for a short time and attempted to stare him down. When he allowed me to win, I decided to be honest. "I guess I do think a lot—little scenarios, mostly rememberings, nothing that would interest you." Well, at least partially honest.

"I'm sure you're right; I wouldn't be interested in what you're thinking."

"Well, maybe some of it would interest you, but I guess I just can't tell you everything. Not yet."

"Not yet. Well, it's probably not very important," he said with a wave of his hand.

We both fell silent. And then a need to understand welled up within me. "Michael, do you actually want me to tell you everything? As in *everything?* As in how we made love, how we slept? That's not really important, is it?"

"Only to you, Tess. What's important to me is how what happens between you and Stephen makes you feel, how you react. What's important to me is that *you* understand what you're feeling when you experience something and when you rerun these scenarios through your head."

"As I said, I love Stephen's body, but I don't like Stephen. Is that strange?"

"Maybe what you have to understand is what it is about Stephen's body that you feel you love, and what needs you have that his body satisfies," he answered, ignoring my question about being strange.

"You certainly know how to ground things, don't you?"

"It's hard to catch a bird on the wing."

"What are you into? Eastern mysticism?"

He took my hand between his own. "Whatever it takes to help you understand whatever it is you have to understand." And then he smiled at me until I smiled.

The week had been a tumultuous one: five showings of a sprawling, five-bedroom, Spanish-style ranch home on Tuesday and Wednesday, which amounted to a lot of admiration but no sale. Then, of course, there was Stephen's Monday visit, and Michael on Tuesday, which had left me thoughtful. But I couldn't be bothered with mind-benders, I had a lot of work to do if I was going to finish filling the order for the evening's meeting of Coffee, Cake, and Criticism, the book club that met the third Thursday of the month at the library. I had already made three dozen chocolate chip cookies early in the morning. Last week I had made and frozen one dozen mini-cheesecakes that had to be filled with fruit. And I had to make a pineapple upside-down cake. I had cut holes in the tops of the cheesecakes and was filling them with blueberry and cherry topping when the phone rang. "Hello."

"Tess? It's me. . . ." It was Janet. ". . . I had to call. I'm in the middle of clients, but I'll be off for lunch in about an hour. You going to be home? I've got something to tell you."

"What?"

"Not now. Wait till I see you. Are you going to be home?"

"All day. What is it?"

"Not now! See you a little after noon."

At twelve-ten Janet came bursting through the door. "I don't have a lot of time. I have to stop at the bank for Terry before I go back to the office. How about some coffee?" she said, heading for the pot.

"Now, what's the important news? You finally got a court date, right?" I asked, setting out a plate of cheese, crackers, and raw veggies I had put together for our lunch after making the batter for the cake.

"Bless you. I'm starved!" she said. "And, yes, David said we're set for the second week in May. Absolutely for sure this time. But that's not my news."

Once we sat at the kitchen table, Janet spilled. "Well, Tess, do you know Angel Santos, from Harold Bradford's office? You know, the district attorney? Well, Angel was in our office this morning, and while we were waiting for her X-rays she told me about the break-in, and I had to call you immediately—"

"What break-in? I don't know what you're talking about. No one broke in here."

"No, no, not at your house—at Stephen's."

"Stephen's? Start over, Janet, I don't know anything about this."

"No. Of course you don't. God, I'm not doing this well at all."

"You're not doing WHAT well?!"

And Janet told me the bare bones of a story . . . about how the police had answered a security alert at Stephen's townhouse Sunday afternoon . . . about an unidentified witness outside the house who told the police of sounds of violence coming from the second floor of the house, and then disappeared . . . about the police breaking in and finding Stephen in the bedroom, not in danger, but in flagrante delicto. "And, Tess, you'll never guess who was with him—that awful Dorothy Oberman!"

DOROTHY! HE WAS WITH DOROTHY! I couldn't believe my ears. I barely heard Janet's editorial comments about Stephen's lack of taste . . . Dorothy's lack of scruples . . . their combined lack of class and overabundance of brass. "Janet," I broke in as I felt myself breaking down, "Stephen was just here on Monday. I . . . we slept together—"

"The man is OUTRAGEOUS, Tess! I can't understand why you continue to be involved with him. Get a divorce and get it over with! It's not going to get any better," she finished gently, compassionately.

We fiercely munched our meager repast to the last of it without further conversation; the loud crunch of celery, cauliflower, and crackers somehow sufficed. Besides, what more could be said? The details of the break-in were known only to those who had been there.

Janet left at twelve thirty-five, never imagining for a moment the complexity of The Details as they'd actually happened. But before the day was out, I would learn all The Details from one who had been there, and that night they would keep me awake when I played them back like a bad movie in the theater of my imagination.

MGM PRESENTS

"FATAL DETAILS"

Based on a true story
Color by RealityColor, Inc.
Starring:
Stephen "The Prick" Fineman
Dorothy "The Pig" Oberman
and featuring:
!!Why, The Little Traaamp!!
(and we don't mean Charlie Chaplin)

It was not a dark and stormy night. It was four o'clock on a cold, damp Sunday that was fading away like a drab watercolor painting left out in the rain. Stephen turned in bed onto his left side and curved his body, still heated from lovemaking, around the back of his lover and cupped his hand around her right breast. She smiled to herself as he kissed the nape of her neck, because she knew they would make love again soon—as soon as his body dozed off the postcoital fatigue. She waited, half awake, half dreaming, anticipating the shared benefits of his remarkable recuperative abilities.

Outside, a cream-colored Ford sedan coasted by Stephen's townhouse, stopping for a moment to observe the forest green Volvo station wagon in the driveway. The Ford disappeared around the corner, and then returned, parking in front of the house. The driver appeared agitated, and sat for a time with the motor off, staring at the house before lighting a cigarette.

A warm puff of air smelling of sex escaped from beneath the light bed covers past Stephen's nose as he shifted his body to relieve the pressure on his left shoulder. Aware of his erection, he pressed into the smooth white buttocks in front of him and massaged the breast in his hand. The lady whimpered soft sounds of acquiescence. She turned to him, and their lips and tongues met in an erotic commingling of tastes and smells. Impassioned, they emitted simultaneous moans of gratitude for each other's presence. Together they felt the electric tingle of nerve ends, the heat of skin . . . they heard the soft lapping of water in the mattress beneath them . . . the sudden explosion of sirens—SIRENS! The security alarm! Footsteps on the stairs . . . running up the stairs. The entangled couple bolted upright, pulling the covers up to their chins, searching each other's startled faces for explanation.

Dorothy Oberman burst through the bedroom door, her bright red mane flaring wildly from its dark roots, her painted eyebrows arching high above blackly outlined eyes that appeared as though they were going to pop out and fall upon the bed for witnessing the treachery of the ever-faithless lover. But it was not Stephen she addressed in a shriek of unimaginable dimension. "BITCH! WHORE! Get out of MY BED!" she hurled at Stephen's guest from the foot of the bed, shaking a small pudgy hand that clutched the house key Stephen had given her—for *his* convenience, not *hers:* he had *not* given her the code for the alarm. With her other hand she snatched down the bed covers, exposing the abashed couple, who now shrank from each other. Stephen turned and fumbled with the alarm panel on the wall behind the bed until the siren was quieted, while the nude woman, tight-lipped and narrow-eyed, slipped from the bed. But she did not try to cover herself, did not attempt to escape her attacker's scrutiny. *Eat your heart out, Pig!* she thought to herself, walking defiantly to the mirrored dressing room beyond Dorothy, displaying, with a slow, careful gait, her admirably perky breasts and enviably cheeky ass.

"WHORE! You goddamned CUNT!" Dorothy called after her. "Don't you ever come here again or I'll RIP your face off! You leave MY man alone or I'll cut your TITS off!" Her words spewed forth with beads of foamy spittle. When she turned again to Stephen flattened against the bed, he saw tears of fury drag a trail of black mascara down her inflamed, trembling jowls. Stephen thought he had never seen a woman as ugly as Dorothy was just then, and yet it was she his eyes were fixed upon, not the mirrored image of the silky, trim figure across the room. He was fascinated by Dorothy's extravagance of emotion, her coarseness of tongue; he was excited by her overabundant form quivering with rage. And as the dressing-room mirrors reflected myriad beauties hastily donning clothes, Stephen only had eyes for the Harpy before him who was slowly, outrageously disrobing, exposing quarterback shoulders turned soft . . . pendulous, blue-veined breasts . . . a pouch of striated abdominal flesh bisected by a deep, brownish scar running from navel to evidential black triangle . . . thick thighs dimpled with cellulite . . . knees like swollen faces. She stood naked in front of the bed until her rival emerged from the maze of mirrors. The clothed figure walked past Dorothy and Stephen, flashing a contemptuous look of incredulity at them both. Stephen watched as she silently left the room; he listened with a sense of relief as she descended the stairs and exited through the front door. He then turned his attention back to the perspiring body approaching him. Saying not a word, Dorothy got into the bed, causing Stephen to bob up and down ridiculously as her weight created great waves in the water mattress. Stephen allowed her to envelop him in an embrace, to stroke his penis to an erection that disappeared into the vast cleft of her sex when she climbed atop him.

After closing Stephen's front door behind her, the *other* other woman paused below the open bedroom window to give her inner chaos and outer composure a chance to equalize. She was having a hard enough time believing the scene her eyes had just witnessed, and hearing the faint sounds of passion escaping from the room above took her yet another step further from how she thought reality should feel. And when the police showed up in answer to the alarm, the woman shamelessly fell upon the two officers with a quick but vivid tale of sounds of violence coming from the upstairs window of Stephen's house. She left them breaking through the front door. This is like being in a Woody Allen movie, she thought, glimpsing the policemen's forceful entry into the house through the rearview mirror of her Volvo just before she turned the corner. And, as with Woody Allen's movies, she wasn't sure if it was comedy or tragedy.

But I hadn't *yet* learned The Details when I burst into tears soon after Janet left my house. What she had told me was enough to keep me in tears as I boxed the cooled cookies, as I wiped the counter, getting ready to put the pineapple cake together. Dorothy again, I thought. What kept him going back to her? What did she have that I— No. I wouldn't let myself think like that. He'll pay for this. He'll pay for my pain. I remembered Monday night . . . first the soft loving, then the hard facts. He'll get his, I thought . . . and I'll get mine. I reached for the ripe pineapple next to the sink, brought it to the counter, and began twisting off its serrated top when I suddenly realized that I hadn't spoken to Sandy all week. Surely Sandy "You Heard It Here First" Solomon must have heard about The Break-in. And she hadn't called me! It wasn't like her to try to spare me the details. So I put the pineapple down, wiped my hands, picked up the receiver, and punched in Sandy's number.

"Hellooo!"

"Sandy. Did you hear about Stephen's little fiasco?" I blurted.

"God, yes, Tess. I was afraid to call you. You going to be home for a while? I'll come over."

Sandy walked in as I finished cutting the pineapple into rings. "Hi, stranger," I said.

"God. I'm sooo sorry, Tess. How did you find out? I should have told you. But there's a little more to this than you've already heard."

"How much more?"

"Well, this is kind of haaard," she said, taking off her forest green parachute-silk bomber jacket, laying it on a kitchen chair.

"Sounds like coffee time," I said, pushing to one end of the counter a bowl of cake batter, the cutting board full of pineapple, and the large, buttered pan. Sandy settled on a stool at the other end of the counter and I joined her with mugs of coffee. She said nothing as I got up to get milk from the refrigerator for her coffee and, while I was at it, retrieved the jar of maraschino cherries I would need for the cake. "Okay, so talk to me," I said, stirring sugar into my coffee.

"I don't really know how to say this. . . . You've been such a great friend and all. . . ."

I couldn't imagine what was about to come out of her mouth, but judging from her reddened face and downcast eyes, it was obviously something she didn't want to say, and probably something I didn't want to hear. So I consciously relaxed my shoulders and back and concentrated on listening to Sandy with my stomach, not my heart or head—a technique for unemotional, nonreactive listening I had read about years ago in some pop-psychology article.

But nothing I could have done would have prepared me for ". . . I've been in touch with Stephen, Tess."

Every organ reacted: My head exploded; my stomach heaved; my heart stopped; my spleen stewed; my gall bladder burned. I pictured myself starring in *The Exorcist*— my head spinning around and green guts spewing from my mouth. "You what?" I queried quietly, feigning calm, looking her straight in her long, black, lowered lashes.

"Oh, I only saw him a couple of times. It wasn't anything, really . . . but—"

"But why? What possessed you? . . . How? . . . I'm really at a loss, Sandy. Maybe you better start from the beginning," I said, bewildered, befuddled, deflated, as the old picture of Stephen and Sandy embracing in my kitchen developed in my head like a Polaroid photo.

She began, "Actually . . . remember one night, a few years ago, Charlie and I were here for dinner? The night Charlie got called to the hospital just as we were sitting down to eat? It was during a teeerrible thunderstorm? Well, you had called us into the dining room, and I walked through the kitchen, where Stephen was picking at something from a dish on the counter. And as I walked by him, we hugged. . . ."

The EMBRACE! So I was right! It was special.

". . . I don't know why, we just turned to each other and hugged. It was like the whole world disappeared, Tess. I don't know how else to explain it to you. Anyway, for years I guess I coveted him a little. And I felt the attraction was mutual . . . you know."

No, I didn't know, I didn't want to know.

". . . But, of course, you're my best friend, Tess . . ."

And how do you treat your enemies, dear Friend!

". . . and I neeever, eeever thought of cheating with Stephen . . . until you two separated. . . ."

And THEN? Bitch!

". . . Even then it was only a fantasy, because, well, I was still married to Charlie, and I was seeing George. . . ."

And God knows who else was turning through your revolving bedroom door!

". . . And then after the accident . . . you know, when Charlie and . . . well, after the accident, Stephen came to see me . . ."

BITCH! You never told me that, I thought as I stood up in a fit of nervous energy, pulled my ingredients before me, and began arranging the pineapple rings and cherries in the bottom of the cake pan.

". . . and he was so kind, and so sensitive," Sandy continued, ignoring—maybe understanding—my sudden frenzy of activity. "Nothing happened, Tess. Honest. He just told me he would be there for me if I needed an ear, a shoulder. . . ."

A PRICK?!

221

". . . Tess, it's not that I didn't believe you when you told me all those things about Stephen; it's just that I thought, well, I guess I thought maybe he would feel less threatened with me—I mean, you're so strong and all. . . ."

You thought, BITCH, that he lusted after your gorgeous little body.

". . . And then . . . well, you know how I was feeling about myself? And then you told me how good in bed you and Stephen were? So I started to think about how, if he was so good for you, maybe he'd be good for me. . . . After all, you weren't living with him anymore . . . and you had David . . ."

I stared at Sandy, dumbfounded.

". . . so I called him."

"YOU called STEPHEN! What could you possibly have said, Sandy?"

"Don't be so naive, Tess," she said.

I felt the chill of her contempt-born-of-guilt pour over me. BITCH! SLUT! I could have strangled her—twisted her gorgeous little head off, like the top of a pineapple. . . .

Instead, I picked up the bowl of thick batter and dumped it over her head. I watched the yellow mud coat her silky black hair, slowly spread over the grossly padded shoulders of her scarlet cotton-silk-blend sweater, and drip off the tips of her prized boobs. Her hands went up in a startle reflex and her mouth dropped open long enough for me to stuff a maraschino cherry in it. She wiped batter from her eyes.

. . . She wiped tears from her eyes as my tears dripped into the bowl of batter I was mixing furiously with a wire whisk. "How *could* you, Sandy."

"Tess, I didn't mean to hurt you. You have to understand. I didn't think you'd care . . . with David in the picture, and everything. I only did it once, Tess. Hooonest. And you were right about him, and I got what I deserved—I mean, you can't imagine the shock . . . Dorothy just breaking in on us and the alarm blaring away—"

222

SANDY! HE WAS WITH SANDY! Sandy was the *other* other woman, the police's unidentified witness! I felt the blood drain from my head, my heart—which stopped midbeat—my entrails. I thought if I looked down at my bare feet I'd see all my blood draining out of my toes like little spigots.

"You were there! It was YOU?"

That's when she told me *all* The Details. . . .

I was stunned . . . too stunned to react.

". . . You were sooo right, Tess, the man's an animal, and he's still screwing around with that old bag! I mean I reeeally can't understand it."

I reacted. "YOU can't understand it!" I erupted.

"It was terrible for me, Tess. You just can't imaaagine . . . the man is an absolute aaanimal!"

"And YOU, my dear, are a perfect ASSHOLE! Of course you don't understand. You're a self-centered, conceited little SNOT who doesn't have a whit of understanding or compassion for anyone else!"

Now it was Sandy's turn to blanch. Actually, we both blanched. She couldn't believe I had said what I said—and neither could I. Sandy started to cry and apologize to an embarrassing degree—embarrassing to me, that is, until I began to believe that she was more hurt than I, conceding to myself that, in fact, I was trying to break away from Stephen . . . that I did have David . . . that Sandy was still recovering from a devastating series of events . . . that she was vulnerable, and Stephen was a shit . . . and that they both got what they deserved in the end . . . and that Dorothy The Pig had got a taste of what she deserved into the bargain.

"Okay, okay, Sandy. Stop crying. I want you to know that it hurts a lot to know that my best friend would gamble with our friendship, with my feelings. But I'll forgive you . . . this time," I said, turning back to my cake batter.

"Oh, Tess. I promise. I'll never, ever do anything to hurt you again."

"So. Tell me . . . did your little scheme work?" I probed coolly, undeniably curious.

"Did it—? OH! Did it *work.* Well . . . yes," she answered in a small voice.

"As they say, every cloud has a silver lining," I said, supporting my friend who was still a friend but not the same friend—or perhaps I was not the same friend.

"Now, it didn't happen right away," she began spilling all in the wake of forgiveness. "I mean, not the first time we did it, but the third time—"

"The THIRD time!"

"Are you sure you want to hear this?"

"Every word."

"Well, by the third time I was so hot . . . and he was so insistent that I be satisfied . . . he tried everything . . . I mean *eeeverything.* And I just did . . . well, not *just,* but with a little concentration I did. It was sooo exciting, Tess. And then when I was waiting for him to start again—"

"AGAIN?"

"Well, then the sirens started—"

"STOP! I don't want to hear that part again. Just tell me how you had the nerve to lie to the police that it sounded like someone was being killed up there? That was brilliant!"

"I don't know, Tess. But I was sooo angry that when the police pulled up, I didn't even stop to think. I just ran up to them and said it!"

"Incredible, Sandy. I didn't think you had it in you," I said, beginning to understand that there was a lot in Sandy that I had missed.

"I didn't think I had it in me, either. I mean—"

"I understand what you mean. Well, maybe some more good will come of this," I said, already rehearsing in my mind what I was going to do as soon as Sandy left.

"I see you've still got tooons of work to do, Tess, so I'll get out of your way. Talk to you later," she said. "Okay?" she added with a touch of uncertainty as she walked toward the back door.

"Sure, Sandy. Talk to you later."

* * *

"Stephen, it's Tess," I murmured sweetly into the phone after Sandy was gone, after my cake was finished, after I had settled into a comfortable corner of my sofa in the family room. "I've thought about what you said and I decided to help you." I turned my eyes upward as I uttered these deceptive words, savoring every syllable that rolled off my splendidly forked tongue. "Why don't you come over tonight and we'll talk about it."

"I'll be there, Tess!" he said, elated, ecstatic, inside-out with delight.

Hanging up the phone, I pictured him rubbing his hands together, thinking that he had won. And then I headed for my shower; it was Super Bitch that Stephen was going to have to deal with tonight. Stephen, I thought as I stepped into the steamy cubicle, *now* you're going to get fucked! Yes. Not only pineapple cake would be upside-down when the steam cleared.

DEVIL'S FOOD CUPCAKES

Cake

1 3/4 cups sifted cake flour
1 1/2 cups sugar
1/3 cup cocoa
1 1/4 teaspoons baking soda
1 teaspoon salt
1/2 cup shortening
1 cup milk
2 eggs
1 teaspoon vanilla extract

Preheat oven to 350°F. Line cupcake pans with paper cups.

Sift flour, sugar, cocoa, baking soda, and salt together into large bowl. Blend in shortening and 2/3 cup of the milk. Beat 2 minutes at medium speed. Add the rest of the milk, the eggs, and vanilla, and beat 2 more minutes. Fill cups about two-thirds full and bake about 20 minutes on lower shelf, until centers rebound to the touch.

Remove cups from pans and cool on a rack. Makes 24 cupcakes.

Frosting

2 one-ounce semisweet chocolate squares
1/2 teaspoon vanilla extract
6 tablespoons unsalted butter

Melt the chocolate with the vanilla in the top of a double boiler. Off the heat, beat in the butter, a little at a time. Then place the top of the double boiler into a pan of cold water and beat the chocolate mixture until it is cool and creamy. Spread on top of cupcakes.

CHAPTER 12

Devil's Food Cupcakes

All the windows in my house were open, as were the sliding glass patio doors in the family room and kitchen, on the first Thursday of May, which was also the first warm day of spring, a season that was slow in coming this year. Trees were still greening; the usual brilliant explosion of spring flowers was, instead, a slow drizzle of color. Well, it's finally warming up, I thought. Sooner or later we late bloomers all warm up and take off. I was blending shortening, milk, flour, cocoa, and sugar in the mixer, which would soon emerge from the oven as devil's food cupcakes for Lisa Gross's seven-year-old daughter, Alison, to take to school for her birthday party on Friday. Lisa had ordered a traditional birthday cake with sugary white icing and pink and blue flowers, but Alison had other ideas. It would be devil cakes—as she called them—or nothing, and they were to be frosted with chocolate fudge, she informed her mother. And she wanted her name on each one . . . just Ali, not Alison . . . in script, in shocking pink with a silver candy dot over the i.

"I'm so sorry, Tess," Lisa had said to me over the phone late Wednesday afternoon when she called to change her order from boring birthday cake to daring devil cakes as per her daughter's instructions.

"No problem, Lisa. You tell Ali that she made a very good

227

choice, and a birthday girl should always have her choices," I said.

All girls should have their choices, and not only on their birthdays, I thought, watching the batter become thick and smooth, remembering what my mother had said to me when I told her Stephen and I were separating . . . that I had asked him to leave . . . that women these days have options. "You're a married woman," she had said, "you have obligations. YOU HAVE NO OPTIONS!"—a dictum that had left me paralyzed for days. But I had remained steadfast. Stephen left, and I found out that options beget options, that life is not the straight road my mother believed it to be, but a series of forking paths requiring an endless series of choices. Lulled by the slowly turning bowl, I reviewed the events of the past week surrounding my most recent choice. There was Stephen's visit last Thursday evening to discuss, in strictest confidence, our pact . . . the long weekend filled with ambivalence about The Pact and such considerations as my promise to Stephen that I'd say nothing about it to anyone . . . my Tuesday meeting with Michael, when I told him, in strictest confidence, of The Pact, and agreed to run everything by an attorney to make sure I couldn't get hurt . . . my Wednesday evening visit with Alan Garfield, Millie's attorney husband, who discussed The Pact with me, off the record, in strictest confidence.

Later, David stopped in, unexpectedly, in time to sample a cupcake still warm from the oven. He came to tell me, in strictest confidence, that Stephen was leaving the office and his practice, and that he was going to be indicted for embezzlement. I, in turn, told David that I had known for over a week but that I felt I couldn't say anything . . . because Stephen had taken me into his confidence. David, looking hurt, said something about my skewed sense of loyalty, and I pouted, feeling guilty, guiltier than if I had broken my promise to Stephen. So, in strictest confidence, I spilled, telling him all about The Pact. And when he expressed concern for my welfare, I told him about my visit with Alan, and he said that I should have come to him—had

228

I forgotten that he was a lawyer, too? When I didn't answer, he said, "I'm trying to understand, Tess. You aren't easy."

That was odd. I thought I was very easy.

Stephen had been surprisingly easy, I related to Janet, in strictest confidence, over tea and imperfect devil cakes the following night, explaining The Pact to her. "Stephen has some cash and a fortune in unregistered bearer bonds that he wants me to keep for him in a bank box, in my name," I said.

"You're kidding! Why would he do that?"

"He said he can't trust anyone else."

"But why would he have to involve anyone else? He's a smart man; he could figure out some way to do it himself. This doesn't make sense, Tess."

"Well, I think it's his way of maintaining a connection with me through this awful mess. And my cooperation won't go unrewarded," I added.

"Thank you, Dr. Faust. Did you consider that maybe he's involving you so he can *blackmail* you into taking him back, or—God, Tess, this sounds really awful—maybe he's trying to corrupt you so you'll be as bad as he is, and—"

"And then I'll *want* to take him back. Thank *you,* Dr. Freud. Don't worry, he's not that smart."

"It doesn't take a brilliant mind, it takes an evil mind, Tess. And we all know—"

"I think you're getting carried away, Janet."

"Okay. So maybe I am. But I'm sure this isn't legal, Tess."

"Legal, illegal. Let's not talk so black and white. I explained everything to Alan Garfield—hypothetically speaking, of course—and he said nothing can happen to me . . . as long as I don't know anything about any of this, which, of course, I don't. I mean, I'm just a dumb little housewife whose husband asked her to keep some papers—in sealed envelopes—in her bank box."

"Sealed envelopes? What would that prove?"

"Well, Stephen will mail the cash and bonds to himself and give me the unopened envelopes. That will prove they're his property."

Janet slumped in her chair and rolled her eyes. "Tess, this does not sound kosher."

"Well," I conceded, "Alan did raise an eyebrow at the whole thing, and he said that as an attorney he couldn't advise me to be involved in it, but, strictly as a friend, he told me I shouldn't worry."

"Some friend! Will he be your attorney when they indict you? No, no! Scratch that. If that's the kind of advice he gives, maybe you wouldn't want him for an attorney."

"Don't worry, David will defend me."

"Get serious, Tess."

"Look, Janet, no one can prove I knew what was in the envelopes . . . and that presumes that I'll even get involved and be asked to open my bank box . . . which won't happen because Stephen and I are separated."

"I don't like the whole thing, Tess. Then again, there are possibilities here. Such as, you could run off with everything, and he wouldn't be able to say anything to anyone."

"A key point, my dear."

"As I said. Possibilities."

"No. I mean a *key* point, literally. He keeps both keys."

"Dumb pun, Tess. Of course you know you could tell the bank you lost the keys and have the box drilled."

"I never would have thought of that."

"But I did."

"Well, I'd never be able to do anything like that. However . . . if the keys happened to come my way—"

"Yes?"

"Mmm. . . . Let's just say we never know what we're capable of doing until we're tested."

"That's a little gray for you, isn't it?"

"I'm learning, I'm learning."

"Now, another key point. What was it you said about rewards?"

"If he dies, I'm a very wealthy woman."

"Fat chance. Then again . . ." She paused, catching my eye. ". . . you could kill him!" We both laughed.

"Well, as long as he's alive, I'll have his undying love . . . and twenty-five thousand dollars," I said.

"Right. I notice he sweetened the pot with hard cash. Wasn't taking any chances, was he?"

"I think I did okay."

"I don't know, Tess. It sounds like a devil's pact to me." She paused again before asking, "You didn't sleep with him, did you?"

"No, I didn't sleep with him."

"You turned him down?"

"He didn't ask."

"Oh. How'd that make you feel?"

"Honestly? I guess I felt disappointed. But I think that was strictly ego. I did good, Janet, believe me."

"I don't know. I'm still not sure I understand what *you* believe you're doing."

"I feel like I'm in control for once. You see, if I have control of Stephen's money, I have control of *him*. I like that. I don't know what's going to come of it, but—"

"But who's in control of *you*, Tess? This just doesn't sound like you at all."

"So . . . you could say the devil made me do it."

"That I'd believe."

"And even if I never touch it, it feels nice having all that money under my control," I told Sandy the following Friday morning in my kitchen, in strictest confidence.

"I wish I could say the same. You know, Charlie's estate still isn't settled," she said, changing the subject.

"What's the hang-up?"

"Charlie's insurance policy has a double-indemnity clause in case of accidental death, and they're holding off payment because of the unusual nature of the accident . . . or something like that."

"What does the Great Malcolm Westmeyer, Esquire, say?"

"That I shouldn't worry . . . that I'll come out okay. But he didn't say for how long I shouldn't worry! All I know is there are letters going back and forth between Malcolm and the insurance company, which result in letters from Malcolm's accounting department to me advising me of my tab. One thing's for sure, Malcolm Westmeyer is going to come out of this okay."

"I'd say you won't do too badly either, Sandy."

Sandy averted her eyes and nibbled tiny bits of a chocolate chip cookie. "Um. You know, Tess, Charlie had lots of properties, but by the time they're sold, after I deduct the sales commissions, taxes, and legal fees, I'll be left with diddly," she said. "And, um . . . maybe you could sell them for me . . . you know . . . as a frieeend?"

"How's that?" I questioned.

"Weeell. You could charge me a low commission rate, and I could give you cash, and we'd both make out well."

"Sandy! I can't do that. I mean, if we were talking your house . . . well, it could be worked out. But we're talking big numbers in commercial property, maybe hundreds of thousands in gross profits, tens of thousands in commissions. There's no way to hide that kind of money."

"But it won't be a problem hiding Stephen's money in your bank box?"

The nerve! "Hold on, Sandy. I'm not doing anything really wrong," I said, feeling like a criminal . . . feeling very sorry that I had mentioned The Pact to Sandy, who, I was finding of late, was not exactly who I thought she was.

"I'm sorry, Tess, but you can't imagine how aaawful this is. After all I've been through . . . and now I'm going to be left in the poorhouse!"

"Spare me, Sandy. You're going to be fine!"

"That's what Malcolm keeps saying, but I think he's only concerned about how fine *he's* going to be."

I was growing impatient. I had promised myself that I'd never do this, but I couldn't help myself. . . . "If you want to see financial problems, look at Janet," I started.

"But she only has one child."

"Come off it, Sandy! Janet has to manage a job and the house, which, by the way, is mortgaged to the hilt. And she has to take care of Sean. Can you even begin to imagine the emotional energy alone that raising a child like Sean requires? And she's doing it essentially alone. All Leonard does is send checks. She has to be a father and mother to that child. You'll never have to work unless you want to. And your house, which was paid off by mortgage insurance, is kept immaculate by Estelle, your full-time housekeeper, who also helps you with your two very normal kids."

"Janet didn't have to buy a new townhouse. She could have rented an apartment."

I couldn't believe she had said that. I didn't know Janet when she had found her single-story townhouse, but I remember her telling me about her search for a ground-level apartment that could be fitted with extra-wide doors for Sean's wheelchair . . . and how it was an impossible mission . . . and how, when she looked at the development she lives in now, which was just being built, she almost kissed the sales agent when he showed her a ranch unit, and she almost kissed the builder when he agreed to customize the doorways for her at no extra cost. I remembered all this, and I wasn't even there at the time. Sandy was. But I let it pass. I did remind her, however, that when Janet finally landed a decent-paying job with Terry, her ex-husband tried to cut back on her support. "She had to pay an attorney to help her hold on to whatever money she had!" I screeched.

"But it didn't go to court. She settled with him."

"And how did she settle? In exchange for his not cutting back on child support, she agreed to give up half of her alimony after three years when he convinced her she'd be remarried by then—and her lawyer agreed! I notice *he* didn't marry her."

"Okay, okay . . . so you're right," Sandy admitted, backing off. "But, Tess, this all gets sooo complicated," she whined.

Things appeared a lot less complicated to Judge Bennett in the Montgomery County courthouse, as Sandy and I heard from Janet and David that evening in Janet's living room: "Tess, it was divine! I almost kissed the judge! And you should have seen Leonard, he was positively *livid*. . . . I was waiting for him to jump up and down in a fury and crash through the floor like Rumpelstiltskin. . . ." Janet went on and on, her green eyes brilliant with glee. ". . . And David was incredible, you should have seen him—like a knight in shining armor. . . . I did kiss *him*, Tess. You *were* incredible David."

David sat smiling until Janet came up for air and a sip of wine, and then, "Disraeli said, 'Justice is truth in action.' All we did was tell the truth," he protested modestly. We applauded, and then David stood up to take the stage. He related the details of the story, playing all the parts himself, a veritable one-man show—quite unlike the reserved David we thought we knew so well, obviously pleased with himself and the result of his efforts. "Picture this," he started. "Kendall, Lenny's attorney, was quoting all kinds of figures, pleading relative abject poverty—relative to other physicians and kings, I suppose—and denying the promises he had made to Janet, calling her a liar and a greedy bloodsucker and casting all manner of aspersions. Then, after letting Kendall go on for a while, the judge leaned forward and cut through all the bullshit with a wave of his hand—which happened to be holding a letter. 'Mr. Kendall,' the judge said, 'I have a letter here from a doctor who states that in his professional opinion, this child—this *handicapped* child— NEEDS to go to camp in the summer . . . NEEDS to go to this particular camp. Now, you've inundated the court with a confusion of figures, Mr. Kendall, can you manage one more, please? Could you tell us how much money Dr. Meyer managed to put in his pension fund last year?'"

With this, Sandy and I squealed and kicked our feet like two-year-olds. We were getting the picture.

". . . And Kendall told the judge that the records showed fifty thousand dollars, but that the real figure was only forty thousand . . . and the judge's very bushy right eyebrow flew up to meet his hairline. 'The camp costs twenty-eight hundred dollars, Mr. Kendall,' he said. He noted Janet's meager income, her scant IRA, and ordered Lenny to pay for last year's camp tuition *and* expenses, and to pay for camp and expenses *this* year!"

234

"And wait till you hear this!" Janet added. "On the way out of the courthouse Leonard and his attorney were in front of us, and we heard Leonard say—loud enough for us to hear—that he was sure the judge wasn't swayed as much by his big income, as by my big tits . . ."

"You're not serious! What a slimeball!" said Sandy, aghast.

". . . so I caught up with him and told him that he was right, because, considering my financial situation, my breasts were probably my biggest asset!"

"You didn't!" said Sandy, appalled.

"You're one of a kind, Janet!" I cheered. "You've really got balls!"

"I do now—Leonard's! Do you think I should frame them or bronze—"

"JAAANET!" Sandy cried.

"Actually, with your guts, I can't believe you used to let Leonard push you into lopsided settlements," I said.

"I guess it was a power thing. You know. He has the money—I have to take care of Sean. I was always afraid that if I made waves he'd cut us off. In fact, I was almost ready to settle with Leonard again today before the hearing when he offered to pay this year's camp fee if I agreed to pay for last year. You know, half a loaf and all that. But David insisted that the judge hear the case."

"Aren't you glad you did? Next time you won't be so quick to settle. In fact, after this maybe there won't be a next time. Maybe Leonard's learned a lesson," I said.

"Now, there's a great title for an obscene movie— *Leonard Learns a Lesson.*" Janet laughed, shaking her head, and then sobered. "It *was* obscene, you know. I can't imagine how Leonard allowed it to go to court. Wasn't he embarrassed? I mean, he's supposed to be a profes-sional . . . a parent. He's supposed to be a man." She tried to squelch the emotion that seized her, but tears escaped from her eyes. "Anyway," she sniffed, "I hope you're right, Tess, but the man's a bulldog; when he gets his teeth into something he doesn't let go."

"I can be pretty tenacious myself, Janet. Just let him try something again," David jumped in, clearly enjoying his role of protector.

"You really were wonderful, David," Janet said, giving David a hug.

"It's true, David. We're all impressed," Sandy added, clearly impressed.

Make that *admired* protector, I thought in a flash of jealousy that caught me by surprise, shamed me. I pushed the mean little thought away. Yes, what David did best was nurture, protect, I thought, beginning to understand just how important these qualities were in our relationship, finally admitting to myself that what I needed was someone to take care of me. It crossed my mind that if it were up to David, I'd never be out in the rain without an umbrella, I'd always eat a good breakfast, I'd never, ever get lost, and . . . well, yes . . . I'd always get my boo-boos kissed. Okay, so I was older . . . so I made more money . . . so I was the female . . . but *he* was so good at caring, at taking care.

"Oh, Tess! I almost forgot the best part," Janet cried, bringing me back. "The judge asked David for an accounting of his fees—he was going to make Leonard pay them! When David told the judge he wasn't charging me anything, he ordered Leonard to pay for my trip to Maine for visiting day at camp for last year and this year."

"Can he *do* that?" I asked.

"Can he? He did," David replied.

"Well, here's to a happy ending." I raised my glass in a toast.

"And here's to Sean, a brave little guy who has a very brave mom," David added.

"And here's to Judge Bennett," Janet finished, "who had the distinct pleasure of giving the devil his due."

PEARS FLAMBÉ

Poached Pears

1/2 cup sugar
1 1/2 cups red wine
1 1/2 cups water
3 cloves
zest of 1/2 orange
zest of 1/2 lemon
1-inch piece of vanilla bean
4 firm, slightly underripe pears
4 tablespoons Grand Marnier

Simmer sugar in wine and water until dissolved. Add cloves, zests, and vanilla bean. Simmer 20 minutes.

Take pan off heat. One at a time, peel the pears and drop into liquid. Barely simmer about 3 minutes, until pears are tender. With a slotted spoon, transfer pears, standing up, to a shallow, flat platter. Warm Grand Marnier. Ignite 1 tablespoon Grand Marnier and pour over warm pear. Repeat for each pear. When flames go out, allow pears to cool and then refrigerate, covered, several hours.

Crème Anglaise

1 cup milk
1 cup heavy cream
vanilla bean from pears
4 egg yolks
6 tablespoons sugar
1 1/2 teaspoons cornstarch

Bring milk, cream, and vanilla bean just to a boil and remove from heat. Let stand 10 minutes. Slowly beat egg yolks into the sugar until mixture is pale and creamy. Beat in cornstarch. Vigorously whisk milk mixture into the egg mixture. Return to very low heat and cook, stirring, about 15 minutes, until the sauce is thickened. Do not boil. Remove from heat and take out the bean. Cover and refrigerate.

The Assembly

Place each pear in a pool of crème anglaise in a dessert bowl. Serves 4.

CHAPTER 13

Pears Flambé

Ken Briskin, a clean-shaven, slim six-footer with dark brown, neatly styled hair, hazel eyes, manicured nails, and polished shoes, was a newly divorced orthodontist when I met him at a singles social at a hotel in Cherry Hill, New Jersey, in the middle of June—a fund-raising event sponsored by the Variety Club. This was not an event I would have chosen to go to on my own. I was, after all, in a relationship with David. Then again, there must have been some reason I agreed to go with Sandy when she asked—begged—some reason other than her insistence—"Oh, Tess, you haaave to come with me! It's only ten minutes from the bridge. I'll drive . . . I'll take you to dinner first!" she had implored. "Janet has another date with what's-his-name, Bones—you know, the chiropractor—and I just cooouldn't go alone. I've never been to one of these things. I'd be teeerrified!" Some reason other than my ego—"You're sooo good with people," she had wooed me, "and men reeeally like you, they'll talk to you." Perhaps I was, in fact, trying to pull away from David, just a bit, as our relationship grew closer; but I wouldn't have admitted it to myself at the time. That would have meant admitting that I was as attached to him as I later realized I was . . . later, as in while being embraced by Ken Briskin in his restored, historical Philadelphia townhouse . . . but that was later.

* * *

Yes, *later,* as in *last night,* I thought the morning of July 7 as I fished eight firm, ruby-fleshed pears from their simmering California red wine bath and set them two by two on a platter to cool. They look like chubby little bodies flushed from a hot tub, I thought, smiling, reaching for the squat bottle of Grand Marnier and the blue box of matches. Flaming the pears with the orange liqueur was my secret step in the otherwise standard recipe for the dessert I was making for Millie's dinner party the following night—chilled poached pears served in crème anglaise. I uncorked the bottle, lit a match, poured an ounce or so of the golden liqueur over a pair of pears, and then touched the lighted match to the top of each, setting them passionately ablaze. After igniting the last pair, I stared at the soft blue flame, remembering the details of the social I had let Sandy drag me to not quite a month ago.

Sandy and I hung around the corners of the room dimly lit by tiny bulbs covering the dark ceiling like a starry sky. We each nursed a single drink for about two hours, trying not to talk to each other. Sandy was perfectly coiffed, perfectly made-up, and attractively costumed in a red linen—linen amazingly never looked rumpled on Sandy—straight skirt, matching V-neck, short-sleeved, collared shirt that showed off her finer points, and matching (I couldn't believe she'd found them) red sling-back high heels. She talked to one or two other women who also were trying not to talk with their own friends. I, demurely attired in a long khaki skirt, long, off-white bulky cotton sweater, and flat sandals, observed the crowd feeling somewhat condescending because I, after all, had a lover . . . someone I'd see the following night. So, while Sandy was briefly involved in a conversation with a permed fifty-plus-year-old brunette in a tight black silk jumpsuit, Ken Briskin walked up to me smiling the smile of one who had found a familiar face in a crowd. "Well, you look like someone my age who's probably read, or at least heard of, *Ulysses.*"

"It's on my bookshelf, waiting. I wink at it at least twice a week," I said, smiling. "But I'd guess you're younger than I am."

"Thirty-one, next month," he offered.

"Thirty-five, in two months," I followed. Out of the corner of my eye, I saw Sandy, who was to my left a little behind Ken, watching us.

"I'll take you out for your birthday," he said.

"I'm already busy," I said, instinctively protecting David's territory.

"I had a feeling you weren't going to be easy," he said. "Just don't tell me you're already taken."

I noted that Sandy had moved next to me and was smiling at Ken. "Oh, no, nothing like that," I sort of lied. "It's just that I always spend my birthday with family," I totally lied, totally ignoring Sandy.

"Well, we'll talk about your birthday when I take you out for my birthday."

"Hiii!" Sandy interjected, extending a hand to Ken. "I'm Sandy Solomon, Tess's friend. We came here together. Actually, I dragged her here because it's the first time I ever attended one of these functions," she rattled on, holding Ken Briskin's hand, sucking his eyes with hers. "Tess wasn't interested in coming because she's pretty much spoken for—"

"Oh! Is that so?" he asked, dropping Sandy's hand, dropping his smile, turning his eyes to me.

"I—"

"It's sooort of true, isn't it, Tess?" she said before I could get two words out.

"Not really," I finally managed.

"I knew you were too good to be true," Ken said to me, while Sandy, now standing close—very close—to Ken, realized she had gone a bit too far. Grabbing Ken's arm, she tried to make it better. "Weeell," she said, "maybe not . . . what did you say your name was?"

"Ken. Ken Briskin."

"Maybe not, Ken Briskin. I guess I'm a little more enthusiastic about Tess's suitors than she is."

"Then I'd like to call you. Could I have your number?" Ken asked, almost turning his back to Sandy . . . who looked devastated.

"Sure," I replied, rummaging through my pocketbook. Not wanting to appear pretentious, I pushed my business cards aside, wrote my name and telephone number on an old supermarket receipt, and handed it to Ken. I was aware that Sandy was watching, and that she was thinking that it was *she* who had come here looking for a date, not me. But I wasn't going to worry about it. After all, it was she who had insisted that I come. And besides, I thought, guilt slowly usurping arrogance, who knew if he would actually call me? And even if he did . . . maybe he had single friends.

"We really have to go, Tess," Sandy said, glancing at her watch.

"It was nice meeting you, Ken," I said, shaking his hand.

"It was my pleasure, Tess. I'll call you. By the way, my birthday is July 6. You're not busy, are you?"

"I am now." I tried not to look at Sandy.

"Great! And maybe you're not busy next Friday?"

"Call me."

"I'm sorry," I said in the car as we crossed the bridge to Philadelphia, although I immediately wondered why I was apologizing.

"For what?" Sandy replied, not convincingly.

"I'm not sure. But I think you're disappointed."

"There wasn't a soooul there that I would have wanted to go out with. That's not your fault. But," she continued, "you didn't have to ignore me when the one nice guy in the room came over to us. . . ."

Us?

". . . You could have introduced him to me before I finally had to introduce myself. . . ."

My heart dropped to my stomach. Mea culpa! Mea culpa! I mentally beat my breast. She was right. I had ignored her. I had ignored her and I knew I had ignored her. I don't know why I had ignored her. I can't believe I had ignored her.

". . . Frankly, Tess, I had the feeling you were trying to

242

ignore me and keep him all to yourself. I mean, especially after you had told me that you were *only* going along for the ride."

"I didn't do it on purpose, Sandy. I didn't realize you were standing next to me . . . and then, when I did see you, I didn't want to interrupt him to introduce you . . . and you actually didn't give me a chance." But it was no use. How could I ask her to excuse my behavior when *I* couldn't excuse my behavior? I had already forgotten about *her* behavior.

What an evening that had been! A real eye-opener, I thought, wrapping the dish of pears and placing it in the refrigerator to chill overnight. And, speaking about eye-openers, there was last night! I grabbed a sponge, wiped the stovetop and counter, and poured the hot poaching wine with its bits of lemon and orange peel into the sink, mentally making a list of ingredients I had to buy for the custard sauce I planned to make Friday afternoon. Just as I finished cleaning up, the phone rang. It's Sandy, I witched as I picked up the phone. She wants to know how my date with Ken went last night. "Hello, Sandy!"

"Hiii! How'd you know it was me?"

"I took a wild guess."

"Sooo. How was Braces' birthday dinner?"

"We had a nice time."

"God, Tess, you're sooo understated! Where did you go? What did you do?"

"Well, we went to dinner at Le Petit Champignon—"

"Did you have lemon mirror cake for dessert?"

"That would have been disloyal to Marv!"

"And you *are* loyal. By the way, Tess, what did you end up doing about a birthday present?"

"Listen, I can't talk right now. I just finished poaching pears, and I've got to take a shower, get dressed, and be at a settlement by one o'clock—the Spanish ranch. It finally sold, but the buyers are nuts—would you believe they wanted to test the electric can opener before they would sign the agreement?—so I don't want to be even a minute late."

"When can you talk?"

"Breakfast tomorrow. It's Janet's Friday off, give her a call. Tell her I've got an interesting breakfast story."

"Well, okay. Sounds intriguing. Can you give me a hint?"

"Um. If you get a phone call from Ken, don't be surprised."

"Me? From Braces? What's the story? I thought he was mad about you! I mean, *three* dates in two weeks . . . and now he wants to call *me?*" She sounded confused but, judging from the sudden lilt in her voice, victorious.

"I'll tell you tomorrow."

"Now! Tell me now. Did he remember me? Did he ask you for my number?"

"Yes, he remembered you. Listen, I've got to go. I'll see you in the morning, about nine-thirty at Mykonos? And don't forget to call Janet."

"I won't. You've got me so curious!" she bubbled.

A crack of thunder awakened me Friday morning at six-thirty. Lightning flashed above my bed, momentarily brightening the blackened sky beyond the skylight. It was pouring. A wonderful day to stay at home, I thought, and then remembered that I was meeting Sandy and Janet for breakfast. But that wasn't until nine-thirty, so I didn't have to get up until eight-thirty, so I had time for another two hours of sleep, I figured, burrowing farther down in bed, sandwiching my head in my folded king-size pillow to block the rumble and crash of thunder, pulling the sheet and comforter over my face to block the morning light, the flashes of lightning. I felt myself drift. . . .

Sandy and Janet weren't at Mykonos when I arrived, but Stephen was sitting in a booth near the front of the diner. I sat down across from him and he asked the waitress to bring me a cup of coffee. Then he got up and sat down beside me. "So, you've been screwing David. How long has that been going on?" He looked odd, drunk or drugged . . . something.

"It's none of your business, Stephen. Are you all right?"

"I'm sick. You made me sick. You betrayed me . . . you and David. You always loved him, didn't you? He always loved you. I know that. Did you think I was blind?" He put his hand to his temple and I noticed it was bandaged.

Oh, my God! I thought. I can't go through this again! Not his whole hand! So I didn't ask.

"You don't care about me anymore, do you? You didn't even ask what happened to my hand." And he thrust his bandaged hand in front of me. And it started to seep red, to weep, it started to swell.

No! I don't want to see this, I thought, and I tried to get up, but he held me to him, against his feverish body, puffing his hot breath into my face . . . and I struggled to get free . . . and I tried to scream for help, but I was too constricted to make a sound . . . and I heard a siren . . . it was an ambulance coming for Stephen, to take him to the hospital . . . or was it the police? was he going to jail? . . . and the siren got louder and louder as I struggled harder and harder, trying to free myself from his constraint, from his suffocating, sour breath.

. . . My alarm was blaring as I awoke, finding myself entangled in my bed covers, straining against unyielding sheets, suffocating beneath my pillow. A dream. What a terrible dream, I thought, finally freeing myself from the twisted linen, pulling the pillow from my face and breathing fresh air. And I could see through the skylight that the sky was clear and bright. The storm had passed. *That* storm had passed.

"Sooo! What's with Braces?" Sandy asked even before we were seated, while we waited in the foyer at Mykonos for Janet.

"I gave him your number because I decided that I wasn't going to see him again."

"He turned out to be kinky?"

"Oh, there's Janet. Let's go."

Once seated, Sandy pressed on. "Sooo! Was he kinky?"

"Is who kinky?" Janet asked.

"Ken," I answered. "And—"

"Aha!" Janet interrupted. "It was The Third Date with Ken Wednesday night. Details, please!"

"Okay, okay," I said. "But you're going to find this very uninteresting."

"A first sexual encounter with someone new is never uninteresting—to hear about, that is," Janet retorted. We all laughed.

"Why do you assume I slept with him?"

"Well, it *was* your third date. Rule of thumb and all."

"Maybe by *your* thumb."

"Well, didn't you?" Sandy jumped in.

"Do you want me to start from the beginning . . . or the juicy part?" I teased.

"From the beginning," said Janet. "Context, Tess. I need context!"

"Okay. In the beginning was heaven and earth—"

"Tess, PLEASE!" Janet scolded. "Fast forward to the evening of July 6."

"Okay. The evening of July 6 Ken picked me up at seven—looking extremely dapper and smelling wonderful —and took me to Le Petit Champignon, where we enjoyed a delicious feast of— "

"Skip the dinner, Tess, and get to dessert—dessert as in once you left the restaurant."

"Right. So we went back to his beautiful townhouse, where he gave me a gracious tour, and then fixed me a drink in the kitchen—"

"The KITCHEN! Why do you always end up in the kitchen?" Sandy blurted impatiently.

"It wasn't her fault, Sandy," Janet explained. "If you'll note, the man didn't have the right moves. He should have fixed her a drink first, and *then* given her The Tour, which, naturally, would have *ended* in The Bedroom." More laughter.

"Hey! Are you going to let me tell this story or not?"

"Go, go, go," said Janet.

"So he fixed me a drink in the kitchen and we stood by the counter chitchatting, and then there was a lull in the conversation and he sort of looked like he wanted to kiss me—"

"What's *sort of* mean?" Sandy broke in.

"Sort of, as in he stared forlornly at me with watery eyes, and the vein that runs down the middle of his forehead was sort of sticking out and throbbing."

"So then?" they asked in unison.

"So then . . . I kissed him."

"*You* kissed *him?*" Sandy questioned.

"I kissed him and he dropped his drink on the floor and put his arms around me and kissed me back with great ardor."

"With Great Ardor!" Janet repeated to Sandy. "And?" she questioned me.

"And it was nice."

"Nice! It was *nice?* Is that all you have to say about glasses smashing on floors and GREAT ARDOR? NICE!" Janet exclaimed.

"It was nice. And that was it."

"THAT was IT!" she exclaimed again.

"That was it. I've never experienced anything like it before, but although his mouth was nice—very nice—it was the wrong mouth."

"I think I've heard this in a song somewhere," Janet mumbled.

"What I mean is, well, everything was right, right, right . . . but somehow it was all wrong. Understand?"

"Not in a million years," Janet answered.

"And I was worried about *him* being kinky!" Sandy sighed.

"No, listen. Let me try to explain."

They were all ears.

"I was really looking forward to this date. The guy is young, very attractive, a professional, bright, somewhat intellectual, an interesting conversationalist, he has a quirky sense of humor . . ."

"He likes her puns," Janet explained to Sandy.

". . . he asks lots of questions, doesn't just talk about himself, dresses well, smells good, and he's a really good

247

kisser, which I had learned when he kissed me good-night after our second date . . ."

They sat taking in every word, not knowing where I was going.

". . . so I was looking forward to our third date, and I thought maybe we'd fool around just a bit—get to know each other a little. But when the opportunity presented itself, something inside me turned off. It was like someone flipped a switch, pulled a plug, something. And all I could think of while we kissed was, 'They're the wrong lips . . . they're not David's lips,' and I suddenly missed David terribly and I couldn't wait to get home to call him—"

"I must be going mad," Sandy broke in. "I could have sworn you just said that you were in love with David!"

"I guess I did, didn't I."

"Well! It's about time," said Janet. "We were wondering how long it would take you to figure it out."

"You knew?"

"A friend always knows," said Janet.

"So is that when he asked for my number?" Sandy asked again.

"Well, yes, that's when I gave him your number."

"Ken, we have to talk," I said once his lips had left mine, while he clung to me, rocked me in his arms.

"We have all the time in the world to talk. Right now all I want to do is kiss you."

"That's what we have to talk about," I said, trying to be gentle.

"All right," he said, sobering up, pushing the broken glass with the side of his foot into a pile. He led me by the hand to the study next to the kitchen, where we sat together on a tan leather love seat. "Now. What's so serious?"

"Me, I'm afraid. I just realized that I'm serious about someone I've been seeing."

"And that someone isn't me."

"Right. Ken, you're a very attractive and desirable man, but—"

"But you're in love with someone else."

He's so intelligent . . . so grown-up, I thought. "Right. Honestly, if I had known I wouldn't have led you on, but I wasn't aware of it myself until I became attracted to you. That doesn't make much sense, does it?"

"It does to me. In fact, I take it as a compliment."

After I thought about it, it made perfect sense to me, too.

"He must be the suitor your friend Sandy mentioned."

"Yes." I was mustering a second apology, but Ken beat me to it.

"I'm sorry if I embarrassed you. But I have to tell you that I'm very attracted to you, and if you ever find yourself . . . that is, if you ever find that you'd like to see me, I'd like you to call me."

I was sorely tempted to take his number and hide it away . . . just in case. But I thought of all the women's business cards Stephen had stashed away over the years, and a wave of nausea choked back a positive response. "You're incredible!" I finally said. "Listen. You are just too, too nice to let go completely. Would you be interested in calling a friend of mine?"

"It depends. It wouldn't be Sandy, would it?"

"As a matter of fact, yes."

"She's a pretty lady . . . a little hungry, but pretty."

"Not hungry, just anxious. She's a widow and she doesn't have her sea legs yet. I think you two would enjoy each other."

"So do you think he'll call?"

"I'll bet he does. He said you were very pretty."

"Did you call David when you got home?" Janet asked.

"Better than that. I drove over to his apartment and gave him the birthday present I had planned to give Ken."

"I'm so glad you're home, David," I said when he answered the door in his bathrobe at 12:15 A.M., very surprised.

"So am I . . . now," he responded. And he kissed me and held me.

And I wanted to tell him that I had been to dinner with

this guy, Ken, who was one of the nicest men I have ever met, and one of the best-looking, and one of the smartest. *But it was really weird, David,* I wanted to say, *it was weird because being with Ken made me miss being with you. And the more he wanted me, the more I wanted you.* But all I said was, "I have a present for you."

"Oh, right! Ken's birthday present," Sandy squealed. "What did you finally decide to give him?"
"Me."

Ken did call Sandy, about a week later, and after that I saw very little of her. So it turned out to be a passionately paired summer: Sandy and Braces, Janet and Bones, me and David. It was funny that Sandy never came up with a nickname for David. It was also funny that we didn't triple- or even double-date. We all went our separate ways. I know that Janet spent a lot of weekends and days off at her man's shore home, but she'd call me occasionally when he wasn't sleeping at her place. Sandy all but disappeared. During the day it seemed like Jonathan was always with Sandy's mother or the housekeeper, and Rebecca was at camp. Ken's patients must have been at camp, too. At night, Ken didn't leave Sandy's until the wee hours—"Of course I can't let the children find him here in the morning," Sandy told me during a rare phone call. But it was Janet who told me that Charlie's estate was finally settled and that the insurance company had honored the double-indemnity clause. She had heard it from her mother, who had heard it from her sister, Sylvia, who was Sandy's mother.

I was busy with a steady flow of dessert customers, and real estate agreements and settlements that had been spawned in the spring by families who were moving into the area and wanted to be settled in their new homes before the school year started. And I was busy with David, although I still hadn't shared my revelation with him—that I loved him. What if I told him and he said, "Tess, I'm sorry, but I didn't mean for this to get so serious. I just wanted us to be friends—friends plus sex." What would I do? So I said nothing. I enjoyed our summer together and continued to keep a part of me away from him.

"Why do you think I can't tell him?" I asked Michael the last Tuesday of July—the last Tuesday I'd see Michael until he returned from a weeklong meeting of psychologists in Maine, and then a three-week family vacation in Woodstock, Vermont. ("Clay courts! And grass courts, too," Michael—an avid tennis player—had told me the week before.)

"Why do *you* think you can't tell him?" he answered my question with one of his own.

"You know, Michael, I really hate it when you sound so shrinkish."

"I'm sorry. I didn't mean to sound . . . shrinkish," he said, perceptibly shrinking from the word itself. "I only thought you might have a better idea of why you can't tell him than I have."

"The fact is, you already know why I can't tell him, and you're just waiting for me to figure it out."

"Help me!" he pleaded to the ceiling. "Tell me"—he turned back to me—"why are you still trying to do both our parts? Why don't you make it easy on yourself? You do your part and let me do mine. I promise I won't think you're dumb if you answer a question to which I may already know the answer, if you promise that you won't think I'm dumb if I don't know all the answers you think I know."

"You've got a deal."

"Good. Now we're getting somewhere."

"I'm afraid."

"Of what?"

"I'm afraid of rejection."

"I'll buy that. See how easy this is?" And we both laughed.

And I gave him a big hug when I left and told him to have a good August, and that I'd miss him.

David called to tell me about Stephen's indictment the second Wednesday of September. I thought it interesting that Stephen hadn't called to tell me about it himself, although the truth was he hadn't been in touch much since leaving his practice. Maybe it was because he knew about David and me. Neither of us had told Stephen, but once he left David's office we were more relaxed about our affair. And word gets around.

David had learned of the indictment through legal contacts. The newspaper carried a small item about it the following day. It could be a year or two until the matter would be settled—trial, appeals if necessary—until Stephen would have to go to jail—if he had to, which he probably would, according to David. I called Stephen to tell him how sorry I was. He thanked me for calling, for helping him save his pension. He asked how David was.

"He probably knew all along," David said to me Saturday night over pasta primavera at La Diva, our favorite local Italian restaurant.

"Do you think so? He's never said a word."

"I'm not surprised. Stephen's a funny guy. We were friends and office roomies, but he shared very little of his life with me. Obviously, other than a few mutual ventures, he didn't share much of his business with me either, and he rarely said anything about his personal life. It was a real surprise when you two split the first time, and even more of a surprise when you got back together. What surprised me most was that you and Stephen made it as long as you did."

"Why?"

"Wishful thinking, maybe," he confessed.

"Really? You really thought about me when Stephen and I were together?"

"You didn't know? No, of course you didn't. You were so involved with Stephen."

He rubbed his hand over mine on the table. "There's a poem, Tess, written by Emily Dickinson. It reminds me of you." And he reached into his pocket, took out his wallet, and retrieved from a small compartment under his driver's license a folded, worn piece of paper on which a poem had been handwritten. He gave it to me.

Unfolding it, I began to read it to myself; I continued to look at the paper even as David recited the poem to me word for word:

"The Soul selects her own Society—
Then—shuts the Door—
To her divine Majority—
Present no more—

Unmoved—she notes the Chariots—pausing—
At her low Gate—
Unmoved—an Emperor be kneeling
Upon her Mat—

I've known her—from an ample nation
Choose One—
Then—close the Valves of her attention—
Like Stone—"

My heart was beating so hard I lost my breath. I thought I'd swoon—yes, swoon, like in ye olde days—as his depth of feeling overwhelmed me. "That's so beautiful . . . and so sad," I said after a quiet time. "And it made you think of me?"

"Because you're beautiful. And because it used to make me sad to see you so closed to loving."

I tried to swallow the lump of feeling that rose in my throat, and managed to ask, "How long have you had that in your wallet?"

"Since the day after I first met you . . . when I fell in love with you."

The lump won. I wanted to embrace David right there in the restaurant and tell him that nobody had ever said anything like that to me before. Nobody had ever made me feel the way I felt just then: loved—in love.

"And? But?" Michael questioned on Tuesday.

"But. But I couldn't move, I couldn't say a word. I sat there and cried without making a sound, holding myself. It was as if the whole world had disappeared, including David, and I was alone with my feelings."

"What were your feelings?"

"Pain. I was hurting. And I couldn't understand where the pain was coming from. Certainly not from David. So it had to be coming from inside, from myself." I waited for Michael to say something, to encourage me to go on, because what I had to say was difficult. For a moment, just a moment, I even foolishly wondered if he would understand. But I was on my own. Michael was going to sit quietly, attentively, and wait for me. "Then I remembered sitting here with you, how I felt loved. And I looked up and saw David sitting back in his chair watching me . . . the way you do . . . but different somehow—he needed me. Only I could bridge the distance between us, I realized. At that moment it was David who was in pain, and all I wanted to do was ease his pain."

"I do love you, David," I said, reaching across the table, putting my hand on his. Grasping my hand, he smiled through pressed lips and nodded slowly. Tears ran into his beard. And we sat there for a long time, feeling relieved and grateful for each other.

When I finished relating the story to Michael, I felt a small sense of loss. "I feel sad, Michael. I feel like I've let something go."

"What's that?"

"I feel that I've moved away from you."

"Part of you has . . . with my blessing."

He leaned over and kissed my forehead, and I understood that nothing had been lost, only changed.

"Do you realize this is the first Sunday brunch we've had in months?" Sandy reminded Janet and me as we settled into our booth at Mykonos on a warm Indian summer morning late in September. Although once we were into our first cups of coffee, it felt like we had never missed a Sunday. But we

254

did have some catching up to do. By now we were all aware that Bones, the chiropractor, had moved into Janet's house. Sandy and I had finally met him—and were reminded that his name was Arthur Segal—at Janet's house Friday night. She had invited us to dinner, an event that also gave Janet an opportunity to meet Ken Briskin. It turned out to be a nice evening. Arthur, not yet married at thirty-seven, was a huge man who looked like he could crack your bones quite literally, but he had a gentle, friendly manner that invited ease. He was clearly mad about Janet, who was clearly mad about him, as was Sean. "Tell me again about the time you ran a sixty-yard touchdown at Temple!" he had begged Arthur on his way to bed after Janet kissed him good-night. Ken was clearly delighted to see me—much to Sandy's chagrin—but he was clearly crazy about Sandy. "I owe you, Tess!" he said to me sometime during the evening while standing behind Sandy, wrapping his arms around her as she squealed, loving the public display of affection as much as the affection that inspired it. He was as affable and charming as I had remembered him to be. And David and I were clearly in love and loving every minute of it.

"Thanks again for dinner, Janet," Sandy said once the coffee was poured and orders were taken. "It was a nice night. Ken thought you all were great."

"It was nice. Thanks, Sandy. Arthur enjoyed it, too. We'll have to do it more often," she replied, understanding, as we all did, that we probably wouldn't do it often at all. But whenever we did do it, it would be nice.

"So what's the story with Arthur? Are you going to get married or anything?" Sandy asked.

"For right now, it's 'anything.' We're very happy just the way we are. I think we're going to play house for a while and then go from there. We both want to be sure. But, between you and me—and not a word to anyone, either of you—I think I can safely say that marriage is a definite possibility."

"Oh, Big Secret!" Sandy teased, disappointed that Janet didn't have any real news to spring on us. "Can you do any better than that, Tess? You and David were positively gloooowing!"

"You do have a way of putting things, Sandy."

"So?" Sandy pushed.

"So I'm not divorced yet." What I didn't say was that until that very minute, I hadn't thought of Marriage, and neither had David—at least, he hadn't brought it up. Marriage . . . Tess Ross, I mused.

"Tess, what are you nodding about?" Sandy asked, bringing me back to brunch.

"I was just thinking. . . . Well, Sandy, what's up with you and Ken? You looked very cozy the other night."

"Weeell . . . he really is wild about me. And the kids like him a lot. He's very good with them. He said he always wanted children, but his ex-wife—she's a radiologist—didn't. I think that was one of the reasons for the divorce—besides her affair with the hospital administrator."

"Well, he seems like a sweet guy—and cute. And Tess tells me that he's pretty bright."

"And he's got money," Sandy added. "He drives a Mercedes and he has looots of people working for him in his practice, so he has lots of time off. It's been a great summer. He's taken me everywhere. We even took the kids to Disney World for three days when camp was over. It's sooo nice not having to worry about finances!"

"You went to Florida? That's one I didn't hear about," Janet chimed in.

"Don't feel bad, I didn't know about it either," I said. "So what's it going to be with this guy, Sandy?"

"Oh, I don't know. We're taking it one step at a time. I'm just clearing up all of Charlie's estate business."

"I thought that was taken care of over the summer. Janet said that—"

"That's true, but there were loose ends. Like my attorney, for instance. You wouldn't believe the enooormous bill I got from him just last week. I can't imagine what he does to warrant it. I swear they make it up as they go along."

"Now, now, Sandy, let's not disparage the legal profession," Janet defended.

"I guess with your successful day in court and David's

new standing in Tess's life, we'll never be able to tell another lawyer joke," Sandy agreed.

"We'll just have to pick on doctors," Janet offered in compensation, "but we'll have to be careful to spare orthodontists and chiropractors."

We all laughed at the evanescence of our alliances, and I thought of pears flambé—how hot they burned one day . . . how cold they were the next—and I stopped laughing.

ORANGE BOMBE GLACÉE

Bombe

1 quart vanilla ice cream
1 cup water
1 envelope unflavored gelatin
1 cup sugar
4 tablespoons lemon juice
1 cup orange juice
1 tablespoon grated orange rind
3 egg whites
1 cup heavy cream
candied orange peel
fresh mint leaves

Line a 2 1/2-quart mold with about 1/2 inch of softened vanilla ice cream and place in the freezer.

Sprinkle gelatin over 1/4 cup cold water and let stand for 5 minutes. In a saucepan, mix together 3/4 cup water, sugar, lemon and orange juices, and orange rind. Add the gelatin and heat, stirring, until the gelatin and sugar dissolve. Chill the mixture until it thickens and then beat it to a froth. In a separate bowl, beat the egg whites until stiff peaks form. Fold them into the thickened mixture. Whip the cream until soft peaks form, and fold it into the mixture. Spoon the mixture into the ice-cream-lined mold. Cover with wax paper and freeze for several hours. Unmold and decorate with candied orange peel and mint leaves. Serves 8.

Candied Orange Peel

3 oranges
2 cups sugar
3/4 cup water
3 tablespoons light corn syrup

Peel oranges with a vegetable peeler, removing the colored plus a little of the white part, and cut the peel into 1/8 x 1 1/2-inch strips. Simmer in a pan of water for about 15 to 30 minutes, until tender. Drain and cool.

In a saucepan over low heat, melt 1 cup of sugar in 3/4 cup water and the corn syrup. Add the peel and cook over low heat until much of the syrup has been absorbed, about 15 minutes. Remove from heat, cover, and let stand for an hour, and then drain. Lightly toss the peel in a plastic bag with 1 cup of sugar.

CHAPTER 14

Orange Bombe Glacée

When I was a child, my very favorite summer treat was an orange Creamsicle, a vanilla ice cream Popsicle coated with orange ice. Memories of this cool sweet and its context—Atlantic City shore, hot sun, hot sand, salty air—washed over me like a refreshing ocean wave as I prepared orange mousse for an orange bombe glacée. A frozen dessert of molded vanilla ice cream filled with orange mousse, orange bombe glacée is no more than an inverted Creamsicle. The bombe was to be the finale of Carla Herman's Friday-night dinner party for six at seven-thirty.

I noted it was five to one. I'd made delicate chocolate lace cookies, to be served with the bombe, in the morning; the dome-shaped metal bowl lined with an inch of vanilla ice cream was in the freezer. The dessert would be constructed and frozen solid by five—along with a small one in a custard cup I was making to indulge myself. I'd unmold the bombe glacée onto Carla's silver plate, decorate it with mint leaves and candied orange peel, and have it in her freezer before six, I figured, whipping egg whites to a froth.

Janet had called earlier to ask if I could meet her for lunch at the diner. She had the day off. And, by the way, did I know where Sandy was? she had asked. I hadn't spoken to Sandy for three days. And I was too busy to go out to lunch, but I told her she was welcome to lunch in my kitchen.

I was spooning the orange mousse into the center of the molded ice cream when Janet walked through my back door.

"Wait till you see the shoes I bought at Rosie's!" she said, dropping her pocketbook on the kitchen table, pulling a shoe box from a silver plastic bag imprinted with a black rose logo. The shoes were beautiful. Janet pulled off her sneakers and socks and modeled the sleek high-heeled pumps. "Aren't they wonderful, Tess? Lots of toe cleavage," she said, holding her foot out for me to note the deep V-cut front.

"They're gorgeous. What are they for?"

"My black lace dress. I'm wearing it to Arthur's cousin's wedding next week."

"Great choice. You look wonderful in black," I said, picturing her auburn hair piled on top of her head, setting off the elegant black dress. "You'll be smashing."

"You *do* think it's okay to wear black to a wedding, don't you?"

"Are you kidding? I've heard of at least three weddings in the past year where the entire bridal party wore black and white."

"Next thing you know, brides will be wearing black!" she said.

The sudden memory of a dream I'd had years ago, a week before I married Stephen, sent a chill through me: I was a bride dressed in a long black gown with a long black veil. I have to remember to tell Michael about that, I thought.

"Tess, you look like you've seen a ghost. Are you okay?"

"Do I? I've got to get a little sun on my face. I think I have been pale lately." I finished filling Carla's bombe—and my little one—covered them with plastic wrap, and put them back in the freezer. "Done. Now we can eat."

We sat at the counter nibbling at cold leftover stir-fry right out of the serving dish, sipping coffee, then more coffee while I boxed the lace cookies, and more coffee to wash down pieces of broken cookies. Janet told me she and Arthur were off to the shore for the weekend as soon as Leonard picked up Sean for a rare weekend sleep-over.

"What's the occasion?" I asked.

"Beats me. Every couple of months he gets pangs of guilt, so he asks Sean to spend the weekend with him and The Twit."

"Does Sean like her?"

"It's hard to tell. He doesn't dislike her, but he tells me she's dumb."

"Eleven-year-old boys can be very perceptive."

"And many go downhill from there! Actually, she's nice to Sean, but he says she tries too hard. She tries to do too much for him. I think she embarrasses him. I feel a little sorry for her. She's very young, and Sean says his father doesn't pay much attention to either of them."

"So why does he bother at all?"

"As I said. Guilt—the bond of the absent parent, even the *good* ones. Linda Gordon's husband is just the opposite of Leonard. He'd do anything for his kids from his first marriage. Linda complains that what Jeff would like to do is cut himself up into tiny pieces and feed himself to his children—like fish food. Guilt, Tess."

"Some people don't deserve to have children," I said wistfully, my mind embracing an image of David playing with his nephews, thinking what a good father he'd make; I felt suddenly inadequate as I remembered my mother's admonition, "A man wants children."

"There you go again, Tess! You're pale as a ghost. What's wrong? Are you sure you're all right?"

"I'm fine. I'm fine. I was just thinking—"

"About what?"

"I was just feeling sorry for myself because David would make such a good father and I can't have children." I heard my voice crack.

Janet was off her chair and next to me, hugging me in an instant, and much to my surprise, I was crying like a baby in her arms. "Hey, hey, Tess. What's going on here?" When my sobs ebbed, she pulled away to arm's length, her hands on my shoulders. "You two are going to get married, aren't you!"

"I'm not divorced, Janet, did you forget that?" I said,

262

sounding a bit testy, annoyed at myself for my uncharacteristic emotional outburst.

"But you want to get married. Right?"

"I don't know what I want. I'm not sure I have the right to marry David. He loves children, Janet."

Janet sat back in her seat. "Have you talked to him about it?"

"Not really. We don't talk about marriage. I think he's waiting for me to bring it up, and I'm not ready to discuss it. He knows I can't get pregnant, though. That was a discussion we had when we stopped using condoms."

"So why aren't you ready?"

The unburdening softened me, and I spilled. "First I've got to get divorced, and what with Stephen's legal problems, I don't think this would be a fair time to ask him to have to deal with a divorce, too. He still views me as a major emotional support."

"You're not going to put your life on hold in consideration of a man who never once considered you, are you?"

"I feel I owe him something, if only not to kick him when he's down."

"You owe him NOTHING!"

"Well, we'll see. I have to tell you, Janet, as much as I think I'd like to settle down with David, as much as I love him, I like my privacy, too. I love it when we're here or I'm at his apartment, but I also like it when I'm home alone, doing . . . whatever. Does that sound weird? Do you think I'm getting old and rigid?"

"We're all getting old and rigid. And no, I don't think you sound weird. Everyone likes their own space now and then. I must confess that sometimes I hide in the bathroom; I sit on the pot with the lid closed just so I can be totally alone for a while. The shower is another hideaway, but you can't stay in the shower very long—the hot water runs out."

"Ah, confessions of a water-closet recluse!"

"Oh, well, we all have our little perversions."

"More coffee?"

"No, thanks. I'm already wired for the day. Tess, is David pushing for you to divorce Stephen?"

"David doesn't push. He's the most laid-back man I've ever met. He seems to understand me so well. And what he doesn't understand, he accepts. Sounds a bit unreal, doesn't he?"

"Sounds like a saint. So, even if he won't push, I will. Get it done, Tess!"

"Look who's pushing. Mrs. I'm-Happy-with-a-Live-in. Well, maybe you and I'll have a double wedding."

"Wouldn't that be a hoot!" Janet cried.

"Hey! We'll include Sandy, too. She and Dr. Perrrfect look pretty serious, too."

"Oh, I don't think Sandy's going to wait that long. Last week I caught her trying on engagement rings in Strawbridge's. 'Just to get an idea . . . in case he asks,' she said. She's as happy as a pig in shit with this guy."

"Well, we can't blame her, Janet. After the men she's been involved with, Ken is heaven-sent."

"And loooaded, as Sandy will tell you."

"Yes. Well, hopefully she'll learn that it's not what she needs from him."

"What *I* need is two days on the beach, and it's supposed to be another gorgeous weekend. The way the weather is going, we could miss autumn altogether," said Janet, carrying her mug and fork to the sink.

"Don't worry. By Halloween it'll be cold. Happens every year. Almost overnight."

"Right. So right now I'm off to pack." She picked up her pocketbook and the bag holding her new shoes, and was on her way. I watched from the back door as she walked to her car. "Listen, Tess," she said, turning toward me, "do something fun with David this weekend. You've got to lighten up. If you feel like visiting us at the shore, just give a ring. On second thought, you don't have to call. We'll either be in the house or dead-ass on the beach. Just come."

Janet's kind offer was accepted gratefully. Saturday morning, David and I drove to Beach Haven, where Arthur owned a two-bedroom bungalow on the beach. It had been built by his uncle and aunt—his father's eldest brother and

sister-in-law—thirty-five years ago. When they had died—
he ten years ago, she six years later—the property was left to
their two sons, who had little interest in Beach Haven. So
Arthur, who had fond memories of bare feet on hot tar roads
and the house that used to be the only house on what used to
be a quiet beach in what used to be a sleepy little shore town,
bought it from his cousins. Beach Haven wasn't as quiet as it
had been thirty years ago, but you could still leave your
doors unlocked when you went to the beach, he told Janet.
He really loved the old bungalow built high up on stilts—
now flanked by two large, contemporary homes of cedar and
glass—a staunch survivor of many storms over the years,
with a real masonry fireplace and a huge picture window
overlooking the beach. In the winter Arthur would go there
when the moon was full over the ocean, build a fire, and
watch the white snow cover the silver sand.

We found Janet and Arthur as she had said—dead-ass on
the beach—at about ten in the morning. It was a bit nippy
when we arrived, but the weatherman had predicted clear
skies with a high of seventy-five to eighty, and by eleven we
were able to shed the jeans and sweatshirts we had worn
over our bathing suits. I felt incredibly tired. I couldn't
remember ever feeling so tired, even though my week hadn't
been particularly stressful or busy. So I took advantage of
the soft sand and the warm sun, and dozed in and out as the
sound of the ocean pulled me back to my childhood. And I
half dreamed, half remembered the time when I was playing
near the edge of the water and a huge wave engulfed me, and
I tumbled over and over and over until I didn't know which
way was up, and water was in my mouth and my ears and
my eyes, and I couldn't breathe and I was scared. . . . And
then I half remembered, half dreamed the dream I used to
have when I was a child, where I would be engulfed by a
huge, dark wave at twilight, and I would tumble over and
over and over until I didn't know which way was up, and
water was in my mouth and my ears and my eyes, and I had
to take a breath . . . and I found I could breathe underwater,
like a fish . . . like an unborn babe.

That evening we feasted on hot dogs grilled on a hibachi

on the tiny back deck, and homemade potato salad. After helping to polish off two bottles of wine, David and I graciously accepted Arthur's invitation to stay through Sunday—after offering the obligatory "Oh, we couldn't impose on your hospitality any more," and throwing in the empathetic "You two came here to be alone!"—because after all, we allowed them to convince us, all that wine, and the late hour, and Sunday would be another glorious day. And it was.

Monday was an entirely different story.

"I told you it would get cold by Halloween," I reminded Janet on the phone Monday night, after a gray, drizzly, sixty-degree day, dropping to forty at night, with a five-day forecast of more of the same.

"But there are still two weeks until Halloween."

"And it's still not *cold,* just miserably cool."

"I'm not ready for this, Tess. Neither is Sean. Either it's the weather or he's coming down with something. He's been lethargic since he came home from Leonard's last night. Listen, did you hear from Sandy while we were away? I tried to reach her today and she's still not home. I called Aunt Sylvia, but nobody was home there either."

"Not a word."

Tuesday was an entirely different story.

"Hellooo!" It was Sandy on the phone, awakening me at nine in the morning.

I had overslept. How I hate gray weather, I thought, feeling as gray as the day. "Sandy! Where were you? Janet and I were getting worried."

"Not to worry. What are you doing for lunch? I have neeews! I have something to show you!"

"You're engaged!"

"Nope! Come to lunch and I'll tell all. Janet can make it at twelve-thirty for about half an hour."

I had a settlement scheduled for eleven-thirty that I figured would take about an hour. Leaving room for snags, I told Sandy to meet Janet and that I'd get there as soon as I could.

There were snags. I arrived at Mykonos at one. Sandy and Janet had finished their Greek salads and Janet was half out of the booth when I walked up the aisle. She fell back into her seat when she saw me, folded her arms on her chest, and smiled mysteriously.

"So what's the news?" I questioned as I slipped into the seat next to Sandy, who was suddenly coy.

Janet dropped the bomb: "Sitting next to you, for the first time anywhere, is Mrs. Kenneth Briskin."

I was speechless. "What!" Well, almost speechless.

"See!" was all Sandy said, thrusting her left hand in front of me, the ring finger of which bore a sparkling circlet of chunky round diamonds.

"I'm speechless!" I said. "When did this happen? Where? You didn't tell us? This really *is* news!" Well, almost speechless.

"This is where I came in," said Janet, sliding out of the booth, taking the check with her. "This one's on me, Sandy. Congratulations!" Janet leaned over to kiss Sandy after I had kissed Sandy and moved to Janet's seat.

"Okay," I said, once Janet had gone, "tell me all!"

And Sandy related a story of true love, passion, security —the whole ball of wax—and how she and Ken felt there was no reason to wait, that they both had wasted too many years already, and that if you don't know The Real Thing after three months, you wouldn't know it after three years. Did I detect an oblique reference to me and David in that statement? I wondered. I decided I was being paranoid and that Sandy was only trying to justify her own impulsive behavior.

". . . sooo," she continued, belying my defense of her, "maybe you were wise in not getting a quick divorce to marry David. There must be reasons for your putting it off. I think you would know by now if it was The Real Thing. After all, Tess, you've known David for yeeears."

What I couldn't understand was how we'd got to talking about me and David when she obviously had sooo much to tell me about herself and Ken. I ordered a BLT on toast and some coffee, and then, ignoring Sandy's comments about my relationship, asked her if her elopement had been sudden or planned, if anyone had known about it.

"I guess it was sort of sudden. The only people who knew were my parents and Ken's mother and sister. And we only told them a week before."

"What did your parents say?"

"They were real happy for me. After all I've been through, I think they were glad to see me settled. And they absolutely looove Ken."

"And his mom?"

"She was just happy he was happy. And, being a widow herself, she understood why I didn't want a fancy wedding."

A fancy wedding they didn't have. They had been married Friday morning by Ken's rabbi in Philadelphia. Ken's mother and sister and brother-in-law, Sandy's parents, and Rebecca and Jonathan were the only guests. They all went to dinner afterward at the Four Seasons Hotel, and then Sandy and Ken stayed at Ken's townhouse for the weekend. The real honeymoon—three weeks touring Europe—was to take place next spring, she explained. "You know, those things take time to plan, Tess."

"Well. I'm thrilled for you. You look radiantly happy, and Ken certainly seems like a terrific guy. But I have to admit I'm a little hurt that you never said a word to me. I would have loved to have seen you get married, and I'm sure Janet would have, too. Why the secrecy?"

"I was afraid to say anything. I didn't know how everyone would react. You know"—she lowered her voice—"some people could get jealous."

"Who are 'some people'?"

"Well, I'm sure Janet would love to marry Arthur. And I'm not so sure how you would have taken it. I mean, you'd probably say that it hasn't been very long since Charlie died . . . and that I don't know Ken very well. . . ."

And the further she went, the further behind I followed,

far enough behind to see that the distance that had come between us was not going to be made up easily, maybe never.

"... You understand what I'm saying, don't you, Tess?"

Better I shouldn't get entangled in what she made out to be interpersonal conflicts, but which were, in fact, self-conflict, I thought. I told her that the only thing that was important was that *she* understand. I meant that. I wished her happiness. I meant that, too.

The following Sunday, we tried Sunday brunch all together—the six of us. After we had greeted each other, and Janet and I had kissed Ken and welcomed him into "the family," and Arthur and David had kissed Sandy and given Ken hearty handshakes, Janet said that she had news—Big News. "Sean's going to be a brother," she announced.

We all looked at her agape, not knowing what to say, not sure if this Big News was good news or bad news.

She quickly helped us. "No, no! Not me! The Twit! The Twit is pregnant! She told Sean over the weekend that he's going to have a baby brother or sister—which is probably why he was acting so funny when he came home, Tess. Sean finally told me yesterday."

"But I thought they had an agreement not to have children," I said.

"They did. What poetic justice! One of life's luscious little ironies! I can't wait to talk to old F.F. and congratulate him."

"F.F.?" Ken questioned.

"Fuckface—her ex-husband," Sandy explained with an affectation of disapproval.

The men were blown away by the appellation, and they listened in awe as Sandy, Janet, and I each tossed our own sentiments regarding Janet's baby-in-law-to-be into the cauldron of ill will.

"Maybe she'll have twins!" Sandy offered. "And I hope she knows enough to ask for a full-time housekeeper."

"Not a chance," Janet answered. "Sean tells me she scrubs the kitchen floor herself—on her knees. But twins. Now, there's a possibility. Twins run in Leonard's family."

"A touch of colic would be nice," said Sandy.

"Oh, for sure!" Janet agreed. "Sean was a colicky baby. It almost drove Leonard out of the house."

"I think they should have a girl," I added my own evil. "That means he'll have to pay for a bat mitzvah *and* a wedding!"

"*If* The Twit sends her to Hebrew school," Janet interjected. "But she'll probably have the baby baptized. Leonard would go mad! And his parents would disinherit him! Oh, what a splendid idea."

The men were rapt. David alone was heard mumbling something.

"What?" We turned to him.

"Eye of newt, and toe of frog, wool of bat, and tongue of dog," he repeated with a wicked smile. "It's an old family recipe."

Although Janet had appeared positively thrilled at brunch, and as things, and people, aren't always as they appear, I wasn't surprised to hear her later express at least a little hurt that Leonard had deserted one family to start another, at least a little anger that Leonard's new child might rob Sean of what little attention he was receiving from his father, as well as his inheritance, and at least a little anxiety that Leonard's financial responsibility to his new child might prompt him to ask the courts to decrease his responsibility to Sean. "You'll cross those bridges when you come to them," I said, trying to ease her fears. "Just tell me why it is that I always have bridges to cross. For once I'd like to feel my feet on solid ground long enough to get my balance," she answered.

But her fears soon took a backseat to her delight with the ensuing events related to the baby-in-law-to-be. More Big News was served at brunch the following Sunday, a meal the men chose to skip. "Guess who called ME?" Janet started, and didn't wait for a response. "Old F.F. himself. The man must be absolutely at his wits' end to call ME." And Janet told of Leonard's plea for help, for friendship in his time of betrayal. "I suppose Sean told you . . ." he had started. "Obviously," Janet interpreted to us, "that's what he had in mind when he invited Sean for the weekend." The Twit, said Janet, had tricked Leonard into getting her pregnant— according to Leonard. We all wondered what, sometime later, a judge would wonder: Shouldn't an obstetrician know about birth control? The fact that he couldn't reasonably oversee his wife's taking her pill every day was a loose end that we, The Jury, chose to brush aside, as would the judge sometime later when Leonard would make a public discussion of his private problems. Janet said that Leonard had threatened to have the marriage annulled unless The Twit submitted to an abortion. She had refused. His attorney told him he didn't have a case. He cried to Janet that she was the only one who could understand. And in an effort to evoke a sympathetic response from his former mate, Leonard had instead delivered the most damning provocation: *"You know how I am."* He had begged Janet to talk with his present wife, to convince her that an abortion would be best. "It would be better for all concerned, including Sean," he had said to Janet. "I'm not going to live forever. Wouldn't you like to see Sean get everything he's entitled to?"

"Can you imagine!" Janet said to us.

"What did you say to him?" Sandy asked.

"I said, 'Thanks for thinking of us, Leonard. Don't worry, I'll talk to her. I *do* know how you are.'"

Tuesday night Janet called to tell me that she had received another phone call—from The Twit!

"So, what did you tell her?"

"I didn't have to tell her a thing. She told me! Leonard told her he was going to divorce her and give her and the baby nothing because she had broken their agreement. Of course, she swore that she hadn't missed a pill. Then she said that—wait until you hear this!—she said that Leonard was always crying about how I had raked him over the coals, took him for everything he had, stripped him bare . . . so she called me to get the name of my lawyer!"

"That's wonderful! Did you give it to her?"

"Of course!"

Later, a judge—with a raised eyebrow—would conclude that "even a man with only a law school degree knows that it takes two to have a baby," and that Leonard would be financially responsible for his offspring. This was after Leonard, embittered and embarrassed among his peers, had left his home, and after The Twit had delivered a healthy baby girl and was well into a romantic relationship with the obstetrical resident who had assisted in the delivery—a young single man who, initially, took pity on the young thing who had been taken advantage of by an older, heartless man, and who, finally, was taken in by her. "All's well that ends well, Tess," Janet would say. Ending well, in this case as in most, having more to do with one man's getting what he deserved than justice for all.

Thursday morning I awoke from a disturbing dream of confusion and nausea—something about trying to find something or somebody . . . running back and forth between two houses . . . growing weary and dizzy—to David's gentle hand on my arm. "You okay?" he asked as I rubbed my eyes, trying to gain balance in a bed that refused to be steady. But it was my extra-firm Sealy Posturepedic, not David's water bed. So why was it moving? What felt like a fist in my stomach gave me the answer that I didn't take time to contemplate, and I bolted from the bed to the bathroom and heaved whatever was left from Wednesday night's linguine and clams into the toilet. David was but a step behind me, holding my head, making calming sounds, sounds I hadn't heard since I was a little girl. When I was through, he gave me a glass of water and helped me back to bed. "I guess you're not okay," he said, trying to sound chipper, but sounding concerned instead.

"Do I feel hot to you?" I asked him.

He put his hand on my neck, his lips to my forehead. "Nope. I don't think you have any fever. Maybe a touch of food poisoning, though." And we reviewed our dinner at La Diva, discovering that we had eaten nothing in common but

272

the salad. "So it wasn't the salad," he concluded, desperate to be helpful.

David made me tea and toast with jelly, and when he saw I was beginning to perk up he showered and dressed and left for his office. He called almost hourly, and I told him I was fine, just very tired. And I promised that I'd call the doctor if I wasn't feeling better by the next morning, and he said he'd stay over again that night, but I told him that I was going to bed early and it would be better if he slept at home.

Friday morning was a repeat of the morning before. I called my gynecologist—the only doctor I had—hoping for some over-the-phone remedy, but he told me I should come in to see him, reminding me that my last checkup had been more than a year ago and that we might as well get everything checked out at once. Just what I'm in the mood for, I thought, a pelvic, a rectal . . . shit. Why hadn't I just called the pharmacist? I thought, poised over the toilet.

David arrived about five-thirty. He had called several times during the day—before and after I'd visited Dr. Ebert—and after I told him that Dr. Ebert said I was going to be fine, he told me that he'd be over as soon as he could leave the office.

"How's my patient?" he asked, walking into the family room, finding me bundled in an afghan on the sofa. "Not too good I see," he said, noting a *Brady Bunch* rerun on the television. "Down to rock bottom. It looks like I arrived just in time!" he said, pulling a quart of his mother's homemade chicken soup (for me), a corned beef sandwich (for him), and two Sherlock Holmes videotapes from the grocery bag he was carrying. Just what the doctor ordered, I thought. And he sat down beside me and kissed me and held me, and told me that he loved me and that he was going to take care of me.

"But who's going to make the coffee cakes for Joanne Freed's Saturday-morning meeting?" I teased.

"Take me to your kitchen. I'm a fast teach."

"Just kidding. Joanne said the coffee cakes I have in the freezer will be fine. She didn't want anything fancy. She's only having some of her neighbors in to discuss putting up a light at the corner of Dogwood and Red Oak," I said, holding him close.

"Yep. That's a bad corner. So. What exactly did Ebert say was wrong? Did he think it was something you ate?"

"Not exactly. But he said I'll be fine," I said, and then picked up the ringing telephone.

"Hello, Tess?" It was Janet. Were we doing anything tonight? Maybe we could go to dinner or a movie, she suggested.

"I'm not feeling great, Janet. A touch of something. David's here with chicken soup and a couple of old movies and . . . yes, he is a sweetheart," I said to her, looking at David. "Listen, we'll all have brunch Sunday. Call Sandy. Okay? . . . Good. See you Sunday."

"You will come Sunday morning, won't you?" I asked David.

"Sure. Anything you'd like. Got to keep up on the really important news!"

"You're horrible!"

"I'm sorry."

"No, you're not."

"Yes, I am. Want me to show how sorry I am?" he said, leering at me.

"Later," I answered, getting warm all over, blushing. Blushing! Oooh, what this man does to me! I thought.

I ate the chicken soup and a quarter of David's sandwich. He ate the rest of the sandwich. We fought for the pickle. He won. "Not with your tender stomach," he insisted.

"Now for dessert," I announced, getting up from the sofa for the first time since David had walked into the house. From the freezer, I took the mini orange bombe glacée that I had made three weeks before and had forgotten about, and then discovered when I was looking for the coffee cakes for Joanne.

"That looks interesting. What is it?" David asked when I brought the unmolded bombe into the family room.

"It's a bombe," I said, setting it on the coffee table before us. "It's one of my favorite desserts."

274

"It's a very small bombe," he pouted. "Am I going to get any of it?"

"Nope," I answered, suddenly struck by a pun, "it's all for me. I have a rather large *bomb* for you."

"Oh?" He looked appropriately puzzled.

"David," I started, wrapping my arms around him, "a most remarkable thing has happened. . . . We're going to have a baby."

KILLER CAKE
(CHOCOLATE CHIP FUDGE CAKE)

FROM: Commissary Restaurant, Philadelphia

Cake

6 ounces unsalted butter
6 ounces unsweetened chocolate, chopped
6 eggs
3 cups sugar
1/2 teaspoon salt
1 tablespoon vanilla extract
1 1/2 cups flour
1 1/2 cups chocolate chips

Preheat the oven to 350°F. Grease two 9 x 1 1/2-inch cake tins and line bottoms with wax or parchment paper.

MIX CAKE BY HAND. Melt butter and unsweetened chocolate together over simmering water. Cook to lukewarm. In a large bowl whisk together for 1 minute the eggs, sugar, salt, and vanilla. Whisk in the butter-chocolate mixture. Stir in flour and chocolate chips. Pour batter into prepared pans and bake for 30 to 35 minutes. Do not overbake; cake tester should not come out clean. Cool on racks and remove from pans as soon as cooled.

Frosting

1 1/4 cups sugar
2 tablespoons instant coffee
1 cup heavy cream
5 ounces unsweetened chocolate, finely chopped
4 ounces unsalted butter
1 1/2 teaspoons vanilla extract

Combine sugar, coffee, and cream in a small, deep, heavy saucepan. Stirring, bring to a boil. Reduce heat and simmer 6 minutes without stirring. Remove from heat. Add chopped chocolate and stir until it is melted and blended. Add butter and vanilla. Whisk well. Chill until mixture begins to thicken.

Assembly

Put one cake layer bottom-side-up on a cake plate. Spread with one-third of frosting. Top with second layer, also bottom-side-up. Trim the circumference of the cake. Pour all but 1/2 cup of the frosting on top of cake, spreading it over top and sides. Put the reserved icing into a pastry bag fitted with a small star tip and pipe 16 rosettes around top of cake. Refrigerate if not serving immediately, but bring to room temperature before serving. Serve with lightly sweetened whipped cream. Serves 16.

CHAPTER 15

Killer Cake

"I couldn't have conceived of the kind of feelings I've been experiencing, Michael," I said on Tuesday morning, punning unintentionally.

He smiled at me but said nothing, allowing me to bubble unimpeded.

"I mean, I used to say I wanted to be happy, but I didn't really know what *happy* meant. And David! Well, you should see him! He's insane with happiness! He can't do enough for me. I think he'd like to pick me up and carry me around inside himself. Can you picture it? A big, blond mama kangaroo!"

Michael sat nodding, smiling, beaming—a mother hen watching her newly hatched chick, I mused, not missing the influx of maternal metaphors suffusing my thoughts. "And I was so surprised!" I continued. "I know that sounds strange, but with my history of infertility . . . and my periods have always been irregular so when I miss one, I don't think anything of it . . . and I figured I was gaining weight because I was relaxed, and happy with David—not to mention eating a lot of my own desserts!"

Michael chuckled.

"And when I called my mother, she was so excited about being a grandmother she didn't even mention my marital status! She said she'll be up here this weekend . . ."

Michael nodded and threw me a thumbs-up.

". . . and she said she may consider moving up north. I'm not sure how I feel about that, but I think it's interesting that she'd move away from me but she'll come back for my baby. . . . Well, she's not doing it yet, so I'm not going to think about it."

When I was quiet, Michael asked, "And how did your friends react to your wonderful news?"

"We all met at the diner for Sunday brunch—I'm sure that doesn't surprise you. And even though I was feeling queasy and looked like hell, something must have been shining through, because the minute I sat down in our booth, Janet said, 'Tess, what's up? You look positively ethereal!'" And I recounted to Michael how, when I told the gathered that I was pregnant, Janet practically dove across the table to hug me, all pink-faced and squealing, which made me turn pink and squeal along with her . . . and how Arthur, grinning a bigger grin than the one he displays while describing his sixty-yard touchdown, leaned over and hugged me and Janet together . . . and how they relinquished me to Ken, who was sitting to my left . . . while David, who was on my right, sat back thoroughly enjoying the hug-in, gratefully accepting the handshakes and kisses he deserved as the expectant father.

"Sandy wasn't there?" Michael asked.

"Sandy was there."

"Oh. You didn't mention her."

"Aha! You noticed." And I related to Michael how, while five at our booth were pink and squealing, one alone was pale and silent: Sandy. Until, when the gush had subsided, she said, dripping with affectation, "Well! That *is* news, Tess. I can't believe you didn't call me! I mean, here we all are being so excited and . . . well, is this what you two want? I mean, well, we're so pleased for you, I hope *you're* pleased with your news." And how her patronizing posture momentarily damped the exhilaration of the moment. Until Janet saved the day. "Of course it's what she wants!" she defended me. "It's what she's always wanted!" And Sandy sputtered, "I was just trying to be sensitive to Tess's feelings. . . . Tess knows I'm really happy if she is. Right, Tess?"

"Sandy was jealous," Michael said.

"Sandy was jealous," I confirmed.

"I guess that made you pretty angry."

"Not me. You know I don't get angry."

He laughed in my face. "Oh, I forgot with whom I'm conversing—my placid petunia."

"Okay. So maybe I was a little annoyed."

"A little annoyed. HAH! I'll bet you wanted to punch her out!"

"Close," I admitted, giving in, laughing with him. "Now, you have to understand that I figured she might be jealous—not of my pregnancy, but of the attention I'd get. In fact, on the way to the diner I said to David, 'Watch Sandy. She's not going to be so happy.' And he thought I was being unfair."

"You think she's not happy for you?"

"It's not that. Sandy filters everything through her own little world. She sees others' lives only in terms of her role, or her imagined role. And she doesn't have a very big role in this scenario. Am I making sense?"

"I understand. Do you think that means she doesn't care?"

"I don't *care* if she cares."

"Well, I guess it's not really important," Michael said, dismissing the importance of Sandy with a yawn and a shrug.

I was learning that when Michael said something wasn't important, it meant that he thought I might not have considered how important it really might be. I set him straight. "Of course Sandy's important, Michael. She's a friend. But she's not perfect, just like my mother isn't perfect, and David isn't perfect . . . and you're not perfect. Of course," I allowed, "some are less imperfect than others."

Michael smiled.

I continued rather pretentiously, "If I want to be friends with Sandy, I have to accept her imperfections . . . just as she'll have to accept mine. Although I must admit that lately I've found her hard to take, which makes me feel guilty. . . . Anyway, who knows—she could decide she doesn't want to

280

be friends *with me!* Of course, *we* know, in that case, that it would be because *she* doesn't understand what's important."

Michael kept smiling at me.

"I'm rambling, aren't I?"

"You're great. You're just great. And you're going to be a mommy."

"Right," I replied, turning inward for a moment, enjoying the thought. And then, "I'm going to be a mommy, and David's going to be a daddy, and you . . . well, Michael, I've had some interesting thoughts about you since I've become pregnant."

"Is that right?"

"Yes. I have to tell you, one of my first considerations was where you fit into all this . . . where to put you. . . . I mean, if it hadn't been for you, David and I might never have gotten together, and so I feel you played a big part in my having this baby. At first I thought maybe I'd like you to be the baby's godfather—your surrogate-father role notwithstanding, you're not exactly its grandfather. For one thing, you're too young." We both laughed. "And then I wasn't sure if *godfather* was right, either. What I'm trying to say is that when I thought about it all—me and David and the baby and you—I kept wondering, 'What's wrong with this picture?' You see, as much as I know you care, Michael, I don't expect that you're going to come over to our house and take little Bambino to the zoo. And I don't expect you'll want me to call you every time Bambino gets a new tooth or says a new word. Of course, maybe you'll want to see a picture of us all every few years? But I won't expect that you'll send me a picture of *your* family. All of which made me think of some of our earlier discussions . . . about our unequal friendship . . . about you being a *paid* friend. And I decided that there was some validity to my feelings. Michael, you *are* paid, and our relationship *is* unequal. But now I understand that my discomfort was not with the relationship we have, it was with my perception of it and what I thought it should be. I didn't understand the Therapy Thing. I didn't believe that I could get what I needed from you without your falling in love with me . . . without your thinking that I was uniquely unique, truly special—and it goes without saying that I couldn't think of myself as that special. Intellectually I knew that every person is unique, and, in my own inimitably convoluted way of thinking, I felt that if all people are unique or special then there is nothing special about being special, and that if there is nothing special about being special then you'd have no reason to care especially for me, which only reinforced my feeling unworthy of love. . . . Are you following this?"

Michael was sitting forward in his chair, listening intently with his hands enmeshed under his chin. But he said nothing, which made me feel like I was onto something important.

I continued. "You know, I think I'm solving a mystery here."

No reaction. Or did I detect a trace of a smile?

"Well, until now I just couldn't put together what I felt and what you said, and I kept throwing the *paid friend* bit up to you as if it implied insincerity. . . . Did you ever read Frost's poem about 'boughten friendships'?"

He didn't answer.

"Well, anyway," I continued, deciding that Michael was not at this moment interested in my intellect, but my guts. "You *do* care," I continued, "but not in the way that I thought I needed you to care."

He nodded silently.

"Here, in this room, you let me know that you understand who I am, Michael. You introduced me to me, to that part of me that is not unique but is like everyone else—my guts—and also to that part of me that *is* unique—warts and all, as they say. I guess part of my problem was that I couldn't understand how you could love *all* your warty clients, but that you'd have to in order to help them. So I believed that for a fee you effected a model of loving them, like following a recipe from a book, a model that was good enough to fool them into thinking that you really did love them. And that seemed so dishonest. But what I now know is that you connect with them on a level where we're all equals—at the gut. You could call it a *psycho-umbilical cord."* I smiled. He didn't. I continued, "Now I understand that you don't have to *love* them, not in the popular sense of the word. Does this sound at all religious to you, Michael?"

He ignored my question. "Who is *them?"* he asked.

My face reddened, but I pushed on. *"ME,* Michael. I guess I'm talking about *me.* What I'm really trying to say is that I didn't need you to *love* me, Michael, I only needed you to care good enough—to do a good enough job as therapist— so that I know what it feels like to be loved, to show *me* how to love me, so that I could let someone else love me . . . someone like David . . . and so I could love him. You did that for me. And for that I love *you*—in the popular sense of the word . . . in the popular but unromantic sense of the word . . . well, maybe a little romantic, but we've been through all that before, haven't we?"

Michael smiled.

"I know that I'll always consider you my baby's godfather in a sense, but that *you* don't need that, and my baby won't need that. Does all of this make sense to you, Michael?"

"What you're saying is that you didn't understand how it all fit together and worked, and now you do."

I nodded slowly. "Do you know what you are, Michael? You're a catalyst. You make some extraordinary changes occur, and then you simply drop out of the picture unchanged."

"You think I'm unchanged?"

"Well, I suppose I have had some effect on you, if only by further confirming your abilities as a therapist by being a successful client. And I suppose that you could have learned something new by learning about me . . . because I am unique . . . something that could help to make you even better at what you already do so well, or maybe even something that could serve you in your personal life. Because we are all unique, we do all learn from each other, don't we?"

"Yes."

"So I guess I can feel pretty good about being good enough to do something good for you."

He smiled.

I gloated silently at my arrogance, feeling quite equal for just a moment. And then I remembered the rest of my agenda. "Michael, I have to tell Stephen about the baby. I have to ask him for a divorce, a quick divorce." I tried to explain to Michael how loathsome a task this was for me, knowing that I'd be confronting Stephen at a time when it looked like he could lose everything, while I had it all, and I'd be asking him for more . . . for blood. "I'll feel like a vulture picking at his bones!" I cried.

"Some of my best friends are bone-pickers," Michael teased.

I told him he sounded like Janet, who had asked me why I couldn't take pleasure in the deed. Why I couldn't savor the moment. "After all he's done to you! You should tell him in the middle of Veterans Stadium, thumbing your nose for the close-up camera!" she had said to me on the phone Monday evening. "You should take a full-page ad in *The Philadelphia Inquirer*: DEAR STEPHEN, I WANT A DIVORCE SO I CAN MARRY YOUR ONLY FRIEND AND HAVE HIS BABY. LOVE, TESS."

"Sounds like Janet has some great ideas. Did she happen to mention billboards, or skywriting?" Michael asked.

"Very funny. You know, you're being hateful."

"I'm being hateful? Well, maybe you're right. After all, Stephen's been such a nice guy—"

"Now you're being sarcastic."

"Hmm. I can't seem to get it right today, can I? So I'll be quiet. Tell me what you think you should do."

I understood his point—the one he didn't have to verbalize. "I have to ask Stephen for a divorce," I said, adding, for my own justification, "but I have to do it my way—with kindness."

"Just remember to be kind to yourself," Michael said, with kindness.

* * *

On the way home from Michael's office, I tried to think of exactly what I was going to say when I called Stephen. No. I couldn't ask him for a divorce over the phone. It had to be done face to face. So. Location would be the most important factor, I decided. The Location Thing was a spin-off of my real estate training, it seemed; it was a displacement of priorities in an effort to relieve anxiety, in fact. So a silly but functional inner monologue ensued regarding Where To Tell Him. I didn't want to tell him in my house, which used to be *our* house; someplace public would be better. But not a restaurant; too many people. I was going to show a house on Thursday—north of here, near a park with a lake. It was quiet, open, familiar. I'd ask him to meet me in the parking lot at the lookout. Yes. Perfect.

Wanting to *getitoverwith*, I called Stephen as soon as I got home, before starting to prepare a chocolate Killer Cake for Andrea Snelling's husband's birthday dinner that night.

Harold Snelling was a chocolate freak and nothing, absolutely nothing, would do for his birthday except a Killer Cake, Andrea had insisted. A dense, fudgy cake laden with chocolate chips and covered with a rich chocolate fudge frosting, Killer Cake can do in all but the most extraordinary sweet tooth, according to ardent fans of the famous Philadelphia dessert. But Harold was up to it, Andrea had said. I told her I charged extra if my face broke out or I gained more than five pounds within three days of making it. We had laughed again.

My telephone conversation with Stephen was more somber. I told him I had to talk to him, that Thursday would be good, that I would meet him on the hill overlooking the lake at one o'clock. Yes, he knew where I meant, but why couldn't he come to the house? he asked. "Please indulge me," I appealed. "Sure," he said, sounding incapable of putting up a fight.

My mission accomplished, I set a large ceramic bowl next to the ingredients for the cake on the island counter and began the blending process—by hand with a large wire whisk. As I slowly whisked together the eggs, sugar, melted chocolate and butter, vanilla, salt, flour, and chocolate chips, I was taken by the richness of the mixture . . . by the name of the cake. *Killer Cake,* I thought, picturing a diner dying of pleasure while eating a slice . . . a glutton dying of suffocation while trying to stuff the whole thing down . . . diabetic Stephen dying of it, I thought, an unnamed rage whipping through me. . . .

Later that afternoon, Stephen slipped into the kitchen and spied the Killer Cake sitting on a white pedestal plate in the middle of the counter. He ran his finger through the sweet, buttery icing on top of the cake, sucked it off his finger. He picked at the crumbs on the delicate white doily at the base of the cake and licked them from his fingers. He stuck his fingers into the side of the cake, gouged out a frosted chunk riddled with sugary chocolate chips, and pushed it into his mouth, repeating the cranelike motion over and over until he had devoured the whole thing. I watched him turn pale, ashen, sweaty, as the infusion of sugar flooded his bloodstream. And then I watched as a glistening redness, starting at his feet—he wasn't wearing socks—traveled up his body, indicating his rising blood-sugar level. I watched his ankles redden . . . his hands . . . wrists . . . and then his neck extending from his starched white shirt. And then his face turned red and started to bloat. His eyes and mouth formed great O's as his head swelled like a balloon, growing bigger and redder until it exploded with a mighty KABOSH! leaving his limp body to fall on the white tile floor, spattering it with blood.

. . . What an image! Janet would love that one, I thought, tittering ever so slightly at my morbid sense of justice, at my ability to mete it out so excessively in my fantasies. I continued to whisk, watching the thick batter fold over and into itself. Voluptuous, I thought. This is a voluptuous cake. I'm voluptuous, I thought, voluptuously pregnant. Passionate, I thought, breathing in the sweet, heavy perfume of chocolate. This is a cake of passion. And my heart started to pound as I felt passion rush through me, awakening lust.

And I laughed aloud at myself, at my mercurial emotions, wishing that David would walk in just then.

Standing on the edge of the precipice, Stephen looked smaller than I would have described him. He was short, I noted, surprised that I hadn't seen him as *short* before. He was no more than five-foot-six, though he always claimed to be five-foot-eight. And he was slight—slim-shouldered and -hipped, thin-armed and -legged. But his tummy spilled over the waist of his designer jeans, puffed out his yellow knit pullover shirt. Standing round-shouldered, sway-backed, his posture suggested that of a small boy. Is this what happens to us when we are defeated? Do we become children again? Are we really just children blown up into grown-ups by success? Are we deflated by defeat like pricked balloons?

He had arrived before me and was looking down toward the lake. He looked painfully alone. I felt that if I approached him, touched him, instead of easing his aloneness I would become a part of it. We would be two people isolated from others, and no less isolated from each other. "What's in your head?" I asked, standing a few feet from him.

"Nothing," he responded without turning.

"You must be thinking about something."

"No. Not really. Look down there, Tess. Look at the lake and the blond trees."

Blond trees? I stepped closer to him, close enough to see over the edge of the cliff, to see what he saw below. The huge oval lake was as still and reflective as a mirror, the near end edged by willows, their autumn gold-leafed branches tossing in the breeze like hair—yes, like a woman's blond hair being brushed in front of a mirror, I fancied. Every now and then the sun would flash in the giant mirror, momentarily blinding voyeurs. *"Blond* trees?" I queried.

"They look like heads of hair, don't you think? What a sexy bitch that Mother Nature is. A real siren. Now, there's a lady I'd like to do."

287

"I think with Mother Nature it wouldn't be you who does the doing," I played along.

"Maybe. But what a way to go—sucking on The Big Tit, getting sucked into the center of being."

"You want to be God, don't you? You want to be able to control everything," I said.

He turned on me. "You've been spending too much time with that shrink of yours, Tess," he said. "He's got your head filled with a shitload of psychobabble. Or is it David who's making you so self-righteous?"

I backed away. This wasn't going to be easy, I realized. "Stephen, let's not be angry with each other. We've been doing pretty good for the last few months."

"I'm sorry," he apologized, looking forlorn again. "So tell me, why did you want me to meet you? What's going on?"

"I have something to tell you, Stephen. And something to ask."

"Whatever you want. I've told you that before."

"I want a divorce, Stephen. I was going to wait until—"

"A divorce? You're asking me for a divorce? Now? I thought we had things settled, arranged. I thought we agreed—"

"I agreed to help you, but I never agreed to stay married."

"No. Something's going on here. What is it, Tess?" he asked with growing hostility, stepping toward me as he attacked.

And I retreated, away from the edge of the cliff, until my back was against a large oak.

"Remember, Tess, I *know* you! I want the truth!" he yelled.

"David and I are getting married," I blurted out.

"Yes. Of course, that's it," he said, looking struck. "But I'm surprised, Tess, surprised you couldn't wait until I got my head above water. For God's sake, can't you see I'm drowning!"

"Stephen—"

"Revenge, Tess? Is that what this is all about? It's not like you. David's put you up to this, hasn't he? Sweet, mild-mannered David . . . two-faced prick!"

"It's not like that, Stephen. Really. Let me explain," I begged, trying to appease, to ease the turmoil that gripped him.

"I *need* you, Tess. Don't you understand how much I—"

"I'm pregnant, Stephen."

His body tensed. He looked like a trapped animal, I thought, continuing to talk, hoping to defuse his reaction: "I hope you can be happy for me. . . ."

He flinched.

I'm not doing this right! screamed in my head. ". . . You know it's what I've always wanted, Stephen . . . what I wanted for *us*, but—"

"That's not what you wanted!" he lashed out, taking hold of my forearms, frightening me. "You know what you wanted from me? This!" he yelled, sliding his hands to my wrists, pulling my left hand into his crotch. *"This* is all you really wanted from me!" He pushed the heel of my hand into the softness of his genitals until I could feel the stirrings of an erection. I was aroused by the feel of him, by the hardening of his body, the softening of his eyes. And arousal displaced fear. The slackening of my body, the slight parting of my lips gave me away, strengthened him, set his teeth. His eyes lost the softness that had staved off my fear of him. It seemed a moment frozen, a freeze-frame, our facing each other, raw with feeling. I thought I'd faint from the over-whelming realness of it. What happens now? What do you do when the quake begins, when it's all erupting to the surface, when it can't be pushed back under? I knew even as I felt him release my left wrist, as I watched from outside myself his arm swing back . . . and I couldn't move . . . his lips draw back exposing clenched teeth . . . and I couldn't cry out . . . his eyes squint and his face redden. And my eyes filled with tears even before the blow, just from the thought of it, more from the thought of it than the pain of it. And as I fell to the ground I felt nothing, but heard the crack of skin on skin . . . and as I yelled out I heard nothing, but felt the sting of skin on skin . . . and as my body skidded across the damp leaves I saw nothing, but heard the yelp thwacked from my throat . . . and as I lay, stunned, propped on one scraped and swelling forearm, I saw the red drops, I watched the blood drip into a large, browned leaf—blood from my open, silent mouth.

"Tess!" Stephen gasped. "I didn't mean . . . I'm sorry, I—" and he knelt down to me.

I stood up. And as I brushed my hair back from my face with my fingers I felt the soreness, pictured the shiny blue swelling that would soon be there, and I became aware of the metallic taste of blood. Turning away from him, embarrassed to face him, embarrassed at how I must have looked, I walked back to the edge of the cliff and looked down at the lake, the blond trees. I tried to summon Super Bitch, but old feelings of impotence washed over me. I wanted to close my eyes and be carried to the trees by the wind, be embraced by the trees and rocked to sleep. I swayed to the music in my head: "Rockabye baby on the treetop." I wished Stephen would disappear . . . go away . . . do away with himself . . . shoot himself with the gun he kept in the glove compartment of his car—another *male thing* I didn't understand. A loud crack woke me from my reverie, and I turned to find him standing oppressively behind me, near the big oak, looking up at the darkening sky, as startled as I by the unexpected brilliance of nearby lightning, the disquieting crack of thunder. He's still here, I thought. "You're still here," I said.

"We better go before it pours," he answered.

"It *was* what I wanted, Stephen," I cried. "I wanted our baby. Remember how we tried? Remember my surgery? Maybe if we had succeeded . . . maybe we could have made it work . . . maybe—"

"You mean if *I* had succeeded, don't you!?" he flared anew. "You're the proof! You're pregnant! So it had to be *me*, right? Isn't that what you're really saying? *I* didn't succeed?"

"No, Stephen, I—"

"Well, lady, I've got news for you. The reason you didn't get pregnant with me is because that's the way *I* wanted it. I had a vasectomy, Tess, before I even knew you!"

NO! I thought as his words ricocheted off me, leaving

painful nicks in my consciousness. "No . . ." was all I could say.

"YES!" he yelled.

"I thought it was *me,"* I whimpered. "All those years . . . I thought I had let you down . . . I felt so inadequate. And all that time . . ." Stephen stepped toward me, triggering a rush of adrenaline. "How COULD you!" I yelled. "How could you DO such a thing? How could you LIE to me . . . all that time? And you let me go through surgery! What kind of a man are you?"

"I couldn't tell you," he said, looking at his feet, cowed momentarily by my reproach. "I was afraid you'd leave me. And besides, your doctor said you probably couldn't get pregnant without the surgery . . . so maybe you wouldn't be pregnant now if you hadn't had it. So maybe I did you a favor."

The enormity of his selfishness overwhelmed me; but I held onto my sanity, understanding that later, when I was alone, I could allow myself the luxury of letting go, of breaking down. Now I had to be rational. I had to understand, so that later I could believe that what had happened had really happened. I began to remember the facts. "Your sperm count, Stephen. It was normal."

"I knew someone at the lab."

"Who would falsify a sperm count?" I asked naively.

"The technician."

Then I understood. "A woman, you mean. *Another* woman you slept with before me."

"Not *before* you, Tess. I was seeing her at the time."

"No—"

"AT THE TIME! UNDERSTAND! I've always had women in my life. But I loved YOU, Tess. I LOVE you. The rest are just the way it is for me. It's business, it's men's business. I have no fantasies about my life. It's YOU who have the fantasies—about me, about us, about what I wanted. You have no idea what I want. You have no idea who I am!"

"I, I, I! What about ME, Stephen?"

The wind had picked up, blowing dry leaves around our ankles and clouds heavy with rain across the sky above our

291

heads. Anticipating the cooling, cleansing wetness on my throbbing face, my soiled hands, I stood fast watching the lightning, stroke after stroke connecting the clouds, the clouds and the earth, in an evanescent network of light. The accompanying thunder was deafening: God's warning that great powers were at work, I thought. Stephen watched, understanding that there was little he could do to make a mark on the universe, not understanding that the marks he made on people were more important, still not understanding that every relationship *is* a universe. And I started to hurt, from the inside out. My blood ran suddenly hot and fast. I trembled with rage. . . .

"YOU ARE A SMALL MAN!" I erupted, pointing a finger at Stephen from an outstretched arm. He stepped back, toward the great oak. And, as if I had pointed the way for God, for Zeus, for the powers that leave us essentially to our own folly but drop in for an occasional *gotcha!* a thin, bifurcated streak of light bolted from a place in the sky to where Stephen stood—one prong piercing the grounded leaf filled with my coagulated blood, the other striking Stephen's left shoulder, forming, for an instant, a connection of incredibly graphic moral content. For me. That's for *me*, I thought. Stephen did not cry out, he just lit up, froze as he was lifted off the ground and thrown against the tree in a posture reminiscent of cartoons of terrified cats—the ones that look like they have lightning inside them—and then fizzled and slumped, singed and smoking. But he didn't fall to the ground . . . his feet never touched the ground. I walked over to his body and saw that he had been impaled on a broken branch stump . . . that it went into his back and held him under his shoulder blade. The gold choker chain of naked women he wore had branded his neck, and had fallen to the ground before him in molten eighteen-karat lumps. I saw that his fly had been soldered shut. And then I saw the heart carved into the massive tree trunk just to the right of Stephen's slumped head. Inside the heart was carved *S. K. & L. E. 1961.* Stephen would never have done such a thing for me, I thought. I reached out and touched his left

292

shoulder . . . I supposed his heart had stopped . . . closed my hand around his left shoulder and put my ear to his stilled chest . . . I had heard that's what happens when one is electrocuted . . . closed my other hand around his right shoulder and pressed my body to his. "Good-bye, Stephen," I said.

. . . As I stood there I felt my boundaries fall away, and I waited for a gust of wind to carry my essence off . . . but instead I felt Stephen's arms go around me to hold me together. He's still here, I thought. We were still standing by the edge of the cliff overlooking the lake. I started to cry again, and then the rain came and mixed with my tears, washed away the dirt, the blood, the clouds that fogged me in. I saw how easy it would be to push him over the edge of the cliff. I could picture him plummeting into the lake, a floating island suspended on the cracked mirror surface for just an instant before the water took him in, sucked him into its center, and closed over him.

"Good-bye, Stephen," I said, pushing away from him, pushing against him, pushing him back, horrified at the thought of how far he had pushed me. "YOU'RE A SMALL MAN, STEPHEN! And you're going to get SMALLER, and SMALLER, and SMALLER, until there's NOTHING left of you, and then you're going to understand what it means to be FUCKED!" I raged, irrevocably reclaiming the power that I had so easily, so eagerly relinquished to Stephen so many years before. Then, as quickly as my rage had ignited, it dissipated, and I saw Stephen again as I'd seen him when I first arrived—small and childlike. I walked by him, eschewing his outstretched hands. And I left, leaving him atop the hill in a brewing storm to feel his smallness at the center of his universe.

BOCCONE DOLCE
(SWEET MOUTHFUL)

FROM: Sardi's Restaurant, New York

4 egg whites
pinch of salt
1/4 teaspoon cream of tartar
1 1/3 cups sugar
6 ounces semisweet chocolate pieces
3 tablespoons water
3 cups heavy cream
2 pints fresh strawberries

Preheat oven to very slow (250°F).

Beat egg whites, salt, and cream of tartar until stiff. Gradually beat in 1 cup of sugar, and continue to beat until the meringue is stiff and glossy.

Line baking sheets with wax paper, and on the paper trace three circles, each 8 inches in diameter. Spread the meringue evenly over the circles, about 1/2 inch thick, and bake in the very slow oven for 20 to 25 minutes or until meringue is pale gold but still pliable. Remove from oven and carefully peel wax paper from bottom. Put on cake racks and dry.

Melt the chocolate pieces with 3 tablespoons of water in the top of a double boiler. Whip cream until stiff; then gradually add 1/3 cup sugar and beat until very stiff. Slice 1 pint of strawberries.

Place a meringue layer on serving plate and spread with a thin covering of melted chocolate. Then spread a layer about 3/4 inch thick of the whipped cream and top this with a layer of sliced strawberries. Repeat layers of meringue, chocolate, whipped cream, and sliced strawberries, then top with third layer of meringue. Frost sides smoothly with remaining whipped cream. Decorate top in an informal pattern, using remaining melted chocolate squeezed through a pastry cone with a tiny round opening, and dot with whole ripe strawberries. Refrigerate for 2 hours before serving. Serves 8.

CHAPTER 16

Boccone Dolce
(Sweet Mouthful)

It's funny sometimes, the way things turn out. My mother says that things always turn out for the best. The question is, the best for whom? Another question is, exactly when do things *turn out?* I've discovered that life isn't exactly a series of independent events, each with a beginning and an end. There is only one beginning—birth—and one end—death. What's in between—the middle—is life. The middle is an evolution of events that never *turn out* definitively. Look at my life, for example: I married Stephen and I couldn't get pregnant. And then my marriage failed. So, according to my mother, it was for The Best that I had never had a baby. Whose best? Mine, the would-be baby's, Stephen's? Probably all concerned. But it had Turned Out, in fact, that I *had* married Stephen. For whom was that The Best? Not me, certainly. Perhaps it was The Best for Stephen and he just didn't know it. But, as things Turned Out, we separated and I fell in love with David and now I'm going to have a baby. My mother would say that it was for The Best that my marriage to Stephen had failed, because I was now able to have a child—something I could never have done with Stephen. Certainly it was for The Best for my mother, who wanted nothing more than to be a grandmother, although, according to her, perhaps it wasn't for The Best for her to have been a mother. And I believe it was for The

Best for me; I have always wanted a child. I'm sure it's for The Best for David, too, but surely not for Stephen. Perhaps The Best all around would have been if I had not married Stephen in the first place. Then again, if our marriage was, in fact, for The Best for Stephen, then things would not have Turned Out for The Best for him if we had *not* married, even though, it later Turned Out, we divorced. Now, who is to say that the way Things have Turned Out, as they now stand, is for The Best, and for whom? I suppose that will depend on how the child Turns Out, and how my impending marriage to David Turns Out. For The Best, I hope.

This was the convolution of thoughts in which I was lost as I swirled whipped, sweetened egg whites onto a cookie sheet with the back of a spoon, forming an eight-inch circle that would be baked into a layer of crunchy meringue for perhaps *the* most delectable of desserts: Boccone Dolce— Sweet Mouthful. This creation from Sardi's of New York consists of layers of meringue, melted chocolate, sweetened whipped cream, and fresh sliced strawberries, frosted on the sides with whipped cream, and decorated on top with whole strawberries and drizzles of melted chocolate. Boccone Dolce, in my opinion, *always* Turns Out for The Best—for everyone. Today it was being turned out for David's birthday dinner. He wouldn't let me make a dinner party for him—far too exhausting, he had said—but he'd agreed to my making his birthday cake. Janet and Arthur and Sandy and Ken were to meet us at La Diva for dinner at seven-thirty, after which we'd have coffee and birthday dessert at my house. It had been snowing all morning, the big-flaked kind of snow that falls slowly from a bright sky through crisp, dry air, fleshing out the skeletal trees, covering the ground like a soft, thick blanket. The oven timer buzzed—indicating two finished meringue layers— and the telephone rang simultaneously. I picked up the phone and cradled it on my shoulder as I pulled from the oven the two cookie sheets bearing the lightly browned circles of meringue.

"Hello, Tess?" It was Alan Garfield. He had good news for

me, he said. My divorce from Stephen should be through by the end of the month . . . first week in February for sure.

What a nice birthday present for David, I thought: a wedding date. "We can have a Valentine's Day wedding!" I said, delighted with the news . . . delighted with the way things were turning out.

I returned to my labor of love, slipping the meringue disks onto a cooling rack, placing the third cookie sheet in the oven, pouring the cream into the mixing bowl, watching it triple in volume, burying the spinning beaters, while the *whirrr* of the mixer lulled me into reminiscence. I recalled the day above the lake two months ago, and the late-night telephone call from Stephen a week later when he told me that he would give me a quick divorce, when he told me that he was filing for bankruptcy, that his trial was to be in mid-February, and that he was planning to go away for three weeks in January, alone, when he told me that he was so sorry for so many things he could never make it up to me even if he had another lifetime, that he wished me well and hoped I'd be happy. I had thanked him for his cooperation, for his good wishes, and then I asked him about the trip he was planning. I don't know why I asked him about that; there were so many more important questions. He said he was going to a quiet island—where he could clear his head. It was important to him that I know he was going alone, he said. I told him it was no longer important to me if he traveled alone or not. But that wasn't true. As much as I didn't want to believe it, as I spoke with him I realized there still remained a remnant of a tie between us, albeit a tenuous one. Perhaps it would break with the divorce, or my remarriage, or the sale of my house—I had finally found a buyer—or the birth of my child. I knew it would break . . . and then I wouldn't ask any more questions.

Sandy startled me—she was practically next to me by the time I noticed she had walked in. "Hiii!" she said.

I turned off the mixer. "Boy, did you scare me! I didn't hear you come in."

"I told you not to leave your back door open. You don't

297

know who might walk in. I see coffee's on," she said, walking toward the coffee maker.

"Pour us both a cup, Sandy, and grab some crackers from the cabinet. There's egg salad in the fridge. We can have lunch. The meringue in the oven has another fifteen minutes to go," I said, covering the bowl of whipped cream with plastic wrap, placing it in the refrigerator, and retrieving the soup-bowl of egg salad I had made the day before. "So how's it going?" I asked once we were settled at the counter.

"Not bad, Tess," she answered quietly, clearly a new Sandy—more thought, less vowels. She looked thin, but not drawn, not unhappy. And as I watched her carefully spread egg salad on half a piece of Melba toast, I remembered the afternoon, just a month ago, when she had called me.

"Tess, I have to see you! I don't know what to do!" she cried.

"What's wrong, Sandy?"

"It's Ken. He's not . . . nothing's what . . . oh, Tess, it's all so complicated."

"Okay, Sandy. I'm here. Come over." Well, I thought intuitively as I made fresh coffee and finished making the tuna salad I had planned for my lunch, it looks like the honeymoon may be over . . . before it even begins. Within minutes, Sandy's green Volvo—which, she had told me excitedly only a week before, Ken was going to trade in for a BMW as soon as the new models came out—was parked in the drive and Sandy was walking through my back door, red-eyed and sniffling. But my heart didn't stop, or even skip a beat in dread; she didn't appear that upset . . . not like when Charlie had died, not even like when she had found out about Charlie's affair—more like when she'd told me about her affair with Stephen.

"Tess, you're just not going to belieeeve this," she started, pulling a mug from the cabinet and filling it with coffee.

I got the milk from the refrigerator and sat at the table. "I think I'd believe almost anything these days, Sandy. What happened?"

She took off her red fox jacket, dropped it on a chair, and

sat down across from me. "Okay," she said, looking right at me—and broke into tears.

I took her hand across the table. "I'm here, Sandy. Tell me what's going on," I insisted, beginning to get concerned after all.

"He's BROKE, Tess!"

"What?"

"He's broke. He owes the casinos a fortune."

"Ken? A gambler? I—"

"Can you belieeeve it?"

"As I said, I can believe almost anything," I replied, finally understanding how an orthodontist could have so much time off from work. He was seeing fewer and fewer patients because he visited the casinos in Atlantic City several mornings a week. Then he wined and dined Sandy on the weekends, impressing her by paying for everything with new hundred-dollar bills, which were really short-term loans from the casinos—cashed-in chips, obtained on credit. A nasty little cycle, really. Unfortunately, Sandy liked her position in the loop well enough not to ask too many questions, taking his half-truths about his successful practice and complicated real estate investments at the shore as the whole truth. "But what I don't understand is how you didn't know he was at the casinos so often."

She offered no explanation. There was none, save her own penchant to see only what she wanted to see. *That* was something I could understand.

"Tess, tell me what to dooo. I do love him, you know . . ."

I was glad she said that, because I really didn't know.

". . . and I think he . . . well, I think we need help."

"Things going well with Ken?" I probed, watching Sandy swallow a mouthful while spreading egg salad on the other half of the dry brown rectangle.

"We're working on it," she answered. "Michael's been a big help already. I'm so grateful that you recommended him to us, Tess. He's helping me and Ken understand about the gambling, and a lot of other stuff . . . about both of us. But I think we've got a long way to go."

"I think you're doing great, Sandy. How are the kids?"

"They couldn't be happier. They're absolutely mad about Ken. Would you believe that Rebecca asked Ken if she could call him Daddy? He was thrilled. And speaking of children, how's the little mother-to-be?"

"I'm terrific. And I got some good news today. Save February 14," I told her, explaining Alan's call.

"Oooh! I love weddings! I'm so happy for you, Tess."

"Thanks. I am looking forward to feeling settled—if one can ever feel settled."

"Well, I feel settled. And I owe it all to you, Tess. I mean, what if you hadn't gone to that singles party with me? And what if you hadn't gone out with Ken? And suppose *you* had fallen for him? Can you imagine! But, most important, you sent Ken to *me* . . . and then you sent *us* to Michael." She put the canapé down on her plate and looked at me with a kind of rueful smile. "You know, Tess, a couple of years in therapy wasn't exactly what I had in mind when I told you how Ken and I were going to get to know each other during our delayed long honeymoon—remember the three weeks in Europe we were planning? That really would have been a nice trip, but . . . well, isn't it incredible how this all turned out?"

I was tempted to recount to her my earlier thoughts, but I decided to let it slide and suffice with, "It certainly is. For the best, just like my mother used to say," while running through my head was a song by the Rolling Stones, the one that says that we don't always get what we want, but we just might get what we need.

Dinner that night was delicious. First we shared four different pastas, and following entrées of veal and shrimp we shared a large bowl of green salad tossed with olive oil, balsamic vinegar, and freshly ground black pepper. We also shared four bottles of wine—all except me, that is. I was allowed one glass, David informed me before dinner. Sensing an impending pout, he added, "Besides your being pregnant, we need a designated driver! So it all turns out—"

"I know. For the best," I finished his sentence, chuckling to myself.

Following dinner we returned to my family room, where I set before the six of us espresso and the Boccone Dolce. It was gorgeous. And the taste . . . well, there were no just words!

"Where did you get fresh strawberries in January?" Janet asked.

"They're in all the supermarkets. Aren't they fabulous?"

"What's the crunchy part?" asked Arthur.

"Meringue—it's made of egg whites and sugar, baked to a crisp."

"I can't believe we're still eating! After that dinner! But it's too good not to eat!" said Ken.

And we ate the whole thing. Janet had pulled the empty cake plate across the coffee table to her, from which she and Arthur were scraping the last crumbs of meringue, the last dabs of cream, with their forks, then with their fingers, when the phone rang. I picked up the receiver next to the sofa.

"Hello," I said. And I must have paled as I listened to the voice on the phone, because David jumped from his easy chair and knelt in front of me, his hands on my knees. After hearing a lot of sputtering and half-asked questions, the gathered heard me say, "I'll be there shortly." But when I put the receiver down, I didn't move.

"Tess, what is it?" David asked. "Who was that?"

"It was a nurse from University Hospital," I answered. "I have to go there . . . right away."

"What is it?" David repeated, alarmed.

"It's Stephen. I have to go—he may be dying. . . ." And I pulled away from David and was off the sofa. "My boots. What did I do with my boots?" I asked the floor . . . and found them in the foyer . . . and by then David had his coat on and mine in his hand.

"Let's go, you'll explain in the car," he said, then turned to the others, telling them to make another pot of coffee and he'd call from the hospital.

On the way to the hospital, I told David what the nurse

had told me: Stephen had been brought to the hospital by ambulance in a state of shock; he was suffering from a severe infection; he was accompanied by a friend who had told the doctor that he was married to me.

"But Stephen's supposed to be in St. Kitts."

"I know. He must have picked up something on the island," I said. What I was imagining was tetanus, rabies, typhoid, picturing a tanned, feverish Stephen lying on crisp white sheets with a beautiful nurse at his side. What I found when I reached the hospital was something I could never have imagined.

First of all, what he had picked up he hadn't picked up on St. Kitts. He had brought it—or should I say *her*—with him from Philadelphia: Dorothy. Of course, she was not precisely what made him sick—not to say that finding out he had taken her didn't make *me* sick. Be that as it may, when David and I walked into the emergency ward, the nurse at the desk gave me an envelope containing Stephen's valuables—his wallet, watch, keys—and we were directed to a room. As we walked down the hall, Dorothy came running to us, meeting us halfway.

"Thank goodness you've come, Tess. He's dying and the doctors need your permission to treat him—" she'd started, when a doctor emerged from a room and walked over to us.

"Are you Mrs. Fineman?"

"Yes, I—"

"I'm Dr. Gerstler, and we have a life-threatening situation here, Mrs. Fineman," he said as we walked briskly to Stephen's room. He stopped at the door and turned to David. "Are you a member of the family?" he asked.

"No, not exactly—" David started.

"Then you'll have to wait out here." The doctor took me by the elbow, steering me into the room.

I wonder if Stephen's wife's husband-to-be or Stephen's wife's baby's father would be considered a member of the family? I thought involuntarily as we approached the bed, reproaching myself immediately for the inappropriateness of the thought. As I said, nothing I could have imagined would have prepared me for what I was to see . . . and hear.

Stephen was breathing in short, fast gasps. His skin was sweaty and as gray as his hair; his closed eyes were dark pits, his cheeks sunken. Tubes snaked from every orifice.

"Stephen," I said, touching his arm and recoiling from the clammy feel, from the putrid smell that seemed to emanate from him. "Can he hear me?" I asked the doctor, who shook his head.

And then there was the matter of the huge bulge under the bed sheet, over Stephen's midsection. An enormous erection, was what instantly came to mind, the lewd picture disintegrating beneath a wave of guilt as I realized almost as quickly that the protrusion was some sort of frame designed to keep the sheet from touching him.

"Mr. Fineman has a life-threatening infection," Dr. Gerstler explained coolly. "Fournier's gangrene—a spontaneous fulminating gangrene of the penis."

FULMINATING! GANGRENE! I cringed, and my eyes involuntarily shot to the tent over Stephen's groin. Then the doctor said something about it going untreated for too long, that "the tissues are dying and sloughing away, clear down to and including the *corpus cavernosa*," that "the patient had become toxic . . ." and then more medico-babble about *Hemolytic streptococcus* or *staphylococcus* being the likely villain.

FULMINATING! GANGRENE! TOXIC! reverberated in my head. I looked quizzically at Dr. Gerstler. "Toxic?" was all I managed to say.

He explained, "Essentially, this means that your husband has become poisoned by the agent that infected his penis."

Oh! You mean *lust!* I thought, not believing that I could think such a thing at a time like this, shocked by my lack of compassion.

The doctor took my incredulous look as lack of understanding. "Mrs. Fineman," he tried again, "your husband could die if we don't take drastic measures very quickly, and we need your permission."

"Drastic measures?"

"Surgery."

"Surgery?"

"Amputation."

"Amputation?"

"Amputation of the penis. We may be able to save the testicles," he said, averting his gaze from mine, resting it on my just-obvious pregnant belly.

A lot of good his balls will be without a bat! I thought, my eyes falling involuntarily to the doctor's groin. Staring at Dr. Gerstler's fly, I felt the situation begin to sink in. Amputation of the penis or Stephen could die, the doctor had said.

"Can I get you a glass of water, Mrs. Fineman? Please, sit down, I'm afraid this has been a shock." And he led me from the room to a seat in the hall. "What more can I tell you? Your husband has an unusually severe infection. We must operate soon or I can't promise—"

"How did this happen? I don't understand."

"We're not sure. We understand from Mrs. Oberman that your husband had been in the Caribbean. She also told me that he's diabetic, and that could certainly have been a big factor here," and he continued on about diabetes and poor circulation and the incidence of infection, and then he excused himself and said he'd be back in a few moments, and he disappeared into Stephen's room. He knew all the proper names, all the medical jargon, but he didn't know The Details.

Dorothy knew The Details, and within seconds of the doctor's departure, she was by my side. "David went to make a phone call. He told me to tell you that he'll be back in a few minutes," she said, wringing her hands. And then she told me The Details:

It seems that Stephen had been having a bit of a problem with impotency of late. Understanding that impotency can be a problem in diabetics, he sought the aid of his physician, who told him that his impotency was more likely the result of psychological problems than physical ones, and that perhaps a therapist was in order. Much vexed, Stephen went to a new doctor, who also told him it didn't appear that his problem was caused by his diabetes or anything else of a physiologic nature, and also suggested a therapist. "But what if it *is* my diabetes?" Stephen pressed. "Well, we have had success with papaverine," he told Stephen, explaining the use of the drug, which, when injected into the penis, causes a pharmacological erection that can last a fairly long time. "Fairly long?" Stephen queried. "Upwards of two hours," the doctor replied. Well, that was all Stephen had to hear. Superman in a bottle! "Can you imagine the fun we could have!" he told Dorothy . . . and, I assume, others. But the doctor wouldn't recommend drug therapy—"Not yet. Let's wait and see," he said. So Stephen, who has always had a bit of a problem dealing with delayed gratification, went to his own source: a cute nurse who worked for a urologist Stephen saw a couple of times a few years ago for some nonspecific infection that made him think he had the clap, but he didn't, and when the infection cleared he saw the cute nurse a couple of times. "Stephen Fineman! What a nice surprise," she exclaimed when he called her recently. "Stephen Fineman! What a nice surprise," she exclaimed when he showed her the best time, the longest time.

"He told you that?" I asked Dorothy, who'd told me that last part on a long sigh of resignation.

"He tells me everything," she replied.

I didn't believe he had told her that.

And she continued, "So he brought this stuff with us to St. Kitts. And we used it a couple of times, and it was incredible. He just went on and on and on . . ." she said, looking me right in the eye. Vicious bitch! "And then one afternoon he asked me to inject it. . . ."

One *afternoon?* I thought to myself, picturing their pasty white bodies sequestered in a dark, stagnant little room fitted with a wall-to-wall bed, humping into a sweat while, outside, the glorious sun warmed the silky sand, the blue-green sea and gentle breezes cooled bronzing bodies.

". . . He was a little too smashed to fill the syringe . . ."

In the *afternoon?*

". . . and maybe we were out of clean needles . . . maybe I forgot to change the needle . . . I don't know . . . but at any rate, sometime later, during the night, Stephen woke up. He said his prick ached, and it was all red. Well, we figured it was from too much screwing around. . . ."

Maybe she's not so dumb after all.

". . . But by morning it was swollen and the red was spreading and he was in pain. And then he got a fever and we got scared. I wanted him to see a doctor, but he said he didn't want to be treated on a foreign island. Luckily, we were able to get on a flight to New York the next day. But by then he was in terrible shape. His penis was horribly swollen and it was turning black and blue. He could hardly sit in the plane. By the time we got home, he was almost delirious with pain and fever, and his penis—ohh, it was oozing pus and the skin was all black and peeling off . . . and there was this terrible smell. . . ." Here Dorothy turned pale and her eyes watered. "I've never seen anything so awful!" she cried, bowing her head, putting her hands to her face. "And then he collapsed!" Dorothy clutched my arm with both hands and put her face close to mine. "He can't die, Tess. Please, don't let him die. He's all I have!"

Then you ain't gonna have much, lady, I thought, pitying, but not forgiving. Pulling my arm from her grasp, I stood up and walked to the door of Stephen's room. The doctor and a nurse were behind the curtain that was pulled around the bed. I stood there folding and unfolding the top of the manila envelope containing Stephen's things, attempting to digest The Details, and then I looked down at the envelope. The *keys*, I thought, ripping open the envelope, pulling out Stephen's key ring. On one end, the smaller end, were three keys, two of which were keys to safety deposit boxes, one of which was the key to *my* safety deposit box—the one with all the money in it. And I realized that I had Stephen by the balls in more ways than one. It's funny the way things turn out, I thought to myself, considering the many shades of gray, remembering Michael's counsel: *Be kind to yourself.*

The doctor approached me with the consent for surgery. "Mrs. Fineman, we have the operating room ready for your husband," he said. "All we need is your signature on this form and we'll take him right up. He's failing quickly. If we wait much longer, he might not survive the surgery."

I looked at the doctor, then I looked into the room where

the smell of death was suffocating. I thought of how I had loved Stephen and how he had abused me, misused me, how he had been unkind, uncaring, unfaithful, how he was treacherous, deceitful, and base, how he had embarrassed me, humiliated me, degraded me . . . how he had hurt me . . .

How sweet revenge will be, I thought. Stephen will finally get his just deserts. And I won't have to plunge a knife in him, riddle him with bullets, drop poison in his drink—all I'll have to do is not do anything. It is funny sometimes, the way things turn out. "I'm sorry, Dr. Gerstler, I can't sign that. I couldn't possibly allow you to mutilate him in that way," I wailed, dabbing at my dry eyes with a tissue.

"But, Mrs. Fineman—"

"I know he'd rather die than live without his manhood. Surely you can understand. Surely any man can understand!" I emoted to the ceiling, my hand at my brow.

"But he *will* die without the surgery, Mrs. Fineman!"

"I'm sorry, Dr. Gerstler, but I've made my decision."

Before the morning light was bright, Stephen Fineman's light went out.

The funeral was graveside. The casket was closed. No one would have to remember him lying too still, too rigid, an empty form in white satin. No one would have to recognize as essentially Stephen's the made-over face approximated from photographs. No one would have to guess at how he might have looked when an overwhelming population of microbes wrested him from life—not at all himself. More than a hundred people showed up—mostly women. And he quite lucked out with the weather. It was a cold, clear day, there was no wind, and the sun shone so brightly many of the mourners wore sunglasses to protect their eyes from the glare off the snow. A low rumble of commentary continued among the men during the service, snatches of which I heard quite distinctly: "*. . . wife left him . . . never had kids . . . didn't have many friends . . . indicted . . . died before the trial came up . . . helluva way to keep from going to jail . . .*

307

*liked the ladies . . . wouldn't have had much of a life if they'd
cut off his dick . . . funny the way things turn out . . . for the
best . . ."*

For the best? I wondered, looking to my mother standing
beside me with her classic countenance of concern, remembering her censure when I called to tell her of Stephen's
death by deliberate disregard. "MURDERER!" she had
yelled at me. "But they would have mutilated him, Mom!
Unmanned him!" I had tried to justify my inaction. "Better
you should let him die?" she'd retaliated. "He would have
wanted it that way," I had begged, my self-righteous wall of
rationalization crumbling beneath the realization of my
irresponsibility. "How do you *know* how he would have
wanted it? He was out cold!" she'd impugned. "But—" "No
buts about it. You had NO RIGHT to play God!"

She was right. I had had no right, because, despite what
others might think, allowing Stephen to die possibly wasn't
Best for Stephen . . . although it might have been, had he
said so . . . but he hadn't . . . so we'll never know. And not
knowing makes it Not Right, I reasoned, the sweet taste of
revenge turning bitter with contrition.

The short service concluded, the women were now filing
past the coffin. They were crying, and each had something to
say as she passed, placing a flower or a bit of earth on the
coffin. I couldn't quite make out their words, but I recog-
nized many of them. Of course Dorothy was there, her eyes
black and blue with smeared mascara and eye shadow, and
so was Sandy in her long black coat and black boots. I saw
the blonde from the airplane, and various medical techni-
cians and nurses dressed in white. And Wonder Woman was
there, walking on her toes to keep the spiked heels of her
black patent leather boots from sinking into the soft earth
around the open grave.

Turning to me, my mother asked, "What are they saying,
Tess?"

I left her standing behind the rows of now empty chairs
and walked toward the line of women by the coffin. As I got
closer, I could see their tears, squeezed out of angry red
eyes—tears of rage, not sorrow. I couldn't hear their words,

but their lips were moving, and it looked like they were all whispering the same thing: *"She should've . . ."* *"She should've . . ."* something. I got a little closer and watched their thinned lips: *"She should've cut it off."*

"Well?" my mother asked when I returned to her side.

"They're agreeing with you, Mom. They're saying that it would have been Best to have saved his life," I said, relaying the sum if not the substance of their words.

. . . "We don't have much time, Mrs. Fineman," Dr. Gerstler said, holding a chart with the consent form in front of me.

Overwhelmed by the irony of it all, understanding that there is no revenge as sweet as justice, I reached for the glint of the silver Cross pen in his hand. "Where do I sign?"

David was in the shower when the doorbell rang, and by the time I got to the door the UPS man had gone, leaving a cube-shaped package addressed to me on the porch. I didn't recognize the return address. Settling back into the sofa in the family room, I peeled the brown paper from the package, revealing a layer of gift-wrapping. I carefully removed the pretty opalescent bow and the shiny white paper embossed with blue and yellow hearts, and opened the white cardboard box to find a cuddly soft, light brown Gund bear nestled amidst leaves of pale blue tissue paper. "Golly! Gotta Gund!" I said aloud, laughing to myself, and then put the bear down beside me and opened the slate-blue-lined, ivory envelope that was tucked between the side of the box and the tissue paper. In it was a letter written in blue ink on several sheets of ivory vellum stationery enhanced by an embossed, slate-blue border. It began:

Dear Tess,

You might think it strange for me to be writing to you like this, but I wanted to wish you the best on the birth of your baby.

Consumed with curiosity, I turned to the last page to discover the author, and was shocked and appalled to find it was from Dorothy Oberman. But the handwriting was so gracefully elegant, so contrary to the coarseness of the writer, that I stayed my disgust and turned back to the first page, where I read further:

I also want to apologize for the pain I may have caused you in the past. I hope you'll believe me when I say that I did what I did because I love Stephen, and that I would never hurt anyone intentionally. I'm not proud of my behavior, but Stephen and I go way back, before you, and although you may find this hard to understand, when he was with you (even when he was married to you), I felt he was "cheating" on me.

Most important, I want to thank you for saving Stephen's life. That terrible night at the hospital you were holding not only Stephen's life in your hands, but mine, too.

You might think that life is not very good for me now that Stephen has lost so much, including his career, and probably, for a time, his freedom. And his physical "loss" is terrible. But, truly, I feel none of that matters as long as we're together. In fact, he needs me now more than he ever did before. God knows, I need him. And don't think badly of me when I say this, but I no longer have to worry about him being unfaithful to me.

Stephen is still very bitter, but, for what it's worth, *I* feel you did the right thing.

I know that you and I will never be "friends," Tess, but I hope you can forgive me. I wish you happiness.

Most sincerely yours,
Dorothy

Oddly moved, already forgiving, I reread the letter until I was startled by my baby's distant cry triggering the warm, tingly sensation of my milk letting down. I slipped the pages back into the envelope and then into the big patch pocket of my wraparound jeans skirt. But before I had a chance to get up, David had scooped Sam (named for my father) from his bassinet in our bedroom and brought him to me—for the second time in the last hour.

"Time for dessert!" he teased, laying Sam in my arms. "Hey, what's going on here?" he asked, seeing my flushed face and my eyes grown teary with mixed emotions. "What's wrong, sweetheart?"

"Nothing's wrong, David," I answered, pressing my lips to the soft blond down on Sam's head. "Everything is just right. I was thinking how lucky we are, and I guess I was kind of overwhelmed." I unbuttoned my blouse and we both watched in awe as Sam rooted around for my breast and, finally latching on, suckled contentedly.

"Hey! Who sent the cute bear?" David asked, spotting the stuffed toy and its wrappings.

"It's from Dorothy, David."

"Dorothy? You mean Dorothy Oberman?"

"Yes."

"Well, that's a surprise."

"Quite. I'll tell you about it later."

"About what?"

"Later, David," I sighed, the corners of my mouth curling to the barest glimmer of a smile. "For now let's just say that it appears things really have turned out just the way my mother always says—for the best."

NICOLE JEFFORDS

HEARTS OF GLASS

Three women who appear to have everything.

MUSETTE: the beautiful, enigmatic model and actress.

CHARLIE: the society hostess, married to a rising political star.

GWEN: the powerful, highly acclaimed writer.

Yet, beneath the surface, all three are afflicted by a terrible secret. Threatened by shame, humiliation and the loss of all they truly value, their battle to regain control of their lives will call on their deepest resources. Unwillingly brought together in the knowledge of their terrible shared problem, the three proud and independent women need each other's support and comfort. Relying on each other to stay strong and protect their *Hearts of Glass*.

HODDER AND STOUGHTON PAPERBACKS